PEPPER JACK

Jon Pendergrass

authorHOUSE®

AuthorHouse™
1663 Liberty Drive
Bloomington, IN 47403
www.authorhouse.com
Phone: 1-800-839-8640

©2010 Jon Pendergrass. All rights reserved.

No part of this book may be reproduced, stored in a retrieval system, or
transmitted by any means without the written permission of the author.

First published by AuthorHouse 3/31/2010

ISBN: 978-1-4520-0403-7 (e)
ISBN: 978-1-4520-0404-4 (sc)
ISBN: 978-1-4520-0405-1 (hc)

Library of Congress Control Number: 2010903925

Printed in the United States of America
Bloomington, Indiana
This book is printed on acid-free paper.

PROLOGUE

The room was paid for in cash and had been registered under a different name. Lori Long checked and double-checked her reflection in the mirror. She paced around the luxurious hotel room nervously and glanced at the clock on the wall just as she had two minutes before. And two minutes before that. She looked around at the several lighted candles she had strategically placed around the room and appreciatively nodded at the warm glow they gave off. She placed her hand over her heart and felt it beating hard enough for the people in the next room to hear. The horrifying thought of being overheard by the neighbors crossed her mind momentarily and she quickly chased it away. No one had seen her when she checked in and carried her things up to the room from the parking garage. No one saw as she showered and put on the new lingerie she had bought for just this occasion. It took several minutes to properly enjoy the experience and she made sure that every inch of her skin was properly perfumed and lotioned. No one saw as she checked the clock again and paced nervously. She was safe to take her first walk on the wild side and could barely contain her excitement. Twenty-two years of a dull, lifeless marriage had left her open to suggestion and possibility. She had worked long and hard to maintain the same dress size as the day she had walked down the aisle. Her skin was taut and her muscles toned and she was in better physical shape than most women half her age. The face she saw in the mirror was one that her friends secretly wished they could match. Over lunch, one of these friends suggested a way she could recapture some excitement without risking losing her marriage. She gave Lori a name and number of someone she knew could satisfy her thoroughly. The thought of paying for sex horrified her at first, but her friend explained her experience. "Just think of it as an expensive outing. You get what you pay for. Just talk to him and see what you think. Can't hurt anything." Two days passed before she picked up the phone. He immediately set her at ease with his mannerisms and southern accent. They talked again two days later before setting a time for him to come to town.

She looked at the clock again. Still only two minutes had passed. She paced again nervously and wondered if arranging this was a mistake. Reaching for her cell phone, the thought crossed her mind to call and cancel the whole thing. Lori took a deep breath as that thought was interrupted by a knock at the door. She opened it and smiled, making a mental note to thank her friend first thing in the morning.

"Hi."

"I'm Lori…hi."

"It's a pleasure to meet you."

"Thank you, it's nice to meet you as well."

"This is a nice hotel and a nice hallway, but we might be more comfortable inside?"

"I'm sorry, please come in."

The next hour and a half exceeded every expectation she could have imagined. He was patient, affectionate and attentive to every sound and movement she made. Lori's only regret was that she hadn't arranged for him to stay longer. Afterwards, they talked for a bit and agreed to meet again. He dressed and excused himself, kissing her forehead sweetly before leaving. She lay still for what seemed like an eternity, every nerve ending still tingling. Checking the bedside clock, she noted that she had plenty of time before she was expected home. A hot shower would put an exclamation point on the evening perfectly. Steam began to fill the bathroom and Lori thought she heard a knock at the door. She smiled and strolled over to it, wrapping a towel around her. She opened it without looking, purring "Miss me already?" She never saw the knife that plunged into her chest, bursting her heart with one savage thrust.

CHAPTER 1

Jessica Young took a deep breath and closed her eyes. Taking the ornate doorknob in her hand, she shut the front door of what used to be her house behind her and stood on what used to be her front porch. She exhaled deliberately and opened her eyes slowly, ready to face the rest of her life. The "For Sale" sign in the front yard had a "Sold" sticker placed across it. The thought of one last obstacle out of the way lifted yet another weight from her weary shoulders and allowed a smile to cross her face. She turned and caught her reflection in the storm door and considered what she saw. "Not bad for thirty-eight," she thought, "could still use a little work though." She was tall and slender, with a pretty face highlighted by a slightly freckled nose. Her hair was the lightest of strawberry blonde and her eyes were a bluer shade of hazel. Her real estate broker interrupted her immediate train of thought, "Did you get everything you are taking with you, Jessica?"

She sighed and took a moment to gather her thoughts, annoyed by the intrusion of her moment. "You have no idea," she replied with an ever-widening grin.

For as long as she could remember Jessica had lived her life with someone else's agenda coming before hers. She married and was pregnant right out of high school. She had moved twice following her husband as he lost one job and then another. Both times she had given up good jobs with great potential. Then she tried to nurse him through an addiction to alcohol, finally drawing the line when he graduated to more addictive and expensive highs. She spent the last several years working hard, trying to raise her son as best as she could to prepare him for college and his life afterwards. Now he was off on his own and doing very well in his junior year. She had noticed him coming home less and less and becoming more and more self-sufficient over the past several months. She was proud of the man he was becoming and sad about the fact that her "baby" didn't need her as much any more. Six months ago, her boss had called her into his office to let her know he would be taking off a lot of time to deal with his wife's second bout with cancer. It was like an alarm clock going off on her life. "TIME TO WAKE UP, YOUR LIFE IS CALLING!" The next day was the best day she had in recent memory. She put her house on the market, bought a map of the United States and made plans with her friends to meet at a local bar where she promptly downed a Grey Goose Martini, threw a dart over her shoulder without looking and turned to find it had landed on Memphis, Tennessee. She smiled and the thought of living the next several years playing catch up on a life she wanted to have but had yet to realize.

CHAPTER 2

The Blue Monkey had been a Midtown Memphis mainstay for going on ten years. It was one of those places where anyone and everyone felt welcome. The guy you won five games of pool against might well be your best friend's lawyer. Or your girlfriend's brother's teammate on the over-35 Men's soccer team that plays on Wednesdays and comes in after to raise a glass to how good they were "back in the day." There was live music two or three nights a week and any time there was a big basketball/football/fill in your favorite sport here game, you could bet that it was on the big screens at the Blue Monkey. The bar itself was patterned like an old neighborhood pub. There was a lot of wood and a lot of brass fixtures spread through the three different levels of seating. The main bar ran the length of the main room, dividing it into two separate areas. Jessica had called it home since she had moved to town four months ago. She enjoyed the job because she got to meet all kinds of people and she made decent money so she didn't have to eat into the considerable savings she had brought with her. It also allowed her to take classes at the University. The current class was pottery and design. She loved trying (and mostly failing) to create something beautiful with her hands. There was an innate freedom in answering to exactly no one when creating something. This was the third job she had worked and the third class she had taken to prove that fact to herself and exactly no one else. That very thought caused a smile to break across her face as her pottery wheel slowed to a stop and the pile of clay in front of her resembled…well, nothing. She laughed and called the teaching assistant over. "I've really got to get to work; can I come back and try this again Monday?" The teaching assistant laughed and shrugged her shoulders. "You're auditing the class so whatever you want to do. I'll be in the studio from one to four." Jessica mulled that over and made a mental note to check her work schedule. She smiled at the fact that she didn't bother making an actual note in a planner or anywhere else. The "old Jessica" would have written it down and then double-checked that against an Outlook calendar she kept on her home P.C. She packed up her things and headed to her car.

Traffic wasn't bad as she headed to the Monkey as the regulars called it. She walked in about five minutes late and smiled at the manager as he looked animatedly at his watch. It had become a running joke because she was never terribly late but never terribly on time either. She let him know early she didn't need the job but she loved the job and the staff and the regulars loved her back. He shrugged his shoulders and she stuck out her tongue at him, putting an exclamation point on their unspoken conversation. The crowd was larger than usual this early on a Thursday. She had been looking forward to a quieter shift so she could catch up with her friend and co-worker Melanie Pitts. Melanie was twenty-eight years old and also a professional student. She had the tough but cute bartender look about her and never wanted for attention from men wherever they went. Dark brown hair with blonde highlights fell loosely past her shoulders. She waved at Jessica as she walked by. They wouldn't get a chance to catch up until later though as the Memphis Tigers were playing at Ole Miss in basketball. It would mean a busy but hectic crowd all night and the chance to walk away with a pocket full of tips. Since both universities were well represented in the Memphis area, who won or lost didn't matter tonight. There would be a ton of people in various stages of inebriation to deal with. She scanned the bar quickly as she scarfed down her favorite Pepper Jack Chicken sandwich. Not recognizing anyone, she finished and got on with her shift.

CHAPTER 3

Thursday night in the nation's capital. Jackson Pritchard surveyed the city from the balcony of his penthouse suite. He took a long pull from his bottled water and stepped back inside. Taking a glance around the oversized sitting room, he thought of the movie '"Pretty Woman" with Julia Roberts and Richard Gere. When pressed as to why he stayed in the penthouse, Richard Gere's answer was simple, "It's the best." The Jefferson Hotel was considered by many to be one of the best. It was elegant without being overstated and had been a favorite with the Washington political crowd for decades. His room was a contrast in styles, furnished with antiques, yet wired with Internet ready extensions so that no traveler was too far away from work. Jackson slid into the chair in front of his laptop and logged on. His first stop was his personal bank and investment accounts. He sighed audibly as the numbers still hovered just below seven figures. This was his target. Seven figures free and clear and he could slow down, get off the road and enjoy his life outside of hotels, travel and work. It was a goal that he had set years ago and was seemingly unable to reach. Reviewing his portfolios, he realized that the bad news was that the market was down by any broad-based measurement. The good news was that he was still investing, albeit conservatively, in stocks and funds that over the long run had ALL performed well. Once the market went back up, the reasoning went, his investments would be worth that much more. He searched his brain for the term and smiled as he was rewarded with "dollar cost averaging." He clicked out of that screen and looked over his itinerary for the next few days. The convention kicked off tomorrow with an informal reception. There was a series of seminars on Saturday followed by a black tie dinner that night. Everyone who was anyone in D.C. was supposed to be there and Jackson looked forward to rubbing elbows with the "beautiful people." His guest wouldn't be arriving until tomorrow morning so he had until then to prepare. He looked over the materials he had requested on the convention so he could be prepared. "Young Professionals' Responsibility for Development in Third World Countries." Jackson raised an eyebrow. Laughing to himself, he went over the number of conventions like these he had attended; keeping track was impossible. He put the materials down next to his computer and logged off. Pushing back from the desk, he checked out his closet to make sure everything he needed was there. From a full set of custom cut evening clothes down to proper spa attire, Jackson was a master of details, leaving nothing to chance. Closing the closet door, he was greeted by an up-close and personal view of himself. Six foot one, very fit with sandy blonde hair, blue eyes with a twinkle that suggested a level of mischief few successfully managed and a boyish face. He moved to the spacious bathroom, complete with separate shower and oversized bathtub, brushed his teeth, taking extra care to floss thoroughly and then washed his face. He went back out to the king sized bed in the sleeping area and dropped down onto it. Satisfied with its firmness, he picked up the phone and dialed the front desk confirming his wake up call and clicked through the channels on the TV to catch the end of SportsCenter. After twenty minutes or so, he had his fill and reached over and clicked off the light switch.

CHAPTER 4

Sharon Milligan turned on the lights as she entered the foyer of her house. Dubbed a "McMansion" by the media, the 8000 square foot estate was a sign to those that knew her that she had arrived. Forty-six years old and one of the most successful businesswomen on the entire West Coast. On the cover of business magazines across the country and the society pages locally. She had worked her way up through the ranks of a Seattle dot com, learning every business nuance she could pick up along the way. Struck with several consumer oriented business solutions, she had hung out her own consulting shingle by age 40 and parlayed her expertise into a privately held buyout firm that had successfully bought several companies and transformed them into the tigers of their respective industries. Unlike the takeover robber barons of the 1980's, Sharon's approach was to build them up and maximize the selling possibilities of buy low/sell high. Her own net worth was somewhere over half a billion and growing. She considered herself extremely well-versed in everything she did…except dating. Her taste in men bordered on comedic, which led her to become involved with a series of men with as-yet unnamed neuroses. The last of those moved out of her place after six months to go "find himself." Married and divorced twice with no children. She was considered by most to be breathtakingly beautiful, an exotic combination of her Irish and Italian parents. Long thick curly black hair framed the high cheekbones and laughing eyes that both of her parents encouraged from an early age. She sighed as she dropped her keys on the hallway table and moved to the kitchen to pour herself a glass of wine. She would check her messages and e-mail afterwards, hoping for a message from her latest "victim." She thought this one just might be different. He was a bit younger but Sharon found him full of life and adventure. They had spent five glorious days at a small, secluded island in the Caribbean where he had done nothing but dote on her. He had arranged the entire thing and she had let him, finding great enjoyment and freedom in someone else being in charge for a change. They had met through a mutual friend, and she had found there was a quiet power in him that was most attractive. They had connected on several levels and she hoped that this connection could help overcome whatever issues she would surely uncover by their next get-together. Selecting a nice Pinot Noir, she reached for a glass in the cabinet and set both on the counter. She turned to retrieve a corkscrew from her kitchen island and shrieked loudly as she came face-to-face with an intruder. She froze momentarily before composing herself and asking what he wanted. She assumed it was a he although she really couldn't tell. Sharon was tall and stood face to face with the intruder that was covered from head to toe in black. A sheer black material covered the intruder's face making any identification impossible. "What do you want?" Sharon asked quickly, trying to control her emotions, "My purse is in the hall…." She never finished the sentence as the intruder plunged Sharon's own butcher knife deep into her abdomen and then pulled hard upwards. She fell slowly to the Spanish tile she had overpaid to have installed after her last marital disaster. Her face moved from pain to a confused sort of relief as her last breath left her lungs. The intruder dropped the knife on the lifeless body and moved out to the foyer. Her purse was indeed there and about $250 in cash was quickly transferred to a large black duffel bag. The supposed top of the line security system was rearmed and Sharon's murderer quickly and quietly slipped out the back door.

CHAPTER 5

Seven-thirty A.M. came early in Washington D.C. The alarm clock went off followed five minutes later by the ringing of a telephone wake-up call. Jackson rolled over and dealt with both, sighing and lying still for a moment, remembering what his day held. He pulled on a sweatshirt and shorts, tied a pair of well-worn Asics Gel running shoes and headed out the door for a quick run. The morning air was crisp and clear and Jackson was amazed once again at the amount of activity this city generated. People seemed to move in bunches. He was reminded of an ant colony with streams of worker ants moving to and fro, accomplishing the one task they were assigned and moving on their way. He wondered what his place in the colony was supposed to be and if he would ever get to find out who the queen was. His run went quickly and smoothly; he covered a flat, easy five miles effortlessly, returning to the hotel after about forty-five minutes. He grabbed a quick glass of orange juice on the way back up to his room. He changed out of his clothes and shaved and showered leisurely, enjoying the lack of schedule this morning. The next couple of days would be very much the opposite and the freedom was one of the things he looked forward to. Jackson finished and turned the shower off, reached out for a fresh, oversized towel and dried off thoroughly.

Grabbing a clean pair of boxers, he dressed casually in khakis, a button down polo shirt and loafers. Checking his itinerary again, he arranged to have the limousine pick him up at the hotel at 11:30 with champagne and strawberries stocked. That would put him at the airport at around 12:15 or so depending on traffic. His guest was scheduled to arrive at 12:45, which gave them a good part of the afternoon to catch up before a meeting she was scheduled to attend at 5:30. A reception was scheduled for 7:00 and the rest of the evening was open to whatever happened from there. Jackson double-checked his wardrobe, the case of wine he had ordered and the candles that he had arranged around the suite. He called room service and confirmed orders to be on stand-by for both 4:00 and 10:00 that night. Light appetizers and fruit and cheese and meat trays. Deserts for later. And a case of bottled water. Thinking over every possible change in plans was one of the many talents that made these weekends that much smoother. Assured that he had thought of everything, he sat back on the larger of the couches in the sitting room and turned the TV on, relaxing until the limo got there.

CHAPTER 6

Jan Eberhardt checked her watch and was satisfied that she was on time. She had packed everything she needed and figured that Jackson would provide the rest. The convention was a perfect cover to get back together with him and it had been far too long since they had shared a weekend. And much, much too long since they had shared a bed. Her flight from Atlanta to Washington was a short one and they had scheduled some free time for each other.

"Honey? I've got the car packed, are you ready?"

Her thoughts were interrupted by her husband of five years. Her third husband. They seemed to all lose their charm around the four-to-six year mark. This one was easy, programmable, and had given her the one thing the previous two hadn't: a child. Their daughter was a very precocious three and would surely follow in her mother's footsteps. Jan straightened her suit in the mirror and checked her make-up at the same time. Her thin physique was toned by her six day a week workout regimen. At thirty-eight years of age, being in competitive shape was one of the several accomplishments she was proud of. Her three books had sold well and her infrequent lectures were sold out and limited only by the lack of free time her schedule allowed. She was generally regarded as an expert in the field of renewable resources, a subject that fired her passions. Having moved up to partner in two different firms, she had opened and closed her own consulting firm and now was the CFO and a member of the board of a large multinational corporation. There was their huge home in a gated community outside of Atlanta, the cabin in Telluride, Colorado and the beach house in Florida. Life was fantastic and she couldn't want for anything more...except a man to satisfy her on many different levels. Her husbands fell short repeatedly and her friends and family focused on things that really didn't matter to her deep down. In Jackson, however, she had found a kindred spirit--someone that could speak intelligently on any number of different things and loved to listen. She had worked through different levels of thoughts and problems while lying across his chest. The mere thought of their last "convention" quickened her pulse and subconsciously caused her to lick her lips. That thought was quickly interrupted by #3, "There you are, ready?" She nodded a quick ascent and grabbed her bag and headed to the Lexus idling in the driveway.

CHAPTER 7

The sun had risen over Seattle and Detective Will Swift stepped out on his front porch. He looked around for his newspaper wondering where the paperboy had hidden it this time, stomping his foot on the ground at the same time. This habit had developed years ago after his fourth and fifth surgery to rebuild his knee after twelve years of being a star running back had destroyed it. A thick cloud of steam rose from his oversized coffee mug and provided a nice contrast to the cool fall air. He saw the tip of the paper peeking out from under the hedges lining his sidewalk. He chuckled as he mentally added another tally to the inventive places the paperboy had found to challenge him. It had to number over forty now. Walking back in the house, he kissed his wife on the cheek as she drank her from her own mug. "What's on your plate today, baby?" she asked.

"Not much, light day since we wrapped up the Carlson case." Although a pretty open and shut case, the double murder/suicide of the upper middle class family had still taken its toll. "There but for the grace of God go I," had crossed his mind more than once over the course of solving the case. "I should be able to pick up little Will from school."

"Great," she answered, "I have a little shopping to catch up on." She leaned in to kiss him again and was interrupted by his cell phone going off. The text message came through with a "911" at the end of it.

"Or maybe not," Will said. Dialing the familiar number, he waited through three rings before his partner of five years answered.

"Menking."

"Hey G, what's up?" Will asked.

"This one could be ugly, partner." He quickly detailed what he knew, catching Will up to speed. He hung up the phone shaking his head and sighed deeply.

"Scratch the Daddy taxi, this one is going to be on CNN for weeks and weeks."

His wife looked puzzled, "Why is that?"

"Because the victim is worth about half a billion more than you and me, baby."

CHAPTER 8

Jackson smiled broadly as Jan walked down the concourse and out through security. Propriety demanded a handshake and a cordial welcome to the national's capital, but propriety gave way to passion as they relaxed in the limo on the ride back to the hotel. Her lips were soft and his arms strong and waiting. Several minutes of passionate kisses seemed to last a lifetime to her. Finally they pulled themselves apart and began to catch up. It had been only four months since their last time together and Jan made a mental note for their next separation to be much shorter. They talked and laughed, toasting each other with champagne and finishing the bottle on the trip back to the hotel. The bell staff carried her luggage up and unloaded everything for her review. She looked at his wardrobe, compared it to hers and with a look over her shoulder announced they were going shopping. On the drive to and between the hotel and Jan's favorite stores, which had been strategically alerted by Jackson, she made and received no less than fifteen phone calls and made arrangements for four different meetings, a brunch and agreed to appear at another function after the first of the year. Jackson never ceased to be amazed at her organization, her ceaseless energy and her single-mindedness when it came to getting things done. He sat back and enjoyed the ride and the glass of wine he had poured as she finished up her last call. "That's it, I promise," she said with a smile. She reached for her own wine glass and her phone rang again. She scanned the caller ID and grinned sheepishly, "I do have to take this but it will be short." As she arranged another meeting, Jackson moved behind her and began to kiss her neck and shoulders softly. She playfully tried to shoo him away, but he simply switched sides. By the time she had finished her phone call, he had her completely flustered. She began to protest but he simply covered her lips with his and pulled her body down to him. She giggled like a schoolgirl as his strong hands encircled her waist, drawing her nearer. A few minutes later, the limo pulled to a stop and the driver announced they had reached their destination. They stepped out and Jan adjusted her clothing which had been rumpled somewhat by Jackson's playfulness. The pair then set out for a shopping adventure limited only by how quickly they could use her credit cards. Ninety minutes and two very satisfied commissioned salespeople later, Jan and Jackson returned to the hotel with four new outfits each to satisfy whatever appearances needed to be made. Jackson had selected the stores and salespeople carefully, knowing full well their penchants for handling high maintenance clientele. They earned their money well with Jan and everyone involved was supremely satisfied. The limousine dropped them at the front door and the bell staff delivered the fruits of their labor to their suite. Jackson tipped them handsomely and the bellmen retreated to the exit quickly, thanking Jackson for his generosity. Looking at his watch, he advised Jan that they had a couple of hours before they had to be at the reception. She answered him from the suite's bedroom and asked if he had put out the "Do Not Disturb" sign on their front door. He accomplished this quickly and walking into the bedroom, was greeted by the sight of Jan's final item of clothing falling to the floor. She turned her head over her shoulder and asked why he was so overdressed for their closed-door meeting.

CHAPTER 9

Jessica shared a three-bedroom rent house in Midtown with her yellow Lab, "Max." A very easy drive to both work and the University, it was reasonably priced and in a great neighborhood with people always walking around or working in their yards. She had decorated it in a style she referred to as "eclectic cluttered." There were remnants of every art class she had taken including easels and the odd canvas here and there, plants that she hadn't quite killed yet and the several pictures she had brought with her from her old life. Strolling into the kitchen, she dropped her keys on the counter and leaned down to unclasp the leash from Max's collar. Late fall weather in Memphis was as unpredictable as every other season was and today was no exception. Nearly seventy degrees with a Spring-like breeze had encouraged Jessica to spend the day outside before she had to go to work tonight. She and Max had gone about two and half miles around the neighborhood and now she was going to enjoy the warm sun on her back deck while reading a book. She poured herself a tall glass of water and grabbed the book, heading toward the back door. She was interrupted by the sound of her cell phone ringing. Answering it with an out of breath "Hello," Jessica was pleased by the sound of her friend Melanie's voice. She sounded somewhat tired and Jessica asked if she had just gotten up. Melanie confirmed that she had and wasn't at all sure where she was. Jessica laughed and asked if she recognized anything. "Hold on a sec," she answered and Jessica could hear a door opening and closing. "Ok, it looks like I am down in Harbor Town at the Arbors. Can you come get me?" Jessica assured her she was on the way as she grabbed her keys and shut the door behind her.

Twenty minutes later, Melanie plopped down in the front seat of Jessica's Honda laughing loudly. Jessica looked toward the apartment Melanie had come from and a tall, dark and young guy wearing a pair of khaki cargo shorts waved at them. "He's cute," she said, her voice asking the "Why not" question they had asked each other many times. "And dumb, brainless, and worth about three minutes in bed. I've been more satisfied riding the merry go round horses at the Fair!"

Both women shrieked hysterically as they drove away. A couple of minutes into the drive, Melanie's cell phone rang and their boss was on the other end. He asked why a certain young man was calling here and asking for her with the explanation of the cell number she had given him being disconnected. They shrieked again, laughing all the way to Melanie's apartment as she recounted the evening in distressingly accurate detail.

CHAPTER 10

Detective Swift nodded in acknowledgement to the uniformed officer standing watch at the door of the Milligan house. "How's Marcy doing Bobby?" he asked.

"She's good Detective, should be finishing up her last couple of classes this spring and then hopefully sitting for the Bar after that. She wants to save the world one unwinnable case at a time."

"A lawyer with a conscience is a rare thing indeed. You should be very proud."

"I'll let her know your good thoughts. Thanks for asking."

Will took a sip from his coffee cup and walked into the crime scene. Wondering to himself why he continued to spend $5.00 on a cup of coffee, he surveyed the scene in quiet reflection. Groups of people hovered around different rooms gathering evidence, clicking photographs and dusting the odd doorknob and countertop for fingerprints. In the living room, another uniform officer tired to console and question a hysterical Hispanic woman that proved to be the maid. Will walked past that scene and into the kitchen where he found his partner, Art Menking. Art was a salty old-school cop with thirty years experience and enough stories to convince any rookie to switch professions while they were still ahead. "Where's mine?" Art asked nodding towards Will's coffee. Will shrugged his shoulders and held the large cup out towards his partner as a concessionary offering. "Too expensive for my taste anyway," came the growled reply. "What a shame, pretty lady, ton of money, lived alone. The maid found her this morning. She had missed a few meetings, which was entirely uncharacteristic for her. The maid gets here about 10:00, discovers the body, and calls '911.' Everything checks out with her--she's legal and the victim was paying her insurance and withholding taxes, the whole nine yards. It looks kind of like a robbery, but it doesn't quite feel like it. The purse was gone through and it looks like a computer upstairs was accessed sometime before she was killed. The tech guys are going through that now. That's her lawyer." Art nodded in the general direction of a calm, authoritative figure with a suit that probably cost as much as a month's salary of both detectives combined. At the mention of the word, the lawyer looked up and walked in the direction of the detectives, talking loudly as soon as he came within earshot.

"I want a detailed accounting of everything that leaves the premises. Miss Milligan's affairs have always been very private and it is my intense desire that they stay that way."

Will looked at the lawyer somewhat wearily and announced, "Me too. Too much publicity and I can't do my job Mister..."

"Carey. Michael Carey. I have been in the employ of the Milligan family for the past thirty years and consider them as important as my own family."

"Good, then we are agreed. I will have to rely on your knowledge and expertise to tell me her story so we can figure out what happened here. How about my office this afternoon around four o'clock?"

"Four is fine. I will see you then."

"Thank you counselor," Will answered with a forced smile. He watched as the attorney worked his way to the front door with a sense of amusement. "Love those guys...." He said to no one in particular. He walked into the kitchen and found Sharon Milligan lying on the floor in a pool of blood. Her eyes were open and Will wondered if the expression on her face was one of pain or surprise. His partner followed closely and confirmed they were finished taking pictures so he could examine the body more closely. Will lifted the bottom of the silk blouse she was wearing and found a large slash from her belly button half way up her body. "Was there a weapon found?"

"Yes, a butcher knife was found on the body. One of her own."

"Any prints?"

"Not on the knife. Several around the rest of the place, hers, the maid, along with a host of others. She entertained here semi-regularly. It seems like half of Seattle has been here in the past six months."

"Our invitations must have gotten lost in the mail. Any family, significant others around?"

"There's a sister that lives close, I have a uniform picking her up now and taking her to the station."

"Ok, that'll have to be where we start. Take the maid's statement and remind her not to go far, we may need to talk to her again soon. We'll talk to the sister and the lawyer at the office. Let's find out if there was a boyfriend or anything. Tell the guys to be extra careful and tag everything. This one has to be done by the book." Will sighed deeply and shook his head, agreeing with his partner about this being a shame. "Ok, Miss Milligan, who killed you?"

CHAPTER II

The convention center meeting room was decorated ornately with antique furniture and fixtures arranged atop Oriental rugs. A few hundred people milled around, talking to anyone and everyone and attempting to be seen talking to the right people. Jan and Jackson entered separately at discretely appropriate times, taking in the surroundings and speaking with great familiarity to those they knew. Several of Jan's close friends were in attendance and commented on the absence of her husband, which she quickly explained with business that he needed to attend to at home. Jan and Jackson were very careful to only to be seen together in groups of other people and to come and go separately. Jackson attended several different conferences around the country all year long so his appearance raised no eyebrows among those present. They each had a few drinks and worked the room thoroughly. Jan set a few more meetings for the following day, including a breakfast meeting with a few industry heads that were after her to sit on their Board of Directors. Taking a pre-planned verbal cue, Jackson excused himself and called for their limousine. Twenty minutes later Jan joined her partner in deception who was already half way through the bottle of chilled champagne he had waiting.

"Did you see everyone that needed you to see them?" he teased.

"Behave, there are some very important people in there and I was happy to see them."

"Well, I was hoping you were happy to see me."

"I think I showed you earlier that I was happy to see you. More than once." She took the champagne glass that he offered.

He raised his glass and toasted, "Here's to that and more of it!"

They entered their hotel room as always, Jan on her cell phone and Jackson opening the door. He lit a fire in their fireplace and dimmed the lights. He poured them each another glass of champagne and checked to make sure that everything was as he had arranged it. Jackson moved to the oversized sofa across from the fire and turned on some soft music. A minute or two later a relieved Jan plopped down next to him. She took the glass he had poured for her and took a sip, quickly replacing it on the table in front of them. She gave him a look that he knew intimately and he replaced his own as well. He stood and offered his hand to her and they danced a slow, sultry dance around the room. Their lips met with the slightest of touches, their breathing becoming as one. Careful not to miss a beat, he caressed her face with his right hand while sliding the other downward. He took great care in undressing her slowly, looking deeply in her eyes the entire time. Jackson kissed her passionately once more and then stepped back and allowed her to undress him as well. When she finished, he moved quickly back to her and they continued their dance, their passion growing with each movement. Their kisses grew hotter and wetter and their feet moved more slowly. She took his hand in hers and led him through the open doors behind them. The fireplace was two-sided and filled the bedroom with a warm glow. The temperature was almost as high as the desire between them. They knew each other's bodies thoroughly and began to show off their knowledge. She led him to the bed and pushed him into it and onto his back. She climbed in on top, kissing him deeply once more and lowering herself onto him for what would be the first of several times over the next few hours.

CHAPTER 12

Will Swift walked out of the interview room giving the maid a few minutes to regain her composure after breaking down into tears for the third time. He had talked with the sister, the lawyer and now the maid and he wasn't any closer at all to identifying a lead in the case. Far from being frustrated, he knew that solving murders was much more difficult than was shown on television. In fact, he couldn't recall the last time he had wrapped up a case in fifty-seven minutes, not counting commercials. He strode into the break room and poured himself a fresh cup of coffee, wondering to himself how station house coffee could possibly beat what his wife brewed for them at home. His partner stuck his head in and asked him how the interviews were going so far. Will caught him up to speed and then inquired what the crime scene had turned up. Art told him that the perp had seemingly been very thorough. They hadn't turned up prints they couldn't account for or any fibers or other identifying marks or fabrics they could use. They were certain that robbery was out as a motive because a safe holding nearly a million dollars in cash, bonds and artwork was left untouched, not to mention the jewelry and other valuables in plain sight that any experienced thief would have taken. He went on to say that the tech guys were going to dig through the computer under the watchful eye of the family attorney in the morning. Will thought it was a good idea for Art to be there just to make sure that procedurally everything went according to plan and that the tech guys and legal teams didn't get in each other's way when it involved evidence. He then told his partner that he was going to check the database for similar crimes or patterns found in other crime scenes to rule out a repeat criminal. They headed to the door to go their separate ways, agreeing to meet back up in the morning for breakfast at Will's house and to catch each other up. Reaching the door, their Lieutenant greeted them rather gruffly and they spent the next fifteen minutes recanting their stories again. A slight man, with a pale complexion and pointed face and demeanor, Lieutenant Phillip Morse reminded Will of the Frank Burns character from his favorite old TV show, "M.A.S.H." His boss had gotten his own command after a few unremarkable stints in auto, vice, and finally internal affairs. The jury was still out on whether he would succeed here and be promoted again. The office pool currently stood at $450 and Will had two years and one month before he was transferred or moved somewhere else. Morse, as he liked to be called, suggested they go over the victim's computer files to see if they uncovered any irregularities and then check the database to see if the crime fit any other unsolved murders. He then asked to see both detectives' interview notes so he could offer any insights. They looked at each other for a moment before looking back at their boss and letting him know that their notes weren't typed up yet. He shrugged his shoulders and suggested that he would happy to wait for them. He turned and headed toward his office as the two detectives looked at each other in stunned silence. Will pulled his cell phone off his belt and dialed home, "Well, I was right about one thing honey.... this is going to be a lot of fun...oh wait, I meant to say frustration, work and overtime. I'll be home as soon as I can."

CHAPTER 13

Shelby Farms is one of the larger parks in Tennessee and the largest in the Memphis area. Located on several hundred acres of land, one of its main attractions is a man-made lake with an asphalt trail that completely encircles it. It draws runners, walkers and in-line skaters of all levels of expertise. It was one of Jessica's favorite places to come and walk Max and get away from the mundane trials of every day living. She and Max were working up a sweat and enjoying the mid-Saturday morning quiet when a rollerblader skidded to a crash in front of her. She stopped short to check on him and he quickly stood back up. He smiled at her and said, "I told my friends that you looked like the kind-hearted type I have been waiting my whole life for." She rolled her eyes and stepped to the side and moved around him. He moved to stop her, saying, "How can you not see that fate has brought us together today?"

Taking a deep breath, she answered him. "I'm sorry I wasn't more sensitive to your feelings. What's your name?"

"Jeffrey. My friends call me Jeff."

"And are those your friends over there?" she asked pointing to two guys more interested in the goings on than they should have been.

"Why yes they are. Which one do you think should be the best man?"

She smiled at him and walked in the direction of his two friends. Reaching them, she asked the friends their names as well. "Well, well, Michael, Josh and Jeffrey. What a compelling trio you all must have made back in your fraternity days. I'm going to speak slowly and use small words so hopefully your little pea brains can process what I am saying. If you ever want to find a woman that you can truly be happy with, you will need to first of all stop treating them like game to be hunted and then mounted. Come on lines, pick up lines, drinks bought in a bar, wagers on who can score before everyone else…all these constitute pathetic excuses to hide behind a pitiful front so you wouldn't possibly have to come face-to-face with the idea that a woman might see one inch behind your 'I'm the man' persona that is tired and not attractive in the least little bit. Now if you will excuse me, I am going to go home and enjoy an hour or so with something battery-powered that has about the same level of intelligence that three of you combined have and the ability to satisfy much more than any of you could ever hope to."

"Now just wait a minute!" Jeffrey barked, his face red with embarrassment and anger.

"Max, OUCH," Jessica pointed at the three men. Max responded with the fur on his neck standing up and growling from the pit of his stomach. All three quickly backed up, holding their hands in the air like they were being held at gunpoint. Jessica and Max moved around the trio and walked back to the car, Jessica grinning from ear to ear and trying hard not to burst into laughter.

CHAPTER 14

There was an audible buzz that arose over the floor of the Convention Center as the meetings moved into their final day. Jackson moved around the crowd easily, greeting the few people he recognized and watching Jan work the crowd tirelessly. She was treated somewhat like a celebrity. She signed a few books and other autographs and stopped to have her picture taken a few different times. Jackson had been taken aside by one of the hospitality brokers to ask his opinion on the convention and the hotel where the guests were staying. Jackson politely let him know he had made his own arrangements and couldn't comment on what he didn't know about. Jan witnessed the exchange and smiled to herself, then waved to catch his attention. She took his arm and they walked to one of the many booths around the hall. There, she introduced Jackson to an attractive, serious looking blonde in a power suit, handing out literature on alternative fuel sources. "Jackson, I would like for you to meet my good friend Meredith Gregory. Meredith, this is the gentleman I was telling you about, Jackson Pritchard. Jan and Jackson exchanged furtive glances as he shook Meredith's hand.

"It's a pleasure to meet you, Ms. Gregory. Any friend of Jan's is a friend of mine." Jackson guessed her to be her in mid-to-late twenties and single, frustrated and somewhat self-conscious with the way she shook his hand.

"Please call me Meredith, my friends all do."

"Meredith it is then."

Jan chimed in, "Meredith is going to be in Memphis for meetings Thursday and Friday this week. Maybe you could show her some southern hospitality?" Mentally scanning his calendar, Jackson looked at Jan with a serious look and then smiled broadly at Meredith. "It would be my pleasure. Where are you staying?"

"I'm not sure. My company typically makes the arrangements."

"Please, allow me to take care of everything. I believe Jan can vouch for my skills in that area." Jan and Meredith both smiled and nodded in agreement. Jackson handed Meredith a card that read "Hospitality Consultants Inc." and contained his cell phone number. "Call me and let me know when your flight is scheduled to arrive and I will have your plane met."

They shook hands again and Meredith excused herself to talk with a group that had gathered in front of her booth. Jan answered his question before he asked it. "She has done a lot of free promotional work for us and has personally made me a good deal of money. She wants to come to work for me and I think she would make a great addition. I can't hire her yet but want to show her my gratitude. Send me the bill for everything." Jackson smiled again and they continued their walk through the meeting hall. They were interrupted yet again by her cell phone. She covered the mouthpiece and asked him to meet her back at the hotel. They had an hour or so between the last meeting and the dinner and she wanted to relax and freshen up a bit. He agreed and left the convention hall, letting the limousine driver know to wait for Jan. He grabbed a taxicab and headed back to the hotel. The room had been cleaned and their formal wear for the evening had been dry-cleaned and hung neatly in the closet. Jackson arranged them so they could change quickly once they had finished relaxing. Going back downstairs, he went to the bar and ordered a chicken sandwich and a beer. There was a football game on the flat screen TV in the corner and he took it in, enjoying his food and talking with the bartender. About the time he had finished his meal, his cell phone rang and Jan informed him she was on the way over. He charged his meal to the hotel room, including a generous tip to the bartender and headed back upstairs. Going into the spacious bathroom, he began to run a steaming hot bath in the oversized tub and added a few scents and bubbles to the slowly rising water. He had just turned the water off, undressed and stepped into the hot bath when he heard the doors to the suite open and close.

"Honey, I'm home!" The joke never seemed to grow old to her.

"I'm in here," Jackson answered.

"Ooooh, that sounds promising." Jan entered the bathroom, waving a cloud of steam out from in front of her face.

"Well, satisfaction is just one of the many services I provide."

"Tell me something I don't know lover boy." She quickly undressed and joined him in the tub, sliding over to him and kissing his lips gently. "Now, please tell me that I didn't upset you earlier. I thought I remembered that your schedule was open this weekend."

"Yes, it is open and no, you didn't upset me. A little heads up would have been nice though. You did kind of put me on the spot."

"I know and I am truly sorry baby. I meant to talk to you about it earlier, but I forgot and didn't remember until I saw her in there today. How can I ever make it up to you?"

"I'm sure I could think of a few ways," he answered. The smile in her eyes told him she had already thought of a few and she started with the first of those just then, reaching below the surface of the water to find him firmly waiting for her.

CHAPTER 15

"You didn't!"

"I did!" Jessica answered Melanie as well as two other girls they worked with at the bar. They howled hysterically, picturing one of several guys that would most likely try to attract their attention tonight.

"So...you went home. Then did you..."

"Did I what? Oh that? Well yeah! I'm not about to let three assholes make a liar out of me!"

More shrieks of laughter, enough to get the attention of Jesse, the pretty, uncomplicated, eternal college student that worked the bar with them. He wandered over. "You know, between Melanie sleeping with them and you not, you are going to seriously damage the psyche of the patrons here at our lovely establishment."

"Hell, as long as they keep tipping, they can be as damaged as they like," Melanie answered.

Jesse shrugged his shoulders and wandered back away and wiping the bar down a bit.

"So why do you think you went off on them like that?" Amber was newer to the staff and a junior at one of the smaller local colleges.

"Probably because it was just so blatant. It was like he just knew he was irresistible and couldn't wait to show it off to his buddies. I almost kicked him in the balls."

"I think I would have paid to see that," Melanie chimed in.

"Yeah, me too," replied Jessica with a thoughtful look on her face.

The bar manager walked in and called a quick meeting. "SEC Championship game tonight. This place will be packed with a bunch of drunken football fans screaming and yelling all night long. Just be your normal charming selves and everything will be fine. I've got a few more door guys coming in so everything should run smoothly. Oh, and I got a call from Mitch over at Sidestreet. He said that someone is trying to pass off fake twenties, so make sure you keep an eye out for them. Said the guy stung them for close to $200 a couple of weekends ago."

CHAPTER 16

The ballroom was a picture of elegance. If the reception and seminars were about being seen, the banquet was about looking better than every one else. The banquet staff was dressed formally, the music elegant and everyone in attendance was outfitted in tuxedos and formal gowns. Jackson surveyed the crowd as he entered, smoothing out his classic, conservative Armani tuxedo. He and Jan had arrived separately as always and she was already working the room. She would be seated at the head table although she was not on the presentation schedule. Jackson was strategically seated next to Meredith Gregory and he looked forward to getting to know her a bit better. He began to make his way through the room, talking to the people he had met and spending a few minutes with those that were the most entertaining. He and Jan were seemingly circling the room on opposite sides and their eyes met every now and again. It seemed that she blushed a couple of times but Jackson dismissed that and blamed the lighting. He took one of the glasses of champagne being handed out by the wait staff and planned to keep and nurse it through dinner. Being intoxicated was never a viable option in his line of work with "control" being the optimum phrase. He finally worked his way to where Jan was holding court with a group of ten or so people. One of the travel vendors that Jackson had met the previous day shook his hand warmly as Jackson searched his memory for the man's name. Darrell Arthurs. Same last name as his high school business teacher. Darrell was apparently on his third or fourth glass of champagne as his speech was slightly slurred. "Have you met Jan Eberhardt?" he asked Jackson admiringly. "She's wonderful, knows more about her stuff than anyone you have ever met." Without waiting for an answer, he pulled Jackson over and began to introduce the two. Jan smiled broadly and let Darrell know that they had met previously. Jackson took a moment to take her in. She was impeccably dressed with the red strapless gown he had laid out for her. It was a little longer than floor length and trailed behind her neatly. She offered Jackson her hand, which he took and kissed lightly.

"I remember being charmed by you at the last conference we both attended, Mr. Pritchard. What brings you to our little corner of the world again?"

"Business, a man has to earn a living. Sometimes work is harder than other times."

"And this time?" she asked earnestly.

"Occasionally hard, but the conference has been entirely pleasurable."

"I'm pleased to hear that. If you will get with Meredith Gregory and give her your information, she will make sure you get on our mailing list. We very much appreciate your support and look forward to having you again."

Jackson smiled and bowed his head slightly. "Thank you, you are too kind." He excused himself from the group and made his way to his table where he found Meredith already seated. She was talking with an older gentleman that was several inches inside her personal comfort zone. Jackson noticed she was trying to escape his attentions and he rode in to help. He leaned in and kissed her on the cheek, lingering a moment longer than a business acquaintance typically would. "I'm sorry I am late babe, I couldn't get my tie to work. How does it look?"

Meredith turned in her chair, somewhat startled at first before she recognized him. She stood and fiddled with the tie. "It looks fine Jack. You always worry too much about nothing. Have you met Congressman

Gill?" She nodded in his direction, stifling a laugh as the gentleman attempted to hide the defeated look on his face.

"I have not had the pleasure, I'm Jackson Pritchard." The smell of bourbon overwhelmed the cheap cologne the man was wearing.

They shook hands and the Congressman excused himself, mumbling a half-hearted reason to slide away to another group of people.

Meredith smiled and then looked appreciatively at Jackson. "Thank you so much. The Congressman is a huge supporter of our cause, but when he's had a bit to drink, he's a little…"

"Aggressive?"

"A very politically correct term, Mr. Pritchard."

"Please, Jackson or Jack."

"Which does Jan call you?" she asked with a smile.

Jackson paused for a moment and then nodded, "She prefers Jackson."

"Then how about I call you Jack?"

"I would be quite pleased. Thank you."

"You know, your mother would be quite proud of your manners. She must have worked very hard on that."

"My grandmother actually. My mother died when I was very young." Jackson answered.

"I am so sorry, I didn't mean…"

Jackson raised his hand, "No apology necessary, there was no way you could have known. It's quite all right. I never knew her; she died before I was a year old. My grandparents raised me and we are still very close. My grandmother would be very pleased by your compliment." Jackson excelled at letting people off the hook. Looking around, he noticed people beginning to move to their tables. "Shall we sit down?"

The dinner was a formal seven-course affair that put normal banquet fare to shame. Jackson and Meredith got along well and the conversation at the table was an animated discussion on whether global warming was a serious threat or not. Jackson found himself in the minority, questioning the "science" that the others at the table offered. Eventually the group agreed to disagree with the addendum that they could all do more to at least be environmentally friendly. They were finishing up dinner as the speaker took the podium. He gave a fairly standard if not boring presentation and appeal for more research and development and financial support. The general consensus at their table was that they would have been better off continuing their own conversation from earlier. The speaker ended and the crowd responded appreciatively. Jackson wondered out loud if they were applauding because of the topic or because he was finished. Meredith punched his arm lightly and the shared a quick laugh. The emcee for the evening closed and thanked everyone for coming and directed to them to various websites for more information and exhorted them to keep up the fight. A small orchestra group began to play at the other end of the banquet hall and the patrons all moved in that direction. Jan was making her way across the ballroom with champagne glass in hand.

"So what is it you do that would bring you here?" Meredith asked.

"Jan didn't tell you?"

"Not really. She said you were in the hospitality business and that you had worked together for three or four years. She did say you were charming and engaging. I think she sold you a bit short there!"

"Again, you are very kind. I am a consultant in several areas of hospitality. I write some travel articles. Make recommendations to different hotel groups, travel agencies, stuff like that."

"I read all the time and I haven't seen your name anywhere, have you been published?"

"I write under a pseudonym, Tyler Jackson."

"I recognize that name; I remember reading your article on St. Kitts. But why not use your own name?"

"I like the anonymity of it. It ensures that I am treated like everyone else and doesn't sway my opinion of the places I stay or services I use."

"Makes sense."

They talked a while longer and finished their respective drinks. A few individuals stopped by to extend their greetings and they noticed Jan finally making it to them.

"Did you kids enjoy dinner?" she asked.

"It was both informational and entertaining," Meredith answered for both of them.

"Fabulous. And your Memphis trip?"

Jackson and Meredith exchanged glances with Jackson answering this time. "I'm making the arrangements for Thursday and Friday night and will get back with Meredith when they are ready. Those are the two nights you will be in town, right?" he asked to both.

"Yes, I fly in Thursday morning, have meetings both days and then fly back out first thing Saturday morning," Meredith replied.

"Perfect. Now if you ladies will excuse me, I have an article to write and an early flight myself. It has been a distinct pleasure." He took both of their hands and kissed them, bowed slightly and made his way to the exit.

About an hour later, the door to the hotel suite opened and a slightly inebriated Jan strolled through. Jackson got up from the sofa and clicked off the TV. Walking behind her, he took her coat and purse and hung them up in the closet. He went to the bar and asked if she wanted a nightcap.

"I was thinking that you were the nightcap, and yes, I would definitely like a taste." She strode over to him as he was pouring them both a glass of champagne. He handed her one and toasted, "To another successful conference." She finished her glass, took his glass and finished it as well, placing both of them on the bar. She wrapped her arms around him, pulling him closely to her and kissed him deeply. Taking a step back, she turned around and asked him to unzip her. He did and with two long strides, her gown fell to the floor and she stepped out of it and moved to the bedroom. He quickly followed, closing the door behind him. The pair fell into the already turned-down bed and made love passionately for the next three hours before falling asleep in each other's arms.

CHAPTER 17

Club 152 in Memphis is a hotspot on Beale Street that moves to a different beat than the other clubs in the Historic district. Most of the traditional establishments are bastions of the traditional music of the Street: The Blues. Most had live acts six or seven nights a week that wailed and howled the Blues as well as anywhere in the country. A favorite of both tourist and local crowds, Club 152 was a dance club, pure and simple. The first floor was the general interest floor. Pay a cover and get in. The music is typically hip hop/rap dance music or techno and the dance floor is packed. Whether it's a DJ or a band, the music will be overwhelmingly bass-driven and be played until the last dancer leaves the floor. The second and third floors played different types of music depending on what night it is and if they were open to the general public or treated more like a VIP room. Tonight, all three floors were open and packed. Techno on the 1st floor, 70's and 80's music on the 2nd, and Hip Hop/Dance music on the 3rd. A tall, attractive brunette was all over the 1st level dance floor. She had come by herself as usual and drank a bit too much, also as usual. She danced by herself at first, swaying to the beat of the music while listening to and watching the band play. She rarely had to buy her own drinks and this night was no exception.

She drew the attention of three guys in the bar and they competed for her attention, all with the initial step of buying her a drink. She always enjoyed the attention and loved the fact that she could drink without spending any money. Each of the three was pretty good looking and each treated her very nicely. After an hour or so of vying to be her first choice, one of the three shrugged his shoulders, effectively giving up and moving on. The other two dueled for a while, first at the bar and then on the dance floor. She then made her decision by wrapping her arms around the neck of the taller of the two and kissing him hard on the mouth. They moved their bodies in unison on the dance floor for the better part of the next hour, stopping only to catch their breath a bit and to refresh their drinks. As the night grew later, their movements became more and more suggestive until they were grinding their hips together and pressing their lips and tongues until they became as one. They occasionally bumped into the couples dancing around them, finally catching the attention of one of the bartenders who promptly alerted a bouncer. "Guido" had worked as a bouncer at several clubs on and around Beale over the past few years and was known as a very nice guy that new how to do his job very well. Guido approached the couple and got their attention, letting them know to keep themselves under control or it was time to move on. Both nodded their heads and agreed to behave themselves. And they did for a while. An hour or so and three drinks later, their movements were more erratic and they were on the verge of causing a severe disruption. Guido quietly asked them to leave and began to escort them out of the club. The young man took her hand and prepared to leave. She yelled for him to get his hands off of her and threw her drink in his face. When he protested loudly, Guido came back over to shut them down. The brunette was crying at this point and accused her stunned dance partner of trying to take advantage of her. When Guido asked if they were together, she shook her head "no" and when challenged, asked if he even knew what her name was. With a look of surprise, he answered "Shelby." She then asked about her last name. When he couldn't answer, Guido quickly and calmly escorted him out of the club. He advised the spurned young man to forget about it and go home and sleep it off. At the very least, he should go anywhere else but back in 152. The wanna-be suitor stayed angry for a minute or so until his friends joined him and they headed down Beale to see whom else they could pick up. Back inside, the young lady had regained her composure, had her tab taken care of by the manager and waited for fifteen minutes with a new drink, listening as the band closed out this set. Satisfied that she was okay and in no danger from her "assailant," Guido walked her to the door and sent her on her way. She turned to Guido as she walked down the street, gave him the finger, and laughed all the way back to her car, got in, and drove herself home...alone again.

CHAPTER 18

Jackson awoke early and surveyed the luggage he had packed the night before. He turned his laptop on and logged on, confirming his travel plans, checking his e-mail and his bank balances before logging off and loading it into his carry-on bag. He called down to the concierge and confirmed a car for him and a limousine later in the day for Jan before ordering breakfast. He shaved and showered and dressed in comfortable travel clothes that would make it easily through security and took his luggage to the foyer by the front door. A few minutes later, there was a knock at the door and room service was announced. Jackson let him in and signed for the check, again including a generous tip. He pushed the cart into the bedroom and sat on the edge of the bed, gently waking Jan with a soft kiss on her cheek. She awoke with a smile and stretched, opening her eyes and gazing at him affectionately.

"Do you think of everything?" she asked, surveying the breakfast in front of her.

"I do my best, love."

"And you are the best."

"I'll attribute that to my thinking of everything as opposed to some sort of taste test by comparison," he answered with a wink.

"Of course that is what I meant. I am happy that you and Meredith hit it off by the way."

"Yes, we should talk about that since my ride will be here in about twenty minutes," he said glancing at his watch, "and I need to know what you have in mind for her. She doesn't seem to know what to expect."

"She and I are having lunch today and I will encourage her to let herself be charmed by you."

"This isn't how I usually work. I don't know anything about her."

"She has my full confidence and recommendation. I already had her take a full physical with the idea of hiring her. My firm is successful and well known, but it's still small and insurance is expensive. There's a copy of the physical in the envelope over there on the nightstand along with the rest." He leaned over and kissed her again. He stood and poured her a cup of coffee, adding two sugars and placed it on the table next to her. He walked over and opened the envelope and counted out ten thousand dollars in addition to the physical results.

"You can't see the whole thing, but you can see there that she is in good health and is disease free. Unlike me, she can still have babies, so you will have to be careful in that regard."

"So the menu is whatever she wants then?"

"Yes, just don't be better with her than you are with me lover boy!" She playfully threw a pillow at him.

"Never. I know how you girls talk. This is more money than usual though."

"Just a little extra to say thank you for letting me run a little roughshod over your usual referral policy. And just to say thank you for being you. You still know how to make me feel special. I miss that."

"I just listen. You do the rest." Jackson smiled and sat back down. He leaned over and kissed her lips gently, noting the coffee taste lingering.

"You're sweet…and flattery does still get you whatever you want. Now go and catch your plane before I get all sentimental again. Oh, are we still on for March?"

"It's on my calendar and I am looking forward to it. Haven't skied in a while."

"I'm looking forward to it too. Call me after next weekend. I would like to hear how it goes, minus the gory details!"

"So you are going to tell her or not?"

"What, that you are an escort? I don't think that's a conversation you just broach over breakfast. 'Oh and by the way, your date in Memphis next weekend is paid for.' Just take her out and show her anything and everything she wants to see and if it goes there, well…go there!"

"Ok, I just wanted to be sure that we were on the same page. Appearances and expectations are big in both our worlds."

"I know all too well. Now go before you miss your plane."

"Have a safe flight back." They kissed again, this time quickly as if concluding their business together, interrupted when the bedside phone rang, announcing that his car was ready and waiting downstairs. He asked to have the bell staff come get his bags and hung up the phone. He kissed her on the forehead, stood and headed to the door. He turned and caught her eye, bowed slightly, then left, closing the door behind him. An hour later, he caught the first flight out of D.C. to Memphis. Sitting in first class, the flight attendant asked if his trip was successful. He smiled broadly, leaning his chair back and closing his eyes. "It seems so, thank you for asking." She smiled in return, making a mental note to pay more attention to the handsome stranger.

CHAPTER 19

Jessica awoke early as always on a Sunday morning. Sundays were typically her days to get things done at her own pace. Today would be a little bit different because she was covering a lunch shift. Still, she didn't have to be at the Blue Monkey until 10:30 so she could at least enjoy her coffee and get the bulk of her house cleaned. The back deck provided the perfect setting for a private cup of coffee while the rest of the world slumbered along. The December air was crisp and cool, sending the smallest of shivers up her spine. She smiled at the sensation and sipped slowly, savoring the flavor while she mentally mapped out the rest of her morning. She enjoyed her silent surroundings for a long thirty minutes before coming inside and changing out of her robe and into one of a few men's dress shirts she had inherited over the past few years. Wearing one was a good reminder of feeling sexy, but on her terms. She turned the CD player to a random setting, not sure of what was waiting in the 5-disc rotation and turned the volume up loud. Following a preset pattern, she worked her way through the house, cleaning each room from the top down and finished with the floors. Because her time was short today, the sweeping and mopping would have to wait until after work. She started in the bathroom first with Aretha Franklin asking for "Respect." Along the way through the bedrooms and living room, she heard different songs by Fleetwood Mac, Liz Phair, and Trisha Yearwood. She finished the bathroom and kitchen singing the words she knew to Alanis Morrisette's "Uninvited" and started dusting the place to "Sweet Child of Mine" by Sheryl Crow. She finished up her cleaning with a flourish singing "What I Am" by Edie Brickell at the top of her lungs. Having satisfied her need for feminine self-actualization, she cleaned up and changed and readied herself for a rare lunch shift at The Blue Monkey.

CHAPTER 20

The plane touched down at Memphis International Airport. Jackson gathered his carry on bag and said good-bye to "Cindy", his new favorite flight attendant, making sure to save her cell phone number in his own. It took him about twenty minutes to retrieve his luggage and make it to his car, a black extended cab Jeep Wrangler. It came with a hard and soft top, but whenever he parked it for a few days, the hard top stayed on. A few minutes later, the windows were down and he was on his way to Midtown. He was in the process of buying a condo in one of the new high rise, multi-purpose towers being built along the Memphis skyline. During the finish out, he was renting a three-bedroom bungalow close to Overton Square. Exiting off the I-240 loop, Jackson noticed his stomach alerting him to the fact that he was hungry again. A quick run down Madison left him a few choices open on a Sunday late morning. He bypassed two of the national chains represented and wasn't in the mood for anything exotic, bypassing both an Indian and a Thai restaurant. He drove further on Madison, looked to his left and saw the Blue Monkey, turned and parked and headed inside.

CHAPTER 21

The crowd hadn't picked up yet although Dave, one of the regular Sunday guys, assured her that it would. November and December meant NFL football with every game available every week with the right satellite package. And of course they had that. Dave was working the bar and Jessica had picked up the three tables currently being occupied. They were all at various stages of their lunches and Jessica was already knocking out some of her side work so that she could leave as soon as her shift was over. She was in the middle of rolling silverware when a handsome one-top walked in and sat down at a table across from the bar. She gave him a bit to get settled and comfortable and walked over and handed him a menu. "Would you care for something to drink while you are...?"

He caught her glance and let her string her words longer. "Waiting for you to finish your sentence?" He immediately was taken by the laughter and life in her eyes, unsure as to their color and hoping her might look deeply enough to find out.

She laughed and he smiled back in return. He asked her what was on tap and she ran through the selections, domestic first and then imports. He ordered a "Fat Tire" which showed he at least had a little taste. "I'm ready to order too. Your Pepper Jack Chicken sandwich with fries. Had it before, it's good."

She took his order and went back to the bar, putting his order in and grabbing his beer. Dropping it off, she made a loop around her other tables, taking care of their various needs and then gravitating back to her newest table. "Have I seen you in here before?" she asked.

"Maybe, I've been in a few times. Been a little bit though. I have been traveling with work."

"Fun, what do you do?"

"Consulting work, mostly in hospitality. Just got back from a convention today."

"Did it work for you?"

"You could say it went well. I would." He raised his beer in toast to himself.

"Well cheers to you then." She smiled and walked back to the bar. He laughed at himself and took another drink from his beer. He took in one of the larger screens where a college basketball game was being played. He pulled his laptop out and typed up a few thank you letters to the contacts he had made over the weekend and started putting his thoughts together for a freelance article he had in mind for The Jefferson Hotel. A few minutes passed and Jessica appeared with another beer in hand. "I took the liberty of bringing you another one. I hope you don't mind."

"Not at all, it's nice to have someone anticipate your needs for a change."

"I couldn't agree more. So what are you working on?"

"Just catching up on some paperwork, nothing exciting."

"With sports on TV?"

"Is that so hard to believe?"

"You just separated yourself from 95% of the male population in Memphis."

"Is that such a bad thing?" he posed, raising an eyebrow and cocking his head to the side.

"I suppose not," she said, glancing downward quickly and stifling a smile.

"You should let more people see you smile, it looks good on you."

She shuffled a bit uncomfortably. "Thanks, ummm, I'll go see if your food is ready."

Jackson looked again at the screen and got lost in the game for a few minutes. Jessica made her way to his table and brought his food, quickly excusing herself to check on her other customers. The pepper jack chicken sandwich at the Blue Monkey was one of the best in Memphis. Several minutes went by and he had made quick work of the plate in front of him. Jessica came back around and asked if he wanted another beer. He politely declined, citing the need to catch up on a week of being out of town and asked for his check. He paid with cash, including a handsome tip and left his table cleaner than it was when he sat down. Jessica merely had to carry a glass and plate and run a quick dishtowel over the table and it was ready again. She casually dropped the dishes off in the kitchen and stepped out the back door for a quick breath of fresh air. She saw Jackson get into his Jeep and drive away, nodding her head and smiling.

CHAPTER 22

Monday morning was always Jackson's morning to sleep late. The majority of his work was done on weekends, and he did chores and caught up on his housework after he caught up on his sleep. The phone woke him up before his alarm did and he was surprised to find his computer repair shop on the line. "Good morning Mr. Pritchard, this is Danny McAlester from The Computer Doctor. Looks like there is an upgrade that came out for your laptop and the warranty covers it. When can you bring it in?"

"What? Upgrade? Sorry, I was asleep. You want me to bring my computer back in?"

"Yep, the manufacturer has sent an upgrade out and your computer will work much better with it."

"How long do you need it for?"

"Just a couple of hours. I am pretty open this afternoon if you just want to drop it by. I can have it back for you before five."

"Ok, I will bring it by, thanks for calling." Jackson hung up the phone and looked at his clock, only slightly upset at it being 9:30.

Danny hung up the phone as well and said, "You're Welcome." He looked across the room at the receptionist and she smiled and waved in return.

Jackson dozed for a few more minutes, mentally reviewing his "to do" list and now adding another task to it. He got up and walked to the front door, retrieved the waiting newspaper and unrolled the rubber band from around it. He scanned the business page first to see if there were any stories that caught his eye. Not seeing anything of note, he unfolded the sports page and retreated to the bathroom. Several minutes later he turned on the hot water and proceeded to shave and shower, letting the hot water stream over his body. He placed both hands on the shower wall, letting the heat and steam awaken his senses. Thoroughly refreshed and awake, he blended a breakfast smoothie and drank it down while finishing the newspaper. He went back to the bedroom and pulled the portable safe from under the bed. It was fireproof and contained some important personal papers and after last night, a total of about $25,000 in cash. He took about $500 for some walking around money as well as to start the deposit process. Jackson preferred to make small deposits in different branches so as not to arouse any suspicion or raise any IRS red flags. Placing the money in his pants pocket, he closed the safe and scrambled the four combination dials and slid it back under the bed. He grabbed a backpack that was sitting by the door as well as his laptop and headed out the door and jumped in the jeep. His first stop was the bank near the midtown office of his computer repair guys. He deposited $300, thanking the clerk for her attention and headed over to the computer shop. He was greeted warmly at the front door by Shelby Powers, the firm's receptionist and aspiring technical know-it-all. She had worked there for about two years but had never been taken seriously by any of the techies for one simple and shortsighted reason: she was much too pretty. Jackson and Shelby had spent a weekend together several months ago and it was quite evident that she had been and remained quite enamored of him. From time to time, a random text message would appear on his phone, reminding him that she could and would be the best thing to ever happen to him. It had been cute and first, but now was more of a minor annoyance. "Have you given up on the rest of the women in the world sugah?" Shelby asked teasingly, her southern drawl dropping the 'r' off the end of the word.

"Maybe," Jackson replied, "I'm still not sure I could handle you in anything but small doses."

"Baby steps suit me just fine. Would be good practice for later."

"Maybe next week. Is Danny in?"

"He is, but he is tied up at the moment. He told me you would be dropping your laptop off. I'll give it to him."

"Ok, and I can pick it up when?"

"It should be ready before your pretty little face is sitting down to eat lunch."

"Well, I have a few appointments, but I will be back later this afternoon."

"I can't wait."

CHAPTER 23

The police station that Will Swift called home was a throwback to the days when the buildings themselves instilled a sense of respect that had been lost in modern, cookie-cutter architecture and contracts awarded to the lowest bidder. It was a four-story, inefficient but grand looking building in the heart of downtown Seattle. The holding cells were dark, old and musty and the building lost power with each strong thunderstorm that blew through. Still, Will thought of this as hallowed ground where he could best think and work his way through any problems that needed his attention. He got in around 7:30, before most were at their desks and poured a steaming cup of nearly undrinkable coffee. Whoever the early riser was, they made their coffee strong. Will stirred in a little cream and sugar and headed to his office. Art was waiting there for him, drinking his own cup of coffee. Will thought about that for a second and asked, "Did you make this?"

Art nodded affirmatively and asked his partner why without raising his head from the report he was reading.

"No reason." Will made a mental note to get his partner some Starbucks gift cards. "What are you looking at there?"

"It's a report from the tech guys. They haven't found anything out of the ordinary or anything missing, although there are a few weekends on her calendar that have absolutely nothing on them."

"And that's something because…"

"Because every other day going back three years has at least three or four entries on it."

"Interesting, have we found a personal journal or diary or anything?"

"Yes, but nothing in those about those weekends."

"Anything about boyfriends or people we haven't heard anything about yet?"

"Nope, she seems to have been pretty lousy at dating. Maybe she needed a middle-aged cop to take care of her."

"We'll never know now will we?"

Will chuckled at the look of irony on his partner's face. "I guess we won't. Shame."

"Ok, let's get back with the family to see if there are any other places she would have kept information. Maybe a safe deposit box or even there at the law firm. There's got to be something out there somewhere. Check with our favorite lawyer friend to see what he knows. Follow up with the family and friends about the schedule gaps and see what you can find out. If we focus on those gaps, I am betting they lead us right where we need to go. In the meantime, I'll check the wire to see if anything matches this MO."

CHAPTER 24

Jackson's second stop for the day was the Talbot Heirs Guesthouse. Situated in the heart of downtown Memphis, Talbot Heirs is unique in its approach to hospitality. It is composed of several different suites, all unique in shape and décor. Jackson had utilized the guesthouse before and the woman behind the front desk gave him a smile of recognition as he walked in. He quickly made arrangements for Thursday and Friday night in Suite 4, a favorite of his. It was decorated with a southern theme, including a four-poster, wrought iron bed, a huge walk-in kitchen, with separate bed and bathrooms. The view was spectacular, taking in a good part of three separate skyline views. Jackson confirmed that the kitchen would be fully stocked and that there was plenty of desk space for Meredith to work as much as she needed while she was in town. His thoughts drifted to their last conversation and he smiled fondly at the memory. He found her to be intelligent and charming and a part of him wished that they had met under different circumstances. Confident that everything would be taken care of, Jackson walked back out to the Jeep, started it, and headed east to the University of Memphis where he had an early afternoon class. The traffic was heavy but moved quickly as he reached campus. He quickly parked and found his way to his Italian III class. For a few hours every week, Jackson took time out from the world and learned a little more of the old and beautiful language. The hour and a half passed quickly and he packed up his bag and left. Strolling leisurely through the hallway, he reached in his pocket and found his cell phone. He dialed the number Meredith had given him and listened while the phone looked for its owner. Getting her voice mail, Jackson left a message detailing what he had planned to this point and asked that she get back in touch so they could confirm their arrangements. He was just hanging up when he turned a corner and ran right into someone coming the other direction, sending both of them sprawling and scattering their belongings across the hallway. Apologizing profusely for not paying attention, Jackson scrambled to gather and separate their things for several seconds before looking up and with an expression of wonderment said, "It's you!"

Jessica had finished catching up her independent study in her pottery class and was hurrying to get back to her car. She didn't have anywhere specific to go as she was off work tonight, but she was ready to get home and change for a quick run and a light dinner. She was looking over her planner for the next few days and reveling in the idea of not having a lot of extra curricular things planned. She had her head down and didn't see Jackson as he barreled around the corner, sending her and her purse sprawling across the hallway. She looked up, ready to scream her head off at the idiot not paying attention when her face filled with surprise and she said, "It's you!"

They shared a laugh and spent the next few minutes retrieving their things. Standing, they figured out they were parked relatively close to each other and headed to their respective cars.

"So you are a student?" Jessica asked.

"I wouldn't say I am a student. Just taking a class in Italian. It's good for business." He smiled at the thought. "What brings you here?"

"The same thing I guess. I missed out on a lot of opportunities when I was younger and I guess I was just making up for lost time with my pottery class."

"Sounds fun, what did you make today?"

"How about I tell you about it over a bite to eat? I'm starving!"

"Great minds must think alike. What sounds good to you?"

"There's a barbecue place over by my house that's really good. Hole in the wall joint. I can call ahead and get us a good table."

"Sounds good, about twenty minutes?"

CHAPTER 25

While the shop was closed for lunch, Shelby was making her modifications to Jackson's laptop. She placed a tiny GPS tracking device behind one of the internal drivers and stretched a tiny wire to the power source. She cleared the insides of dust and wiped down a few of the surfaces before replacing the cover. Once everything was put back together, she turned the computer on and logged in using the back door she had installed when she had hacked into his system. She ran a couple of diagnostics to make sure everything ran normally and once satisfied, she logged out and turned the computer off. She felt much better now that she could ensure the safety of the love of her life and her future husband.

CHAPTER 26

Three Little Pigs Barbecue was one of the better-kept secrets in a city known for barbecue places. Jackson and Jessica had met outside and walked in together. An older black woman sat up front by the door and greeted Jessica warmly as she walked in.

"Hey Nattie, is my usual table ready?"

"Chile, you goin' sit where you feel like anyway."

They sat at a booth half way back; Jackson looked around for a moment, taking the place in. The menus looked like they were printed in the 1980's and were stained with barbecue sauce. The tabletops were glass-covered with red checked table cloths pressed underneath. A younger black woman approached the table with an order pad in her hand, chewing a piece of gum animatedly.

"Hey girl, you want your usual?"

"Hey, that would be great, two of them?"

"Sure, what do you want to drink?"

"Diet Coke for me and…" she looked at Jackson for his answer.

"Coke, please."

"On the way, sugar." She walked away from the table, returning a few moments later with their drinks.

"How are your classes coming?" Jessica asked.

"Girl, I don't know that I am cut out to be a mom and a student. I just run out of time all the time."

"Well, if I can help, you just let me know. I can watch the kids if you need a break to study. It's not like I haven't already raised my own." Jessica often laughed at herself when she talked.

"Be careful, I might just take you up on that." The waitress retreated again to take care of her other tables.

Jessica looked at Jackson and found him staring at her. "What, do I have something in my teeth?" She self-consciously reached for her mouth.

Jackson turned his attention and watched as the waitress dealt with the other tables in a much more detached manner. "No, I am just not sure I can remember the last time someone ordered for me. It was…refreshing." He nodded in the direction of the waitress. "You must know each other well. How long?"

"About two months now I guess. She's really a bright girl; she could do a lot with her life if she had some help."

"Are you going to be the one to help her?"

"Maybe," she answered with a laugh and a look of mock indignation. "Why shouldn't we help each other?"

"Would she do it for you in a pinch?"

"I don't know. Maybe, I hadn't really thought about it. I think the point is that people helping each other has to start somewhere. So why can't I be the first?"

"You can be I suppose. No one really thinks that way any more."

There was a moment of awkward silence that was interrupted by the waitress bringing their food. "Here it is, two lunch plates. Spicy, just like you like it sweetness."

"Thank you Lisha."

"Let me know if you need anything sugar." She winked in Jackson's direction, laughing as she walked off. Jessica stifled a laugh as well as Jackson peeked around the mountain of food in front of them. Two of the largest barbecue sandwiches he had ever seen along with beans, slaw and a side of fried okra. They were quiet for a bit as they dug into their food. It wasn't the usual first date "I've run out of things to say" silence. It was more of a comfortable silence between two people enjoying each other's company.

"I can't say I know anyone that has taken Italian before. What brought that about?"

"Any number of reasons I suppose. I like to learn and feel like I am wasting time if I am not learning something. I seem to pick up different languages pretty easily. Plus it helps with work."

"Yeah, you did mention that. What do you do that learning Italian would help?"

"I'm a consultant. Hospitality. Write some articles, meet with hotel groups, travel agencies, things like that. So I travel a good deal. I haven't gotten to go overseas as much as I would like though. Hopefully that will change soon."

"What would make it change?"

"I don't know, retiring, finding something better to do. Fishing or something. What about you? Are you a professional bartender?"

She laughed again and shook her head no. A mouthful of food kept her from answering for the moment. "No, I enjoy it though. I haven't been in Memphis that long."

"How long are you going to be here?"

"Who knows? I'll be here until the wind changes I suppose." She smiled at the obscure reference.

He regarded her for a moment, said "Mary Poppins" and took a bite of his sandwich.

She stopped and stared for a moment, her jaw dropping slightly, before returning to her lunch.

"Speaking of movies, I have to go to the Italian Film Festival on Saturday down at Peabody Place. It's for class. I think I am the youngest person in the class by like thirty years. Are you working Saturday?"

"I think I am working the late Saturday night shift, what time is the festival?"

"All day. Starts around noon I think. I have to sit through at least two of the movies and translate as much as I can. It could be fun though. What do you say?"

"Sure, sounds like fun. In the meantime, how's your sandwich?"

Jackson's mouth was too full to answer. But he smiled really big.

CHAPTER 27

It was five minutes until closing when Jackson burst back into the computer shop. He mumbled a quick apology to Shelby about forgetting his head if it wasn't attached. Shelby looked back at him and said, "Don't worry, I'll never forget about you."

Jackson grimaced and started to protest, but thought better of it and left that conversation alone. She handed him the laptop inside its case and he reached for his wallet. She held her hand up and told him that there wasn't a charge because it was a vendor issued upgrade. He shrugged his shoulders and thanked her.

"So when are you going to take me out again Jackson?"

He sighed deeply, "We've talked about this before, Shelby. We had a couple of laughs and that was it. I thought we had gotten past that."

"Just a reminder, sweet thing. Say what you want but no one has ever made love to me like that before. That can't happen unless there is some kind of deeper connection at work."

"We didn't make love. We fucked. And you are right we fucked well. But there wasn't anything behind it and you really need to move on." Jackson retreated from the conversation and from the storefront. He wasn't sure what provoked that outburst or the emotions behind it.

Shelby watched him go and nodded her head. "I'll move on when I am ready," she hissed. "And you will thank me…you will."

CHAPTER 28

Melanie was on the way to work her shift at the Blue Monkey when her cell phone rang. It was Jessica on the other end. "Hey love, where did you go after class? I waited for a few and didn't see you."

"I ran into that guy that I told you about--the one that was in on Sunday. He takes a class in Italian. We went and had a late lunch afterwards."

"Italian? Who takes Italian?"

"Apparently someone does if they offer classes in it. He spoke a little at lunch."

"At a restaurant or at your place?"

"You're just wrong. Not everyone falls into bed minutes after they meet someone. SLUT!"

"I am NOT a slut...I'm a gourmand."

"You're a what?"

"A gourmand...I enjoy things to excess."

"A gourmand applies to food."

"Oh? Well...what do they call someone that enjoys sex to excess?"

"A SLUT," both women shrieked with laughter.

"So when are you seeing Mr. Wonderful again?"

"I don't know that he is Mr. Wonderful. He is nice to talk to…and to look at as well!"

"Sounds serious."

"Hush. We are going to an Italian Film Festival on Saturday. He has to go for class and asked me to go with him. It sounds like it could be fun."

"Sounds like a snooze fest to me. But for your sake, I hope I am wrong."

"Me too. Yeah…me too," Jessica said with a million thoughts racing through her head.

CHAPTER 29

Will Swift sat in his son's school gym, watching his basketball team play. His wife had gone off to the bathroom when his cell phone rang. He recognized the number and answered, "What's up G?"

"Plenty, we may have a lead on the lost weekend for our victim and there also may be a match on the MO. The boss is on the way in and would like to see us both."

"Man, my boy is playing and he is doing well!"

"Keeping his shoes tied this time?"

"Ok, that's cold. Tell him you couldn't find me for a while. I'll be there when the game is over."

The game ended in a scintillating victory with a final score of 10-8. Will was beaming from ear to ear as his son hit the game winning shot with about four minutes left to play. He gave the budding basketball star an exuberant fist pump and his wife some money to get ice cream on the way home. Then he broke the news about heading to the office. She was disappointed but understanding and little Will was entirely focused on the thought of the ice cream. He drove to the precinct where his wife let him out and he promised to have Art bring him home as soon as they were done. His kissed his wife good-bye, lingering for a bit and mouthing the words "I love you" silently to her. Will then reminded his son to get some ice cream for him and he would enjoy it when he got home. His son looked up and said "Ok Daddy."

The office always looked a little different at night. There wasn't the normal din present in the daytime and Will thought more than once that he could get twice as much done at night than during the day. He worked his way through the maze of cubicles to Lieutenant Morse's office and found his partner waiting along with their boss. "Glad you could join us Detective Swift, how was the ballgame?" Will was sure that he saw his boss flash a smile. "My son plays in the same league. I think they scored 6 points in their last game."

"We hit double digits tonight. It was an offensive explosion."

The lieutenant looked at Will's partner. "Catch us up to speed then Detective Menking."

Art cleared his throat. "Well, in talking with friends and family, we figured the blank spots in her planner were romantic get-aways. The problem we have is there is absolutely no mention of whom they were with. The ex-boyfriend says it wasn't him and can back it up. He also has an alibi for the night Sharon Milligan was killed. We are checking with the bank to see how the money was moved around for those weekends to see if we can nail her movements down. It's just a matter of a couple of days before we get that."

"What about the M.O.?"

"Oh yeah, we got three hits on the national database. Stabbings happen all the time, but there are three unsolved that are at least close. Well-to-do woman with a single stab wound. Robbery the initial motive, but like ours, something didn't feel right. One is in St. Louis but happened the same day as ours. The second one is in Nashville, happened about three months ago. Victim found in a hotel room actually in the shower. It was sent to a sex crimes squad because everything in the room screamed "hook-up." They are checking the victim's computer to find any possible leads. The trail looks pretty cold though. Then the last one was in San Jose about a month ago, but it looks like a suicide. That one should be wrapped up soon."

"So Nashville it is. Got the name of the detective handling the case?" Will asked with a sigh.

CHAPTER 30

Jackson drove east towards his house and felt a familiar gnawing at his stomach. He looked down and said, "I just fed you." He laughed at his own warped sense of humor, but knew the gnawing was for something altogether different. He dialed the cell phone number he had dialed after many of the jobs he had done.

"Dr. Reynolds office, this is Debbie speaking."

"Hi Debbie, it's Jackson Pritchard. Is the doc in?"

"No, I'm sorry, she is lecturing on Mondays now. Has been for a while actually. Do you need to set an appointment?"

"Absolutely. Does she have time tomorrow?"

"Let me check. Yep, I can squeeze you in about 4:30. Your normal 90 minutes?"

"I hope that's all it takes."

Jackson pulled into a liquor store on the way home and grabbed a bottle of bourbon and a two-liter bottle of Coke. He took his time getting home and once there, cooked up a little bit of pasta. Jackson was a good cook when he had the time. He ate, cleaned up his mess and poured himself a tall bourbon and Coke and settled in with some music, starting with his favorite John Lee Hooker CD. Four and a half CDs and five drinks later, he stumbled into the bedroom and fell into bed.

CHAPTER 31

Meredith Gregory got in from the office a little after 9:00 PM. Pretty typical for a Monday. Saving the world one person at a time was going to take a while, she thought to herself. She put the Chinese takeout down on the counter top and opened a bottle of wine. Nothing fancy, just something to wash a busy Monday away. She checked her voice mail and noticed there was a message from a number she didn't recognize at first. She pressed play and smiled when she heard Jackson's voice on the recording. She replayed it again, visualizing him leaving the message and hoping that he was looking forward to the weekend as much as she was. Flipping on the TV, she went through her DVR and speed watched Oprah and a couple of finance/news recaps. Her friends from school and from the gym talked to her about People magazine and the latest reality show on TV. She watched Bloomberg and read Fortune and Forbes. Finishing her dinner and the quick clean up afterwards, Meredith strolled into the bedroom and changed out of her skirt and blouse, having left her suit jacket in the car. Her bra and panties quickly followed and were replaced with an oversized football jersey and boxer shorts. She thought better of it and went into the bathroom and turned the water on in her antique bathtub. Hot water began to slowly fill the tub and steam filled the bathroom air. She walked through her high-rise condominium, making sure the doors and windows were locked and dimming or turning out the lights. She grabbed a few lighted candles and took them into the bathroom along with her refilled wine glass. Testing the hot water with her toe, Meredith turned the tap off and slid out of her clothes and into the water. The heat instantly drew the tension and stress from her day and she melted into the contour of the tub. Soaking for several minutes with her eyes closed, she mentally went through the next couple of days to make sure that everything could get done and she could get to Memphis for her working vacation. She was having lunch with Jan on Tuesday and speaking to a couple of college classes on Wednesday before catching a flight Thursday morning for meetings both days. Meeting with Jan. Hopefully that will go well. Jan could make her career path to the top much shorter. She knew everyone and would be a great mentor. Membership has its privileges, she thought. She finished her glass of wine and settled back down in the water again. She began to soap her arms, relishing the feel of her soft, supple skin. Her hands moved downward under the surface of the water and slowly traced the length of her long legs. They found a familiar spot between them and for the next several minutes, Meredith enjoyed a very hot and satisfying bath.

CHAPTER 32

Morning came very early for Jackson. He awoke to a moderate hangover and the blaring alarm clock he had set last night before his self-medication. He sat up in bed for a few minutes, trying to clear the cobwebs out of his head. He took a quick glance around the bedroom and then at his clock and saw that it was 7:00. He stretched, got out of bed and grabbed a quick shower before packing a bag and heading to the gym for a workout. He took a couple of warm-up laps around the elevated indoor track before stretching and working through a strenuous chest and triceps workout. He followed that with about twenty minutes of abdominal work and burned it all into his muscle memory with two quick miles on the treadmill. Sweat poured from every pore on his body and smelled a bit like bourbon. He went through three towels, taking care to wipe down the weight benches and the treadmill he used. He bought a protein-based sports energy drink and drained it on the way to the car. His cell phone rang and he was pleased to hear Meredith's voice on the other end. They talked for several minutes and confirmed her flight arrangements both in and out of Memphis. She probed to see if she could extend her stay a little bit, but Jackson was pretty direct about having prior commitments Saturday afternoon. They exchanged more small talk as Jackson drove through a newer bank branch he hadn't been too before and made another cash deposit. Another phone call beeped in on her phone and Jackson took the opportunity to cut their conversation short. He warmly told her good-bye and let her know how much he was looking forward to having her in Memphis. She chuckled a bit and clicked off the line. He got ready to throw the phone in his bag when it rang again and the called ID showed it was Jessica.

"Good morning, what a pleasant surprise to hear from you."

"Really? Ok, well good morning to you too." Jessica's voice betrayed a little surprise at how excited he seemed to hear from her. "Am I interrupting anything?"

"No, not at all. I just finished a workout and now I am heading home to catch a shower and get my day started. What are you up to?"

"Well, I am volunteering over at the soup kitchen over on Madison. I do it every Tuesday and Thursday for lunch. Care to join me? There might be a prize in it for you."

"Really, what kind of prize?"

"I can't tell you before you answer. What kind of surprise would that be?"

"Good point. Um, do I have time to shower?"

"Sure, if you can be there inside an hour, I'll give you the VIP tour." She gave him the address and directions and was ready to hang up the phone.

"Hey wait, what's the surprise?"

"Not so fast cowboy, you'll find out when you get there. If you're lucky, that is. If not, well, we'll have to see." She laughed at her own sassiness. He heard it and liked it and told her so. "Flattery will not get me to reveal the surprise any more quickly. Nice try though. I'll see you in a bit. Dress code here is pretty relaxed. Our guests need to be as comfortable as possible."

"Thanks for the tip…and for the invite. It was…unexpected."

"Life should be that way, don't you think? Bye." She sang and stretched out the last word playfully as the phone went dead. A car horn interrupted Jackson from the quick daze he had fallen into as the traffic light in front of them turned yellow. The car behind him screeched its tires and sped around him. Jackson waved back using four more fingers than the other driver. He smiled again and sped home to shower and get to his newest appointment for the day.

CHAPTER 33

It was a perfect day for a power lunch in downtown Atlanta. Jan Eberhardt walked in and was warmly greeted by the staff and managers of the Women's Club. She was escorted to her usual table and was pleasantly surprised to see Meredith waiting for her there. There were two waters with lemon on the table and menus ready for her perusal. Meredith stood and the pair kissed each other on the cheek.

"Congratulations. I can't remember when someone beat me to my own table. You are going to do well in the world, I predict."

Meredith smiled broadly in return. "Well, I like to be on time. I think it shows that you are serious about yourself and the meeting you are attending. My father always told me to be serious about yourself and other people will take you seriously as well."

"Sage advice. Does he give it often?"

"He died about five years ago. Dropped dead at work of a massive heart attack. The doctor said it was genetic, my mom thinks it's because he never smiled. I think I prefer my mother's version."

"Well then, maybe you should practice your smiling. It seemed like Jackson had that effect on you. What all did you two talk about?"

"Not a lot. He told me a little about his consulting work, traveling and things like that. He seemed really nice. And really good looking!" She giggled a bit. "Not movie star good looking, but more-I don't know-street smart and confident. Usually you only see that level of confidence in lawyers or someone trying to sell you something. How do you know him?"

"He and I have worked together for three or four years I guess. He's really good at what he does." Jan smiled, quickly recollecting the previous weekend's adventures. Her husband had greeted her upon her return and promptly demonstrated the vast difference between himself and Jackson. It had taken less than five minutes thankfully. She sighed, "Jackson is pretty unique. He is very selective about the work he does and I think it's only on a referral basis now. I consider myself pretty fortunate to have found him."

Meredith looked a little confused.

Jan continued. "Don't worry about it. Just listen to a piece of advice. Enjoy your trip to Memphis and the southern hospitality I am certain he will show you. If you want more, go for it. He would be crazy not to let you. Then, when your trip is over, stay in touch with him if you want…but don't expect anything and don't lose focus of the goals you have set for yourself. You'll thank me for both someday. Now, what looks good on the menu?" Jan hid her face, pretending to look over the offerings, hoping she hadn't given too much away.

CHAPTER 34

Jackson parked his Jeep outside the hundred-year-old church that housed the homeless shelter and soup kitchen and walked inside. He asked the first person he saw where the volunteers reported and was directed to the back. There he found Jessica slicing some carrots and tomatoes to be put into salads. She turned as he walked in and a broad smile formed and stayed on her face, even after she said hello. "Aprons are over there," she pointed to the pantry at the end of the kitchen. "Your choices today are to cook, serve, and clean or to cook, serve, and clean."

"I'll take the first one then."

"Good choice," she said with another smile.

The volunteer coordinator came around and assigned duties to everyone. Jackson was in charge of spaghetti noodles and sauce. He had two stoves with four huge pots going; two for sauces, two for noodles. The recipe he was handed seemed pretty basic and he was ready to question it when the coordinator stopped him before he got started. "All of our recipes are very basic, some might even say bland. Our guests don't need any more challenges in their diets, so we stay away from a lot of the spices." Jackson nodded his head in understanding and returned to his stirring. Occasionally he caught sight of Jessica and she seemed to be smiling every time their eyes met. Once the cooking was done, they began to serve the "guests" as the staff and volunteers referred to them. The plates were filled with pasta, salad, and some fruit. Jackson seemed to enjoy walking through the dining area and refilling drinks and talking with the guests. A couple of times, he found himself sitting and listening to someone telling one story or another. Two hours later, the last guest had eaten and Jackson and Jessica were elbow deep in hot, soapy water. The last pot was scrubbed and dried and the volunteers shook hands and headed out. Jackson walked Jessica outside to her car.

"It was really sweet of you to come, I'm glad you made it," Jessica said, shuffling her feet awkwardly.

"I had fun…really. Thanks for calling me."

"And so patient. You haven't even asked me about the surprise."

Jackson's face showed that he had forgotten about it. "So…what is it?"

"I was going to make you earn it, but I think you did already. And then some. The owner of the Blue Monkey gave me floor tickets to tomorrow night's Grizzlies game. Interested?"

"Are you kidding me? Floor seats? We can insult the other team and they can hear us. How much fun is that?"

"Exactly why I would want to go."

"I'll go one on condition."

"And that would be?"

"Dinner is on me."

"Done."

Jackson looked at his watch. "I hate to cook, serve, and clean and then run, but I have an appointment in about twenty minutes. Thank you again for a good day though. I'd like to do it again sometime."

"I don't know. The staff said the noodles were a little overdone."

"Really?"

"Yes," she said while shaking her head "No."

"Cute…and very convincing."

"I do what I can. Thank you for noticing."

"You're welcome. I really do have to go. They charge me whether I go or not."

She leaned forward and hugged him and gave him a soft kiss on the cheek. "I am working tonight. Come by if you get a chance, I'll get you another Pepper Jack Chicken sandwich."

"An offer I surely can't refuse. Thanks again for today. See ya," he called over his shoulder.

Jessica gave him a subtle wave, biting her lip gently as she watched him leave. She caught herself daydreaming, giggled at herself and walked to her car.

CHAPTER 35

Dr. Lauren Reynolds had been a practicing therapist for twenty-two years. She had a very successful practice in East Memphis, housed in a small but neat building in a large office park. The leather chairs and couches were pricey but comfortable and Dr. Reynolds looked very much at home here. She was an elegant looking woman in her early fifties. Her kids were grown and she was increasingly bored by both her marriage and her practice. But there was the occasional client that presented different challenges and also had a life outside the walls of her office that allowed her to live somewhat vicariously through others. When she saw Jackson Pritchard's name on her schedule for the day, she smiled a bit. At least there would be some good stories. Jackson walked in two minutes before he was scheduled. Like always. He had a Coke can in one hand and a cell phone in the other, which she reminded him to turn off.

"So what's it been Jackson, eight weeks, ten?"

"Longer actually, almost four months."

"Really, it hasn't seemed that long."

"I checked the calendar. It's been a while."

"So what brings you in?"

"Same thing I suppose. Still trying to reconcile who I am with what I do. Ready to retire but don't have the first idea of what I would do with myself."

"You like the traveling and the writing, why not start there?"

"It would be like putting a drunk to work in a bar, don't you think. Sounds like fun but not a very good long-term decision, business or otherwise."

"Maybe, what do you think?"

"I think we agreed that you wouldn't ask me psychobabble questions like that."

"You are right, my apology. So why now? Why the desire to change what has been a pretty successful few years."

"Not sure. I thought you could tell me. I can't quite get the bank balances over a million dollars which is when I told myself I would retire."

"But you keep spending money on your adventures…as anyone with money should. But once you get close to your goal you start spending money again. So what else?"

"I just don't want to do what I do any more. I met someone a few days ago and I can't stop thinking about her. I woke up with a hangover this morning and went for a workout to get over it. She called me after and invited me to lunch…sort of."

"Sort of?"

"I met her at a soup kitchen and we worked for three hours serving lunch to the homeless. She has lived in Memphis for just a few months I think and she volunteers in her spare time, she knows the waitresses at the places she eats. She's just…different."

"Younger, older? Tell me about her."

"I don't really know. She's a little older than me I guess. She moved here after her son went off to college. Threw a dart on a map and hit Memphis if I remember the story correctly."

"Interesting, what was she running from?"

"Again, I don't know. Nothing. Something. We haven't really talked about it. But she is just so alive. You can tell in how she talks and how she walks and how she acts. She does what she wants because she wants to do it. Or so it seems."

"And this is why you want to retire? Have you talked to your clients about this?"

"I haven't talked to anyone about this yet. You're the first. And she isn't why I want to retire. I think she is more of an embodiment of why I want to quit. I can't imagine anyone like her wanting to be with a guy like me."

"You mean a guy that has sex for money?"

"Something like that. Okay, exactly that."

"Like you say, you don't have sex with all of your clients."

"And like you say, I do have sex with some."

"Good point, I'm glad you pay attention. If you think about it for a minute, she seems to like you so far and doesn't know what you do. So she likes you regardless of what it is you do. So that's step one. Step two will be to reconcile what you do or if you retire what you did. If you move forward with this woman or any other woman, you're going to have to come clean about it."

"I figured that. Should be a pleasant conversation."

"Well, don't put the cart before the horse just yet. Maybe you should work on seeing her again before you make plans for the rest of your life."

"Good call. She might be a cat person."

"Cute, yes, she might be a cat person. Or she might snort a little when she laughs."

"She doesn't."

"Ok, let's put this to one of your favorite things. We've talked about classical music before. What's your favorite song?"

"There's so many. If I had to pick one, I would say 'Pourquoi Me Reveiller'."

"By whom?"

"Well, that's easy. Pavarotti."

"Okay, but why his version and not Placido Domingo's or Jonas Kaufman's?"

"You've been studying," Jackson teased.

"Don't change the subject."

"It's hard to say really. I just prefer Pavarotti. He has such range and power behind him. You can almost feel him singing."

"Exactly. It's the subtlety of taste. Relationships are no different. What makes someone perfect for you may make them unattractive to someone else."

"Okay, I can see that. But what if she is the one and I am not her one? Or what if she can't deal with what I did for a living?"

"I like that you just used the word 'did'."

"I did? I did, didn't I?"

"Yes, which is the first step you need. I've told you for three years now that you won't ever be able to love or be loved until you retire as you so eloquently phrase it. Stop getting paid to be someone's companion or you will never truly be a companion to anyone else."

"Simple as that?"

"Simple as that."

There was a long pause before Jackson spoke again. "That's it? Three years I've been coming here and that's what you come up with? That's the profound life changing advice that you choose to impart? Do I get a refund or something?" He was laughing hard and she joined him. "Where did you get your degrees again, a Cracker Jack box?"

"The first one maybe, medical school was a bit more involved."

They laughed for a good while. Jackson finally caught his breath and wiped a tear out of his eye. "Wow, that felt good. Retire. Well, no time like the present. Any suggestions for notifying my clients?"

"Just tell them. Your success has been built on the fact that your clients trust you. Trust them and tell them what's going on. Hopefully they will appreciate you and your honesty."

"I'll see what I can do. I have one this weekend that's too late to cancel. I'll start talking to the others though and get it worked out. Promise."

"Don't promise me, promise yourself. Keep me updated, I look forward to hearing how it goes. How about you come back and see me in a month or so."

"Done. And thank you."

"Don't thank me yet. You have some difficult conversations and choices ahead of you. I'm proud of you for the steps you have taken so far. Now understand, we have just started and will have a lot to work through when you are ready. I wish you luck."

"Thanks, I just might need it."

CHAPTER 36

Will Swift walked into the office and found his partner sitting at his desk. "Find something?"

"Maybe. I'm hoping for an early Christmas present. Are you going to be on Santa's naughty or nice list?"

"My wife hasn't told me yet. Holding out hope for naughty though." His smile spoke volumes.

Art grimaced. "TMI, partner, TMI." He shook his head slowly for emphasis. "The tech guys went through her computer at work and found a reference to 'Jackson' just before the five-day vacation she took. Still no idea where she went, but there are nine different Jacksons in her corporate address book." We are chasing them down now. Her rolodex is in the evidence we took though."

"Good, see who they are and where they were the night Milligan was killed."

A burly desk sergeant yelled over the office background noise. "Hey Swift, I got a Detective Franklin from Nashville on the phone.

"Thanks Tom." He picked up the phone. "Swift."

"Detective Swift? This is Joe Franklin from Nashville, returning your call."

"Thanks for calling me back, Joe. Listen, you caught a homicide a few months back and I wanted to see if you cleared it. Name was Long I believe?"

"Lori Long, yeah, I remember it. Still open. No good leads either. A pretty open and shut case if we could ID anyone."

"What are you missing?"

"A name. Let me back up a second. You have a lonely housewife that missed out on the sexual revolution. She has her family life, does the mom thing and then wants to play a bit. Problem is her husband checked out on the marriage a while back. She ends up in a hotel room gutted like a fish. Autopsy shows that she had sex within twenty minutes before she was killed."

"Assault?"

"The sex looks consensual. No bruising or restraint marks."

"Well, sounds pretty simple. If her husband wasn't involved, then she met someone there. Her date did it. Or maybe the butler. Is there a butler?"

Both men chuckled. "No butler. I'm inclined to agree with your first answer. The date did do it. But we can't figure out who the date is. The husband reported her missing the night it happened. She checked in alone, under an alibi, paid cash. No one saw her go into the room. A housekeeper found her the next morning. The trail stops cold there."

"Nice. Any other leads at all?"

"Possibly. Security cameras picked up about a dozen people coming and going in the lobby that couldn't be identified by the staff as guests. We are tracking those leads down now. Only one of them was in our system, so its tough sledding finding out who the other eleven are."

"I guess it would be too much to hope for to have cameras in the hallways."

"You got it."

There was a pause in the conversation as both men tried to wrap their arms around the story. Will broke the silence. "Okay, we'll chase down whatever we can on our end. If you think of anything else or find anything, please let me know. I appreciate you getting back with me so soon."

"You got it. Raining in Seattle today?"

"Not yet. Give it a bit though. Rain in our fair city is never too far away."

CHAPTER 37

The Blue Monkey was on Jackson's way home from Dr. Reynolds' office. He drove by once and saw the crowd was kind of sparse. Still kind of early for a Tuesday, he guessed. He circled back around the block and found a spot near the side door. He walked in and was greeted by the manager. "Hey there, saw you here the other night. You going to be a regular around here?"

"Maybe, I heard you have a good chicken sandwich."

"A good wait staff too. Would like to keep it that way too."

"I'll make sure to tip them well then."

"You do that. Be careful with one in particular. She's kind of my favorite. Not as tough as she wants everyone to believe. People can't help but like her though. She makes everyone feel better about themselves instantly. Kind of her thing."

"I've noticed. Think she could bottle whatever it is?"

"Funny. Just go easy. That's all I am asking. I can be an ass sometimes, that's kind of <u>my</u> thing. But to show you that I can be a nice guy as well--that chicken sandwich is on me."

"I appreciate it, but..."

"It wasn't an offer, it's just how it is."

"Well then I thank you in advance." Jackson bowed his head slightly in recognition of the gesture.

The bear-like manager nodded his head and found a reason to be somewhere else. Jackson walked in and took a seat at the bar. Jessica turned to find him sitting there and her face lit up immediately. Jackson laughed. "You know, if you keep doing that, I might come to expect it."

"I can think of worse things."

"True. Hey, I heard a rumor about an unbelievable chicken sandwich. What can you tell me about it?"

She gave him a mock frown like she was searching her memory for that story. "Not sure, I'll check with the guys in the back though. They deal with the chickens much more than I do. The ones I see are typically seven or eight drinks deep in liquid courage before they can do one thing or another."

"You know, that's a great name for a shot."

"What's a great name for a shot?"

"Liquid courage."

She paused. "It IS a great name for a shot."

"Every good bartender has a signature drink. Maybe yours is called "liquid courage."

"What do you think it should taste like?"

"Drinkable, but kind of bitter. It has to taste like you are doing something you don't like doing or even want to do so you can accomplish something big."

"Sounds good. So nothing frou-frou?"

"Nah, you don't need courage if you have frou-frou. Just a trash can handy when all is said and done."

She laughed. "Words of wisdom if I have ever heard them. Something with a bite then. Crown and the like might be a bit too smooth. How about Evan Williams and something?"

"Sounds good to me. Let me know when you have it figured out. Do I get a cut of the proceeds?"

"I'm thinking no. Mike would have something to say about that."

"Mike?"

"The manager. Big teddy bear that is picking up your tab tonight."

"You heard that?"

"No, he told me he was going to chat with you. He's protective of all the girls here. Harmless until someone does something mean. Then he's not so nice."

"I'll try and remember that."

She noted his tone turned a bit more serious. "Please don't think anything of it. I would hate for anything to ruin, well…your chicken sandwich. It's very important that you enjoy that sandwich. I take these things personally."

Jackson tried to suppress a laugh but couldn't. "You win; for the sake of the sandwich I won't be concerned with the big teddy bear."

"As long as your priorities are in the right place."

Jackson raised the glass of Fat Tire she had poured him. "Here's to priorities."

She raised a glass of water in return. "Here's to liquid courage… and a really nice day." Her smile was second only in size to his at that point.

CHAPTER 38

Shelby Powers unlocked the door to her Midtown apartment and threw the keys on the hall table. She looked around at the organized clutter and grimaced. Her place really should be much cleaner than this, she was thinking. She heated up some leftover Chinese food and settled down in front of her computer. There were two-oversized Dell flat screen monitors attached to a tower system she had built herself. The system was designed with both speed and security in mind. Logging on, she clicked a few keystrokes and ran threw a few e-mails. After being online for five minutes, her system challenged her with a prompt, requesting the quote of the day. Shelby had preprogrammed this system to challenge the user to ensure privacy and security. Today's quote was from the movie "Who Framed Roger Rabbit." Shelby loved the freedom of the "Toon" characters to act however they chose. The main heroine of the movie, Jessica Rabbit said at one point: "I'm not bad, I'm just drawn that way." That always made her laugh. She then logged into a chat room to see if any of her online friends were there and was only a little disappointed to find none. Clicking over to another website, she logged in through a back door she had developed in order to hide her movements while online. Once accomplished, she sent a trace out and smiled when it showed that she was in Providence, Rhode Island. She finished her dinner and opened a bottle of Corona. Taking a long sip, she accessed an online banking site and checked her balances. Everything seemed to be in order, so she logged out and onto another site, this one overseas. The site was triple password protected and guaranteed both the safety and the anonymity of its customers. She checked and rechecked the balances as well as the account information. Just the idea of her and the love of her life finally being together made her smile. She had opened this joint account with this in mind. The fact that it had grown to the size it had, made her all the more attractive in her mind. She had read that back in the old days, women came with a dowry and sometimes it was the dowry alone that came before the "Happily Ever After." She made decent money at the computer shop, but lately she had done much better with some of the freelance work she had done. Some of the jobs were bigger than others; tonight's was pretty small. She was supposed to set up a couple of basic security levels for an artist friend's website. She would make sure and leave a backdoor for her to work through, but all in all the job would more than likely take less than an hour to complete. Toasting the technically incompetent with a swallow of her beer, Shelby settled in and got to work and as predicted, finished quickly. Looking at the clock, she realized it was getting late and got ready for bed. She didn't wear anything to bed as she found pajamas constricting and uncomfortable. It also slowed her down on nights like tonight when the only one telling her good night would be one of the several "toys" she owned and made use of more often than she would care to admit. Peering into the plastic container she had pulled from under the bed, she selected one of her old favorites, turned off the light and prepared herself for a satisfying night's sleep.

CHAPTER 39

Jessica's shift ended at 11:00. She cleaned up a bit and stocked some of the glasses she had used through the night. She cashed out and figured out that she had walked with a couple hundred dollars. A good night for a weekday no matter how you looked at it. Smiling, she relived a few of the better moments from the past two days. It had been a while since she had smiled about someone like that and she was enjoying the feeling. There is just something about someone you can talk to and this guy seemed like just that kind of person. One of the bouncers walked her to her car and she got in and drove home. She walked in the door and was warmly greeted by Max. She plopped down on the couch and scratched Max in his favorite spot, just behind the ears. Planning her next few steps around the house, she prepared to get into bed when her phone rang.

"I had to thank you for that chicken sandwich again. It was very satisfying."

"Mike will be pleased to hear it. Would you like his number?"

"I'm good, thanks though. So how was your night?"

"Not bad. Made some decent money, had some fun. Didn't get drooled on too much."

"Occupational hazard?"

"Depends on your perspective I suppose."

"So, a drunk, persistent, drooling guy drinking cheap beer is a good thing?"

"Not so much."

"Maybe bartenders should wear bibs."

"That would be a much different look I would say."

"I always wear one at the Rendezvous."

"I'd like to see that."

"I'm sure we can work something out. Behave yourself watching Italian movies and we just might go."

"What fun would behaving myself be?"

"I don't remember specifying how to behave, do you?"

She paused, trying not to laugh. "No, I suppose you didn't. Any tips for Saturday then?"

"Absolutely, keep doing what you are doing. It's working well."

"Are we still on for tomorrow night?"

"Yes we are. Now the one thing I am not sure about though is what colors to paint my face. The Grizzlies have confused me with their new color scheme."

"Please tell me you aren't the face-painting guy."

"Ok, I won't tell you. I make it look good though. It's all in the presentation and attitude."

"I'm not sure they would let us on the floor."

"Guess I will have to settle for taunting the other team and ogling the cheerleaders."

"Which do you think would get us thrown out first?"

"Ogling the cheerleaders might get your thrown out by me first."

"Taunting it is then. Who are we even playing?"

"Orlando I think."

"Do they have anyone we specifically need to make fun of?"

"Not that I know of. I am sure we can find someone though."

"This is going to be an adventure isn't it?"

"The basketball game?"

"That too."

"Well then yes. And yes to the other thing as well."

"Good answer. You are good about that."

"I consider it more a function of who I am talking to. It's easier when the audience puts you at ease."

"Agreed. Thank you for my tip earlier."

"You are most welcome. Thank you for the sandwich and the unrivaled attention."

"You are most welcome. We seem to be very polite to each other."

"Is that a bad thing?"

"No, do you think it will continue?"

"The phone call or being polite to each other?"

"Either, both."

"Yes…and yes."

"I hope so. I'm getting sleepy."

"I don't want to keep you from your bed."

"I'm already in it. I need to change though--still in my Blue Monkey clothes."

"You know, the name just makes you want to smile. Don't you think?"

"I never thought about it. It is a funny name."

"Yeah, thoughts like that distract me often. What were we talking about again?"

"I'm too sleepy to remember."

"Oh yes, sleep. I need to go too. Early workout planned in the morning and then I need to catch up on some work. Where should I meet you tomorrow?"

"Pick me up here?"

"Sounds nice, what time?"

"The game is at seven. How about five-thirty and we can have a drink before we go."

"Sounds even better. I can't wait. Oh, where do you live?"

She gave him the directions and they talked for a few minutes more before telling each other good night. Smiling again, she got up and changed, getting ready for bed. She lay back down and moved Max over so that he only took up a little over half of the bed. She chuckled softly to herself, thinking that this was going to be fun indeed.

CHAPTER 40

"Good morning Detective Swift, this is Michael Carey calling."

"Well good morning, counselor. What a great way to start my day." Will's voice was thick with unmasked sarcasm.

Sharon Milligan's lawyer heard it and appreciated speaking with a fellow cynic. "You could schedule a morning wake up call with me if you like. I charge $300 an hour. That's about five dollars a minute and worth every penny, I think."

"I'm sure you do, was there a reason you called besides soliciting business."

"Solicitation is expressly prohibited in my profession, Detective. You of all people should know that. And yes, I did call with something specific. In reviewing Ms. Milligan's financial records, we have found that about half a million dollars is missing. We think it is somehow related to the gaps in her calendar that we can't account for."

"Half a million dollars? Is that all? How is it we are finding about this only today?"

"Detective if you were missing twenty dollars from your account, do you think you would notice it right away?"

"Probably not."

"We're talking about the same thing, just on a different scale."

"Interesting scale. Has your team been able to trace any money going out that hasn't been accounted for?"

"Not to that level. She kept significant amounts of cash at home and at the office just in case. The majority of it has been accounted for. My client didn't mind spending money. In fact, she rather enjoyed it."

"Any spending habits you didn't agree with?"

"I'm sure I don't know what you mean Detective."

"I'm sure you don't. Any other leads on the name 'Jackson'?"

"Not so far. But if we do find anything out, you'll be the first one to know, Detective." Michael Carey smiled as he hung the phone up; his ability to mislead the simple-minded was one of the things that made him such a good lawyer. His team was well on its way to finding this "Jackson" and taking back a large sum of money that didn't belong to him.

Will Swift looked at the phone as he hung up the receiver and shook his head. "Lying bastard."

"I'm sorry?"

Will was startled by the unexpected voice of his Lieutenant and he turned to find his boss smiling and holding two cups of coffee.

"I took the liberty of bringing you a cup of MY coffee instead of the sewer water your partner makes. Has he used any of the Starbucks cards you gave him?"

Will smiled both at the fact that his Lieutenant had an idea of what was going on in his squad room as well as that the stories surrounding him might just be wrong.

"I got a phone call from Sharon Milligan's lawyer. He's a lying bastard."

"Kind of redundant phrase don't you think? Lawyer...lying bastard..."

Will chuckled and then took a sip from his coffee mug. "I suppose so. I just hate talking to them, especially when you know they are hiding something. Just a smug..."

"Aren't they all?" The Lieutenant finished his unspoken thought.

"Point taken. He let us know that about $500,000 is missing from her estate. I thought about sending our tech guys over to work with his team to see if we can trace it. I also think they have an idea of who this unknown 'Jackson' is. If they get to him before we do, we may never clear this case."

"Ok, call the honorable counselor and request to send a crew over under the guise of tracing the money down. Have Menking join them as a supervisor or something and see what he can sniff out."

"Done. Thanks Lieutenant."

"Please, it's Phillip...or Phil. I hate Lieutenant. It makes me feel like some young pup that hasn't earned his stripes yet."

"Well, I'll work on it. How about just plain 'boss' for a while?"

"That will work. Let me know if you need anything else Detective."

"Thanks, Boss."

CHAPTER 41

"Meredith Gregory."

"Hey Meredith, it's Jackson Pritchard. Is now a good time to talk?"

"Absolutely. How are you Jackson? I mean Jack."

"I'm well, thank you. And Jackson is quite all right. Again, whichever you prefer. I'm very much looking forward to your visit. Is everything still on schedule?"

"As far as I know, I'm looking forward to it as well. Will you be picking me up at the airport?"

"Of course, I'll pick you up and take you wherever you would like to go."

"That's awfully sweet."

"Not at all, it's my pleasure. Are you going to want a car while you are here?"

"Do you have a car rental agency as well?"

Jackson laughed. "No, just making sure you have everything you need."

"That's very thoughtful. My meetings are downtown so I don't think I will need one. What all are we going to be doing when I am not working?"

"That's up to you. There are all kinds of things going on downtown, so I am certain there will be something that will capture your attention."

"I can't wait. I have meetings up until I leave. If anything comes up I will call you though, ok?"

"Sounds great. Enjoy your meetings and I will see you at the airport."

CHAPTER 42

Jackson left the gym sweating hard after a good workout. His schedule was pretty light, but he still found it hard to focus as he was looking forward to the game later on. He breezed through his Italian class, noting that the film festival began at 1:00 on Saturday. He made cash deposits in a couple of different banks and called ahead to confirm the reservations at the Talbot Heirs. The front desk manager confirmed that the kitchen would be fully stocked including the wine and champagne that Jackson had ordered. Another phone call and Jackson lined up a limousine to pick up Meredith at the airport. Finally, a couple of calls to club managers on Beale that Jackson knew to see what was going on and to arrange for VIP access. They knew Jackson well, knew he would take care of their respective wait staffs and never cause a scene. He typically put a little something in their handshakes as well. Tossing his phone into the passenger seat, he checked the clock on the dashboard and noted that he still had three hours before he had to pick Jessica up. He cranked up the volume on his Kenwood CD player and sang along to his favorite Stone Temple Pilots song. He drove out and hit the I-240 loop and cruised around Memphis and lost himself in the traffic and the music. The hum of the engines calmed him somewhat and he sang along without regard for who might be watching. A fleeting idea popped into his head and he turned down the music and scrolled back through his phone and redialed the Talbot Heirs. He explained that he would like the suite reserved for one additional night, although the probability was he wouldn't use it. The manager was puzzled, but appreciated the extra room night being sold. Jackson thanked her and hung up, scrolled through the phone again and extended the limousine another night. Satisfied with the extra arrangements, he again tossed the phone into the passenger seat. Before it landed, it was ringing again. Recognizing the New York area code, he answered it and greeted Sarah Trammell warmly.

"It's been far too long pretty boy."

"It's always far too long, how have you been?"

"I've been well, thank you for asking."

"I'm pleased to hear it."

"I miss the Southern accent and your gentile mannerisms."

"If memory serves me correctly, we will remedy that next week. Tuesday through Thursday. Las Vegas. The Bellagio. I'm very much looking forward to it."

"I'm pleased to hear it. I e-mailed you a copy of my itinerary earlier, did you get it?"

"I haven't been home all day, but I will check it when I get in. Will you be traveling alone this trip?"

"Unfortunately no, but I have arranged for several opportunities that we should be able to take advantage of."

"His handicap must be getting lower then."

"His handicap? His long and short strokes aren't nearly satisfying enough."

"Interestingly, I was talking about golf this time."

"Plenty of golf courses around Las Vegas thankfully."

"And you haven't picked up the game yet?"

"Actually I have but I have other plans for my free time on this trip."

"Sounds serious."

"I hope so. My attention has been somewhat diverted recently."

"Really, why?"

"When was the last time I saw you?"

"Labor Day weekend."

"Because that was the last time a man was able to satisfy me."

"That would be diverting. And something we shall have to remedy Tuesday evening."

"Tuesday morning actually. I arranged for an earlier flight. He has meetings all afternoon and won't get in until late that evening. Can you get in Monday night?"

"I already scheduled myself to be there. You have a penchant for changing plans at the last minute."

"You know me all too well."

"It's my pleasure."

"I'll see you in Las Vegas."

"Until then."

Jackson pressed "End" on his phone and regarded it for a moment. He sighed deeply and headed home to change and get ready for the game.

CHAPTER 43

The evidence room at Will Swift's precinct was in the basement and held the allure and ambiance of a bear cave. He imagined the smell was about the same as well. He pulled the box marked "Milligan" off one of the wire mesh evidence racks that looked like they came with the building. The box was three-quarters full with different bits and pieces of Sharon Milligan's life. Will sat it on the nearest table and opened it. He immediately found the Rolodex he was looking for and began to turn through it, looking for anyone with the name Jackson. As his partner had previously referenced, there were nine business associates with the last name of Jackson. He found their respective business cards immediately and set them to the side. Each had been questioned regarding the five-day weekend as well as the night Sharon had died and A) had solid alibis but more importantly B) had exactly ZERO motive. Each of them profited immensely from his relationship with the deceased and would not benefit at all from her untimely death. He closed the roll-top lid and replaced it in the box before thinking better of it and returning it to the table. He opened it and began to scan through other letters of the alphabet, looking for a card that might be misfiled, filed by company name or someone that might have Jackson as a first name. Fifteen minutes or so passed before he found the card of one Jackson Pritchard with an 800 number and an e-mail address. Will had seen different approaches to advertising one's business, but rarely did the adage of "less is more" apply to a business card. He made a note of both the number and the e-mail address, replaced the card and took the ancient concrete stairs back up to his office.

His partner was away from the office and the Lieutenant's door was shut. Will dialed the number he had written down and was greeted by a computer generated voice mail message after just one ring. "Phone must be off," he thought to himself. He identified himself as well as the message he was leaving for Jackson Pritchard and asked that he call back before 5:00 Pacific time. "More than likely another loose end that just needs tying up. Probably won't even call me back," he thought to himself. He dove back into some of the reports his tech guys had generated regarding Sharon Milligan's schedule as well as the money that she had spent recently. The frustrating thing here was that the deceased had been very private as well as very thorough when it came to protecting that privacy. She compartmentalized things well and seemingly kept her business and personal lives completely separate. "We'll get there Sharon," Will said to no one in particular, "We'll get there."

CHAPTER 44

Jessica answered the door dressed casually but stylishly and surprised Jackson with a hug and a quick kiss. They both lingered for a moment, only breaking away when the silence lasted longer than normally comfortable. "Ummmm, I think we skipped a step," Jessica said somewhat breathlessly.

"I think you are right. Care to try again?"

Surprisingly, she stepped quickly into him, wrapping her arms around his neck and guiding his lips to hers. Their kiss was soft and slow and full of feeling. He lifted his left hand to her face and stroked her cheek lightly as their lips pressed tightly to each other. It lasted only for ten seconds or so, but the feeling behind it made it seem much longer than that. Jessica reluctantly pulled away and stepped back. Their eyes locked for an additional moment and then broke away as well. There was a satisfied silence for several seconds. Jessica broke it, "Well, how about that drink?"

"Yes, how about it." Jackson's reply was more of a statement of relief than anything else. Something in each of them had been touched. Something that neither of them had felt for a very long time. Something that every single soul longs for at some point in time. Something that few ever find. Each had approached that feeling before, but had never reached its completion. Both felt the mixture of exhilaration of finding such a thing and the unsure nervousness inherent in the desire to keep what you have found.

They finished their drinks and headed downtown to the FedEx Forum. Jackson had arranged for a parking spot not too far from Beale Street, giving them only a few short blocks to walk. They held hands and crossed a couple of busy streets, mingling easily with thousands of other people heading to the game or to their favorite Beale Street watering hole. The evening air was cool and crisp and Jackson reveled in her company. The drive downtown had felt as natural as two old friends on a regular get together. Conversation seemed to come very easily between them. Now, as they crossed the street and approached their destination, Jackson could feel the assured confidence from her gloved hand. Tonight, she would follow wherever the evening took them.

The basketball game was a blast. They agreed that everyone should sit courtside at least once. Drinks and food brought to you. A very attentive wait staff handling anything and everything one might need. Jessica commented more than once on how much faster the game seemed to move in person than watching it on TV. She showed a little court savvy as well, catching a wayward pass from the Orlando Magic's point guard. She held the ball up over her head and blew a kiss to the appreciative crowed that roared at the gesture. The hometown Grizzlies won an exciting game, scoring the last six points to win by three. The noise was so loud that at one point, Jackson couldn't hear himself think. Once the game ended, the pair floated with the crowd that seemed to move as a living organism. Neither wanted the evening to be over, so once they reached Jackson's Jeep, the only question was where to go next. Jackson looked at Jessica and asked matter-of-factly, "Dance, eat, or play?"

"What kind of games?" she asked coquettishly.

"Pool, shuffleboard, bowling. Whatever sounds good to you."

"Tell me more about dancing."

"There's a reggae band over at the Pinch, the usual stuff on Beale or we could find a higher energy club if that's what you had in mind."

"Reggae sounds fantastic actually."

Jackson turned the key and they set off for the Pinch District. One of the oldest neighborhoods in Memphis, it had been nicknamed The Pinch because it was first settled by Irish immigrants in the mid-1800's. The Irish typically had a "pinched" look to their faces and the name stuck. The district had seen revitalization plans come and go but there always remained a core constituency that maintained businesses and residences here. The result was a hometown feel of the restaurants and bars versus the touristy feel to the clubs on Beale Street. Jackson pulled the Jeep into a parking lot and they made their way to the bar. There was a small line outside but the bouncer waved Jackson and Jessica up and into the club. They got their hands stamped without paying a cover charge and were led to a quieter corner and given a small table with a direct line of sight to the band.

"I feel like something tropical, something with an umbrella in it," Jessica said over the crowd.

"Not 'Liquid Courage'?"

"No, but I have been working on that. It's still a great name for a shot!"

The noise of the crowd mixed with the band made it difficult for them to hear each other, so they leaned in closer to hear each other.

Jackson paused, "So how did you like the game?"

"Is that what you really wanted to ask me?"

"Not really."

"Ok, give it another shot. Or, why don't you just kiss me and then take me out to the dance floor."

"That's where I was going."

"Quit stalling."

Jackson leaned in and kissed her again softly, this time with a more familiar and fun feeling, matching the atmosphere and fitting right in with the rest of the crowd swaying to a classic Bob Marley tune. A waitress came and Jackson ordered for both of them and then took Jessica by the hand and led her to the dance floor. They moved and swayed together for a song and then returned to their tables where their drinks awaited them. They drank and talked closely, Jackson telling a story or two and Jessica laughing more than she could remember laughing in recent memory. He asked the waitress to keep an eye out for them as well as on their table and together they covered the dance floor for the next hour. They danced closely, moving around as if they had danced together for years. He anticipated her next move and spun her around confidently. The kissed a few times on the floor, tastefully so. Jackson got the attention of their waitress again and she brought them a couple of longnecks. Another hour and the club was packed. There was little room on the dance floor and the crowd pressed the pair closely together. They were standing and moving closely more than they were dancing, but it was all the same to them. Jackson finished his last beer of the night and led Jessica back to their table. She ordered another drink and they sat and talked and laughed and talked some more. Sitting closer than they were earlier, they spent the next hour or so people watching. They laughed long and loud at some of the approaches, requests, and rejections they saw. At one o'clock or so, Jackson looked at his watch.

"I hate to be the bad guy, but I have an early day tomorrow."

"I see how it is, get some courtside seats and then bail at the first opportunity!" Jessica smiled confirming her teasing.

"You caught me. The seats were great. I have had a great time tonight."

"Me too, so how's the rest of your week looking?"

Jackson took a drink of the water sitting in front of him and regarded his feet before he answered. "I have a potential client in town tomorrow and Friday, so I will be working around their schedule."

"What kind of client?"

"A travel client. She's a higher up in one of the professional organizations that does a lot of travel business."

"So how does that help your business?"

"A number of ways actually. If I can get different organizations on board, I can get their calendars for the year and kind of precede them into the cities they travel to. I make recommendations for convention space, restaurants, hotels, and all kinds of other services that go into their conventions and shows."

"So they pay you to know their tastes and desires and make recommendations based on that."

"Exactly."

"Sounds like fun."

"It can be--it can also be tedious and frustrating. That's why I try to get to know them as well as possible. I do ok, I suppose."

She batted her eyes at him, "Do we really have to go?"

"Well, since we need to stop by the cheese store to go with your whine, unfortunately yes." Jackson punctuated his answer with a wink. He got the waitresses attention and made a sign for a check. She pointed over to the manager who made a show of putting a piece of paper in his pocket. Jackson bowed his head and folded his hands as a show of thanks and helped Jessica out of her chair. On the way out of the bar, he handed the waitress a couple of twenty-dollar bills and thanked her for her attention.

Once outside, they noticed the temperature had dropped and they walked quickly to the Jeep hand in hand. Jackson opened the door for Jessica and closed in quickly behind her, getting in on his side, turning the engine over and cranking the heat up. Jessica reached over, took his chin in her hand and turned it towards her. She leaned in and kissed him as deeply as they had at her house earlier. A minute or so passed before they eased away from each other. Jackson stared with an amazed on his face and simply said, "Wow." Jessica smiled back at him and buckled her seat belt as Jackson backed the car out of the space and drove out of the lot.

CHAPTER 45

Jackson was waiting for Dr. Reynolds when she arrived at her office at 8:30 Thursday morning. She took one look at him and laughed, unlocking the front door and making a sweeping "go on in" gesture with her free hand. Jackson went through the office door and found his usual chair across from the couch in her office.

"You beat my assistant here. So what's the big emergency Jackson? You go four months and I don't hear from you, now it's twice in a few days? Have you started any medications I need to know about?"

"Thank you Dr. Reynolds, first for seeing me on such short notice and second for treating me with a sense of urgency and decorum."

"You are welcome. And don't bother with the sarcasm. Remember, I know you well and know where that comes from."

"Fair enough. I don't know that it is a big emergency. I had a date last night with a beautiful woman that may actually be more beautiful outside than in, I made the decision to retire this week and then am reminded that I am booked out for the next few weeks and months. Then I was reminded earlier about how good I am at my job. But I can't imagine doing what I do and trying to be with this woman in any capacity. Although I think she could possibly be 'the one.' How could

I be her 'one' though, doing what I do? Could someone that might be the one be able to get past that? Where could it go from there? Tying the knot, kids. Oh my God, can you imagine me having to tell my son or daughter that their father may the most exclusive but best value for the money male escort in the Southeastern United States?"

"Whoa there. Hello horse, I am placing this cart right here in front of you." She paused to let that sink in. "Is this the same woman we talked about the other day? And to answer your other question, no, I can't imagine having to have that conversation. Are you that good at your job?"

"Yes, I believe I am. And what I am paid kind of backs that up."

"And what makes you good at it?"

"I listen. I pay attention. I pay attention to what women say that want and what they don't want. I pay attention to what women want but can't or won't ask for. It seems like I am great at anticipating what they want or need, but if you simply pay attention, the rest of it typically works itself out."

"So are you doing the same thing with Ms. Wonderful?"

"No...well, yes. Maybe, I don't know!"

"Wow, you answered that one question in four different ways. I'm not sure that I have had a patient do that before." She smiled at Jackson reassuredly.

"I'm glad you are enjoying yourself."

"I'm sorry. Please understand--you met someone. You two are beginning to date. It's perfectly natural to think that THIS person is the one. That's why most people date specific people in the first place."

"But there is something different, there's a connection I can't explain. Something I haven't felt before. It's in the way that we talk to each other, look at each other. Something in her kiss."

"Have you slept with her?"

"No."

"Good, are you going to?"

"Well, I hope so. I think that's another reason that people date, isn't it?"

"For some people, yes. Have you told her about your job yet?"

"No, and that's part of why I didn't take it any further than it went last night. I can't even imagine how I could have that conversation any time after we had sex."

"Ok, well that's a start I guess. So when are you going to see her again."

"Saturday. I'm taking her to an Italian Film Festival."

"Really? Sounds interesting. A little different, but then again you seem to do things a little differently. Are you still working this week?"

"Yes…and I am supposed to be next week as well."

"Ok, well once you are ready to step back and have the conversation with her, I'll be here. Just for my own understanding, what is it about this woman that makes her so different?"

"I'm not sure exactly. She just has this presence, kind of like she is unaffected by everything around her. In my experience that is rare. Rarer than rare."

"And your clients are so different?"

"Wow, I hadn't thought about that. Not really. Well, not the long standing clients anyway. The others tend to weed themselves out rather quickly." Jackson turned his head and laughed softly.

Dr. Reynolds narrowed her eyes, observing him closely. "What did you think about just now?"

"What, just a second ago?"

"Yes, you answered the question and then whatever you thought about made you laugh."

"You're good you know."

"I do know. So what was the thought?"

Jackson paused as he gathered his thoughts. "It was a woman I met with about four months ago. Another client had referred her and I flew up to Ohio to meet her. Very serious, had the corporate dry-cleaned suit and the hair with the bun in the back pulled so tight that she could barely smile. I think she was a VP of some sort of service company. Anyway, after about ten minutes of conversation, I was ready to pay for dinner and get the hell back on the plane."

"That bad?"

Jackson sighed. "You have no idea. A major league pain in the ass. She had a desperate little laugh like she was hoping to be funny. I got the feeling that the only time she was the center of attention was at work. You know, people kissing her ass because she's the boss."

"That's a tough assessment to make in ten minutes don't you think?"

"Not really. First, it's my job and second, I confirmed that diagnosis with the woman that referred her. Turns out she had accidentally let it slip that she knew a 'professional'," Jackson made quotation marks with his fingers, "and the woman badgered her into making the introduction. It was the longest hour of my life. Well, there was that one time in New Orleans." He laughed at his own joke.

"Cute. So why remember that now?"

"I don't know. We were talking about Jessica and the Ohio woman is exactly the opposite."

"Did you ever work with the Ohio woman?"

"Stick up the ass woman? That's typically what I call her when I tell the story. And no, I don't need to get paid that much. I heard someone say once that you define yourself by the company you keep. I think too much of myself to keep that company."

"And the right answer always comes back to your way of thinking. Did you ever think that might be the root issue? No? Well, maybe something to think about. Now if you will excuse me, I have a client coming at 9:00…who had an appointment!"

CHAPTER 46

Jackson headed downtown and stopped off at a bank, making a quick deposit. He arrived at the Talbot Heirs and triple checked the hotel arrangements. Completely satisfied, he left his car to be valet parked and stepped outside, waiting for just a few minutes for the limousine to take him to the airport. The car was elegant yet understated. It had been furnished with the idea of business meetings in mind and stocked with soft drinks and water. Jackson checked his watch and smiled at the fact that he was precisely on schedule. The driver pulled into the taxi/limousine lane at the terminal and waited as Jackson walked inside. He found the flight and terminal he needed and waited for Meredith to appear. Fifteen minutes later he saw her struggling with a briefcase and two carry-on bags and rushed over to help.

"Could you use a hand ma'am?" Jackson asked with an official sounding voice, approaching her from behind.

She was focused on trying to handle her bags and answered without looking up. "Oh, that would be great. I am supposed to be meeting someone but they are apparently running late."

"Well, people can be unpredictable at times. How ugly was the person you were expecting?"

Meredith looked up quickly with an astonished look on her face. "What kind of question is…ahhh, Mr. Pritchard."

"I asked you to call me Jackson. Now, can I take those bags off your hands?"

"Gladly. I try to not check any luggage if I can help it."

"So this is for how many days?" Jackson asked with a laugh as he pointed in the direction of the limousine. They walked and talked at the same time.

"Two, maybe three depending on how the first two goes." She smiled somewhat seductively.

Jackson returned the smile. "Flexibility can be a very good thing. Do we have time to take you to your hotel room before your first meeting?"

Meredith checked her watch and frowned, it doesn't look like it. I have to be at the Convention and Visitor's Bureau in about twenty minutes."

"We'll get you there and take your things over to the room. You can call me when you are done. I'll wait for you there and pick you back up."

"I added one meeting and now it looks like I will be tied up from now until about 6:30 or so."

"Not a problem. I have a few things to do today, so I will take your bags to your room and send the car back to wait for you. It's at your disposal today and tomorrow." He handed her a room key. "This is the key to your suite. When you are done, you can go freshen up if you like. I have a few different dinner options available depending on what you want to do and we can go from there."

"Do you think of everything?"

"I'm not sure, how am I doing so far?"

"Let's just say that I can't wait to see what dessert brings."

CHAPTER 47

Jessica walked over to one of her several lunch tables and asked, "Who saved room for dessert?" Both businessmen protested animatedly and she handed them their already separated checks. They were semi-regulars, not nearly as funny or good-looking as either of them thought, but were above average tippers. They were nice enough though and she had had to politely decline each of their advances only once. Jessica was fairly certain that neither knew that the other had taken that step or had been shot down. "Men and their insecurities," Jessica thought, "At least they tip well." She walked into the kitchen and sat the dirty dishes she was carrying on top of the stove. From there, she walked to the sink to grab a dishtowel, stumbled a bit and almost fell into a sink full of soapy dishwater. Her arm soaking wet, she realized that the dishes were in the wrong place and went to go pick them up as she dried her arm at the same time. Reaching for the dishes, the towel she was using caught fire and she shrieked loudly, dropping it to the floor and stepping on it. The day manager walked in just as she picked up a plate and realizing it was too hot to hold dropped it to the floor where it smashed into a dozen pieces. Jessica covered her mouth and eyes.

"What the hell is going on?"

"What? Ummm, nothing. A bit clumsy today I guess."

"Okay, please exit stage left before you destroy what's left of my kitchen."

"Okay, thank you." Jessica made a hasty retreat to the bar area where Melanie was waiting with a bemused smile on her face.

"Earth to Jessica, come in."

"Huh? What? I'm sorry, just a little preoccupied today."

"Was he that good or just that big?"

Jessica threw an unburned towel at her. "Shut up! And I don't know about either. He dances amazingly well, he listens to every word I say before answering or telling a story, he opens doors, is amazingly polite and he kissed me like I have never ever EVER been kissed in my entire life."

Melanie paused several seconds to let the effect build up. "Ever?"

"EVER."

"Wow, that's a pretty strong statement."

"He's a hell of a kisser." Jessica bit her lip and shuffled her foot nervously.

"So when are you going to see him again?"

"I don't know. Maybe Saturday. He has a client in town today and tomorrow and said that he could be tied up but would call me if he could get away."

"Sounds serious. Like I seriously need to go throw up. Did he send you flowers?"

"No, I don't think he is the meaningless gesture kind of guy. He seems to be the more wait to get to know you and do things that have some meaning behind it kind of guy."

"Wow, and he has you babbling as well. Are you sure you didn't dance the horizontal mambo?"

"I think I would remember."

"You never know, there was that one guy that gave me rufees."

"He didn't give you rufees; you woke up before he did and figured out that he was WAY uglier than you remembered. Plus, he wasn't your boyfriend at the time…he lived three doors down from your boyfriend at the time and you thought you were going to get caught."

"Well, I didn't remember part of the night."

"You had ten shots of tequila."

Melanie got a dreamy look in her eye. "Oh yeah. Now HE was big."

"You're incorrigible."

"Does that mean hard to satisfy? Because there have been several times that boys couldn't...but men sure could!"

"I'm not listening to you."

"Sure you are. And loving every second of it."

"Maybe a little."

"So, what's your age limit?"

"Up or down?" Jessica thought about that momentarily. "Wait, why are we talking about this? Jackson is in his mid-thirties. That's my limit."

"Ugh, you really like him don't you?'

Jessica bit her lip and fidgeted back and forth, shuffling her feet. "Yeah, a lot."

CHAPTER 48

"Hello?"

"Yes, I need a reservation for one, the Pepper Jack chicken section?"

"We don't take reservations sir, but I believe I could squeeze you in. If you're lucky."

"I think I am. It seems that way so far anyway."

"So far?"

"Sure, I met this very interesting woman. She's going to an Italian Film festival with me. Can you imagine someone actually saying yes to that?"

"Not really. Is she ugly?"

"What? Absolutely not. She is stunning, actually."

"Crazy? Developmentally challenged?"

"No, and no."

"Maybe she is on lithium or something."

"Maybe. Are you?"

"Not that I know of. Not sure I would tell you if I knew though. I do get all of those little brown bottles confused."

"I can see how that might be difficult."

"So how are the client meetings going?"

"Okay I guess. She's tied up until after dinner. I am kind of on my own for a while. And hungry."

"How long before you can be here?"

"Twenty minutes or so."

"Why haven't you left yet?"

"Oh, good point. I'll see you in a bit."

CHAPTER 49

Will Swift was sitting at his desk reviewing a couple of reports for the case when the Sergeant yelled over, "Swift! Line two!"

"Swift."

"Um, yes. Detective Swift? This is Jackson Pritchard calling from Memphis, Tennessee. You left a message for me earlier."

"Yes, Mr. Pritchard, thank you for calling. Do you have a couple of minutes to talk?"

"Sure."

"Well, your name came up in the midst of an investigation I am part of. Do you know a Sharon Milligan?"

"Umm, yes. She's a client of mine. Why do you ask?"

"When was the last time you saw her?"

Jackson thought back to a conversation he and Sharon had previously. She was very conscious about her image and wanted very much to keep everything between them buried as deeply as possible. So the Caribbean was out of the question. "August I think. There was a convention in Seattle that we had a meeting around."

"You haven't seen her since then?"

"No sir."

Will listened carefully to his voice. Even the coolest customers betrayed themselves by changing their tone or cadence or the level of formality in their speech. "Can you remember where you were the weekend after Thanksgiving?"

"Sure, I was skiing with some friends out in Colorado. Telluride. Had never skied there before. They had early snow this year."

"How about last weekend?"

"I was in D.C. Why? Is something wrong?"

"I don't think there is anything wrong where you are concerned. You have proof of these trips you took?"

"Sure, I keep receipts of every thing. I'm self-employed so I have to, taxes and all."

"Fair enough. I appreciate you calling back. If I have anything else, I will contact you again."

"Can I ask what this is all about?"

"Well, since you didn't know her well, I'll let you know why I am asking. She was murdered last weekend."

"Holy...wow, what? How? Why?"

"We don't know the particulars. Your card was in her Rolodex. That's why I called. Just chasing every lead we can. If I have any other questions, I'll call you."

"Sure, anything I can do to help."

"Thank you, and thank you for calling back." Will hung the phone up and crossed Jackson's name off his list. "Strike fourteen."

CHAPTER 50

Shelby ate lunch at her desk as usual. She was checking her e-mail as well as the overseas accounts she had set up, when she noticed one of her markers had been disturbed. Shelby had been very careful in setting up the account and made sure she had included a few technical markers. These were bits of code that she added that ran in the background and ran in a certain pattern until someone came through and tried to access the file it was attached to. In this case, the file was an encrypted and numbered bank account with a little over half a million dollars in it. Shelby liked checking on the planned dowry she had prepared for Jackson and knew he would appreciate the gesture very much. She thought that if they had that much money, he could retire from the dirty job he did and they could live happily ever after. Who couldn't love someone that thought that much about someone else's life, future, and happiness? Getting back on track, Shelby entered a few different tracer queries into the system to try and get an idea of who was checking her out. Her mind raced for several moments as she retraced the steps she had taken to cover her tracks both where the money and she were concerned. The mental checklist completed, she turned her attention to the results of the queries the system had prepared. Three separate inquiries, all tracing back to the Seattle area. Digging deeper, she followed the pathways through the Web, making sure to cover her tracks at the same time. The first led her directly to the Seattle Police Department. That was expected, given the circumstances. The second and third seemingly followed the same trail, although they began from two completely different starting points. She traced one and followed it back through a series of firewalls and other obstructions. The trail ended at a server of a Douglas Jimmerson, private detective. The final path led back to a law firm. Shelby thought about both for a moment and began to make sense of it. The firm more than likely represented Sharon Milligan and was attempting to track down her assets. The firm probably retained the detective and the parallel tracks were the detective showing them what he had found. Shelby pondered this for a while and decided to have a bit of fun with both. She hacked into the firm's server and planted a series of viruses and timed them to go off daily each 9:00 A.M. beginning the following Monday afternoon. With three days of system wide failures, the firm would easily be paralyzed. Then she turned her attention to the detective. Searching through his hard drive, she found several pictures of kids, angry e-mails between him and an ex-wife, bank account balances at the bare minimums and credit card balances at the opposite end of the spectrum. Feeling a pang of remorse, she decided to spare his system and chose instead to lead him on a wild goose chase. She laid a false trail of bread crumbs that would take him away from the accounts she had set up and if he was any good, would take him instead to a small, non-traceable reward set aside and addressed to him. The thought of playing Robin Hood made her smile. She quickly composed the note she would leave attached to the $25,000 prize she would leave. "Dear Douglas, Congratulations on following me this far. As you know now, I have been onto to you for some time. I hold no ill will toward you at all, realizing that like me, you are being paid to do someone else's bidding. Doing some checking, I realize that you need this little token of my appreciation much more than your employers do. Therefore, keep the money and tell them the trail went cold. Keep this our little secret or I will bring this to their attention, which could be an issue for you and them. Remember, you followed the trail that I set up, so it will be very simple to show them how you got here. I'd much rather you used the money and took care of your family. Best wishes. S." She wondered how long it would take for him to get there, and wrote a quick program that would alert her to the money being taken. Having finished the task of throwing off the bloodhounds, she switched programs and checked on her beloved and what he had been up to lately. She had installed a few spyware trackers into his system and was able to access his schedule, his e-mail and some other simple programs. The encryption software the firm had sold him was too powerful to get around so far, but she would figure it out soon. She noticed he was working this weekend and part of next week and felt bad for him having to work that hard. She had become somewhat familiar with his clientele and knew in her heart that they would never treat him as well as he deserved. No one would ever treat him as well as she would. Sighing, she logged out and clicked back over to the company computer system and surfed the Web while she finished her lunch.

CHAPTER 51

Jackson redialed Jessica's number. "Hey, can I get a rain check on that sandwich? I got a strange phone call; one of my clients was killed recently."

"Oh no, that's terrible. Did you know them well?"

"Pretty well, we had done some business pretty recently. I need to make some phone calls to see what I can find out."

"No problem. If you need to talk later or whatever, give me a call."

"Thanks, you're the best." He hung up the phone and dialed Meredith's number, getting her voice mail. He left a message explaining he had some work to do but would be a phone call away when she finished with her business." He hung up and sat for a moment, thinking through his next few steps. The phone call from the detective had shaken him up a bit. He replayed the conversation in his mind, checking to see if he had given away any information he would not have wanted to. Unable to come up with anything, he searched his phone for numbers in Seattle to see what he could find out. Dialing Sharon Milligan's home number, Jackson was greeted by an automated voice mail that advised him to leave a message after the series of beeps. He hung up and dialed her office number. A perky receptionist answered and Jackson asked for Sharon's Executive Assistant by name.

"Ashley Danielson."

"Hi Ashley, it's Jackson Pritchard."

"Oh hi, Mr. Pritchard. How are you? I guess you heard the news."

"I did, it's awful. What happened?"

"No one is really saying. I heard a maid or something found her in her kitchen and that she had been stabbed to death."

"What!" Jackson heard himself almost screaming. "Who would want to do something like that? What are the police saying?"

"Not anything. They have interviewed everyone here at least once if not twice and sifted through all of her documents."

"Are they getting anywhere?"

"It doesn't seem like it. They have had her body for almost a week and still no announcements or anything."

"When's the funeral?"

"That's the other thing. They aren't releasing her body yet. It may be a week or so according to one of the attorneys I talked to."

"Do me a favor?"

"Sure thing."

"Call me when they make the arrangements. I would like to fly up and pay my respects."

"Good. It will be nice to see you again. You can stay with me if you like."

"That's a very generous offer. But, I wouldn't feel right putting you out like that."

"It wouldn't put me out at all. In fact it would be my pleasure."

Jackson wondered to himself if she was really hitting on him while they were talking about a funeral. "Why thank you. I appreciate you doing that for me." He gave her his cell phone number and hung up. He thought again for a moment and redialed the restaurant. Jessica answered on the second ring. "Blue Monkey."

"You answer the phones too? A jack of all trades."

"A girl has to do what a girl has to do. Did you find out what happened?"

"Not really. She was murdered though."

"What? Oh my God, that's crazy."

"Tell me about it. It was just a few months ago that I saw her."

"What are you going to do?"

"Now? Nothing I can do. A detective called and questioned me earlier. That was kind of odd. Still got a sandwich for me?"

"Absolutely. Come on and get it."

"I'm on the way."

CHAPTER 52

Will Swift checked his voice mail and e-mail and found nothing new. He went through his file notes and nothing jumped out. He checked and double-checked the medical report, the physical evidence report and all fourteen interview reports they had conducted to this point. He sighed and rubbed his temples as he stared at the computer with bleary eyes. Thinking back to his training classes, he went through all the steps he knew to uncover something, anything that would point him in the right direction. A particular conversation he had with a crusty old now-retired captain came to mind when Will was still in property crimes. "Rookie, whenever you get stuck, make sure and follow the money. The money trail will always lead you to the bad guys." Will picked up the phone and dialed the IT investigator's number.

"IT, Gray."

"It's Swift. You got a second?"

"Sure Detective. What's on your mind?"

"The money."

Twenty-five minutes later, Will walked into the IT offices. He quickly spotted Jeremy Gray across the room and made his way over. They shook hands.

"Detective, good to see you as always."

"Thanks, are you still getting speeding tickets by the dozen?"

"Not since I got the badge. Life is much better now."

Jeremy Gray was a mildly competent computer hacker. He had been successful in hacking into several low-security corporate websites but not much beyond that. Twice he had gotten through the first level of security of a government site but had been discovered and gotten caught each time. The second time he had been sentenced to community service and found that he had a knack for duplicating what other people had done when hacking into websites. He simply lacked the imagination to find his own way. He logged in and showed the Detective what he had done and retraced his steps as best as he could. The trail went cold all three directions he went. As close as he got was that it started somewhere in the South. Initially, everything pointed to West Tennessee, but now he wasn't so sure. Trying his best to explain the ins and outs of computer hacking, Tech Grade 2 Gray lost Will in the first five minutes of his explanation and then promptly lost himself somewhere thereafter, leaving both men with perplexed looks across their respective faces. Will thanked Jeremy for his time and asked if he had saved any of his work. Gray nodded and handed him a disc that showed his movements in and out of the different websites he had worked through. The two men shook hands and Will left the office, dialing his cell phone as he walked down the hall and out of the building. He searched through his phone until he found and dialed the specific number he was looking for. An answering machine answered with a series of beeps the only indication that the caller had reached anywhere.

"It's Detective Swift, pick up Jonas." There was a pause for several seconds and then Will heard the phone receiver pick up and then subsequently get dropped. It shuffled around for a few seconds until a cheery voice picked up. "Detective! So good to hear from you."

"Save it. I need to trace a hacker. Can you do it?"

"Does it rain often in our fair city?"

"I'm on the way over."

Jonas Fisher was a hacker in the truest sense of the word. He had hacked into Top Secret or higher clearance government websites as well as the best protected corporate sites anywhere. He had gotten bored and retired until drawn back into one last job where he was paid top dollar to infiltrate a series of sites that turned out to be a sting operation with Will Swift at the end. Facing five years in prison, Jonas worked out a deal where he became a consultant to the police force, training them on tracking hackers. He also had a handshake deal that in exchange for information and the occasional hack, the police would turn a blind eye to his online activities as long as he didn't do anything big. Jonas made more money these days legitimately as a consultant. Companies hired him to infiltrate their systems and patch the holes. He lived in a nondescript apartment building in a nondescript neighborhood. Twenty-nine years old and dressed entirely in black clothing that looked like it had been worn a few times since it was washed last, Jonas opened the door with another warm greeting.

"How is my favorite detective?"

"Tired and broke. How is it that I bust you and you probably make five times what I do just by playing on your computer?"

"The world is a funny place detective."

"I'm not laughing Jonas."

"You should be. I do it every day. At myself. How else could I have been caught by someone as brilliant as you?"

"And yet, you were. That's got to chew on you right here." Will balled up a fist and stuck into his stomach.

"So what are you bringing me Detective? Did you forget your vo-tech locker combination?"

Will laughed at that one. "I heard someone say one time that even a blind squirrel finds a nut. Speaking of, how is your love life?"

"Touché. So whatcha got?"

"Not sure. Working a homicide and it looks like the victims' computer system hacked to the tune of a half million dollars. The cyber trail has been filtered and the tech guys can't seem to pick it up."

"That's my kind of tune. Shocked, by the way, that your guys can't find anything. Did Tech Specialist Gray remember to turn the computer on before he used it?"

"I'm sure he did. See if you can pick up the trail and see where it goes."

"I could be busy doing something else you know."

"True, but the city will pay you and you will get my good will at least for a while."

"Nothing could warm my heart more."

"I need a name and number."

"I have you on speed dial."

CHAPTER 53

Meredith Gregory checked her watch and listened as the last of the presentations were made in the last of her meetings for the day. They seem to be running mostly on schedule if not just a few minutes late. For the past hour, she had been distracted from the presentations being made by the thoughts of the weekend and what Mr. Jackson Pritchard might have in store for her. Her fingertips traced the skin of her face and she smiled slightly at the possibility. The final presenter summarized his points neatly and thanked the board for their time. There was a slight round of applause and the meeting began to break up. Meredith packed her briefcase up and stood, making her way out of the conference room. She was stopped twice by business associates, and spent a few minutes catching up on what each was up to. The conference room opened into a long hallway that led outside and to her waiting limousine. She climbed in the rear and made a call on her cell phone to Jan Eberhardt. Jan had sent Meredith as her envoy, both as a test to see how she would handle it as well as someone she thought would represent her interests well. She was right as usual. They spoke for several minutes while the car wound it's way through the streets of Memphis. It turned down Second Street and made it's way past AutoZone Park. Meredith had grown up as the youngest child in her family with five brothers. All played various sports, the most popular of which was baseball. It had been a favorite of hers even as a young girl and she had fond memories of watching her brothers play from the stands. She took every opportunity she got to watch a game in whatever city she found herself in when the games were being played. Out of season, she still enjoyed touring the stadiums. She made a mental note to see if Jackson would take her back by tomorrow. The limousine stopped in front of Talbot Heirs and Meredith stepped out. It wasn't quite what she expected from the outside and with a puzzled look on her face she walked in the front door. The front desk manager greeted her.

"I see the same look from many of our first time guests. Is there anything I can help you with?"

"My room was arranged by a friend and I am already checked in. Can you direct me to my suite?"

"Absolutely Ms. Gregory." He pointed the way to her room with a smile.

"How did you know my name?"

"It's my job ma'am. Is there anything else I can do for you?"

"No thank you. Umm, wait. How about a six o'clock wake up call?"

"Consider it done."

Meredith opened the door to her suite and was pleasantly surprised to find her host in the kitchen slicing some vegetables. A blues song she couldn't identify was playing on a stereo and Jackson was drinking a bottled beer.

"Well, aren't you full of surprises? What are you listening to?"

"We have to work on your musical recognition. This is what Memphis music is all about. 'I'm in the Mood' by John Lee Hooker. Doesn't get much better than that." He held up a plate. "Cucumber? Tomato?"

"I didn't picture you being a health food person."

"I'm not. Health food is tofu and soybean burgers. These are vegetables and they are fresh from the farmer's market. I even got you some ranch dip if you like. Drink after a hard day at the office?"

"I think I will. What do you have?"

"I remember you drinking martinis in D.C. I have stuff to make those. I also have some wine and beer. Choose your poison."

"I think a glass of wine will do nicely. It was a long day today. I'm going to go get out of these clothes. Be right back." She sang the last few words and walked out of the room. Jackson snacked on a couple of fresh tomato slices while he waited. He finished his beer and thought about opening another one. Instead, he opened a bottle of Pinot Noir and tasted it. Satisfied, he poured a glass for Meredith and set in on the bar. A few minutes later, Meredith reappeared, dressed casually in a blouse and jeans. Jackson noticed her bare feet.

"See you fit in well down here, no shoes and everything. I just have mine on for show."

"You're silly. So what kind of time do you have tonight?"

"I have tonight and tomorrow night free. You have me at your disposal." He bowed slightly as he said it.

"Are you hungry?"

"Kind of. Definitely will want to eat in a while. Do you have a taste for anything?"

"Not really. You are the Memphis guy, so I figured I would leave it to you."

"Fair enough. Two distinct tastes of Memphis within a couple of blocks. Barbecue at the Rendezvous is a Memphis tradition. Automatic Slim's is more nouveau cuisine. Kind of a trendy place to eat and be seen."

"Do you have a preference?"

"Nope, just depends on what you have a taste for."

"Let's be messy. Barbecue sounds good."

Jackson smiled. "A woman after my own heart. I'm ready whenever you are."

CHAPTER 54

Douglas Jimmerson walked into his office and plopped down in front of his computer after sitting through a 12-hour stakeout. His patience had paid off and he was rewarded by snapping a dozen or so pictures of a couple emerging from a hotel room after a night of secret lust. They were married, but not to each other. He checked his e-mail and found nothing of interest and then began to follow the money trail he had found the other evening. The downtime on the stakeout had given him a few ideas how to work around the seemingly dead end he had previously run into. A few keystrokes led him down the now familiar path he had blazed. He smiled broadly as his first idea yielded a way around the first roadblock he encountered and then again as he found the trail leading in the direction he initially thought. A few more keystrokes and he came upon a file he hadn't seen before. He isolated it and ran a virus scan, finding nothing. He opened it and almost choked on the beer he had opened when he found a letter addressed to him. He read and reread the letter and wondered how in the heck someone had gotten onto him that quickly. Thinking further, he imagined that he had to be on the right trail. Now came the moment of truth. Take the money and run or push farther and try and catch whoever was behind the letter. It took just a few seconds. He clicked his mouse a few times and suddenly became $25,000 richer. A few more clicks and he shut down the tracer programs he had been using. He checked a few more places in his computer to make sure he wasn't being tracked by any spyware or had picked up any viruses along the way. Satisfied, he shut his computer down and headed out to the bank to redistribute his newfound money.

Shelby was sitting at her desk at home when an alert popped up on the screen. She clicked a few buttons and smiled as she saw that the money she had left behind had been taken and sighed in relief as she checked the activity that had followed. Feeling emboldened, she checked in on Jackson Pritchard to see what he was up to. Surprisingly, he hadn't logged on much in the past few days and she wondered what he was up to. Her cell phone rang and she silenced it, not interested in the boy that was on the other end of the phone. She made a mental note to stop giving her cell number out as she was certain that it would upset Jackson to know that she drew so much attention.

Another notice was issued when Mr. Jimmerson transferred that money. Jonas Fisher smiled and felt like a spider with a new meal stuck in his web. He typed on his keyboard for several minutes and wound his web tightly around his prey, literally salivating at the pursuit and capture. He picked up his cell phone and dialed Detective Swift's number. Will answered on the third ring.

"Swift."

"Detective. How is your evening going? Playing hide the salami with Mrs. Swift?"

"Not yet Jonas. Speaking of, when was the last time you had sex with someone else actually in the same room?"

"Ouch, a little testy tonight are we?"

"Not me. Was there a reason you called me?"

"Absolutely. I haven't found your hacker yet, but I have found someone else that was looking for them. It seems this competitor of yours can be bought. Do you have a price as well?"

"I wouldn't know Jonas. But please continue your story."

"You sound busy. Are you sure this is a good time. I could call you back…"

"JONAS...please, continue." Will struggled to maintain his composure.

"Well, it looks like the hacker caught on to the fact they were being tracked and left a little package for the person that was tracking them. Does the name Douglas Jimmerson ring a bell?"

"Yep, small time detective, kind of an ambulance chasing version of what we do. I think he was kicked off the force a few years ago. Nice enough guy. I've had drinks with him a couple of times."

"Touching. I am envious of such male bonding."

"Cute. Send me the information. I'll drop some doughnuts off for you tomorrow."

"Too easy detective. Too easy." He closed his flip phone and looked back at the computer screen. He clicked a few more keys, activating two separate search programs he had written. "After all, information is power," he said to no one in particular.

CHAPTER 55

The Rendezvous restaurant is a long-standing institution in downtown Memphis. It hadn't originated the idea of dry ribs, but many people would argue they perfected it. The restaurant was also one of the most well known barbecue restaurants from coast to coast. Additionally, The Rendezvous had pioneered the business of packaging and shipping meals via another Memphis tradition, Fed Ex. Meredith and Jackson also noted that they moved people in and out very efficiently. They were sharing a rack of ribs and enjoying the fixings along with it while surveying the flow of people. Meredith was amazed at the efficiency of the waiters, another attraction of the restaurant. Most of them had worked here for years and had a reputation of knowing their clients as well as anyone, anywhere. They never wrote anything down and ruled their sections absolutely while thoroughly entertaining their guests. They were among the highest paid servers in the city. Meredith was enjoying herself tremendously but noticed Jackson wasn't.

"Is everything ok Jackson? You've been kind of quiet since we got here."

"I'm sorry. Kind of a tough day. I find out that a client and friend of mine was killed recently."

"That's terrible, I'm so sorry. Is there anything I can do?"

"No, but thank you, offering is very nice. How did your meetings go today?"

"Excellent, I think we just added to the bottom line of the Eberhardt empire."

"She's a big fan of that. And of you it seems."

"Funny, I was going to say the same thing about you."

"Well, she's very good at developing a loyal following. Has she talked to you about working for her?"

"She hasn't offered anything, but it seems like the conversations are leading that way."

"You could do worse. Much worse."

"Well, hopefully the picture will clear up soon. So what's on your agenda tonight?"

"Nothing specific. I understand you have meetings beginning early tomorrow. I have some arrangements and things to make since I am traveling all next week. Since your last meeting is at 2:00 tomorrow, I figure we can enjoy a Memphis downtown Friday night and have you sufficiently worn out for your flight Saturday morning. The car is at your disposal tomorrow."

"Sounds good. Are you going to walk me home?"

"Of course, I wouldn't dream of leaving you on your own in my fair city."

"You're sweet. My knight in shining armor."

They polished off the ribs and Jackson paid the tab. They quietly walked arm in arm back to her hotel and to the door of her suite. Jackson began to recount the plans for tomorrow as Meredith unlocked the door. Successfully unlocked, she turned and quieted Jackson with a kiss and pulled him into the room, locking the door behind them.

CHAPTER 56

Jessica woke up early on Friday and opted to take Max out for a brisk walk. She chose Harbor Town, a neighborhood that was designed to include both retail and residential development. One of its amenities was a wide running/biking trail that paralleled the Mississippi river to take advantage of its scenery. She wanted to clear her mind and get ready for the practical exam she had coming up in her pottery class and so she could really get her mind around this "thing" with Jackson. It had been only a short while since her decision to take care of herself first and foremost. She had chased away more men than she cared to remember and had congratulated herself each and every time. Something about Jackson made her want to rethink that strategy entirely. He was funny and intelligent. He made her feel good about just being her and she truly enjoyed every second they spent together. Then a thought of doubt crept in. "What's wrong with him...what do I not know?" She tried to block the thoughts out, reasoning that everyone had a past and everyone had issues. Her stride quickened as she pushed the pace a bit. Max trotted along next to her, wagging his tail in oblivious enjoyment. She cleared her mind again and thought about the day's schedule. Test this morning, a little shopping afterwards with Melanie and then working the night shift. She wanted to get a new outfit for the film festival tomorrow. She dialed her friend's phone number and hung up when the voice mail answered, remembering the cute, drunk lawyer her friend had left the bar with the night before. Her phone rang just a few minutes later.

"Hello Madonna how's the hangover?" Jessica asked suppressing a laugh.

"Madonna?"

"You know, like a virgin? Only, you know, not?"

"That's mean. I'm not feeling very good about myself this morning and need to talk."

"I'm sorry, sweetie, what happened?"

"I let him come over to my house!"

"What?!?! That's against your rule!"

"I know. But then after he came inside, he came inside…and outside…and then inside again."

Jessica could hear her smiling. She slapped her forehead lightly saying, "I always fall for it."

"Sucker, oops, wait, that's me. You did call me though, what's up?"

"Where's Mister Multiple?"

"I sent him out for coffee and doughnuts."

"You're too much. I want to go shopping later. Before our shift."

"Okay, pick me up?"

"Sure, noonish, be ready, be dressed and be alone."

"That gives me plenty of time for another legal brief. Has to be, I have his boxers."

"I'm bringing you a home STD testing kit. Goodbye." Jessica sang her farewell with an exaggerated singsong voice. She laughed and cranked up the CD player and sang as loudly as she could, interrupted a few minutes later by her cell ringing again. She turned the volume down and answered. "I'll have you know that you interrupted Macy Gray."

"What can I say, my timing is impeccable."

"Be nice, I like her music."

"I'll be nice, but only because you're going to see Italian movies with me tomorrow."

"I'm actually looking forward to that."

"I'm glad to hear it, I am too."

"So how did it go with your client last night?"

"Prospective client," Jackson corrected. "Not too bad, I was out a little later than I expected. Hazards of the job."

"Was it enjoyable?"

"I think so. Would hate to have my entertaining abilities questioned."

"Did you need something? Or did you just miss me?"

"I actually called precisely because I missed you. Tonight might be later then last and I wanted to, well…I just wanted to say 'Good morning'."

"That's awfully nice."

"Maybe. Are you working tonight?"

"Yep, but Melanie and I are going shopping first. You know, Girl time."

"I hope you enjoy yourself. Can I call you later?"

"I hope you do."

CHAPTER 57

Will Swift knocked loudly on the apartment door with a bag of doughnuts under his arm. He waited for several seconds before knocking again. Glancing at his watch, he was ready to dial Jonas' number when he heard the locks being worked on the other side of the steel door. It opened and a clearly disheveled Jonas appeared on the other side in a tattered bathrobe.

"Detective, what a pleasant surprise. Wait, it's not a surprise. And hopefully it's pleasant. I'm not holding my breath though. What time is it?"

"7:00, the early bird gets the worm, didn't they teach you that in school?" Will handed him the bag of doughnuts and reached down and retrieved the cardboard coffee holder with the pair of coffees in it, squeezing through the doorway.

"Yeah, but who wants a bunch of worms?" Jonas watched the detective enter with a quizzical look and sarcastic tone, saying "Um, won't you come in?"

Will surveyed the apartment quickly, noting the four Samsung oversized flat screen computer monitors as well as the server rack on the far wall. He counted three servers that looked like they were networked and then one other standing alone. He scanned the rest of the apartment, noting the clutter and trash strewn throughout. "Nice décor, what do you call it, Nouveau Trashy?"

"My maid took the year off, is there something I can help you with detective?"

"Absolutely, you can tell me what else you found out about this mystery hacker."

"I told you what I knew last night."

"Now, why do you want to start with me this morning? I brought you doughnuts and coffee and everything."

"I'm at a loss detective, what else do you think I know?"

Will moved close to Jonas, stopping about six inches away from his face. "I'm certain you told me everything you knew when we talked last night. I'm equally as certain that as soon as you hung up the phone, you dove back into cyberspace and dug and tracked and searched every nook and cranny you could until you found out much more. You probably fell asleep at your computer," he leaned in closer. "See, I think there are keyboard marks on your face. A definite improvement."

Jonas leaned back. "Doesn't your wife make you brush your teeth in the morning? Ever hear of a breath mint?"

"Don't change the subject."

"I was getting there. I did search a bit last night but didn't come up with anything. I might look again tonight, but was working on a different project last night, one that I am certain is much more entertaining, ergo challenging and is definitely paying me more money. And I slept in my bed last night if you must know." He took a long drink from the coffee cup. "Ugh, what is this?"

"It's coffee. Regular coffee. From a doughnut shop, not some half-caff, creamy, frothy, coffee flavored dessert in a biodegradable cup with a sleeve. Enjoy, it might put hair on even your chest."

"You stopped at a doughnut shop?" Jonas snickered. "I suppose clichés are based mostly in the truth. Whatever, you could have at least put a little something in the coffee."

"It's in the bag genius." Will nodded in the direction of the table where the doughnuts were. "So when I come back tonight, you're going to fill me in on the rest of the story?"

"Depends on what you are bring me, there's a diner a couple of blocks from here that does a fantastic patty melt."

"I know the place, you give me what I need and you'll have patty melts for a month."

"I'll hold you to that detective. What makes you so sure I will find anything anyway?"

"Because you find what you set your mind to finding. And then I find you. Funny how that works isn't it?"

A deadpan look from Jonas was the all the answer he needed. "What time should I expect you detective?"

"You can expect me when I get here...and not a minute sooner."

Jonas raised his coffee cup in mock toast and nodded at the detective as he showed himself out, closing the door behind him.

CHAPTER 58

Jackson set the treadmill for a five-mile run at an eight minute pace. He preferred to run outdoors, but the familiarity of the gym appealed to him this morning. His evening with Meredith had not been unsuccessful, but he had been troubled to find himself thinking of Jessica for most of the night. He had awakened and rolled over to find himself looking into the face of the beautiful woman he had spent the night with. Then he had promptly moved quickly and quietly to the restroom and vomited. That thought was stuck in his mind as he worked his way through the road-racing program. The other reason he had chosen the treadmill was so that all he had to do was run. No thinking about his path or dodging traffic, just step after step of focused reflection. He ran through the cool-down portion of the workout and switched the treadmill to manual, adding another three miles. Afterwards, he stepped off and reached for a pair of towels, wiping down his machine first with one and then mopping his sweat soaked face and hair with the other. He moved to another area of the floor and stretched for several minutes, working the lactic acid from his muscles to ensure a minimum of soreness once he had cooled off. While he stretched, his mind wandered back to the previous night. He knew he could keep up the façade for one more evening, but the question kept coming back. Why? Why spend one more night with a stranger when he could be spending it doing something that made sense. And what made sense to him was Jessica. Getting to know her, learning all about her and in the process learning about himself as well as them together. That made sense. He finished stretching and went back to the desk where he had left his bag. Opening it, he saw that he had missed two phone calls. The first was from Jan Eberhardt and the second was Meredith whom he had missed by just a couple of minutes. He walked to his car and got in, started the engine and pressed redial. She picked up on the second ring, sounding a bit out of breath, "Hello?"

"Hey, it's Jackson, sorry I missed your call."

"It's ok, sorry I missed you this morning. So if a handsome guy has a breakfast cart left for you at your bedside, does that count as breakfast in bed?"

"Did you get out of bed to eat?"

"No."

"Well then, I would say it counts."

"Thank you for breakfast, that was very thoughtful. It would have been nice to share it with that handsome guy though."

"I checked with room service, they said that was extra."

She laughed, a not displeasing laugh at all. "You're cute. And amazing, thank you for last night."

"I think you did most of the work, so I should be thanking you."

"Do you plan on repeating that performance later?"

"I don't think so. I hate people that repeat themselves; it shows a tremendous lack of imagination in my way of thinking. Original thinking...that's much more impressive to me."

"I think I like the sound of that. What do you have planned for us tonight?"

"Something a little different I think. There's a newer place I'd like to check out first. Kind of a newer style lounge in an older atmosphere. Plus I know the bartender."

"You seem to know a lot of people in the bar business Mr. Pritchard. That might cause some to be concerned with your liver."

"My liver appreciates your concern. I don't treat it as badly as you might think. I typically indulge in quality as opposed to quantity. My liver appreciates the changes in scenery. Whoa, I missed my turn. Don't you hate it when that happens?"

"I do, and apologize in advance for distracting you."

"I accept your apology and insist that when we are face to face again, there will be absolutely zero distractions."

"You have a unique way of raising the bar when it comes to expectations Mr. Pritchard."

"I thought we had moved past the formalities Ms. Gregory."

"Face to face, yes. You're much more fun to play with on the phone when speaking formally however."

"As are you as well. You're a worthy conversational adversary, Ms. Gregory."

"I look forward to continuing this conversation later."

Jackson pulled up to his house and parked the car, opened the door to his house and dropped the keys on the hallway table. Still sweating from his workout, he scanned the newspaper. He checked his watch and planned the rest of his day according to the time he had left. Then he called Jan Eberhardt back.

"Took you long enough sweetness. I'm beginning to feel left out a bit."

"You know better. But you also know I rarely answer my phone when I am working."

"I do know that. And I also know you weren't working when I called. I know this because I called you after talking with Meredith this morning. You do good work."

"Who would know better than you?"

"Apparently I don't know as well as some. Sounds like you had a successful first date."

"We had a very nice night."

"She sounded very satisfied on the phone. I'm not sure I was quite the satisfied after our first encounter."

"You wouldn't open up nearly as quickly."

"Call it being successfully guarded."

"Touché. So to what do I owe the pleasure of your phone call?"

"Just checking in, seeing if you had enough to take care of my girl the right way."

"You know I wouldn't do anything but."

"I do know that. I'd like to send you another token of my appreciation. Shall I mail it or would you like me to send it the usual way?"

"Send it the regular way, and thank you very much."

"No, thank you. You just helped me land some top talent for my company. I'll show my appreciation again in Colorado."

"I look forward to it."

Jackson hung up the phone and threw it on the couch. He looked over the paper and went through his mail quickly. Stepping to the back of the house, he undressed and showered quickly. Once done, he toweled off and climbed into bed, setting his alarm for four o'clock, time enough to get rested and ready for the next couple of days.

CHAPTER 59

The second stop on Will Swift's tour of Seattle was the office of one Douglas Jimmerson, Private Detective. Will opened the front door of the office to find the reception desk empty. It reminded him of an old film noir setting and Will half expected Humphrey Bogart to walk through the door at any moment. By the looks of things, it had been several months or longer since anyone had worked there on an ongoing basis. The computer on the desk was dusty and outdated. The yellow sticky notes on the desk had faded and the writing on them was illegible even up close. A jacket and umbrella hung from the coat stand in the corner indicating that Douglas was there. Will crossed the space to the door marked "Office-Private" and knocked on it. He waited for a few moments with no response and tried the door handle. Finding it open, he peeked in and found an office that was in total disarray. A rumpled man in his late forties slept on the sofa with a half empty bottle of vodka on the coffee table in front of him. Will shook his head and laughed softly to himself. He cleared his throat loudly, hoping to awaken the sleeping detective. A moment later he did it again and asked, "Douglas Jimmerson?" Still nothing. He reached over and grabbed an ice bucket half full of water and paused for a moment before dumping the contents on the sleeping man. Douglas jumped up in shock, sputtering a bit as the ice cold water choked him momentarily. He yelled, "What the fuck!" and looked around to see the intruder standing in his office, holding his badge up a foot or so from his face.

"Good morning Douglas, sleep well?"

Douglas took a minute to clear his head, rubbing his eyes and focused his attention on the floor, trying to get his bearings. "I don't know about sleeping, but I passed out pretty stylishly I think. And who might you be?"

"Detective Will Swift, homicide. Did you get my messages?"

"I did, figured you were selling tickets to the Policeman's Ball or something."

"Cute. If I were, could I put you down for say, $25,000 worth?"

Douglas raised his head, his eyes narrowing in disbelief.

"You see Douglas, I don't care about that money. As far as I can tell, it has nothing to do with any crime. But what I do care about is how you got there in the first place. Because the trail you followed to get it is exactly the same trail that showed up at a law firm that paid you a nice little retainer about a week ago. That law firm just happens to be the firm that represents Sharon Milligan."

"Never heard of her." Douglas paused for a second to gather his thoughts. "Do you have a warrant? Am I under arrest? Or are we just having a conversation between colleagues?"

"None of the above. My colleagues don't drink their dinner and pass out at work."

"Well, I guess we don't have anything else to talk about do we then?"

"Maybe not, of course there are a few issues outstanding with a couple of outstanding warrants you have. Your license is out of date, as is your permit for the pistol you have under the sofa pillow there."

Douglas sighed and looked at the ground. "What do you want?"

"I want to know who you are working for and what you found?"

"Well you know who I am working for…"

"You mean Michael Carey."

"Yes, Mr. Carey asked me to see if I can find out who got into Ms. Milligan's computer system and got away with a good bit of money. Said I would get a cut of it. Up to ten grand."

"So why did you stop?"

"I think you know the reason Detective."

"I do, but does Mr. Carey?"

"Nope, he still thinks I am working on the case. Those were the instructions I received along with the money."

"From?"

"Some anonymous donor that goes by the name of 'S'."

"And why would this one-initialed benefactor be so...generous? Some kind of quid pro quo?"

"It would seem that way. I did take a day or two off."

"And drank your ass off. Now what I want you to do in the meantime is nothing. I want you to report back to Mr. Carey that your search is still ongoing. The things I know about you came from your department file. Sucks what happened with your ex. Women can be pretty vindictive. But what you could do is stand up like a man, clean yourself up and come rejoin the rest of the world. Who knows, you might even get to see your daughter again. I am going to try and take care of that end for you. I'll be back in touch."

CHAPTER 60

Friday night and the temperature had dropped as rapidly as the sun had disappeared over the Mississippi River. Winter announced itself quickly as always in Memphis. The cold air lay still over the city like a blanket left outside over night, making everything in the world seemed pressed more closely together. Jackson and Meredith stepped out of the limousine and climbed the stairway in front of them. Molly Fontaine's Lounge was rapidly becoming a hot spot on the social scene in Midtown Memphis. Situated in the Victorian Village, it was housed in a restored Victorian style mansion with over a hundred and fifty years of history. It had sat vacant for a number of years as downtown Memphis had withered and emptied, only to be reborn through a series of revitalization programs that had brought people and businesses back downtown. The current owner bought it from a long established Memphis family and had renovated it to its current condition. Meredith Gregory fell in love with the place the second they walked in. The lighting was subdued and the lounge was divided up into several rooms, retaining its former shape as an historic home. They removed their coats and handed them to the hostess who immediately took them to the rear of the house. They had dressed up for the evening, Meredith in a classic little black dress and Jackson in a sport coat, black pants and no tie. As they walked through, they noticed that each room they passed was decorated differently with only one or two tables and chairs in each room. The feeling was that of being at an invitation-only soiree set in whatever time period your imagination allowed. Jackson led Meredith to the nearest bar and greeted the bartender by name. "Hello there Hannah, how are you?"

"Why, Jackson Pritchard. To what do I owe the privilege of your company this fine evening?" She spoke with a thick accent that Meredith couldn't quite place.

"Your company is my privilege indeed. Hannah, allow me to introduce my friend Meredith Gregory. Meredith is in town for a series of meetings and has deigned to lower herself to be seen with the likes of me. Meredith, this is Hannah Delacroix."

Meredith smiled broadly and extended her hand. "It's a pleasure to meet you. Your accent is lovely, where is it from?"

Hannah returned her smile politely before responding. "I'm from just down the river in New Orleans. You could say I was kind of drawn here I suppose."

"And why would that be?" Jackson goaded.

"You've heard the story before."

"But she hasn't," he answered, nodding in the direction of Meredith.

"I'll tell the story, but what to drink first?"

"Bourbon and water for me," Jackson answered and looked at Meredith quizzically.

"I'll have a glass of Merlot."

"House ok?"

"If you think it's good, sure." Meredith had a tendency to look down before she spoke, a trait that Hannah and Jackson both picked up on.

Hannah turned to the bar to replace a couple of bottles she had been using to fix the last round of drinks. Meredith took the opportunity to size her up while her back was turned. Hannah had a head full of thick curly hair that was charcoal black. She was slender although not skinny with an admirably thin waistline and a full-sized chest that bounced with every step she took. As she turned back to the bar, Meredith noticed she had deep blue eyes that looked as if they had seen more than most people would in a lifetime. Hannah smiled sweetly at Jackson and cleared her throat.

"The Molly Fontaine house drew me here like it has drawn many others--it is inhabited by spirits."

"You mean it's haunted?" Meredith asked, taking a sip of her wine.

"You might say that. But not haunted like most people would picture. There aren't any chains rattling or ghosts jumping out of closets or anything. When someone says a place is inhabited by spirits, they are more referring to the history of the building and a presence of the supernatural."

"I'm not sure I follow."

"There are absolutely places that are haunted. Malevolent spirits can inhabit a place and make it a downright nasty place to be. More often, a spirit will be drawn to a place for what it represents. When that happens, the place can and usually does take on a sort of aura that attracts those that are sensitive to that sort of spirit."

Meredith took another drink and looked at Jackson, who simply smiled and nodded in Hannah's direction.

"Ok, first a history lesson. A successful cotton farmer and merchant built this house back in the late 1800's. He lived across the street in a house similar to this one but larger. His family had thousands of acres of farmland both south and east of here. He built this house as a wedding gift for his daughter's pending marriage, but she caught one of the fevers that spread through Memphis and died before she could marry. Heartbroken, he closed up the house and moved away. The day he died, the house he lived in caught fire and burned to the ground. Two separate eyewitness accounts describe two ghostly figures leaving the house as it burned and walking across the street to this house. The fire seemed to follow all the way to the front porch and then was stopped by some unknown force. It burned for three hours this way until it died out. The house sat vacant for almost fifty years and then was purchased by a couple that renovated it and other properties around the Midtown and Downtown areas. They lived in the house for just over a year when the husband took ill suddenly and died in one of the upstairs bedrooms.

He died the same date as the daughter of the merchant. The daughter's name was Molly Fontaine. Anyway, the woman couldn't bear to live here so she moved and boarded up the house as well. She reopened it after she had opened some other businesses and renovated it to what you see today."

"That's so sad! You said the husband died in the house. Where?"

"I'm not exactly sure where, but I was told it was in an upstairs room not open to the public. I have walked around up there a bit and one of the rooms is much colder than the rest. From time to time down here, a cold draft will filter through one or more rooms, even though none of the doors or windows has been opened or closed."

Meredith felt her skin crawl and she shuddered as if a cold draft had blown over her skin.

"So what drew you here?"

"The story mostly. I'm a bit of a wandering soul and a bit of a romantic as well. I believe I can sense when Molly is around and hopefully can help her ease her suffering, if she wants me to anyway."

Meredith's eyes grew wider. "Believing that really brought you here? And keeps you here?"

Hannah nodded her head. "Absolutely. Look around. And not just here, but anywhere you want to go. What's the one thing that motivates people to do something?" She paused for a moment to let the question set in. "Belief. Belief in something. People fight wars, make life changing decisions, go to church, work for a specific company, any number of things, simply on the basis of what they believe."

"So Mr. Pritchard, what do you believe?" Meredith asked, catching him slightly off-guard.

Jackson refocused his attention and answered, "I believe I will have another drink. If you please, Hanna." He finished his drink with a flourish and placed the empty glass back on the solid, antique looking bar.

"Uh huh," she replied shaking her head slightly back and forth.

"Jackson believes in manners and respecting other people's beliefs," Hannah answered for him. "He's a pretty rare soul for that." She blushed involuntarily and turned her head.

Meredith cleared her throat and nodded, understanding the bartender a bit more clearly. "I believe I am happy that he has shown me so many interesting things in your fair city. I hope we get the chance to explore some more the next time I am here."

Her answer surprised Jackson somewhat and he raised his glass in an impromptu toast. "To new things. And new friends."

Hannah and Meredith joined him, "To new friends."

CHAPTER 61

Evening was turning into night in Seattle as well. Will Swift dug the cell phone out of his pocket. "Hey baby, how was your day?"

"Good, are you going to be home soon?"

"I think so; I do have a couple of more stops to make and then should be there. How is everything at Swift household?"

"Everything is good, as always baby. I'd rather not cook though-- think we can go grab some burgers or something?"

"That sounds great. I'll call you on my way home."

"Great, I love you."

"Love you too, baby, see you in a bit." He smiled and hung up and laughed softly at the good fortune he often felt in regards to the wife and life he had chosen. Or that had chosen him. He sometimes was uncertain how it had all come about, instead focusing on making sure that it all stayed together. He peered inside the window of the martini bar he had been directed to. It was no different than any of 1000 newly founded martini bars across the country. It was trendy, overpriced, and a place for those who needed to be seen to see each other. Will wasn't here to be seen; rather he was here to take the next step to find who had killed Sharon Milligan. He entered the bar, quickly scanning through the most recent batch of beautiful people that had filtered in on a cold December evening before making his way through the crowd. Seeing his target, he took off his jacket and sat down, interrupting the cozy conversation of the well dressed couple who regarded him with mouths wide open.

"Why Detective, I am surprised to see you. Do you come here often?"

"Oh no, the food here isn't very good. I much prefer to eat places that emphasize food rather than presentation. I hear the presentation here rocks though. So who is your friend?" Will nodded in the direction of the beautiful if not very intelligent looking blonde across the table from the attorney.

"Detective Swift, may I introduce you to Jaycee Rose. Jaycee, this is Detective Swift. Now, if you have something work related, I would ask that you call my office."

"Well, that's the funny thing, counselor. I did call your office and your secretary was under the impression you had gone home for the evening. So I called your house and spoke to your wife. Lovely woman." Will noted with pleasure Jaycee's head whipping in the direction of her dinner companion. "She was under the impression that you were working late. So I called back to your office and let your secretary know that you were working late and that it was important that I reach you. Subpoena important. She suddenly remembered that you might be dining here with a friend. Lucky for me, she was right."

"Well, as you can see, now isn't a good time..."

Jaycee interrupted his sentence, grabbing her purse and standing up and away from the table. "I think now is a perfect time Michael. I would be happy to give you all the time you need. And by the way, my cell phone number will be different tomorrow." She stormed off in a huff.

Michael and Will both watched her walk out of the restaurant, cell phone in had and seemingly arranging for a ride. "I'm very sorry to interrupt your dinner plans. Had you ordered already?"

Michael frowned and then shrugged his shoulders. "We had, but she never really eats. There's a small house salad coming if you are interested."

"More of a meat and potatoes guy, but thanks."

"So I am guessing you have made some progress then?"

"Some, not nearly as much as I would like. This point in my investigation reminds me of another investigation I closed a while back."

"I guess that doesn't happen very often."

"Me solving cases? Or asking if someone would like to hear my story rather than just telling it.

"The second. I am certain you solve enough cases to keep the streets free of criminals, which incidentally helps me to sleep better at night."

"The sarcasm thing doesn't really work for you. You should try something different. How do you act when you are playing ambulance chaser? Is it the direct plea to the heartstrings, I mean wallet?" Will noted that Michael's face flushed momentarily with anger.

"My apologies. So your story?"

Will made a show to pull out a small spiral notebook and write slowly, saying out loud: "Note to self, Carey didn't like question about profession, didn't answer." He dotted the sentence loudly and put it back in his pocket. "I'm sorry, just making myself a little note. What did you ask me again?"

"I asked if you were going to tell me that story, it sounds intriguing."

"Certainly. So I was investigating this high dollar burglary. Making some decent progress and narrowing down on who/what/where, all that good stuff. Anyway, I am in this bar, asking some questions about the wheelman. Do you know what a wheelman is?"

"Yes."

"Great, just wanted to make sure you were keeping up. Man, is your food not here yet? How long ago did you order?"

"An appropriate amount of time ago, detective. I am sure the food will be here momentarily."

"That's good; I would hate for your dinner to be cold or delayed. I always get a headache when too much time elapses between meals." Will quit his purposeful rambling and stared at the increasingly frustrated lawyer across the table.

"And?"

"Oh, I'm good, I ate about four hours or so ago."

"I was referring to the wheelman you were questioning."

"Oh that, so anyway I am making some nice progress and the bartender says, 'There was another guy in here asking the same questions just yesterday.' It turns out that the company that insured the property had someone sniffing around and conveniently forgot to tell me. Didn't share information, basically didn't play nicely in the sandbox."

"And what happened as a result?"

Will made a point to lean in closely and lowered his voice. "I caught the guy anyway and then had the person that ordered the parallel investigation arrested for obstructing justice. I made sure the case went in front of a judge you and I both know that dislikes meddling attorneys very much and the guy got three years. Served eighteen months. True story."

Will noticed Michael swallow very hard and take a long drink from the glass of wine in front of him. "Fascinating," the attorney said, using his best poker face. "Now is there anything else you need? Because if not, I am going to attempt to eat in peace and forget today happened."

Will shrugged his shoulders slightly, "I'm good." He paused for a moment and then added, "You would be wise to remember that."

CHAPTER 62

A couple of hours after Hannah's story, Jackson paid the bar tab and escorted a moderately intoxicated Meredith to the front door where the limousine was waiting for them. On their way out of the bar, he checked his receipt and noticed that the bartender had included her phone number and requested that he call her sometime. He pocketed the receipt silently and joined his client in the well-heated car. She took her jacket off and asked him for his. Jackson handed it to her and poured them each a glass of champagne that he had chilled while they were inside. Meredith placed them in front of the window that divided them from the driver and slid back into the seat next to him.

"So what is our next stop sir?" she asked playfully.

"Well, are you hungry?"

"Not for dinner," she replied, lowering her voice seductively.

"So what..."

Meredith interrupted him with a kiss, lifting herself off the seat and straddling his lap. Jackson reached up and caressed the side of her face lightly. She pressed tightly against him as he traced his fingertips along her neck. He slipped his hands under the straps of her dress and slid them down off her shoulders. She lifted her arms over her head and he lifted the dress up and off with one swift motion. Meredith broke the kiss and unbuttoned his shirt deftly. A couple of minutes later, she had completely undressed him and had moved down between his legs. Jackson reached for the intercom, "Driver, how about a trip around the loop?" At the same time he raised the divider between the front and back seats giving them a measure of privacy.

About twenty minutes later she caught her breath, "Oh my God, where did you learn how to do that?"

"Playboy. Letters to the Editor when I was younger. It really does pay off to read the articles."

"Thank you Hugh Hefner then. That was amazing, definitely worth the price of admission."

"Admission?"

"Ok, maybe worth sitting through the hokey ghost story."

Jackson pondered that momentarily. "You didn't like Hannah's tale of belief?"

"Don't get me wrong, she told it well and I am sure it sells a few more drinks than otherwise would have been. It just seemed a bit too.... melodramatic I guess."

"Hmmm. I liked the story. Different strokes I suppose."

"Good thing we got on the same page here in the car. Can we revisit this story later?"

"Of course. We should probably get cleaned up for now though." They found their respective outfits and dressed and freshened themselves up. A few minutes later, the limousine came to a stop and the driver opened the rear door. Jackson exited and extended his hand to Meredith as she stepped out of the car and onto Beale Street.

CHAPTER 63

The Blue Monkey was quieter than usual for a Friday night. Several of Jessica's regulars had been in and out, ensuring she would have a good night tip wise, but the down time also left her time to think, and therefore worry, about her date tomorrow.

"So do you think he is as good in bed as he is in your thoughts?" Melanie asked her with a smirk.

"I'm certain I don't know. And I certainly wouldn't tell you. Well, that's not exactly true now is it?" She smiled, both at her friend and at the thought of finding out.

"Would you like me to test drive him for you?"

Jessica's jaw dropped in amazement. "Absolutely not. That's just wrong. I don't want to worry about whatever diseases you have in addition to how good he may or may not be!"

"Probably for the best. He probably wouldn't want to leave my bed anyway."

"He probably would get stuck to the sheets."

They both wrinkled their noses and sang "Ewwwww" at the same time. Then they both burst into laughter, going back to their customers. Jessica waited on several people at the bar and found that she was actually humming to herself. It had been years since she could remember just humming mindlessly. She smiled at that thought as well and thought that smiling that was another pleasant addition to her days lately.

Mike, the bar manager interrupted her silent pondering. "So where is Mr. Wonderful taking you after you sit through some boring subtitled movies?"

"I don't know. And I am looking forward to the movies. I think they will be a nice change of pace. Speaking of tomorrow night, I am still on the schedule, but it looks like you have two more than usual. Can I have the night off?"

"She thinks she might get lucky!" yelled Melanie from the other end of the bar. Jessica fired a wet bar towel at her in response.

"At least someone besides her would be," Mike said quietly, nodding in Melanie's general direction. "One of the extras is a trainee, but we should be ok. I could make a back-up reservation somewhere for you just in case. Make him pay for it."

"Somehow I get the feeling that he will have something planned. And I am sure that will include dinner."

"Well, it better be some place nice. Sitting though those kinds of movies doesn't sound like my particular brand of vodka."

"You and Melanie both. Maybe I am just wired a bit differently."

"I would say so. That's why you do so well here. I just want to make sure that doesn't come back and bite you."

"I hope it doesn't either...but I hope he does, just a little." She winked and poured a couple of beers and delivered them to the other end of the bar.

CHAPTER 64

Will Swift knocked on the dingy apartment door for the second time today. He heard some shuffling once again and a few moments later, heard the gravelly voice from inside.

"Who is it?" Jonas challenged.

"Avon Lady, open the door."

"Avon Lady, what the heck is that?"

"You don't remember the Avon Lady?" Will sighed loudly and pushed through the opening door, which revealed Jonas dressed in an eerily similar fashion, as he was earlier in the day. He handed Jonas the food that he had promised earlier and asked, "So what do you have for me?"

"Interestingly, not much more than this morning. Whoever moved that money and set up the other Detective moves around pretty smoothly. A normal hacker may have not been able to find any trace of them."

"But then you aren't normal are you Jonas?"

"Thanks for noticing Detective. Don't you have any friends or wouldn't your wife actually like having you at home? Oh, wait, I wouldn't want you at home either. Good call on her part."

"Not that it is any of your business, but she and our son went to her mothers' this morning and will be back tomorrow. So you and I could have our own little sleepover if you really wanted."

"While I am sure you could tell some great ghost stories, I think I will have to take a rain check."

"It rains a lot in our city Jonas."

"That it does. So why is it so important to find this hacker, Detective?"

"There's half a million dollars missing. An unsolved murder that they may or may not be involved in."

"Sounds like I might like the guy."

"Why would you say the hacker is a guy?"

"Most hackers are. Anyone that has ever challenged me at all has been. I can't imagine a woman that could do it. If there was I would certainly like to meet her."

"To?"

"Shake her hand, ask her to bear my children, I don't know. Why does it matter?"

"Just curious. It would be entertaining to see you interacting with a woman. First time for everything I suppose. So how long before you think you will know something?"

"I don't know, Detective. Looks like I am going to have to try a few different tricks to work through. I can probably run the first algorithms overnight and have some much better trace information by Monday at the latest."

"Three days, you must be slipping in your old age. Or maybe you lost your confidence, getting busted by an old man like me."

"Highly unlikely. Even a blind squirrel finds a nut every once in a while. You having a wife proves that theory twice."

"Ever the charmer. Have something solid by Monday or I won't be bringing you food. I'll be bringing a warrant."

"For what?"

"You're still on parole. Impeding an investigation could send you back inside, brother."

Jonas sighed. "Ok, ok, maybe a little later in the morning on Monday?"

"Done. Enjoy your weekend Jonas."

CHAPTER 65

Meredith and Jackson walked hand in hand down Beale Street, Meredith taking in the scenery for the first time. Watching people experience things like that was a perk of his job that Jackson truly enjoyed. The street seemed almost alive with tourists and Memphians alike getting revved up on beer, barbecue and blues. Two full blocks of the street were barricaded every weekend and people walked up and down enjoying themselves without worry.

They moved their way up the street to a dance club that blared bass-heavy house music loud enough to entice passersby to come in. Meredith looked up at the sign and asked what the significance of the name "Club 152" was. Jackson's answer of that being the street address seemed to satisfy her. Jackson walked up and hugged a rather surly looking bouncer. They talked for a minute and the bouncer nodded his head to whatever Jackson was telling him. Meredith smiled broadly as they both waved her over and they walked in the club going around the gathered line waiting their turn. Jackson didn't see the tall, attractive brunette that was waiting in that line, instead his attention was focused on Meredith as she sauntered into the club as if she owned the place. The brunette glared at the couple and made a quick decision to get out of line and wait outside for them to come back out. There was a shallow alley just down from the club with a perfect vantage point to see the entrance to Club 152. She ordered a large beer and something to snack on from one of the street vendors and sat down to begin her vigil.

Inside the club, the music was loud and the dance floor was crowded and the air was smoke-filled: the perfect atmosphere for a dance club. The pair navigated through the first floor much like you would a minefield, weaving in and out and around the various tables, patrons and their belongings and employees. Jackson led Meredith to a solid steel door at the far end of the club that was guarded by another bouncer, a very serious-looking, well-built man with a shaved head. Jackson greeted him by name. "Guido, what's going on upstairs tonight?"

"DJ on the second floor. Third floor isn't open yet. Don't know if it will. You know how Friday's are."

"Yeah, how much to go up?"

"For you? Ten grand should cover it."

"That seems a bit higher than last time."

"Inflation. What can you do?" Guido shrugged his shoulders with a smirk on his face.

"I don't have that much on me tonight. But I would gladly pay you Tuesday..."

Guido laughed. "I got you brother. Still owe you for that thing."

"It was my pleasure. Tijuana at New Years is a fascinating place to be." Jackson recalled for a moment the picture of a carrying a passed out Guido out of a local jail in Tijuana a few years back. "Plus, that trip demonstrated my need for a new strength regimen." Jackson watched as Meredith dropped her jaw in surprise.

"Whatever, just don't make me come upstairs and show this pretty lady how a real man dances."

"I am certain she would appreciate the demonstration. How late are you on?"

"Three. Late night. Hate the hours, love the dough."

"I hear you. I'll be at the Y Sunday for a workout and some ball. Be there?"

"I think I can manage, depends on how Saturday night goes."

"Cool, catch you later."

They shook hands and hugged in the same motion and Guido opened the door to a set of metal stairs that led upward and opened to another dance floor just as packed as the one downstairs. The music was more hip-hop but just as loud and Jackson and Meredith worked themselves to the bar that was stacked three deep. One of the bartenders recognized Jackson and waved him down to the end of the bar. With Meredith in tow, Jackson moved down.

"J-man, what's up?"

"Same old Chris, what's up with you?"

"You know me, just working for the man."

"You'll be the man someday soon, I can feel it."

"Yeah, whatever, I can see what you should be feeling. Please introduce us." He clearly enunciated every syllable of the last sentence.

Jackson laughed, "Meredith, this is Chris Ramsey. Local bartender, philosophizer extraordinaire, and purveyor of all knowledge and information that is useless to 99.3% of the planet. Chris, may I present Meredith Gregory, a friend from out of town and a purveyor of things relevant to the today as well as tomorrow. I am certain you two will have nothing to talk about."

Chris shook Meredith's extended hand warmly. "The pleasure is all mine, or would be if you would ditch Mr. Manners over here."

"He does have good manners doesn't he?" Meredith frowned in mock consternation. "Why is that do you suppose?"

"I don't want to spread rumors or anything, but his manners rival those English guys you see on TV, seems like most of them play for the other team if you know what I mean."

Meredith laughed loudly, "I do, but I can personally vouch that he plays for the right team."

"A shame," Chris said shaking his head in Jackson's direction, "you went and ruined a perfectly good white girl." He looked back at Meredith and smiled, "Next time, you should be a bit more selective. Don't just take the first pretty face that is nice and polite. There's a whole lot of fun to be had out here in the real world."

The three of them laughed again and Chris brought drinks for the pair. They sat and talked for a while, finishing their drinks before moving out to the dance floor. It was crowded to the point of not being able to move around much. Instead, they swayed intently to the beat, dancing closely and talking and laughing even closer. She was a good, if not confident dancer and he followed her movements closely with his own. Several drinks later, they made their way back down the stairs and out of the club. Jackson fist-bumped his friends on the way out and they stumbled hand-in-hand up Beale Street and back to the Talbot Heirs. The tall, attractive brunette finished her drink and followed at a discreet distance. They stumbled through the front door of the hotel and found their way to their room, undressing each other as the door closed behind them. Shelby Powers approached the front desk with a distraught look on her face.

"Can I help you, sweetie?" The front desk clerk was her usual chipper self.

"I hope so, I am supposed to be in a wedding party tomorrow for one of my college sorority sisters. Everything is set, but the bridesmaids all got together to throw a surprise thank you brunch for the maid of honor for all the hard work she has done." Shelby was becoming more and more hysterical as she told her story. "The girl that just came in is organizing everything, but I don't really know her and forgot her name and need to talk to her and I saw her leave the party we were having down on Beale Street but I couldn't catch up with her and I don't know how to get in touch with her and I don't know much about Memphis and my dress doesn't look right..."

"Easy now, take a deep breath, everything is going to be just fine. You'll be wanting Ms. Gregory's room them then, such a nice girl. Would you like me to ring her for you?"

"Oh no, she had a man with her, I couldn't interrupt that, Leslie has been too sweet already."

"You mean Meredith."

Shelby covered her face with her hands. "Meredith...Lesley is the maid of honor. I've had too much to drink if you can't tell. You have no idea how much help you have been. Thank you so much!" She retreated from the lobby and out the door, a serious look on her face. She walked back to her car, planning her next steps carefully. She would have to get back into Jackson's computer and find out what she could about this

Meredith Gregory and then she could push her out his life just as she had done with the others before her.

CHAPTER 66

Jackson woke up early as usual. He was thankful he had taken the Alka Seltzer before they had gone to sleep last night, as his hangover was virtually non-existent. He gathered up some clothes and took them into the bathroom, careful to move quietly through the suite. He looked back at Meredith in the bed as she slept soundly. Closing the door behind him, he splashed water on his face, brushed his teeth and dressed. He crept carefully out of the bedroom and into the kitchenette, where he cleaned up a bit and started cooking breakfast. He checked the clock and nodded approvingly as the limo wouldn't be there for another three hours to take Meredith to the airport. Several minutes later, the suite was filled with the savory smells of a home-cooked breakfast. He was getting ready to put a tray together to serve breakfast in bed when Meredith appeared in the doorway, a sleepy tousled look in her hair and eyes, wearing the plush bathrobe the hotel had provided.

"Good morning, sunshine. Sleep well?"

"Good morning yourself. Look at you all hard at work. So that applies to the day time as well as at night then." She smirked at her own joke.

"We all have to be good at something I suppose. Coffee?"

"With just a little milk, thank you. And you are very good at it. So how long have you been doing it?"

"Cooking or having sex?" Jackson answered without looking up. It was his turn to smile at his sense of humor.

She took a sip of her coffee. "Actually, I was referring to having sex for money." Her expression was one of concern.

A look of surprise flashed for a split second on his face before he regained his composure. "Actually, you just described a prostitute, which I am not. The term more accurate to me is male escort I suppose. My business card says 'Hospitality Consultant' which is even closer."

"So what's the distinction?"

"Many of my clients enjoy a non-physical relationship with me. A lot of what they get is event planning and scheduling. Great conversation and a companion that they don't have to work for, especially when their attention needs to be elsewhere."

"And the other crap you were telling me about? The writing and travel articles and all that?"

"That other CRAP is all true. I'm surprised you didn't look that up when you got home."

Meredith felt the light rebuke in his tone. "I did and read a couple of them. They were good. But why do the other thing? You have so much to offer; you're smart and sexy and fun." Her voice changed to one of desperate concern.

"Why what? Why do the job? Or why do this as opposed to look for a relationship. The two can be mutually exclusive I should think."

"Point taken, so why do it for work. Your writing is good; you seem to have a knack for it."

"Number one, writing pays just ok and it's not consistent. I've gotten accustomed to a lifestyle that costs much more than that. Number two, I have a clientele that has come to depend on me and I enjoy working with them. Number three, I'm not going to do this forever, I'm looking to retire sometime in the near future."

"So I was just another job?"

"Would you like the real answer or the work answer?"

She thought for a moment. "The real answer, wait, no the work answer. How about both?"

"Fair enough. The work answer is of course not; you were and are something special. And I can't wait to show you just how special sometime very soon."

"And the real answer?"

"In all honesty in your case it's the same answer. I am very selective about my clients; I'm on a referral only basis at this point. My vetting process is very similar to the one Cabinet appointments go through. It takes at least two or three weeks. I liked you from the second I met you and enjoyed every second that we spent together."

"So why take this as a job?"

"That is an interesting question. And I am certain there are several different answers depending on your point of view. I'm not sure I know everything behind it and choose to defer answering. So, can I ask you a question?"

"Please."

Jackson measured his words carefully. "So how did you figure it out?"

She smiled and looked down at her feet as if the answers were written there. "There wasn't any one thing. But, you were just too ready for everything. Too prepared I guess. Restaurants, cars, all the people you know everywhere you go. It would be tough to pull all that together given a month of getting ready. You pulled it off in less than a week, and you do need to hear this, everything was perfect. I mean really perfect. It's nice being spoiled for a change."

"Thank you, that's nice to hear."

Meredith sighed and got up and grabbed a plate of food and plopped back down at the bar. "Can we enjoy breakfast together? No more work questions, I promise."

"I would like that."

They ate for several minutes in relative quiet. Finally, she dropped her fork. "But how did you learn to do all that…stuff?"

Jackson almost choked on the bite of omelet he had just taken. They laughed for a good bit as he chewed and swallowed. "Do you really want me to answer that?"

"I guess not," she answered with a blush. "I wouldn't mind another demonstration though."

Jackson chuckled and leaned over and kissed her cheek gently, lingering for a few extra moments. They talked for a while longer and confirmed her travel arrangements. Breakfast was finished and the dishes placed in the sink.

"So I am keeping your number. Can I ask you for a favor now?"

"Absolutely. Shoot."

"If you ever do retire, will you call me?"

"You know, I honestly think I might do just that."

CHAPTER 67

Across town, Jessica woke up and smiled at the sun peering in through her window. She checked the clock and stretched, taking her time as for once, she didn't have to rush. The aroma of freshly brewed coffee filled the house and she made her way to the kitchen and shut off the automatic brewer. Thirty minutes, a cup and a half of coffee and half the newspaper later, she moved to the restroom where she took a hot, leisurely bubble bath, taking care to shave her legs carefully, dry her self thoroughly and rub lotion all over afterwards. "I could get used to this," she thought to herself, moving to the bedroom wearing only the towel on her head. Her CD player rolled out an eclectic mix of her favorite music and she sang along as each individual song moved her. Checking the time again, she noted that it was nearing ten and felt her heart flutter just a bit in anticipation of the next several hours. She went through her entire wardrobe and back again, looking for a casual yet breathtaking outfit. A clingy black pullover with jeans and boots caught her eye and she pulled them on. Moving back into the kitchen, she poured a half a cup of coffee and was taking her first sip when her cell phone rang.

"Good morning!" she purred.

"Wow, now that's a greeting a guy could get used to."

"Ya think? Don't be writing checks your body can't cash, especially this early."

"It's not really early you know. How close are you to being ready?"

"A while I think. Finishing this half a cup of coffee could take hours."

"Cute, I have just a couple of things to take care of and will be on my way. See you in a bit?"

"Can't wait. See ya."

As soon as Jackson hung up his phone it rang again. He answered it without looking at the caller ID. "No, really, I'm on the way."

"To Seattle? That's a little early, but I am sure I can find a way to entertain you until Tuesday."

Jackson frowned and looked at the phone's Caller ID. "I'm sorry, I was just talking to someone else."

"And then your favorite Executive Assistant calls instead. It's a sign sweetie, pay attention to it!"

"I just might have to do that. Do you have some news for me?"

"I certainly do. The funeral is Monday at 1:00. If you give me your e-mail address, I can send you all the details." He did and she made a note to send him some personal details as well. "Should I book you a room anywhere or are you going to take me up on my incredibly hospitable offer?"

Jackson paused as if considering her offer. "I'll take care of it on my own, but I do appreciate it. Have the police found anything else out?"

"Not that I know of, but they don't necessarily keep us working girls informed."

"I appreciate your help; I'll bring you something nice for your trouble."

"You in a bow would do nicely."

"Food for thought, Miss Ashley, food for thought."

About 45 minutes later, Jackson pulled his Jeep into Jessica's driveway. He walked to the doorway and brought her a box of Italian candies. "They seemed appropriate," he explained without being asked. Jessica moved closely to him, wrapped her arms around his neck and kissed him deeply. Several moments passed and they broke their affectionate embrace.

"Wow again, are you trying to get me to like you?"

"Maybe just a little bit."

"It's working so far."

"Good." She leaned in closer to him and this time they kissed for much longer. Running his fingers through her hair, he pressed himself away just a bit.

"We won't see any movies at this rate."

She looked down in a mock pout and said, "Ok, I will try to be good. No promises though." She took his hand in hers and they walked out the front door and got in the car.

The drive downtown to Peabody Place took about twenty minutes. The weather was perfect, a cool, crisp December afternoon. Interestingly, he was dressed similarly to Jessica in a black mock turtleneck and jeans with some loafers. Each had a jacket they had thrown in the backseat.

"So what are we going to see today?"

"I have to see at least two movies, one of which has to be in Italian. They are showing six or seven I think."

"Anything specific?"

"I'd like to see 'Il Posto' by Ermanno Olmi. Olmi was one of the founders of Neoclassical Italian cinematography. His movies are typically made up of long, slowly shot scenes. I think it would be interesting to see how he saw things. Then they have a few different movies by Michelangelo Antonioni."

"And he is?"

"Arguably the master of Italian cinema. He is a contrast to Olmi in that he focused on the upper class parts of society versus the lower class. 'Blow Up' is one of his better works and it's in English."

"And you know so much about this because…?"

"Movies are a passion. Always have been. A good one can tell a story and ask questions at the same time. One of my favorite things is walking out of a movie and feeling quiet and at peace. It's like having all of your questions answered with having to ask them."

"Good answer." She leaned over and kissed him again. "I have to say that I enjoy that more every time I do it."

"Please, by all means, continue to help yourself."

CHAPTER 68

Shelby Powers had slept only about an hour. She rubbed her eyes and looked back at her reflection in the mirror. Her eyes were bloodshot and she felt as bad as she looked. But she had accomplished what she had set out to do. Hacking in to Jackson's computer, she had learned a bit about Meredith Gregory from Atlanta, Georgia. She found a phone number and then crosschecked potential addresses where she might live. Clicking a few more buttons, she also found out that Jackson was headed to Vegas and then Seattle next week. Vegas sounded fun, but Seattle concerned her. She wondered if he was digging around or just going to pay his respects to an old friend. Checking her schedule, she noted that she had some unused vacation time that her boss had asked that everyone in the office take before the end of the year. She made a note and sent an e-mail requesting the week off. She included her phone number, half expecting it for the ring immediately. She moved some funds around and found a couple of cheap airline tickets and started running through some of her travel options in her head. A couple of tears ran down her face without her realizing it. She wondered if they were from sheer exhaustion or for the devotion that her beloved was showing to hitting his financial goals. She made a mental note to really show her appreciation when they were finally together again. "It's going to be sooooo worth it baby, just you wait and see," she said, no one else hearing her declaration intended for just one person.

CHAPTER 69

The Peabody Place was busier than usual on a Saturday morning. Located just behind the historic Peabody Hotel, The Peabody Place reflected a national trend of redeveloping urban areas with specific themes in mind. This specific trend had been written about in several publications nationwide and had been dubbed "Shoppertainment" by members of the media. There were restaurants and bars, a dance club, different clothing and music stores, a movie theater and so forth. It was designed to be a destination for the tourists that didn't necessarily want to spend their entire Memphis experience on Beale Street and it did its job well. The movie theater was decorated in a "retro" style with a train station motif. Elevated toy trains made their way around the waiting areas. Jackson and Jessica purchased their tickets and stepped onto the long escalator up to the second level where there was a reception area decorated to resemble an Italian villa and courtyard. Jackson walked over and talked to an older woman that Jessica assumed was his professor. He shook hands with a couple of other people and turned and motioned for Jessica to join him. A couple of quick introductions to some of Jackson's classmates and they made their way further inside. They surveyed a list of events planned for the day and were both impressed by what they saw;

a wine tasting, Italian acrobats and jugglers, a cooking demonstration by several local chefs.

"Wow, these people know how to hold a film festival," Jessica remarked, taking a sip of the wine that Jackson had handed her. She looked down into her glass and remarked about how good it was.

"See how good wine can be without a screw top?" Jackson teased.

"I'll have you know I drink good wine. Maybe not this good, but I always avoid screw tops and wine boxes thank you very much."

"A decision befitting your inherent wisdom?"

"Either that or drinking bad wine at a younger age. Nothing worse than a white zin hangover."

Jackson laughed loudly at that and glanced at the time. "Ok, we have about twenty minutes before the first go round of movies. Would you like the English one or the Italian one first?"

"Methinks Italian first before the wine slows me down."

"Il Posto it is then. Do you want anything else before we go in?"

"Split some popcorn with me?"

"Absolutely, butter or no?"

"No thanks, not a fan."

"Good, I'm not either." Jackson ordered and brought back drinks, some popcorn and an oversized bag of M&M's.

"Goodness, how much did that run you?"

"They have a quick loan window that I stopped by."

"Good thinking, shall we go?"

"Oh yes, lets."

CHAPTER 70

Jonas Fisher woke up slowly and lifted his head from his desk. He yawned and smacked his lips, testing his breath on his hand. He grimaced and stood up and stretched. His computer desk served as his bed two or three times a week as he fell asleep while working. Or surfing...or gaming. The previous night had been work, and he had gotten a lot done. As was the case in many nights, the majority of what he had accomplished had occurred while he was asleep. Years of experience had refined his search instincts, as well as the software he had written to help him find the things he would be looking for. A couple of cleverly crafted algorithms allowed Jonas to peek into virtually any individual's computer he chose. Corporate and government websites were more complicated, but only in the number of steps to take and obstacles to overcome as far as he was concerned. A lesser programmer would have come to the dead ends left by the hacker Detective Swift was searching for, but Jonas had detected a couple of familiar patterns in the tracks that had been left behind and he focused his search around these. He skipped over the sloppy, elementary level work of Douglas Jimmerson, then thought better of it and traced the parallel path entered by the law firm that hired him. He found a mess of files and transfers and a cleverly planted virus scheduled to crash the server on Monday afternoon. Jonas backed out carefully, making a mental note of the virus and how it was placed. He backtracked again, coming to where he had left off before. The tracer program he had developed took over at that point and had followed the trail back to its original source; all while Jonas had slept. He slid into the kitchen and grabbed a Mountain Dew out of the fridge, opening it and taking a drink. The caffeine jolted him out of his weary state and he sat back down in front of the computer. Several keystrokes later, he had arrived at an interestingly sophisticated firewall, considering it was a home computer he was dealing with. There were challenges at multiple levels and each took several minutes to work around. Each level aroused a higher sense of curiosity from Jonas as he was intrigued by the work this fellow hacker had put into keeping their system safe. Nearly an hour later, Jonas struck pay dirt, defeating the security measures he had come across and gaining access to the system. He searched for a few minutes to see who was hacking, wondering if he had possibly played online games with them before. He accessed a file labeled "My Pictures" and was stunned to find out that this hacker was a she. And hot! Dark hair and eyes and a body to die for. Jonas spent the next twenty minutes or so nosing through her files. Shelby Powers, thirty-two years old. Lived alone. Had a little money set aside, but nothing significant to speak of. She had to store the majority of her information somewhere else because there wasn't much to access on her hard drive. He could tell that she had traveled recently and was preparing to travel again. Coincidentally, she had a ticket on standby to come to Seattle! Thinking a bit further, Detective Swift had him checking out someone that potentially hacked and stole money from someone very wealthy in Seattle. "Follow the money trail moron," Jonas scolded himself out loud. Looking further, he could see that she had been looking in other people's files as well. There was a trace program that hit a couple of servers in Seattle. Jonas made a mental note of the IP addresses, sure that they matched the dime novel detective and the law firm that had hired him. The trace program had also been searching through a computer in Memphis, although he couldn't get it to give up whose or where exactly it might be. Jonas tried a couple of end arounds but was stifled each time. He dropped a few well-worded obscenities and stopped the trace. Reaching to log off the system, a chat box appeared on the screen, shocking Jonas to the point of not being able to catch his breath.

"See anything you like?"

CHAPTER 71

Jackson and Jessica strolled out of the theater laughing as much as when they walked in.

"So...you are getting extra credit for this, right?" Jessica faked a stretch and yawn.

"Yes I am, and no, I wouldn't call it action packed either. I did like it though. I liked the dialogue and the director's eye. You could really feel what he wanted to show the audience.

"I saw the older gentleman in front of me doze off."

"And you?"

"I pinched myself a couple of times to make sure I didn't," she smirked.

Jackson playfully nudged her shoulder. "Hungry?"

"Kind of, something substantial sounds good, how long until the next movie?"

"We have about 30 minutes. Do you want to go get some of that pasta we saw earlier?"

"Actually I was thinking a hot dog with everything on it sounded pretty good."

Jackson stopped and looked at her for a moment.

"What?"

"You just surprised me. That doesn't happen very often."

"Was it a good surprise?"

"It still is."

"Good, now about that dog…"

The hot dog and the second movie went down much easier than the first. Still, they were laughing and leaning against each other when they emerged from the movie theater.

"Well, I made it all the way through that one without snoring anyway."

"So you liked it?" Jackson asked hopefully.

"Honestly? I don't think that foreign cinema will ever be my cup of tea." She could tell by the look on his face that he was disappointed. "But can I let you in on a little secret?"

"Certainly."

"I really like the fact that you liked them so much."

"Really? Why is that?"

"Passion is something sorely lacking in the world I think. If you find one or two things that you can be passionate about then you are ahead of about 90% of everyone else. Just a thought I had before."

"I like it. Pretty deep though. How much is it going to cost me?"

"I think dinner would just about cover it."

"Is that right?"

"Yes, that's right. After 5 hours of Italian cinema and movie food, I think I deserve it." Jessica pouted animatedly.

Jackson took his cell phone out of his pocket and dialed a number. "Hey Steph, it's Jackson. Can you fit me in tonight? Sure, we're hungry now. We're downtown, give me about 30 minutes? Great, you're the best." He hung up and smiled.

She beamed in return, taking him by the hand as they headed towards the parking deck where he had left his Jeep. "You're going to make me ask aren't you?"

"Ask what?"

"Where are we going?"

"Oh that, I got us a table at Grisanti's. Have you been there before?"

"No, I've been wanting to go though."

"Some of the best pasta you will ever eat. This is Frank Grisanti's place. His father, John, had the original Grisanti's and it was fantastic. This huge Italian guy walking around letting everyone sample different bottles of wine. Didn't matter who you were, he treated you like family."

"That sounds really cool."

"It was. Frank's has the same kind of wine list. Nothing you can find at any liquor stores around here. REALLY good stuff."

They reached the car and he walked around to open her door. She pushed him gently against the door before he could and pressed her body to his, kissing him deeply. Several passion-filled moments passed before she pushed away again.

"Ok, maybe there should be a ground rule associated with that." Jackson wiped his brow.

She gave him her best innocent look, "Ground rule? For what?"

"Uh-huh. I told you earlier that you could help yourself to a kiss whenever you liked. But ones like you just left me with are entirely too potent. "You're going to have to cut them a little bit or keep them in reserve for when we are in a more private setting!"

"I will try to do better, promise." She looked at her feet and shuffled a bit restlessly.

"OK, now let's eat."

CHAPTER 72

Jonas stared at the screen for several seconds, a look of disbelief reflected on the monitor in front of him. The chat box was towards the top of the screen, seemingly taunting him.

"Hello?"

Jonas decided to answer while safeguarding his system at the same time.

"Who is this?" he typed as he ran the security program that safeguarded his files.

"Apparently I am the person you were looking for. And you really don't need to safeguard anything. I have been in your system for the past ten minutes. If I really wanted to check anything out, I would have already done it."

"Shelby?"

"Yes, and you are?"

"Jonas. You are pretty good you know."

"Pretty good? I think very good."

"How did you come up with the idea of storing your stuff somewhere else?"

"That's an interesting idea, but I haven't done that. I just have it firewalled in a way that no one ever thinks to look for it."

"Now THAT'S interesting."

"Thank you. Now why the hell are you trying to hack me?"

"I was pretty much made to, there's some money missing from one of the clients that a friend of mine is investigating. He asked me to see what I could find out."

"And what have you found?"

"Someone worth talking to."

"That's sweet, but I am already spoken for."

"Lucky guy. Listen, could we talk sometime? Real world I mean. Your security and everything is pretty amazing."

There was a long pause before any other words appeared on the screen. "Ok, can't hurt. Did you hack my cell number?"

Jonas blushed and then laughed because no one could see him. "Yep," he answered guiltily and repeated the number he had found. "When is a good time to call?"

"Give me a few hours, it's about eight here now. Call me about ten?"

"Done, where is here?"

"Memphis, I would have thought you knew that by now."

Jonas smiled again. Sarcasm, a language he spoke well.

CHAPTER 73

Grisanti's sits on the edge of Midtown, on Poplar Avenue, one of the busiest streets in Memphis. It's in a non-descript location but is a favorite of anyone with a real taste for real pasta. Jackson led Jessica inside and they approached the hostess stand. A tall, stunning brunette looked over a long waiting list and up over a crowded lobby and caught Jackson's eye. "Hey Steph," he said to the brunette, leaning over and kissing her on the cheek."

"Hey yourself, handsome. Where have you been hiding?"

"I haven't been hiding, just been working a lot. Was in D.C. last week, heading to Vegas soon. You look fantastic. How's the budding architect?"

"He's good. Always has his nose stuck in a book. He has exams coming up so I don't expect to really see him for the next couple of weeks."

"Sucks for him. I guess I understand focusing on work though." They smiled at each other, as if sharing an inside joke. "So do you have a table for me?"

"Of course, would I ever not take care of you?"

"Not that I know of. I am counting on that of course for when I am old and can't take care of myself any more."

"That won't happen to you. I can feel it."

"I appreciate your confidence. Of course, I may just be flirting with you."

"I hope so, as long as it has been and all I get is a kiss on the cheek? I was almost offended."

"You know better than that."

"I would like to think so." She turned and introduced herself to Jessica. "Make him buy you good stuff tonight. The veal is really good and the wine is better." She led them to their table and once there, hugged Jackson again and smiled again as Jackson slipped what looked like a $50 bill to her. Jessica caught the transaction out of the corner of her eye and smiled. Years and years ago, her grandfather had told her to watch how someone treated people in the service industry if you wanted to know what kind of person they were. As far as she could tell, Jackson passed that test with flying colors. She followed as Jackson wound his way through the restaurant and they came to a quiet table, out of the way of most restaurant traffic. They sat and were attended to almost immediately with bread and water, menus and wine lists. The server seemed to have every facet of each memorized and presented a few of his favorites and a couple of the evening's specials before leaving them.

"So what would you like?" Jackson asked Jessica.

"It all sounds so good, I don't have the faintest idea."

"I thought you might say that. I love this restaurant and eat here when I can. When he comes back, I think he just might surprise you."

Jessica wasn't sure what to think of that, but upon his return found out. Jackson ordered a bottle of Pinot Noir that carried a pretty hefty price to it. The server asked them if they were ready to order and Jackson reached out and touched Jessica's hand.

"She hasn't eaten here before and I am afraid you have presented her with too many good choices. What do you propose we do about it?"

The server smiled and drew a bit nearer to their table. "How about you describe what you really have a taste for and I will see what the chef can come up with?"

"That sounds perfect," Jessica sighed. She thought for a moment and her memory took her back several years to another restaurant where she had been served the perfect dish. It was chicken and pasta and peppers and a few other things that she wasn't quite sure of. She noticed that while she talked, the server nodded as if picturing the dish in his head.

"I think our chef will really enjoy this. The same for you sir?"

"I look forward to his brilliance."

"So, you can just come in and order whatever sounds good?"

"Within reason. Chefs are fun that way. Challenge them and see what they can come up with. It's one of the reasons I love coming here. The chef is really good.

A plate of antipasto was brought to their table along with a steaming hot loaf of bread. Jackson refilled their wine glasses and they talked animatedly non-stop until their meal arrived. Another bottle of wine was ordered and they finished it and along with the last bits of their dinner. The chef came out and they offered him their highest compliments.

As the dishes were cleared away, Jessica leaned back in her chair, fully satiated from the feast they had shared. "That was amazing. It was like a few different tastes blended together and then they came out and presented themselves separately at different times. That was phenomenal." Her sides hurt from laughing so much and she couldn't remember a time where just sitting and talking had been so enjoyable. Jackson was thinking similarly about their evening together.

"So it's almost nine. What sounds good to you? Beale Street? A band somewhere? I have it on good authority that the opera is performing tonight and is exceptional. Or Tunica is just down the road." Tunica had become the mid-south's playground and alternative to going to Vegas. Although the casinos weren't as ritzy and there weren't the same level of VIP's, Tunica had become the third largest destination for gamblers in the country.

"How about we go back downtown and park and just see where we go from there."

Jackson agreed and signaled the server, who brought them their bill. Jackson paid it and they made their way back to car.

CHAPTER 74

"Knock knock, Jonas."

"Man don't you have something better to do?" The exasperation was evident in his voice.

"Yes, but I'm not doing it. Instead, I am sharing my time with you."

"Did you bring any food this time?"

"Nope. But I will order a pizza for you if you like."

"You're a prince among men."

"So what did you find out?"

"Well, your hacker is from Memphis like you thought. Whoever he is, he's good."

"He?"

"Of course he, do you really think a woman could stump me?"

"So sorry, didn't mean to offend your tender sensibilities."

"Offense taken. I actually was worried earlier about whether or not my apartment was clean enough for your visits."

"Spoken like an old never-married woman. You aren't getting soft on me now are you?"

"You should be so lucky. Anyway, the IP addresses lead back to Memphis, unless they were bogus. I can't find any trace of the money. I did find some trails related to your detective butt buddy and the law firm, but they haven't gone anywhere yet. I'm telling you, this guy is good."

"I find it interesting that you are so certain it's a guy. We have several women in IT downtown."

"Right, and they do such a good job that you keep me on speed-dial. I'm sure they do a great job of making coffee and answering the phone. And by the way, I haven't gotten the money that usually comes with being kept on retainer. By definition a retainer is money that you pay to someone to retain their services. You are getting the services and I have yet to see the retainer."

"Are you in prison?"

"Well, no."

"Consider your tab paid in full then."

"Nice, the point is that a woman can't hack as well as a man. Never could, can't now and never will be able to. That's why you needed me to find the money and the money trail that your guys couldn't."

"Point taken. But not agreed with. So when are you going to know something?"

"Depends on what this guy has going on. I'll know more tomorrow or the next day, but what I will know I don't know yet. Sometimes it takes a day or two just to get the lay of the land, get familiar with certain patterns and tendencies. I'll get him though. So what do I get when I do?"

"Well now, this is where our friendship might just take off. There is a reward for information leading to the arrest and prosecution of the murderer. The victim was loaded if you recall. So find me the hacker and that should lead to finding the killer. Are you seeing where this is going?"

"I am detective. And may I say you're a dog for not telling me that earlier. What kind of reward?"

"A healthy one. I can't tell you exactly how much, but it might even get you to turn your computer off for a day or two if you got it. Actually get out and see the sun shine for a change."

"Well now I have some extra incentive to get it done. Of course some walking around cash in the meantime would kind of rock. Can you hook someone up?

"I need something concrete to go on. A name, a number, blood type, something. A step in the right direction is a step towards your bank account. Deal?"

"Done, now shoo, I have work to do." Jonas paused for a moment. "Wow, that's not a phrase I thought would ever come out of my mouth. Congratulations Detective, you just made my mother very happy."

"I'm just here to protect and serve."

CHAPTER 75

Jillian's is an entertainment destination that caters to those over the age of 21 that sits on the southern side of Peabody Place in downtown Memphis. It consisted of three levels of a restaurant, dance club, video arcade and a downstairs "Cosmic Bowling Alley." The cosmic simply referred to the dance music, disco balls, and black and neon lighting. It took a mere suggestion and Jackson and Jessica made their way downstairs, kicked off their shoes and got their own lane. They laughed and drank and bowled, neither of them very impressively. Jackson won both games, but by the slightest margin. Jessica befriended the couple in the next lane and the foursome spent as much time talking as they did bowling. Jackson wandered off to the bar to get the next round and their new friends commented on how great they were together. "It's like you guys have been together forever, how many years has it been?" Jessica could only smile and shrug her shoulders. "We've known each other for about a week now!" She smiled at the surprised look on their faces and then she high-fived the woman who just nodded her head and smiled back knowingly. Jackson came back to their seats bearing drinks and each of the couples drank and finished their game. The neighbors finished first and the two women exchanged phone numbers and promises to call each other. Jackson and the other man shook hands and left it at that. After the couple had gone, they sat and Jessica recounted their conversation and it was Jackson's turn to smile.

"It does seem like longer than a week though. It was last…"

"Sunday," she answered.

"Now you don't know what I was going to say."

"Sure I do. You were going to say it was last Sunday that you came into the Blue Monkey and got the best chicken sandwich you had ever had." She leaned in closer and kissed him softly.

"Well, the Sunday part is right. Not sure about the chicken sandwich though. You keep pushing it and I'm not sure it's the best. I had this chicken sandwich in Telluride one time that made me stand on the bar and yell, 'WAHOO' it was so good."

"Did you actually yell 'Wahoo'?"

"No, but it makes the story better, don't you think?"

"It does actually."

"It was a great sandwich in Telluride, I will say that. The Blue Monkey's is right up there as well though. And the service has been much better by far."

"You're just trying to get back in my good graces now buddy. Flattery will get you everywhere with me, by the way."

"Buddy?"

"Uh-huh."

"You know, there are several things I can deal with. Being called 'Buddy' by you seems to be a preemptive shot. Next thing you will be saying is 'I just want to be friends' or 'it's not you, it's me.' All that means is that of course it IS you. Time to go! Buh-Bye!"

Jessica was back to laughing uncontrollably again.

"And why is three strikes in a row called a turkey? Seems like if you called it 'Triple Shot Power' or something that would be more fun. What do you think?"

"I think you need a hobby or something instead of sitting around thinking about stuff."

"Probably wouldn't be a bad idea. Anything come to mind?"

"I think that since you just beat me twice in bowling, we should go upstairs and you should take me dancing."

"I thought you would never ask!"

CHAPTER 76

Jonas was holding his cell phone, waiting for their pre-agreed on time to call. He was intrigued to find his hands were actually shaking. He put the phone down and paced a bit back and forth, wondering how to begin a conversation with a complete stranger 2000 miles away. He went back and searched through the information he had gleaned from her computer and figured the best thing to do would be to just talk to her. But where to start? "Hi Shelby, it's Jonas, the guy that hacked your computer. How are you?" Yeah, that would work. "You know, your security is good, but I'm better." Sure, better. How about just pick up the phone and say, "Nyah, nyah, nyah, nyah, nyah." Whatever. That's why Jonas preferred the virtual world. The women were gorgeous and didn't say anything. They just stood there with their clothes hanging off...or off altogether. What the heck did he get himself into? He couldn't call her, wouldn't call her. But then what? Turn her over to Detective Dorkelstein? That wasn't going to happen either. He went and grabbed a beer out of the fridge and pondered his next move. He took a sip and sat back down in front of his computer screen, pulling up her picture again. She was absolutely stunning. They didn't make computer hackers like this as far as he knew. The picture had to be a fake. He was considering going back in and searching some more when his phone rang.

"Hello?"

"One of the things that few hackers realize is that when they are in someone's system, someone can turn right back around and get into theirs. How are you Jonas?"

"Shelby?"

There was a hypnotic sort of laughter coming from the other end of the phone.

"Yes, you weren't thinking about not calling me were you?"

"Uh, no. I was just finishing up a beer and something to eat."

"Are you dressed?"

"Yes, are we skipping ahead to the fun stuff already?"

"Not at all, most computer geeks keep a rather limited dress code. Easier access I suppose."

"Nice visual. A bunch of guys sitting around with their Johnson in their hand."

"It doesn't just apply to guys ya know. Although at the moment I am missing the Johnson."

"So you're…"

"Hey, look who showed up to the party. Does that make you uncomfortable?"

"Not at all. I'm sorry, what were we talking about again?"

Shelby laughed. For the first time in a long time she thought to herself. But wait, she was in control of the conversation. "You were trying to figure out how to wiggle out of your clothes without me knowing it so you could take care of whatever just came up."

"Cute. I'm dressed though. Sorry to disappoint you. However, I do like your way of thinking."

"Ok then, so let's talk about why you were poking around in my computer."

There was a long pause before Jonas spoke. "Yeah, about that. It wasn't on purpose really. A guy I know asked me to check out some missing money and the trail led to you. I really didn't mean to snoop."

"Yes you did. But I forgive you. For now. So who is this guy?"

"I don't know him really. He knows me from some of my previous work. Online. Knows my screen name, that's all."

"Your screen name is the same as your first name. It's not a huge leap."

"You know what they say. The best place to hide sometimes is in plain sight."

That thought stuck a chord with Shelby. "You might be right. So have you told him about me yet?"

"No, he's supposed to get back with me on Monday. I'll think of something and throw him off a bit."

"And why would you do that?"

"Why wouldn't I do it?"

"You don't even know me yet."

"Oh, I don't know. We seem to be getting along pretty well so far."

"Two different things, love. Two different things."

CHAPTER 77

Jessica led Jackson from the crowded dance floor and towards the bar. The techno rhythm pounded in their ears and they almost had to yell to hear each other. Jessica made a motion to move outside and Jackson followed closely behind.

"Where did a polite young man such as yourself learn to dance like that?"

"I never had much of a choice. Only white guy on my track team. My teammates went to great lengths to make sure I represented well."

Jessica laughed and fell into him a bit. "I'm a little drunk."

"If you're a little drunk then I am seven feet tall. It is getting a little late too."

"What time is your curfew? Wait, you don't have anywhere else to be do you?"

"On the contrary, I can't think of anyplace I would rather be than right here with you."

Jessica stopped giggling. "That was really sweet. And a bit…"

"A bit what?"

"If I said scary would that be a bad thing?"

"Not if it is where you are right now."

"I've probably been here a bit too long actually."

Jackson leaned in and kissed her softly. "That wasn't scary was it?"

Jessica smiled. "I'm not sure. Can I have another just to make sure?"

It was Jackson's turn to smile. He leaned in and kissed her again, this time with a bit more urgency behind it. Jessica pressed her lips against his and they stayed there for what seemed like all night.

"And that one?"

"A bit scarier. I could get used to that, and that scares me more than I care to admit."

Jackson smiled at her. "Do you want to talk about it?"

"What time is it?"

"About one-thirty."

"Are you hungry? I know an all-night breakfast place that has the best biscuits and gravy. And if you're nice, I might tell you a story or two that would shed some light on this scariness.

Forty-five minutes later they were sitting and laughing in a booth much less glamorous than their previous meal. The laughing had started when they had gotten to Jackson's Jeep to find that the occupants of the car parked next to his couldn't wait to "get a room." "Wow," Jackson had said, "She's pretty flexible." As soon as they had left the parking garage, Jessica exploded with laughter, unable to control herself. They had driven several blocks before she caught her breath. That is, until Jackson added, "and enthusiastic." Five more minutes of laughter. Now the food in front of them was fried and the ambiance was something less than intimate. And they both loved it. He took a drink from a cup of Hot Chocolate that seemed as if it had seen better days.

"So, about that scary kiss?"

"You do get right to the heart of the matter don't you?"

"I suppose. I didn't mean to push though."

"You didn't, I offered. Well, where to begin? What would you like to know?"

"Why your eyes are sad even when you are happy...or laughing hysterically like before!"

"Experience I suppose. Life. After a while it adds up. I have seen people that have been beaten down by life basically. I think we all get to a certain point where the things we have dealt with and internalized for so long, they come out. Some people's hair turns gray, others have sad eyes I suppose."

"Makes sense. They are beautiful though."

"You're sweet. And probably dealing with some sort of carb intoxication from the biscuits and gravy. Told you they were great."

"You were right. Again."

She smiled and then proceeded to tell him her story. The telling of it took about thirty minutes and Jackson asked a few questions here and there. A teardrop rolled down her cheek and he gathered it up with a napkin and then caressed the side of her face with his hand. "Oh, look what a mess I am. Some great date I turned out to be. I think the rule book specifically prohibits crying on the first date."

"Then aren't we both lucky that this isn't our first date?" Jackson smiled reassuringly.

"I suppose we are." She smiled and blushed, looking down at what was left of her breakfast.

"Wow, I would like to see the thought that just crossed your mind."

"Play your cards right and you just might," she raised one eyebrow flirtatiously.

"Check please."

"Good start."

They paid at the front of the restaurant and made their way to his car. Jackson moved in behind her as she reached the car door and wrapped his arms around her waist. He pressed against her and she placed both hands on its side for support. He kissed her neck and she tilted her head back, thoroughly enjoying his touch. The night air had cooled considerably since their day started and she shivered at the chill. Sensing that, Jackson opened her door and closed it behind her, walked around and cranked the Jeep and it's heater up. The cold combined with the breakfast and the conversation had sobered them both to the point of just being tired. The drive to her place seemed much longer than when he had picked her up earlier. About twenty minutes later, he pulled up in front of her house and parked, getting out and walking her to the front door. He paused for a moment, not sure of what to do next, when she opened the front door and held it open for him, not giving him a chance to think or decline the offer.

"Can you get a fire started in the fireplace?"

"At three in the morning?"

"The wood doesn't mind. It will burn either way."

Jackson laughed and in no time had a roaring fire burning in her fireplace.

"I would offer you a drink, but I am alcoholed out for the night."

"I don't think that's a word."

"Well, it should be. It fits perfectly don't you think?"

Jackson passed a thoughtful look across his face and nodded his agreement. Jessica came back in from the kitchen with two steaming mugs in her hand. Hers was coffee and his was hot chocolate. "It seems like you don't drink coffee, right?"

"I do from time to time. Hot chocolate just sounded good earlier."

"I'm sorry, would you prefer the coffee?"

"No, this is great, thanks."

They chatted a little while longer and finished their drinks while watching the fire burn. Jessica had moved next to him on the long sofa facing the fireplace and placed her coffee mug on the table beside her. "Ok, so I told you my story, what's yours?" She folded her legs under her and made herself comfortable.

Jackson swallowed hard and handed his mug to her. "Nothing really to tell."

She placed his mug next to hers and answered, "That's really not fair. I told you everything."

"So what would you like to know?"

"Everything."

"How about I just show you?"

"That will work too."

Jackson leaned over and kissed her softly, letting the two of them come together slowly, adding to the anticipation each of them was feeling. He would remember later that she tasted of rich, deep chocolate. Her skin was soft to the touch and he brushed her face and neck with his fingertips. They kissed slowly at first; enjoying the sensations they were creating. As the passion level increased, they fell into a sensual yet comfortable rhythm. Jackson moved his hands downward, stroking her arms and eventually moving under her blouse. He could feel her pressing against his touch, showing him where and how she wanted to be pampered. She moaned lightly as his hands gently and quickly unclasped her bra and slid it off and to the floor. Jessica smiled and bit her lip lightly and intercepted his hands as they moved in again. Jackson's face showed a puzzled look that Jessica caught and she answered his anticipated question. "I think you need some attention." She pressed him back against the sofa and slid her hands downward, brushing his stomach and reaching his belt. He was visibly excited and she focused her nimble fingers on the task of freeing him from his constraints. His belt buckle proved simple enough and she unzipped his pants and slid her hands inside, grasping him gently and stroking him up and down.

"Oh my," she said with a smiling twinkle in her eye. "I hope I can be as flexible as the other woman we saw earlier!"

"I'm certain that won't be a problem at all." Jackson inhaled sharply as she took him quickly in her mouth. "Oh my is right," he stammered. He could feel the passion building between them as his own excitement level rose quickly. Suddenly he was flooded by images of the past few weeks and drew away quickly from her. He stood up and zipped his pants and mumbled an apology under his breath, unable to look her in the eye.

"What's wrong?" Jessica pleaded.

"Nothing, everything is perfect here, I just can't."

"Can't what? It seemed like you were well on the way!" Jessica laughed a bit, trying to take the edge off her confusion.

Jackson shuffled his feet, looking at the floor. "Oh, I CAN, but I just can't. Not just now."

"Why, is it something I did?"

"No."

"Something I said?"

"No, not at all."

"You're going to have to help me out here Jackson before my feelings get hurt. Am I not pretty enough?"

"You're kidding right?"

"I don't know, am I? You tell me...oh my God."

"What?"

"You're married!" Jessica stomped off in a huff, muttering under her breath. Jackson chased after her and grabbed her arm.

"I'm not married."

"Then what is it then?"

"I can't..."

"We've covered this already," Jessica said growing more frustrated and confused by the second. The pace of their conversation increased. "You can't because..."

"It's complicated, a very long story."

"More hot chocolate then? Coffee? You can't because of me? Because of you?"

"No, no. Nothing like that."

"Because the economy is bad? Your football team lost today?"

"I..."

"You don't like me that way? You just want to be friends?" She was peppering him with one statement after another, raising the tension level with each word. "It's not me, it's you?" Jackson was getting more agitated, shifting his weight back and forth. "You need space?"

"No."

"You want me to respect you in the morning?" She was getting louder ,"Let me guess, I won't hear from you again the second I sleep with you?"

"No."

"You're just reeling me in to break my heart that much harder?"

"NO!"

"THEN WHAT DAMMIT?"

"I'm an escort," he answered, his voice trailing off.

"What? I couldn't hear you."

"I'M AN ESCORT. I'M PAID FOR, SERVICES TO THE HIGHEST BIDDER! HAPPY NOW?"

CHAPTER 78

Time seemed to stop. Jackson watched Jessica's face closely as she processed what he had just said. Interestingly, she didn't show any of the emotions that he would have guessed.

Jessica made a quick decision in her head before speaking very carefully. "I'm happy that you answered me finally, yes. I'm very happy that you stopped before we went any further. Beyond that, I'm not sure just yet."

Jackson looked around for his coat, finding it by the front door. "I'll be going now. For the record, I had a great time today. And the other days as well. You're pretty incredible."

"Thank you, I think so too. But if I am so incredible, why on earth would you want to leave?"

Jackson looked at her with stunned silence. He turned his head a little bit to the right as if he was attempting to decipher a foreign language. "I don't...want...to leave, but I figured..."

"You figured that I would throw you out? I think I am insulted."

Jackson dropped his jacket back down where he had picked it up. "You are the LAST person I would want to insult, trust me. How would that work again?" He asked, shaking his head as to clear out the confusion.

"Why I would be insulted? The time we have spent together over the past week should have answered that for you I would have hoped. What you do and where you are in life doesn't mean anything to me. It's your heart that matters."

Jackson was speechless. His shifted his weight back and forth again, with his arms folded across his chest.

Jessica continued, speaking softly and calmly. "I didn't bring you back here because I was impressed by dinner or by you taking Italian. I was impressed because you worked your tail off at the shelter. Because you have an amazing air about you. You honestly care about people but aren't really sure how to show that side of you to the world. I see that. I want that. I want to know it. I want to know you. Can I do that?"

He nodded his head and breathed deeply, trying to contain the emotion building within him. He succeeded right up to the point that she held her arms open for him. The tears streamed from his eyes and he melted into her arms. She held him tightly as his body shook, racked with sobs as he released days and months and years of emotions that he had worked so hard to hold in.

CHAPTER 79

It took several minutes, but Jackson calmed his breathing and sat up. He was somewhat embarrassed by his outburst, but was comforted by the look of understanding he saw in Jessica's face. She smiled and touched his hand.

"Better?"

"Embarrassed."

"Don't be. It would seem you needed to do that for a while now."

"It would seem so." Jackson excused himself and went into the bathroom and splashed water on his face. The guy staring back at him from the mirror wasn't nearly as big and bad and he had seemed just an hour earlier.

"How about something to drink? Maybe some more hot chocolate?"

"Only if you have some Peppermint Schnapps to put in it."

"Oooo, that sounds good. Two coming right up."

Jackson dried his face and hands and moved back to the living room. Jessica sat on the sofa in front of two steaming mugs. "It needs to cool a bit."

"I guess you would like the story in the meantime," Jackson smiled.

"It couldn't hurt, could it?"

"No, I suppose not. Ok, where to start...I guess it was about seven years ago. I was working at a brokerage firm as an analyst. Great money tracking stocks, writing reports, doing research. Kind of a doorway to bigger and better things and more money. I didn't have the pedigree that a lot of guys did. Great education, but my "Daddy" didn't work there nor was he a big client."

"What were your degrees in?"

"I have Bachelors degrees in English and History and an MBA in International Finance."

"Impressive."

"Thanks. Anyway, I had gotten passed over a couple of times in favor of a "Daddy's boy" or someone similar and was getting kind of fed up with it. Did I mention I was also engaged?"

"No."

"Oh, well I was engaged. To be married."

"Is there another way?"

"Not that I know of, just clarifying."

"Thank you."

"You're welcome, may I continue?"

"Please do." She smiled at the change of pace and tone of their conversation.

"So, we were getting ready for our annual year end Christmas party. Everyone gets their bonuses based on how the firm did and how everyone did individually. The bonus is kind of an indicator of where your career path is headed with that firm. Less than last year means you may want to take a box to work on Monday while hoping your resume is up to date. About the same means no changes in the works. A big bump means your boss will be talking to you about your new promotion sometime soon. There was a trading position that had come open and I really wanted a shot at it. The manager over that particular position and I had talked and he seemed genuinely excited about the possibility of me working under him. I had brought three different stocks to his attention in the past few months that had exploded like I thought they would and he and his clients made a boatload of money on them. It felt like a shoo-in.

"Is shoo spelled with an 'o' or an 'e' at the end of it?"

"Stop it. You're just teasing me now."

"Maybe just a little." They both smiled.

"So the party was at the Peabody. Real swanky black-tie affair. We all drank in the Lobby bar for a while before we went up to the main dinner. We ate and were having a great time."

"You and your fiancée?"

"Yes, we had plenty to drink and the food was excellent. Then the Chairman of the Board got up and made his annual speech about how great things were and how lucky we were to be in the business we were in, yada, yada, yada."

"Three yadas?"

"That's the second time, you have interrupted, do not let there be a third!" he warned in mock seriousness. Jessica bit her lip, attempting a serious look on her face.

"So they passed the bonuses out and mine was a hundred dollars more than the previous year. A very nice bonus sure, but it told me that I didn't get the job that I wanted. One of the other analysts just about came out of his chair he was so excited, and I knew that he had gotten that job. Another legacy case. Nice guy but didn't know the difference between a put and a call."

"I don't know the difference between a put and a call."

"Then you wouldn't have gotten the job either unless your Daddy worked at the firm or spent a lot of money there! Can I finish?"

Jessica laughed out loud this time. "I'm sorry. This is fun though."

"I'm glad my personal pain and suffering is entertaining to you."

"Not that part and you know it."

"I do, but the story will be much better when you hear the whole thing."

"Go ahead then."

"We finish dinner and drink some more. Everyone is pretty drunk. The manager I had talked with before takes me aside and we talk for a while. He explains that he really wanted me in the position, but his hands were tied by the board. I am talented and he really wants me to work under him, he thinks I would do great and all that stuff. I thanked him rather insincerely as I recall and went back to the party. The band had started playing and the dance floor was pretty packed. Slow stuff, kind of catering to the older crowd. I looked around the ballroom a couple of times and could not find my fiancée."

"What was her name?"

"My fiancée?"

"Was there another woman in the story?"

Jackson laughed again. "Ok, you're right. Her name was Samantha. I called her Sam."

"I always thought that Sam was a cute name for a girl." Jackson frowned at her. "Sorry."

"Anyway, I asked a couple of the guys and they said they hadn't seen her. Sam and I had gotten a room in the hotel, so I headed back up there to see if she had gone back to change or something. I open the door to the room and found Sam...and the jackass that had gotten the promotion bent over the bed doggie style."

Jessica grimaced. "Ouch."

"Not for me so much. His pants were down around his ankles and he stood up to pull them up. But he was drunk and he fell over backwards. When he rolled over to try and stand up again, I kicked him in the face like I was kicking a football. Broke his nose."

Jessica covered her mouth with her hand. "Oh my gosh."

"Yeah. I hadn't really even been in a fight before that in my life. Sam rolled over on the bed but didn't bother to get dressed. She looked me in the eye and told me that she was tired of being with someone that would always finish second and started crying."

"You should have kicked her too."

It was Jackson's turn to laugh. "That wouldn't have been a gentlemanly thing to do. In the meantime, Tad had gotten up..."

"Tad? You're joking right?"

"Nope, I didn't say that earlier? What an ass. Anyway, he ran out of the room and told me I was going to be sorry and I told him I already was. So I took the elevator downstairs and walked out of the hotel. My bank was a couple of blocks away, so I walked over and deposited my bonus check. Always thinking you know. I walked back into the ballroom and found a small crowd gathered around young Tad. His father screamed at me that my life was going to be hell as long as he was at that firm. I told him to go fuck himself. I walked over to the Managing Partner and offered my resignation effective whatever day he thought was appropriate. He smiled and said he thought that a month's severance was appropriate. And then he hugged me. He whispered that he hated both father and son and only wished he could have done the same thing that I did. Then the other manager came over and shook my hand and told me that he would have me another job before New Year's. I thanked him and left. I never felt so free in my life. I went back down to the Lobby bar and was enjoying my first bourbon and coke as well as a conversation with a very attractive 40 something year-old woman. We finished our drinks and she asked me if I had any plans for the next night. When I told her I didn't she asked if all the arrangements had been made for the following evening for the awards banquet she had to attend. When I looked confused, she put her hand to her mouth kind of like you did earlier like she had caught herself. She then asked me if JoJo had sent me to talk with her and I told her that I had no idea who JoJo was. She was embarrassed and apologized and told me she would tell me the rest of the story in her room if I was interested. I was. So she asked for a case of wine to be sent to her room and we went upstairs. Coincidentally, it was right above the room I had rented. I checked that out the next day. Anyway, she told me she was in from out of town and had recently separated from her husband. She didn't want to be at this banquet without someone on her arm, so she had asked around and gotten in touch with some woman named JoJo that hired out escorts. Then she asked me again if I was interested. Being drunk enough and unemployed enough, I figured what the hell. We never really discussed a price and when the weekend was up she handed me an envelope with about five thousand dollars in it."

"Did you sleep with her?"

"Oh yes, both nights. I think I was probably better the second night though, being much more sober and all."

"One would think."

"So she asked me to take her to the airport in the limo she had arranged for and to make sure it got back to where it needed to go.

214

During the ride, she said that she traveled a great deal and wondered if I would be interested in meeting her again. I told her that it was an interesting proposition and asked if I could think about it and call her back with my answer. A couple of weeks and no jobs later I called her back and agreed. She was my first and was best client."

"Was?"

"I'm retiring."

"Wow, so your attachment to her and the job kept you from sleeping with me?"

"No, my unbelievably intense attraction to you kept me from sleeping with you without you knowing about this…and anything else you want to know."

"And you are going to stop doing what you do?"

"Yes, I think I covered that already."

"Just clarifying. Are you doing that because you think it's what I would want?"

"No, I am quitting because it is past time for me to quit. I have wanted to quit for a while, but always found an excuse based on how much money I had in the bank or because of how far out I was scheduled. But recently it has been shown to me that it's not how much money you have that's important. There's a whole lot more to life and I don't want to miss another minute of it…with you." He looked at his feet, not sure what reaction the last part would cause.

A tear rolled down her face and she said quietly, "Look at me please." He raised his head and saw her face and smiled sweetly, raising his hand to brush the tear away. "That may be the bravest thing I have seen anyone do in a long time. Thank you." She took a deep breath and continued. "And if you want me, you can have me. I am falling for you so hard, it scares me to death. So please know what you are doing, because I have no idea!"

They fell together again and kissed and cried and laughed and talked and moved into the bedroom and fell into bed and kissed and cried and laughed and talked some more. Several hours later, the night gave way to morning and the sky began to lighten. At some point earlier, they had undressed down to boxers and t-shirts. Jessica looked at the clock and said, "Well, it's official, you spent the night. Can we get some sleep now?"

"I would love that. Where do you want me?"

"I want you to hold me now," she said, turning over and pressing her back into his chest. She turned her head back and they kissed softly yet intimately and within a few minutes had both fallen into a deep and satisfying sleep.

CHAPTER 80

Jonas wiped his eyes, tiring of staring at the wall bank of monitors. He had been hard at work for the past 24 hours, trying to figure out just how this mystery woman had hacked into his system. All his usual backdoors had security measures on them that still seemed in place. He checked five or six thousand other places he thought of when referencing hacks he had done. Nothing clicked. His stomach roared at him, unhappy with the complete lack of food it had been presented. "Shut up," Jonas growled. "You eat when I do. Ok, that was pretty redundant. God, look at me, I'm talking to my stomach." He sprang to his feet as the ringing of his phone startled him.

"What?"

"Now Jonas, is that anyway to greet the new woman in your life?"

"I'm sorry, I didn't sleep well last night."

"I understand. But you really should back up from the computer. You aren't going to find where I got in."

"How did you...?"

"Because we are very much alike. I got hacked a few years ago and it kept me up for literally a week. I almost OD'd on No Doz just trying to stay awake. The person that hacked me finally taught me how to retrace

217

other people's steps by retracing my own. It's kind of like Sherlock Holmes. If you have all the possibilities in front of you, you simply eliminate them logically until you are left with the one last possibility. That's the true scenario, no matter how farfetched it might be."

It was like being hit with a baseball bat. "You came in through the path I followed you and the other detective on. That way, it would look like the work I had already done and I wouldn't check it."

"Wow, you are a quick learner, maybe there are a few other tricks I should teach you."

"How about sending me the diagrams first. I may want to visualize them before putting them into practice."

"Such a naughty boy. I need you to do something for me. The payback could be very nice for you if you do a good job."

"What do I have to do?"

"Go to a funeral and see if someone in particular shows up."

"That's it?"

"That's it."

"Is this not something you can do?"

"No, I will be in another city on Monday and you live there."

"Whose funeral?"

"Sharon Milligan."

Jonas groaned, "I was afraid you would say that."

"Why?"

"Because it's all they have been talking about in the papers out here. Multi-gozillionaire cut down in her prime. There will be cops and security and stuff everywhere."

Shelby chuckled, "Cut down isn't very nice. Accurate but not nice."

"Nor is it nice to laugh about it. I talk about cops and security and you focus on the cutting part. Glad to see we have the same sick sense of humor. You know where they send people like us when we die?"

"I'll save you a spot on the bus I am driving."

"Thanks, so who am I looking for?"

"No one you have ever heard of. I'll send you a picture."

"Boyfriend of yours?"

"Nope, he had a chance once, but he blew it."

"So he's a moron then."

"Maybe just a little misguided. But then, most boys are until the one puts them on the right path."

"So are you the one?"

"For him? Or for you?"

Jonas swallowed hard. "You tell me."

"Do this favor for me and we will discuss that further."

"Fair enough."

CHAPTER 81

Jackson rolled over and opened his eyes. It took him a split second to recognize his surroundings. The cool sheets hugged his body snugly, fitting him seemingly in a cocoon. He turned his head to the side to find Jessica cuddled up in a ball, yawning herself awake. "Good morning," he said as he stretched his arms over his head.

"Good morning, have you seen the movie 'Titanic'?"

"Yes, is this how you greet all of your overnight visitors?"

"You're my first overnight visitor since I moved to Memphis, answer the question."

"Yes, I have seen 'Titanic'."

"There seems to be a difference of opinion among my fellow bartenders and servers on how the movie ends."

"The credits roll?"

"Cute. Actually you are a lot more than that, but I don't want to swell your ego too much this morning."

"That's an awfully nice thing to say."

"I say lots of nice things."

"I've noticed."

"Anyway, at the end of the movie, does Rose die?"

"Yes."

Jessica paused, letting that sink in. "No, she couldn't have."

"So why ask me the question?"

"Because, well, Mike and Jerrod answered the same as you."

"Hence the difference of opinion. How many agree with you?"

"Well, just one."

"Your friend, um, what's her name?"

"Melanie."

"I got the impression before that she wasn't the brightest bulb in the box."

"Be nice."

"No offense intended."

"You're kind of right."

"If you say so. Of course she dies, it goes along with the terrible script. Leonardo DiCaprio shivering in the water telling Kate Winslet that she is going to grow old and die warm in her bed. And that he would be waiting for her. Yuck by the way. And if you look closely, when she is walking back on the ship there at the end, it's all the people that died earlier in the movie that were there to greet her."

"That doesn't necessarily mean she died."

"Well, I guess not, but in this case she did. Sorry."

"You're supposed to be on my side." Jackson rolled over on top of her and kissed her while playfully pinning her arms down over her head.

"I'm on your side now. It's much nicer over here."

"It IS much nicer over here."

"I'm glad you agree."

Jessica lifted her face to his and kissed him in return. He pressed against her tightly, entwining his fingers with hers, as their kisses grew hotter. Jackson brushed the side of her face lightly, sweeping a few stray hairs from her face. Their eyes locked and they both knew it was time. She pushed her hands under his shirt and lifted it up over his head, dropping it off the side of the bed. They finished undressing each other slowly and explored each other's bodies with the tips of their fingers. The bed was warm and growing warmer by the second. The heat between them grew as each of their excitement levels peaked. Everything was perfect. They fit together perfectly and moved together in a perfect rhythm. Together they discovered a level of intimacy that each had only wondered about and few ever attain. An hour or so later, they collapsed into each other, thoroughly spent and very much in love. They kissed and talked closely for a while until each drifted off into a perfect sleep, her wrapped tightly in his arms.

They slept until late morning. This time Jackson awoke first and slipped out from under the covers, trying not to disturb Jessica. He stood for a second, looking for his clothes and was slightly startled when she said, "a little to the left would be nice."

Jackson turned to her voice and blushed slightly, diving back into the bed. Jessica shrieked playfully as he landed next to her and kissed her exposed shoulder.

"Sleep well?"

"Wow, unbelievably well. Are there drugs in that thing?" She playfully pressed her hip between his legs.

"Not that I know of. I can give you a prescription that you can refill as many times as you like though."

"I like the sound of that."

"Maybe you'll like the sound of this as well. Let's go somewhere. Just get away for a few days. Somewhere warm. I'll arrange everything."

"When, today?"

"No, I have to go to Seattle tonight for a funeral tomorrow."

"The client you told me about? Oh…that kind of client?"

"Yes, I didn't figure you would want to go there, but I could fly back, meet you at the airport and we could just go. Do you have a passport?"

"Yes, isn't this kind of sudden?"

"Maybe, can you get out of work?"

"I don't know, I mean I think so. Yes. I'm sure of it. Are you serious?"

"Absolutely. I know just the place too. It's quiet, it's out of the way, beautiful, good food, things to do if we can't figure anything else out to do."

"Sounds lovely. What do I need to do?"

"Pack, get out of work. Shower."

"Shower?"

"I thought you'd never ask." Taking her by the hand, he led her to the bathroom, started the shower and helped her inside, following closely behind.

CHAPTER 82

Art Menking was enjoying a cup of Seattle's finest coffee while he was waiting for his breakfast meeting. The phone call setting it up had come as a surprise and he was interested to see where it was going. His cell phone rang and he saw it was his partner.

"Menking."

"You know it's me, can you not just say hello?"

"I thought I did?"

"Whatever, where are you?"

"Grabbing some breakfast."

"Ok, I'm running a little late, but I will see you at the office."

"Ok." The older detective hung up the phone and greeted his visitor with a nod of his head. He spotted the familiar face on the other side of the diner and was waved over. He stood up, crossed the floor, and nodded his head in recognition. The smiling gentleman was Michael Carey.

"Good morning Detective Menking, won't you have a seat?"

"Don't mind if I do."

"So how is our investigation coming?"

"You mean our investigation like mine and my partner's?"

"I suppose. I do have a vested interest here as well."

"Your vested interest should be in letting us do our job and catch a murderer."

"Absolutely, and I have the utmost faith in the Seattle Police Department. I'm not sure I have the same faith in your partner though."

"Do you want to file a complaint?"

"Oh no!" Michael feigned the surprise well. "Nothing like that. However, as the person presiding over her estate, it is well within my rights to launch my own investigation."

"Sure you do. Just don't get in our way and muck up the works."

"I wouldn't want to do that. My investigators are very thorough. However, I am a man that likes to have a back up plan. Insurance, if you will. Your Detective Swift could come up with something that we didn't. If there's something he finds out, I'd like to know about it. Is that too much to ask?"

"Maybe. If it jeopardizes the investigation, then yes."

"I've already assured you that it wouldn't."

"So what exactly are you asking of me."

"Nothing more than just keeping me informed when there is a new lead or whatever in the case. I'll just follow behind in the shadows."

"Uh huh. And what do I get in return?"

Michael smiled and knew he had his man. "I am a man that also believes in rewarding the people that do good work." He reached in his pocket and pulled out an envelope and slid it across the table. "Just a taste."

Art peered into the envelope and counted ten crisp one hundred dollar bills. "That's a pretty sweet taste." He opened his overcoat and slid the envelope in his pocket.

"My client is missing a sizable chunk of money. As the business lawyer, I want it back. As the family's friend, I want to see the killer brought in and punished. In that we have a common interest and could help each other.

"I'll see what I can do."

"Thank you detective. Would you like another cup of coffee?"

"No thanks, I'm trying to watch my caffeine."

"Good for you, Detective, we should all take better care of ourselves."

"Something we agree on." He patted his coat pocket and excused himself, sliding out from the table and walking out of the shop. He walked the couple of blocks to his car, his mind racing. "Was it a set-up? Was he seriously going to get paid just for information? No harm in that as long as the investigation wasn't compromised. And he really could use the money." He got in his car and drove to the station, feeling much better.

CHAPTER 83

Jackson's flight had gone off without a hitch but lasted entirely too long. Memphis to Seattle was a long flight and his head seemed to spin wearily at the recent turn of events. He checked in to the luxury downtown hotel and found his way up to his suite. He had printed off the schedule and the maps that Ashley had sent to him and planned tomorrow's events accordingly. He kicked off his shoes and sat down at his self assigned task for the evening: Thirty-four phone calls to clients announcing his retirement. It was early evening on the West Coast so he had plenty of time. Even the calls out East wouldn't be too late. His clients' cell phone numbers were programmed into his phone, so the project was simply a matter of dialing and time. His first call was to New York.

"This is Sarah."

"Hey Sarah, it's Jackson. Listen, I want to thank you again for understanding about this week."

"Not at all. I knew Sharon as well. Just not as well as you did." There was a little bit of good-natured teasing in her voice.

"Still, I know you were looking forward to Vegas. I remember the Bellagio all too well."

"Well, you can make it up to me sometime soon."

"That's the other reason for my call. I'm not sure I will be able to anytime soon."

"Really, why is that?"

"I'm retiring, hanging it up. For good."

"I always told you that you were too good to last. So what's her name? There has to be a story."

Jackson laughed and paced a little in the room while he talked. "There is a girl, and her name is Jessica. But I have been planning on quitting for a while. The timing and the girl just happened to come together at the same time."

"I always hoped it would be me you would be retiring for."

Jackson let a loud burst of laughter escape. "Now, now. That's very flattering, but you and I both know you won't be changing your circumstances any time soon."

"I'm teasing sweetheart. And I am very happy for you. Do you have any replacements in mind to recommend?"

"I didn't really think about that. I don't know anyone off hand, but I will see if I can come up with some kind of recommendation."

"I would appreciate that. You know how much I love business trips. Do me a favor? A couple actually…"

"Sure, anything."

"First, tell this Jessica how lucky she is. Second, if it gets serious and you decide to marry her, send me an invitation?"

"I certainly will. And you made me smile. Thank you."

"You're a special guy, Jackson; seriously one of a kind. I wish nothing but the best for you. BUT, if it doesn't work out, you know I will always have a job for you."

"I appreciate that as well. I figure if it doesn't, I'm going to take some time and see the world anyway."

"Take care, Jackson."

The calls pretty much went that way all night. He talked to twenty-seven, left five messages and two simply rang with no answer. He made a mental note to try and get in touch with those via e-mail as well. Night had fallen and Jackson fell into his bed, exhausted from the long weekend. He picked up his phone and dialed it one last time.

"Hello?"

Jackson spoke in a cheesy French accent, "Yes, zees is Francois, calling about your manicure and pedicure zees weekend."

"Only if you paint my toes."

He reverted quickly back to his own voice. "Done."

"So how was your flight?"

"Long and uneventful."

"What have you been doing all alone in that hotel room?"

"Talking on the phone. Talked with twenty-seven people in the past two hours."

"Do you have a phone sex operation as well?"

"Fortunately, no. I was having conversations about my pending retirement though. Too bad I couldn't have one of those press conferences. Man, that would have made today much easier, I can just see it now, 'Well Jackson, what do you think of the state of the world where a young man can retire from your given profession'?"

"You can go to hell is what I think there Chad."

"Who is Chad?"

"A figment of my imagination."

"I am looking forward to experiencing your imagination a bit more."

"Pleasures untold my love."

"I think I like the sound of that. So how did the conversations go?"

"Most of them went about the same. Happy for you...sorry to lose you...do you know anyone that could replace you?"

"Well do you? Twin brother? Anyone you can think of that you could teach?"

"Interesting idea. A school for escorts. I could be the Head Pimp."

"You could recruit from the Chippendales!"

"Have you ever met one of those guys?"

"No, why?"

"Pretty boys with no brains. The reason they wear so little is that they can't figure out how to dress themselves."

Jessica stifled a laugh. "Yes, but no one wants to play with their brains."

"If I or any other man said something like that about women, we would instantly be castigated as being among the unwashed, chauvinistic heathenry."

"Well, turnabout is fair play I say."

"Fair enough. There's a great strip club I would love to take you to."

"Mmmmm, sounds interesting. Are you going to buy me a good time?"

"You are just full of surprises aren't you?"

"Maybe. I have a pretty good imagination as well you know."

"I look forward to finding out. Which leads me to the other reason that I called. Did you get off work?"

"Yes, Mike wasn't very happy, but he gave me the whole week and weekend off. Interestingly, he had exactly zero issues with it until I mentioned your name."

"I'm touched that he remembered me."

"He's a good judge of character and likes who I like."

"That gives me plenty of incentive to treat you well then. Now, after I hang up from you, I am going to call in a few favors and see if I can't get us away to a warm and lush tropical locale for a few days of rest and relaxation."

"Sounds wonderful. Can I do anything to help?"

"Just pack."

CHAPTER 84

The telephone rang seven times before he answered, "This is Jean Pierre." A heavy French Caribbean accent filled Jackson's telephone receiver.

"Jean Pierre, my old pirate friend, how are you?"

"Jackson, you sly dog. How is the lover of many?"

"Not me, Jean Pierre, I am merely an understudy at the foot of your greatness."

"Truer words were never spoken, what can I do for you this fine evening? I should say night, you do know it's late here."

"Is it? My sincerest apologies. I need one of your special packages, maybe three or four days in a hut over the ocean."

"Consider it done, when are you coming to see us?"

"Tuesday?"

"Nothing like advance notice Jackson." His Caribbean accent became a little less friendly for an instant. "Your clients always tend to plan farther ahead."

"Well, that's the thing. This isn't a client. I am actually out of the business. Just had my last client."

"Really? What happened? Wait, it's a girl isn't it?"

"She's not just a girl, trust me my friend."

"C'est l'amour. I love it. You can expect the most romantic week you have ever experienced. Let Jean Pierre take care of everything."

They spent a few more minutes making the necessary arrangements before hanging up. Jackson slumped back against the headboard for a moment and sighed loudly. Gathering a surge of energy, he moved back over to his laptop and fired it up. He accessed his financial accounts and nodded approvingly at the progress he had made recently. Then he bought airplane tickets for himself and Jessica and transferred money to his travel account. Satisfied, he accessed his e-mail and was touched to find several of the clients he had spoken with earlier had e-mailed him with kind words and e-cards expressing their affection for him. One message even contained a marriage proposal if that would keep him available to her. Jackson laughed at that and then spent several minutes and answered all of the messages he had gotten. Nothing else there required his attention, so he logged out and checked the clock. He decided to make one more call.

"Hello?" Jessica sounded sleepy as she answered.

"Hey sleepy head, I'm sorry if I woke you."

"You didn't, I was just resting my eyes."

"Uh huh. Why is that people never want to admit to being awakened by the phone?"

"I'm not sure. Did you miss me that much since we last talked."

"I did actually. I just wanted to say good night and to let you know to pack your bags for warm weather. All the arrangements are done."

"Really? That's fantastic." Jackson could hear the authentic excitement in her voice, breaking through the cobwebs of sleep he had first heard. "And good night to you, too."

"I can't wait to see you. My flight gets in early Tuesday and we fly out early afternoon."

"Where are we going?"

"It's a surprise, but I think you will find it acceptable."

"As long as you are with me, it can't be anything but acceptable."

"Sweet-talker. Get some sleep and I will talk to you tomorrow."

"Ok, thanks for calling and telling me. I'm going to sleep now." The sleep in her voice made her sound that much more seductive.

Jackson smiled and hung up and plopped back down on his bed. He surfed the channels for a few minutes before coming across the late local news. Jackson sat up and paid attention as the lead story was of Sharon Milligan's funeral the following day. The emphasis of the story was the intense security measures that were being put in place to accommodate the large crowds that were expected. A follow up story detailed the lack of progress in the search for her killer. Jackson turned up the volume. "Sources say that the pressure is growing for the Seattle Police Department to come up with a viable lead and they have asked for your help, Seattle. Anyone with information is encouraged to call the number on your screen. If your tip leads to an arrest, you could qualify for a substantial reward." Jackson shook his head and turned the volume back down. A bleached blonde was pointing to numbers on the screen that corresponded to local temperatures. The effects of flying and of a full day finally set in and Jackson pressed a button to turn off the television and another to turn off the lights in his suite. He moved his pillows down from the headboard, slid under the sheets and fell into a deep sleep within minutes.

CHAPTER 85

Michael Carey was fuming. His IT guy hadn't been able to track down where the money went or even how the hacker got through his client's security. He had hired both the computer security and the home security companies. Each had a passable reputation but had been chosen largely because their proposals were cheaper than others that had been interested in the business. That information was known to no one but himself and would stay that way. The detective he had hired wasn't producing anything. Michael made a note to fire him the following day. Now the family was getting restless and offering a reward for information. That would only serve to bring out the nutcases that wanted to make a quick buck. Nothing like being bogged down on a Monday. That could be managed but was more of a hassle than anything else. Lastly, sleeping in the guest room was not Michael's idea of fun. His wife had proven to be less forgiving when she received a phone call from Jaycee, the brainless piece of ass that had walked out on him at a restaurant earlier in the week. He sighed and rolled over, turning the lights out and hoping for better days. He tossed and turn for nearly half an hour before clicking the TV back on, hoping the inanity found there would at least drum him into a coma. Michael was amazed that so many channels could contain exactly nothing worth watching. He gave up and clicked the remote, shutting off the idiot box. He retreated back into his office and opened the files he had been working from in the Milligan case. All her records and calendars had been photocopied and arranged to make it easy for him to follow her tracks for the last 12 months. The answer had to be there, he reasoned, and he had all the incentive he needed to find out what it was. He reached into his desk drawer and pulled out another file. It was a collection of photos of Sharon Milligan that he had a detective take periodically over the last six months. Michael began to cross-reference every picture with the people that were known to him and would have no connection to her murder or the disappearance of her money. An hour later he was half way through the stack and no closer to identifying anyone out of the ordinary. The urge to sleep finally overcame him and he placed the pictures that he had sifted through already face down on the left side of the open folder. Without thinking, he placed the photograph he held in his right hand in the already viewed pile. The trouble being that he never looked at it. The photograph was taken on a recent and clandestine vacation and if Michael Carey had looked at it, it would have been the first person all night that he would not have been able to identify. His first tangible lead to track down. He placed a piece of paper between the viewed and yet to view pictures and closed the file, locking it away in his desk drawer.

CHAPTER 86

Jackson hated funerals. Hated everything about them. Open caskets. Inconsolable family members. Everyone searching to say the right thing but reduced to soulful looks, nods of the head, and the statement "I'm sorry for your loss." This one was going to be that much tougher because the only person he knew well was lying in the casket. He had packed quickly before leaving, but made sure to bring his two best suits, just in case one of them got stained or something spilled on it. It wouldn't be the first time that had happened. Experience is the best teacher. He called down to the front desk and confirmed that breakfast was going to be served for the next couple of hours. He hung up the phone and picked up his cell phone and dialed the last number he had called. He heard the cheerful sound of Jessica's voicemail and left a brief message. His thoughts returned to the task at hand as he prepared to face the day.

CHAPTER 87

Shelby Powers was online as well, checking her future husband's computer for any changes in his schedule. She clicked through his firewall and using his password, moved quickly through the various sites he had recently visited, noting with interest the two airline tickets he had recently purchased. "He knows too many women for his own good," she said aloud to no one in particular. Jessica. Who was Jessica? She searched back through the database of old clients she had downloaded from him and didn't find a Jessica. The flights were leaving from Memphis, so she had to be local. Jessica Young. She checked the white pages and found several in Memphis. But how to narrow them down? A few more keystrokes and she was looking at his directory. No entries for a Jessica. She must be new. So she searched the entries by which had been most recently entered. That one. Had to be it. "J-Pepper Jack." One phone number. Entered a week ago. She dialed the number and a breathless voice answered on the second ring. "Blue Monkey."

"Hi, may I speak to Jessica please?"

"She's not working, I think she will be here for the dinner shift."

"Oh, this is Debra Williams from UPS and we haven't been able to get a package to her. Can you verify an address for me?"

"Um, I don't know if I am supposed…"

"It would be a big help. Is she still on Poplar?"

"No, I think it's on Sheridan."

Shelby checked the white pages and there in black and white was the address of her new nemesis. "Thank you very much, you've been very helpful." Click.

She looked up Jonas' phone number and dialed it.

"Hello?"

"Hello, my strong Seattle man."

"I'm not sure who you have been talking to, but they obviously haven't seen me."

"You're funny."

"You work with what you have."

"Are you ready for the funeral today?"

"Kind of. That's not really my scene. I'm not really sure what to wear."

"Don't you have a suit?"

"Kind of. Should I wear a tie?"

Shelby struggled not to scream in the phone. "Yes, what color is it?"

"My tie?"

"Your suit."

"Oh, it's gray."

"Ok, your tie should be a little on the dark side. Somber for the occasion. No decorations or anything on it. What does yours look like?"

"It's got dice and playing cards on it."

She sighed and clenched her teeth tightly. "You need a new one. Navy blue would be ok, maybe with stripes. Think conservative."

"How long do I have to stay?"

"Until it's over. There will be a service at a church and then something graveside. You will need to go to both in case he decides to go to only one of them."

Jonas groaned. "Man…I don't know."

"Remember what's waiting for you, Jonas."

"I know. When are you coming out this way again?"

"I'm not sure. That all depends on how the next week or so goes."

"And what does it depend on?"

"On whether or not I can take care of my other loose ends. And if you are successful in doing what you are doing for me?"

"Just seeing if the guy shows up?"

"Yes."

"You don't want me to whack him or anything?"

"NO! I mean, no…nothing like that."

"Ok, don't give yourself a hernia or anything. Do you want me to call you when I see him?"

"Does your phone take pictures?"

"Doesn't everyone's now?"

"I guess so. Click a quick picture and send it to me. Then call."

"Will do. Talk to you later. Hey, do you think…" He was speaking to a dial tone. "Nice talking to you too. Geez."

CHAPTER 88

Michael Carey was ready for this day to be over already. The memorial service at the church was very emotional for everyone involved. Family members cried and wailed. There were tears and boxes of Kleenex to take care of them. All of the women needed comforting and all the men had an endless string of questions. Michael wondered if he had a sign around his neck that read "Information." There were questions about the graveside service, the will, and the murder investigation. He needed a drink. Mercifully, the funeral procession formed and headed to the cemetery. He rode in the second limousine following the hearse with a few distant relatives who were uncomfortable with silence. They chattered incessantly about anything and everything and nothing at all. Michael felt a migraine coming on. The procession came to a stop and Michael unabashedly jumped out of the backseat, almost climbing over the couple sitting nearest the door. He dialed one of the preset numbers on his cell phone and said, "I'm here and out of the car, come find me." A couple of minutes later, Douglas Jimmerson walked out from the gathering of mourners.

"Yes boss?"

"Where's your camera?"

Douglas held up the palm-sized camera he had hidden in his hand.

"Nice, wouldn't know it was there unless you were looking."

"And what am *I* looking for?"

"I'm not sure yet. Take as many wide-angle shots of the crowd as you can. I want to see who all is here. Then if you see the ever-present Detective Swift talking to anyone like he's digging, make sure and get clear close-ups. I definitely need to know what angles he is chasing."

"When do I get paid?"

The headache was worsening. Michael closed his eyes and rubbed his temples. "After the service, go get the pictures developed and meet me at my office. You can pick up a check then."

"Good, I hate having to wait on my money."

"That makes two of us."

"What?"

"Nothing. Now get to work and leave the cleavage shots out this time."

CHAPTER 89

Whistles filled the stationhouse as Will Swift strolled through, dressed to the nines in his best suit. One by one, the comments filled his ears.

"Hey honey, you looking for a date?"

"What time does Sunday School start?"

"Are you late for your wedding?"

Swift grimaced and shook his head at the commotion. "You guys need a hobby," he said to all of them, "Or better yet, to get laid." He was on his way to the funeral of the decade in Seattle. One of the elite was being laid to rest and he had a hunch that someone would be there that wasn't supposed to be. Someone that could open the right door for him to stroll through and catch a killer. He called up to his partner and waited a minute for him to come down. "That's your best suit?"

"I don't wear suits often enough to have more than a couple. Plus, they don't agree with me."

"No, it's me that suit disagrees with. I'm taking you shopping for your birthday this year. Better than that, I'll send my wife. She kind of likes looking after you."

"God knows I need it. I'll drive. Would hate to have you get wrinkled or anything."

"Cute."

The drive to the cemetery was about twenty minutes. The two partners talked about their approach in watching the proceedings and whom they thought they might see.

"Why didn't we go to the church?" Menking asked.

"I had someone there undercover. The church and the ceremony were small, invitation only. Family and a few friends. I had Josh Phillips there just in case someone crashed it or something unexpected happened. The cemetery is much more accessible and the public is invited. If someone shows their face, it will be there."

"Gotcha."

"I want you to find Michael Carey and strike up a conversation with him. See if you can rattle him at all. Maybe find out something."

"Anyone else we need to talk to?"

"Not sure. I think there will be more than one person there we need to talk to, I just am not sure who at this point."

The cemetery was the oldest in Seattle and spread across hundreds of acres. Old monuments and markers filled the spaces between winding narrow pathways worn hard by years of use. As they drove nearer the gravesite, they were slowed by a large number of cars and limousines, representing the upper crust of Seattle society. Hundreds of people walked toward the brightly colored tent, ringed by dozens of bouquets and wreaths. Will parked his department-issued Ford Taurus between a Lexus and a Cadillac Escalade, noting the difference with a wry look on his face. He put on his jacket and sunglasses and made his way to the service. His partner saw his primary target and excused himself, saying, "I need to go see that man about a dog." Will turned and made his way through the crowd. He found a good vantage point where he could see most of the crowd while not drawing any unwanted attention. A couple of minutes passed and the service started. Will continued to scan the crowd as a pair of bagpipes began to play a mournful version of "Amazing Grace." The service was dignified and a little long for Will's taste, but Seattle was able to say goodbye to one of its favorite daughters. Just as the service was ending, Will saw Jonas, to his utter amazement.

He was taking a picture of another man with his phone. Will strode over quickly over and smacked Jonas in the back of the head, causing him to drop the phone to the ground.

"Hey! What the…oh, hello Detective." Jonas attempted a crooked smile.

Will pointed at him and then bent down and picked up the phone. "Surprising to see you here Jonas. Admiring young men from afar?"

"I don't know what you are talking about Detective, I figured young men were more your area of specialty."

"Don't move from that spot. If I come back and you aren't here, it will be a long, long night for you." Will turned and spotted the young man as he was walking with the crowd. He pushed his way through and tapped the young man on the shoulder, turning him where they would face each other. "Pardon the interruption sir, but may I ask you your name." He pulled out his badge and ID and showed it. "My name is Will Swift. Detective, Seattle Police Department."

"My name is Jackson Pritchard, I believe we spoke recently."

"Could you follow me just over there?" He pointed back to the area where Jonas was standing.

"Sure Detective, is anything wrong?"

"I'm not sure yet." They walked over where Jonas looked at the ground and shifted his weight nervously. "Jonas, why were you taking this man's picture?"

"Again, Detective, I'm not sure what you are talking about. Have you been drinking before lunch again?"

"No, let's see what your phone shows." He pressed the button to activate the photo gallery, also making a mental note the time showed on the face of the phone.

"There's nothing there Detective." Jonas remained calm, as he had programmed the phone to erase pictures once he had sent them.

"I saw you pointing it at him."

"What? Someone called me and I couldn't see the screen because of the glare. So I held it up to see it better." He was amazed that he came up with the lie that quickly.

"Who was it?"

"It was your wife, she told me to hurry up because she wasn't sure when you would be home."

"I've warned you about that before Jonas, say what you want about me, but talk about my wife and you start losing blood." He scrolled through the phone's history to see the last call. There was an incoming call minutes before, but the number was blocked. "So who called?"

"I don't know. Whoever it was blocked the number and I don't answer calls like that. Did you check and see if they left a message for me?"

Will flipped the phone at him, "Don't push it. Stay close to that phone. I am still coming by later for the information you are supposed to be getting for me." He turned to Jackson, "Do you know this man?"

"No sir, I've never seen him before."

"Good enough." He turned to Jonas. "You can go, I'll be talking to you."

"I can't wait."

Turning back to Jackson, he asked, "How about a buy you a cup of coffee? It's one of many things my little town is known for."

CHAPTER 90

Jackson and Will walked back to Jackson's rental car. Will called his partner and told him the address of the coffee shop. He asked if he had talked with Michael Carey and was disappointed to hear that nothing much came out of it. He hung up and got in the passenger side after Jackson unlocked the car. Jackson slid behind the steering wheel and started the car.

Will directed him along the ten-minute drive to the coffee shop he had in mind. It was one of the dozen or so premium coffee shops that Will frequented. There was an eclectic mix of people inside--studying, writing, socializing and otherwise just being seen. They ordered and sat down at a booth near the window.

"So I'm a little surprised to see you here Jackson. From our previous conversation, it didn't seem like you and Ms. Milligan were close."

"You don't have to be close to have a good business relationship do you Detective?"

"I suppose not, but would just a good business relationship cause someone to get on a plane and fly a couple of thousand miles to attend a funeral."

"I've heard of such things before."

"I suppose so. And that's the story you are sticking with? You had done business together?"

"It's the truth."

"So what kind of business were you doing?"

"Consulting. The nature of which is personal."

"Let me explain something to you. Whatever past transgressions you may have don't interest me in the slightest bit. You have an alibi for the weekend Ms. Milligan was killed. And I believe you when you said you don't have anything to do with it. But, if you don't help me with what I need, then a couple of phone calls to Memphis Police and we start stirring up your personal and business lives. Could be quite the disruption, I might think."

"Could be, I am heading out on vacation tomorrow though. I might just choose to stay on vacation for a while."

"Kind of a Mexican standoff you think?"

"Maybe."

"It would take a simple phone call to get your passport revoked, even temporarily."

"That wouldn't be very neighborly."

"You aren't my neighbor."

"Good point. So why here, why not take me downtown?"

"Because I am not after you. We talk here, you tell me what I need to know and you stay out of the system. I always like hearing a good story over coffee anyway."

"It seems like I have been telling this entirely too often lately."

"What?"

"Nothing, just the story of my life."

"I'll bet it's a good one."

"It is. And yes, I do know Ms. Milligan a bit more than we discussed earlier. She was a client that I worked with for a few years now."

"What kind of work?"

"My card." He slid it across the table.

"I've seen it before, Jackson Pritchard, Hospitality Consultant. Translation?"

"Escort."

247

"I kind of figured something like that. Masseuse was my first guess."

"Among the many services I can provide. Sarcasm is my favorite."

"Whatever, so you had an up close and personal relationship with the deceased."

"Yes."

"Any reason that you or she would have ended it?"

"No."

"Anyone else know about it?"

"Yes, one other person."

"Who?"

"Jan Eberhardt, she's a businesswoman I know from Atlanta."

"Why would she know?"

"They are friends; I actually expected that she would be here today, but I haven't seen her. Anyway, I work only on referral and Jan referred her to me."

"Would this Ms. Eberhardt have a reason to wish her unwell?"

"Not that I know of. I think they were actually very good friends."

"Anyone after you?"

"Again, not that I know of."

"Jealous husbands or boyfriends?"

"No, you have to understand Detective, the women I work with are typically unattached. If they are married it's typically only in name or in appearances."

"So no one upset that you are tickling his wife's fancy."

"I wouldn't think so."

"A better motive might be money."

"Money is a big motivator. The main reason I did what I did."

"What you did?"

"I recently retired."

"Interesting coincidence."

"If you say so."

"So why the sudden change?"

"It wasn't sudden. I had my own business seven years. Never mind what your specific business is, run a business on your own that long and it wears on you some."

"So why quit now?"

"Two reasons. One, I met a financial milestone I set for myself."

"How much?"

"A mmmmmighty nice number."

"I think I understand. Congratulations."

"Thank you."

"And the other?"

"I met someone. Someone surprising."

"I like surprises."

"I used to not. This one was made me rethink that."

"Again, congratulations. You didn't happen to achieve your financial milestone by raking in an extra half million dollars did you?"

"No, why?"

"That's how much went missing from Ms. Milligan's accounts right after her murder." He studied Jackson's responses to gain what information he could from him. At the term murder, he didn't bat an eye. Will knew this wasn't his man.

"I'm not a thief. Or a killer. I'm just a guy trying to get by. Now I have to find a new job. I may relax for a while though.

"I hope it works out for you, honestly. Now, here's my card. If you can think of anything that might help, or if you find anything new out, call me."

"I will Detective, and thanks for the coffee."

CHAPTER 91

Jonas dialed Shelby's phone number as soon as he got out of visual range of the cemetery. His heart rate had nearly returned to normal after the run in with Captain Courageous. He cursed his rotten luck and the Detective's sense of bad timing. The phone continued to ring until it went to voice mail. Jonas grumbled to himself and hung up without leaving a message. A few minutes later his phone rang back and Shelby was on the other end of the line.

"Hey Jonas."

"Hey, I just tried to call you a few minutes ago."

"I saw. I was downloading the picture you sent me. A nice shot you took. Could you not get any closer?"

"It was crowded. And I got rushed by a detective that has a personal vendetta with me."

"A detective? Why is he after you?"

"He busted me a while back and now has me do odd computer searches and things for him."

"So why was he at the funeral."

"Search me."

"Hopefully when I see you. Has he asked you anything about the woman that was killed."

"No, why?"

"It just seems odd that he would be at the funeral I asked you to go."

There were a lot of people there. Probably a thousand or so just at the graveside service."

"Really? That is big."

"Did the guy you took the picture of notice you?"

"Not until the detective pointed me out to him."

"He SAW you?"

"Well, yes. But he doesn't know me from Adam. It's not like he's going to see me again or anything."

"I guess you are right. Did the detective question you at all?"

"Yes, but I played him off pretty well."

"Okay, I guess it could have been worse. Thank you for doing that for me, I owe you one."

"And when are you coming out this way?"

"I'm not sure, but it will be soon. I will make it worth your while."

"You have mentioned that before, I can't wait to take you up on that."

"Good things come to those who wait, my darling."

"Is that so?"

"Yes, but all in good time Jonas, all in good time."

Jonas smiled as he hung up the phone. "A fifty-fifty shot that I ever see that chick. But that fifty percent chance is worth it." He pulled up in front of his apartment and parked his car. He walked into the building and up the stairs and came face to face with Detective Swift. "Been waiting long?"

"Long enough. So what's the game Jonas?"

"Game? This is the second time you've accused me of something today and I still don't know what you are talking about."

"Okay, so where is my hacker?"

"Excuse me?"

"My hacker. The person that hacked in to Sharon Milligan's computer and took half a million dollars." Will got louder. "I asked you to have information for me and you failed to get it and gave me one of the lamest excuses I have ever heard from you. Then you assure me that you will have it for me today and I still don't have it." Will stepped up to Jonas and tapped him on the shoulder. "Then you show up at a funeral you have no business being at and you are taking photos of the mourners. So let me ask you again, WHAT IS THE GAME JONAS?"

Jonas raised his hands in surrender. "There's no game," he said loudly and then more softly, "No game."

"Well, that's good to know my friend. Good to know." He clapped Jonas on the shoulder. "So you have my information for me then?"

"Umm, yeah. About that…."

"Don't tell me, you couldn't trace him.."

"No, I found him and started tracking him. Then he hacked my system and started coming after me!" Years ago, someone had told Jonas that the best lie was wrapped up in the truth.

Will laughed loudly. "Oh no, this is too good to be true. The great Jonas? Hacked? What are your friends in the no-tan club going to say?"

"It's not funny Detective. You have a serious hacker after you and you do what I did, you dump and run. I shut it all down and cut him off before he got any deeper into my stuff."

"Did it work?"

"Yes, from what I can tell, he didn't see much. Not enough time. But he left a virus that I was lucky to find. I went through my system three times just to make sure. That's a dangerous person you had me checking out."

Will stared at Jonas for what seemed like an eternity. "If I find out that there is anything else to this story, you'll be back inside for the twelve years you have left on your sentence. And my favorite judge will ban you from using a computer ever again."

"You can't do that."

"No? Ever see those 'habitual offenders' that just can't drive a car unless they have knocked back a fifth of bourbon before hand? They are riding the bus because they are banned from driving. Or the woman that has bounced or forged hundreds of checks? She lives on a cash basis now. It could happen to you brother, don't think that it couldn't."

"Ok, so you could make it happen. Tough guy." Jonas shook his head. "That doesn't change the fact that I don't have anything."

"All right Jonas, enough beating my chest for one day…"

"You should probably go beat something else. I can see the calluses on your hand from here."

"And I was going to buy you dinner. You just don't know when to stop do you?"

"It's your world boss. Whatever you say."

CHAPTER 92

A typical Monday ended at the computer shop and Shelby floated the idea for everyone to go to happy hour. "How about the Blue Monkey?" Everyone agreed and headed in that general direction. Shelby was the first to arrive and spotted a table with a good view of the bar. She reserved it and ordered a glass of wine and waited for the rest of her crew to arrive. Monday nights can be slow in the bar business and tonight was no exception. Shelby was quieter than usual, a fact that her coworkers commented on. She explained she was just a little tired but that she was enjoying just people-watching. That started a new conversational thread on people watching as a social sport. What Shelby had actually been doing was looking and listening for Jessica Young to show up. An hour or so later, she did. She entered with a hurried look on her face and an oversized manager following her around like a puppy dog. They talked for a few minutes but Shelby was unable to overhear anything they said. She thought this Jessica was cute enough, but nowhere near fitting for someone like her fiancée. The slightly askew wheels in her head turned and came to the conclusion that she must have something on her man. Some kind of secret he was hiding or someone he was protecting.

Something noble. Simple solution then, she had to go. "Sorry Jessica," Shelby thought to herself, "you seem like a nice person, too."

Jessica tied the apron around her waist and finished her conversation with Mike. "So you will come get Max tonight after work then?"

"Yes, I would love to dog sit while you jet around the Caribbean with Wonder Boy. Why do you want me to get him tonight and not tomorrow?"

Jessica chuckled but then spoke a little more seriously. She looked at her feet when she did, not knowing exactly how to frame her thoughts. "Because I am going to pamper myself tomorrow, get my nails and toes done, tan a bit to make sure I don't burn too badly. Although that wouldn't be a bad way to get some aloe rubbed on me. And he's not Wonder Boy; he's different Mike. He talks and doesn't hold back anything. He opened up to me like no one ever has the other night."

"Just be careful. I don't want to see you cry any more."

"I know you don't, and I love you for it."

"Well, at the very least you get to go swim in the ocean and lay in the warm sun while it's freezing up here. Do they have any of those nude beaches down there?"

"Ugh, you would go there. You've been talking to Melanie too much."

"Not talking too, just overhearing. And getting phone calls from every Tom, Dick, and Harry in Memphis regarding her availability."

Melanie walked by and snorted, "You said 'Dick'."

Mike pointed at her animatedly, "You see what I have to put up with?"

"It's impossible to stop her, I've tried."

"You haven't really tried," her friend came back.

"Okay, maybe not. I had to live vicariously through someone."

"Well get ready for a wild, vicarious night tonight baby girl, there are three guys at the end of the bar that are CUTE. And they do love me already."

Jessica shook her head back and forth, "You see? It's hopeless."

"I would invite you to be my wingman, but noooooo, she's saving herself for Mr. Right, aren't you?" Melanie teased. Jessica looked down again, biting her lip. "Aren't you?" She tired to look anywhere else but at her friend. Melanie almost jumped over the bar, knocking an empty beer bottle off to the floor in the process. "You didn't!"

"Didn't what?" She buried her face in her hands.

"You did!" Melanie screamed and hugged her friend tightly. Then she playfully swatted her with the dishtowel in her hand. "Oh my god, why didn't you tell me earlier?"

"Well, I don't know, it just kind of happened and I'm still, well, basking in it."

"Basking? That sounds serious. Was it that good?"

Her face turned a bright shade of pink. She covered her eyes with her hand, "Ugh I can't hide a thing from you!"

"Details, I need details girl."

"No details for you, I don't kiss and tell."

"I don't want to know about the kissing, I want to know about the other stuff."

Jessica bit her lip and bounced up and down nervously. "It wasn't mind-blowing great, but for a first time it was really, really good."

"Ooooh, I'm jealous. But I'm happy for you, I really am. Bring me back something from the islands?"

"What do you want?"

"I don't know, something you think I would bring back."

"I don't want to bring back a disease!"

Melanie covered her mouth in mock surprise. Mike tried as hard as he could, but couldn't stifle the laugh that exploded loudly from within. He looked at Melanie and reminded her that the Monday Night Football crowd would probably start coming in and to get the bar ready. He turned back to Jessica. "Please be careful. You're my favorite Jessica."

"I'm your only Jessica!" She playfully punched him in the arm and moved behind the bar.

Shelby had heard enough. She excused herself from her party, telling them she had a few things to take care of tonight and dropped a ten-dollar bill for her tab. On the way out of the bar, she waved at Jessica and smiled. Jessica looked at her with a puzzled look on her face and turned to Melanie. "Who was that?"

CHAPTER 93

Jackson was exhausted. He dropped down onto the sofa in the living room part of his suite with a beer in his hand. He had shed his jacket and tie in the elevator and now he kicked his shoes off to the floor. He took a long drink and enjoyed the taste and the quiet of the suite. It lasted all of 30 seconds and then his cell phone rang. It was Jan Eberhardt.

"Good evening, you sexy man you. I saw that you tried to call me last night but I was on an airplane."

"Hey, Jan. Where are you now?"

"In your hotel lobby, if I know you at all."

"You are in Seattle? What are you doing here? How long are you going to be here?

"She was my friend long before I introduced you two, sweet cakes."

"Oh yeah, well that makes sense. I didn't see you today, where were you?"

"Out of sight; didn't feel like being seen."

"Gotcha."

"Feel like some company? Meredith is with me, but she is in her own suite. I think she said she missed a call from you as well by the way. Was there anything specific you were calling about?"

"Yes, you can come up." He gave her the suite number. "And I am glad you called, I do have something to talk to you about."

A few minutes later Jackson heard a knock on his door. He got up and strode across the floor and opened it and then leaned against the door frame.

"Hello Jackson," Jan purred seductively.

"Hello Jan, won't you come in?"

"Depends on what position you have me in." Jackson shook his head, looking down at the floor.

"All I have is beer, I wasn't expecting any company."

"I'm good although I will probably need a lot of water later."

"About that, why don't we go sit down and talk for a bit."

"Talking is overrated, but as you wish."

"So how much have you had to drink already?"

"At least one bottle of champagne. Maybe more. Why?"

"No reason, just haven't seen you drunk in a long time."

Unexpectedly, Jan broke down and started to cry. "God, I miss her Jackson. Why did this have to happen?"

Jackson moved next to her and put his arm around her. "I just don't know."

"It doesn't make sense, she didn't have any enemies. Everyone loved her."

"Well, the police said there was a large amount of money missing."

"Was that the guy that was talking to you after the funeral?"

"Yes, I guess you saw that."

"Yep, he looked very serious. I was going to say hello then, but that conversation looked a little deep to me."

Jackson handed her a tissue and she wiped her eyes. "It was. The detective is working hard to find out who killed Sharon."

"Do you think I need to talk to him?"

"I don't know. Can't hurt. He has your name."

"Why?"

"Because he asked me how I came to work with Sharon. At first I didn't want to get into it, but he pushed a bit and I am ready to get it behind me."

"Get what behind you?"

"This, all of it, the reason I called you last night."

She wasn't crying anymore, her tone and posture was much more serious. "Ok, you have my attention."

"Well, to put it simply, I am retiring."

"Really? And why would you want to do that? You're GREAT at it, you get to travel, make very good money, and you get to hang out with me!"

"All very good reasons to keep doing it, but I want to do something different."

"Like what?"

"Something…anything. Travel…actually see the world. And as a tourist instead of as a job."

"You're kind of a tourist now."

"True, but I am typically working the vast majority of the time I am travelling. I'm not getting any younger. I want to see things."

"And who do you want to see them with?"

"Well, that's the other part. I met someone amazing and I have to see if this is going to lead somewhere."

"You have met hundreds if not thousands of women. Why this one?"

"Hard to explain, so I'm not going to. You know me well enough to know that is saying something."

"I do and I am impressed. And a little sad and still a little drunk… and horny. How about one for the road?"

"Thank you, I can't. And thank you for everything. I hope you know how important you are to me."

She turned her head and looked at him with a sideways glance. "I think I do. But not one for the road?" They both laughed. "Okay, well I am off in search of a little satisfaction. Maybe we can have lunch with Meredith tomorrow?"

"I can't. My flight leaves early."

"Take a later one."

"No can do, Madame," Jackson bowed deeply to her. "I am meeting her at the airport. We're flying to a tropical island for some alone time."

"Sounds lovely. Send me a postcard?"

Jackson laughed again. "I will. Take care of yourself Jan."

"Don't be a stranger." She walked to the door then stopped and turned back towards him. "Care to make a friendly wager?"

Jackson tilted his head and smiled. "What kind of wager?"

"A three day weekend at a place of my choosing. No work, no meetings, just you and me."

"And what would we be betting on?"

"That within three months you're bored and back working."

"What if I win?"

"You won't."

"Well, we can't bet if I can't win."

"Fair enough. If you aren't bored then it could only be that this girl is really the one. So I will pay for your honeymoon."

"Tempting. But she's not someone I want to be betting on."

"Wow. With that attitude, you might actually win. Good thing we aren't betting. Ciao. And do stay in touch."

"I will. Be careful out there."

CHAPTER 94

Time flew by in a blink of an eye at The Blue Monkey. Jessica closed her shift and counted out her register. Good tip night as usual. A little extra traveling money never hurt anyone. She felt energized like she hadn't worked at all. The butterflies in her stomach were banging into each other like teenagers at a rock concert. She literally couldn't wait to get home so she could get packed and get to sleep on time. Early even. She would have everything ready so that once Mike picked up Max she could be in bed. Melanie came around the bar and hugged her. "Call me when you can. I love you, girl."

"I love you, too…and I will." She waved at Mike who looked at his watch. He held up one finger and mouthed "One hour" to her and waved. She nodded in agreement and strolled out of the bar on cloud nine and drove home.

About an hour later, Mike left the restaurant's night manager in charge of closing up The Blue Monkey. He got in his car and drove straight to Jessica's house. He was tired and didn't want to belabor the fact that she was going to the Caribbean with this guy she just met. He pulled up and wasn't surprised at all that she had left the light on and the front door was propped open waiting for him. He could see inside the door and saw two suitcases packed and ready to go. He sighed deeply, mentally letting her go. Putting the car into park, he made his way up the driveway and knocked on the door, opened it and announced himself. "Hello?"

Max came bounding down the hallway and wagging his tail. He sniffed Michael's ankles and let himself be petted warmly. "Hey! Thank you so much again for taking care of him while I am away. You're the best."

"I know. It's one of the better-kept secrets in Memphis though. Maybe you could tell a friend or two about me."

"She wouldn't appreciate you as much as I do."

"Right, but she might sleep with me though."

"There's more to life than that and you know it."

"Spoken by someone who has gotten some lately."

She made a face and made a noise of mock shock. "You're terrible."

"You would have to be doing it to be terrible at it."

"Good point." She brought a bag of dog food and his food and water bowls and handed them to him. "Just a cup in the morning and at night, and walk him if you can. I don't want him to get fat."

"I don't think he will change that much in four days. Or five days. Which is it?"

"I think five. I'll let you know though." She hugged him and kissed his cheek then bent down and kissed Max on the head and put his leash on him before handing it to her boss.

"At least I got kissed before the dog."

"You're silly. Thank you again; now go, so I can go to sleep."

"Ok, have fun and good night."

"Good night!" Jessica said as she closed the door.

Mike loaded Max and his things into his car and got in and drove away. "At least she left the light on until we left," he said to Max, patting him again on the head. He drove home without giving the car he passed on his way out of her neighborhood a second thought.

Shelby waited ten seconds after the car drove by before sitting back up. He had been an easy target to follow, walking straight to his car and driving straight to the house. HER house. She fingered the pistol stashed under the driver's seat and wondered if she could go through with it. A vision of Jackson appeared in her mind and immediately she knew she could. Then she remembered another job that needed doing as well and she mentally switched gears. The lights went off at HER house and everything was dark. A report she had read online said on average that people fell asleep within seventeen minutes of going to bed. She would give it thirty just to make sure.

Half an hour later, Shelby slipped in through the back door, pausing silently for almost a minute to let her eyes adjust to the darkness. She had left the pistol in the car. Moving slowly, she found her way to the kitchen and looked quietly for the utility drawer. Everyone had a utility drawer. It's where you kept spare batteries and tape and the little twist ties that came off of the bags that held loaves of bread. And scissors. She was looking for scissors. And she found them. Right where she knew they would be. The surgical gloves she wore freed her from worrying about fingerprints and the fear of getting caught. She moved stealthily through the house to the hallway and found her luggage. She unzipped the main pocket very slowly and took a quick glance inside. A swimsuit and several pieces of lingerie were most prominent. Shelby reached in her pocket and pulled out one of the bullets she had taken out of the pistol and tucked it in the bottom corner of the suitcase. Quickly she replaced the clothing and quietly zipped the luggage closed. The slippers she was wearing allowed her to move without sound as she moved to the bedroom. HER bedroom. Her heart raced and she gripped the scissors tightly in her hand. It would have to be quick. One movement and done. In and out and she was a ghost. Time to go. The bedroom door was slightly ajar as she approached it. She pressed against it slightly and immediately saw the bed where SHE was sleeping facing her. HER arms were wrapped around her pillow and she breathed slowly and silently in and out. Shelby moved forward painfully slowly and approached the bed. She paused and stared at her face and felt a mix of powerful emotions. Hatred for the woman that was trying to ruin her future life. Excitement as adrenaline surged through her veins. And then she noticed just how beautiful Jessica was. Moonlight streamed in through the window and framed her face perfectly. Under different circumstances...she pushed the thought from her mind. She had one job in mind and it was time.

Slowly she raised the scissors and prepared to make the one quick cut needed to do the job. She hoped to get it right so it wouldn't make a total mess of things. She reached out with her other hand and grasped the strands of hair covering her face and with the scissors snipped them off quietly. There were five or six strands, plenty to accomplish the task she had in mind. She raised them to her lips and kissed them softly, freezing as Jessica shifted her weight and moaned softly. Remembering suddenly where she was, she walked softly and slowly backwards out of the room. She moved the door back to where she had originally found it and made her way to the back door. Slipping outside, she checked the street for cars or people, waiting almost a minute before walking out of the yard and up the street to her car.

CHAPTER 95

Jackson stirred early from a restful sleep, beating the alarm clock and wake up call by a full thirty minutes. He shaved and showered quickly and was downstairs eating breakfast by seven. His flight was still four hours away and he relished not having to rush. He was enjoying his eggs and bacon and reading the paper when Will Swift approached. Jackson folded the paper and sat it in the chair next to him.

"Detective, Good morning. Please, join me."

"Why thank you. I haven't eaten yet."

"I haven't even looked; how is the weather outside."

"Nice. It's still cold, but the sun is shining."

"Great, it's much nicer flying in good weather."

"When do you leave?"

"Taxi should be here in about 90 minutes or so." The waiter appeared silently. "Please, order, my treat."

"That's not necessary."

"I insist."

Will ordered and the waiter took his leave. "Thank you, my turn next time."

"Not sure when that might be unless you come down to Memphis. I don't really have any other reason to be here."

"Oh, I don't know. Surely you will come back for the trial when I catch the killer."

"I hadn't thought of that. I just might."

"Do you mind if I ask you a few more questions?"

"No, not at all."

"What kind of woman was Sharon, sexually speaking I guess."

"You don't beat around the bush do you detective?"

"I guess not. There's an unsolved case back in Tennessee that has some similarities and I am trying to tie this case somewhere."

"She was pretty reserved. Nothing way out of the ordinary."

"Way out of the ordinary? As defined by?"

"I don't know, experience I guess. I could be considered an expert in such matters."

"Did you field odd requests from time to time?"

"Yes, but mostly in the interview process. Despite what you might think, I was very particular about with whom I worked. Anything you or any average Joe might consider out of bounds was usually a red flag for me."

"Like what?"

"Anything illegal. Anything violent or leaning towards violence. I have been asked to help play out fantasies where someone is being raped or beaten or things like that and I just wouldn't." Jackson leaned a little to his left and noticed an older woman seated behind the detective straining to overhear their conversation. "Although I did make an exception one time for this nosy woman that was trying to eavesdrop on THE THINGS I WAS SAYING."

The detective looked confused until the woman behind him dropped her coffee cup, spilling its contents all over the table and the man sitting with her. Will and Jackson both laughed loudly.

"And what did you do to her?"

"I embarrassed her. You should try that sometime, it can be rather amusing."

"I bet you are fun in bars."

"People-watching is part of what made me good at my job detective."

"It's what makes me good at my job as well. And you said made. So you are still going to retire?"

"Absolutely. She's worth it."

"Good for you. Ok, so back to Sharon, bizarre requests or anything like that?"

"No. Despite being a supremely successful businesswoman, she had trouble seeing herself as sexy; she simply lacked confidence in being a woman. So I was very attentive. We held hands a lot. Just made her feel good as much as I could."

"Sounds like you were part therapist as well."

"I never made her lie on my couch or anything. Well, not specifically."

"Did she ever talk about being with a woman. Sexually."

"Not to me. I wouldn't think that would be up her alley. I think the main thing that she was looking for was confirmation from a man that she was beautiful and sexy without worrying about whether or not she was rich or powerful. With me there was no hidden agenda so she was free to be herself without having to worry about anything else."

"But she paid you, doesn't that change the dynamic?"

"I suppose it could. Again, I'm not a therapist."

"Now how about this other woman you mentioned yesterday. Jan something."

"Eberhardt. I saw her last night. She's still in town if you would like to talk with her."

"I would. How can I contact her?"

Jackson gave him the number. She asked if I thought she should talk with you and I told her she should."

"Thanks. Cooperative witnesses make my job much easier."

"I didn't witness anything."

"It's just a term. You can give me background and everything I need to get where I want to go. So how long have you known Ms. Eberhardt?"

"About seven years and it's Mrs. Eberhardt. She's married. He thinks happily. She thinks otherwise. I think it's because he is a milquetoast."

"I see. And Jan wasn't happy with that?"

"She was bored. That's one reason she and I began working together."

"And she referred you to Sharon."

"Yes."

There was a silent pause of several seconds. "Do you want to expound on that?"

"Not necessarily. I'm happy to answer anything questions you think are relevant."

"Why would she refer you to someone? Wouldn't she want to keep you to herself?"

Jackson laughed. "Well, my clients know me as someone that can't be kept. Until now I suppose. They also couldn't afford to keep me full-time. So, no I don't think she ever thought to keep me to herself."

"So she just showed up one day? How does this work?"

"Like I said before I work on referral only now. So, someone will call and tell me that they were looking to do some work on a specific weekend. Before we go any further I ask them how they were referred to me. They tell me and I ask for their contact information and call the person they mentioned. I get as much information as I can before I call the person back. Then we set a time to meet and talk. Kind of an interview. I find out the things that I need to know and answer any questions they might have. I explain what I do and how much I cost and if everything goes well, we make arrangements."

"Is that how it went with Ms. Milligan?"

"Yes." Jackson took a drink of water while finishing his breakfast. He pushed his plate to the side and getting the waiter's attention, ordered a mug of hot chocolate.

"Hot chocolate?"

"I've been drinking it more lately. Thinking of giving up coffee."

"Oh, you wouldn't fit in very well in Seattle."

Jackson shrugged his shoulders.

"Did Ms. Eberhardt refer anyone else to you?"

"A few people, one just last weekend."

"And how did that go?"

"Well."

"But you are retiring."

"Yes, she was my last client. Nice too."

"How many clients do you have? Or did I suppose."

"A little over thirty. That seemed to be a pretty manageable number."

"Anyone upset that you aren't working any more?"

"I wouldn't say upset. Disappointed maybe. Less from an attachment standpoint and more from a schedule or routine disruption standpoint I am sure."

"Anyone ever get jealous?"

"Not any that stayed clients."

"So it happened?"

"I had a few that tried to make me a kept man, I just explained to them that wasn't going to happen."

"Any clients go away angry?"

"None that I know about."

"Threats? Anyone tell you they were going to get you or anything?"

"No. I think you may be overestimating my level of attachment my clients held with me."

"Just asking." Will finished his breakfast as well. Jackson got the attention of the waiter and paid the bill, adding a generous tip. "How about I drive you to the airport. It's not far and I am going that direction anyway."

"As long as you aren't put out."

"Not at all, my pleasure. Plus, your former profession is fascinating. I would love to hear a little more about it."

CHAPTER 96

Across town, another breakfast meeting was taking place. Art Menking slid the dossier across the table to Michael Carey looked at it and smiled.

"And this is who?"

"His name is Jackson Pritchard. Apparently he is a rather high-priced escort and had worked for your client."

"What? I never knew of any such a thing." Michael searched his mind for any references to escorts or prostitutes in any of her records and came up blank. Looking at this man's picture didn't ring a bell either.

"He was pretty specific, apparently."

"Well there's your suspect then. Anyone that would sell themselves for money would obviously be a prime suspect in that much money being missing."

"We're searching for a killer first and a thief second Mr. Carey."

"Well of course…as it should be," he stammered.

"Uh huh. Swift doesn't see him as a suspect for the former. He might be for the latter though. I think they are talking as we speak. I'll see what I can find out."

"Fantastic. Our little arrangement seems to be producing fruit already. I'm quite pleased." Michael's mind focused on tracking the man before him down. He took an envelope out of his jacket pocket and handed it over to the detective sitting in front of him.

Art opened the envelope and counted about three times as much as in the previous envelope he had gotten. "Pleasure doing business with you."

"There's still more. Keep me up to date if you don't mind."

"You can count on that. So let's say that you find what you are looking for? What are you going to do with the bad guy?"

"Turn him over to you of course. Once we have recovered what belongs to the estate."

"And if you can't do that?"

"Oh I don't think we will have any trouble doing that. If not, we'll just have to find a way to get it out of him."

The detective smiled. "Just another scumbag off the streets as far as I am concerned."

"When does Mr. Pritchard leave?"

"Today. Not sure what flight. I know it is Seattle to Memphis, that flight switches planes in Detroit I think."

Michael took out his phone and took a picture of the photo in the dossier the detective had assembled and then sent to it another phone. He then called and followed that up with a quick text message. "The photo I sent is a man headed to the airport, get there and see if you can ID him. Call me with info. MC."

"That should do nicely Detective Menking, very nicely, indeed."

CHAPTER 97

The ride to the airport went quickly. Traffic was light, as they had missed the rush hour and lunch hour traffic. Will Swift had switched out of detective mode and was simply talking to Jackson as a guy with advice to give. "It's a good thing what you are doing. You lived outside the lines for seven years and it's time to get back and be a part of society."

"What you don't seem to get, Detective, is that I was a part of society. I filled a very useful role. Say what you want about what I did, but I made thirty plus women's lives better and made them more productive or relaxed or focused or whatever it was they needed on the trips I took with them. Along the way, I have been a full participant in the economy. Hotel suites, food, drinks, rental cars, airline tickets, clothes, tickets to the symphony, movies, I can go on and on. Sure, I made good money, but a lot of people around me made money off of what I did."

"So would you make the same argument about drug dealers? They buy cars and clothes and dinners and drinks and cell phones and a lot of the same things that you do."

"I wouldn't make the same argument. They sell a product that is inherently dangerous to your health and causes more crime in its use and distribution. By the way, when did you become my priest? Or congressman?"

Will laughed. "I'm neither. Just a guy that has seen other people rationalize their place in the world that did similar things like you and watched them flush their lives down the drain. Drugs, pimps, bad people. They usually end up in jail or the morgue. You won't end up there, hopefully. Good for you."

"Thank you, Detective."

"Please, it's Will. You have my card; use it if you get jammed up sometime."

"Thanks, I just might have to take you up on that."

Jackson got out of the car and grabbed his bags out of the trunk. He and the detective shook hands and he gathered his things and headed inside the airport. Check-in was relatively painless and he meandered through the concourse, killing time before his flight boarded. He fished his cell phone out of his pocket and dialed Jessica. She picked up the phone on the third ring, sounding out of breath.

"I didn't interrupt anything did I?"

She laughed. "No, just getting my bags out to the car. I left my phone in the house and ran back in to get it. How are you?"

"I'm good, had a great breakfast with a Seattle police detective."

"And how was that?"

"It was good. The eggs were a little overdone."

Jessica laughed with her whole body. "So are you under arrest? Do I need to not go to the airport?"

"Sadly, you will have to keep our date."

"Not sad for me. I tanned yesterday."

"Good thinking. There's a little island we will have to ourselves for at least a day. Clothing of course is optional."

"Sounds exciting."

"It does actually, doesn't it?"

"Are you at the airport?"

"Yep, boarding in about thirty minutes. I should be there about 3:30 or so and our flight south leaves at 5:30. Oooh, we can grab a sandwich at Interstate."

"Interstate?"

"Interstate Barbecue. After taking me to your favorite spot, I am taking you to mine. You've never eaten there?"

"Nope."

"The best barbecue sandwich you will ever eat, period. Place has been around on Third Street forever. The sandwiches are so good that they opened up a spot in the airport. That one did so well that I think they opened another spot to cut down on the traffic at the other one."

"Sounds promising."

"It is, messy too. You have to have a stack of napkins handy just to eat it."

"Maybe I would prefer to clean you up with something else."

"This imagination thing is something we are definitely going to have to explore thoroughly."

"I'm looking forward to that."

"Me too. I'm going to go get an ice cream before we board. Can't wait to see you."

"Are you bringing me something sweet too?"

"Besides me?"

"That will do...for now."

"Good to know. See you in a few hours."

CHAPTER 98

Shelby Powers got to the Memphis airport around noon. Considering the possibility that it could rain, she had wheeled her car into the parking garage adjacent to the airport in order to keep her car out of the weather. Plus, it made for a much shorter walk to the door. She took her ticket and found a spot as close to the concourse as possible and wheeled her luggage inside. She checked herself and her bags onto the flight at the self-service console, delivering the luggage to the Homeland Security area for further screening. She wondered if they would find anything they would deem a security risk but quickly shook off that thought. The idea of strange men rummaging through her things gave her the willies and she shuddered in response. She packed an oversized suitcase with a few different outfits and got ready for her flight. She printed her boarding pass and went back and double-checked her flight arrangements and then made sure she had packed everything she would need for the quick trip. Glancing at the clock, she saw that she had a good half hour or so before she had to board, so she logged onto her computer and went through her normal surfing routine. E-mail, check. Daily horoscope, check. Hollywood gossip, check. Breaking into to Jackson Pritchard's computer to check up on him. Check. She was hungry so she packed a light snack to carry on in her purse. She grabbed the sections of the paper she had brought with her, including the crosswords and the Sudoku. She liked the fact that the Sunday paper carried the New York Times crossword in addition to their usual offering. She should be able to focus for the entire flight and not be bothered by anyone else.

Logging off the computer, Shelby did a quick once over to make sure she didn't forget anything or leave anything on that was supposed to be off. She repacked her carry on and walked down the concourse to the gate where her flight would be boarding. She was booked on two different return flights, one tonight and another the next morning, just in case she didn't get everything taken care of like she wanted. The flight was pretty full and Shelby was fortunate that only one of the adjacent two seats was taken. She spread out her paper somewhat and began working the first crossword as they taxied away from the gate. The flight itself was uneventful and Shelby was careful to remain unnoticed. To everyone that crossed her path, Shelby was average and unassuming. She could have been any of a million travelers that day. As soon as she left anyone's line of vision, she was forgotten. The very thought caused a cruel smile to creep across her face momentarily. An extra ounce of self control exerted and it was gone.

An hour or so later the plane landed and Shelby followed the inane instructions from the pilot and crew and exited the airplane. Her luggage was already waiting at the baggage claim carousel and she walked directly from the plane and retrieved it. Walking out of the airport, Shelby grabbed the first taxi she saw and gave the driver the address of a high-rise luxury hotel in downtown Seattle. The drive was thirty minutes or so and Shelby never said a word. She nodded her head in agreement with the driver a few times and hummed to herself the rest of the ride. The trip ended and she paid the driver, tipping him an unforgettably average amount. After he had driven away, Shelby walked the six blocks to the hotel that was her intended destination. She entered with a code she had gleaned from the building's "Secure" website. She entered the building and immediately made her way to the service elevator that went down to the basement. She found a bathroom and changed her clothes and added a wig, a pair of gloves that extended past the elbow and dark sunglasses, obscuring her appearance. She extracted the several pieces of the small, snub-nosed pistol she had disassembled before packing it earlier and put it back together. She stashed the suitcase in the janitorial closet and checked her watch, noting the time. She took a back stairwell up four flights of stairs where it opened into the adjoining parking deck. She walked to the middle of the back row, ducking down behind the behemoth SUV parked in slot 96.

Exactly eleven minutes later, Meredith Gregory wheeled her rented Lexus into slot 98 of the parking deck and stopped. She turned the car off and hung up her cell phone almost simultaneously, briefly pondering the symmetry of the two actions done at once. The past two days had lasted longer than she had thought between the funeral and the meetings Jan had scheduled. Thinking back on her weekend with Jackson, she remembered the vow she had made to herself to live her life instead of living to work. Maybe she would go enjoy drinking coffee and watching the rain or go see a movie or something. Out of the corner of her eye, she saw another woman, a taller blonde fumbling with her handbag like she couldn't find something. She turned and asked her if she could help her with something and to her surprise the answer came back, "You can mind your own fucking business" with the flattest tone she had ever heard. Meredith heard a deafening boom and then everything went black.

Shelby surveyed the parking deck and confirmed that they were alone. She walked up to her latest victim and dropped two strands of the hairs from her pocket. Then she dropped two more at the spot where she had waited. The pistol had sounded much louder than when she had fired it the one time before at the range in Memphis. She had bought it from a guy she knew only as Carlos, and he assured her that the weapon was clean and untraceable. She walked down two flights of stairs and dropped the pistol into the trashcan on the lower level of the parking deck after wrapping the last hair in her pocket around the trigger. Then two more flights of stairs and back to the closet where she had left her luggage. She changed clothes again, making sure to repack everything she wasn't wearing. She looked around and made sure she hadn't left anything, grabbed the suitcase and headed back up the service elevator and out of the building. There wasn't a lot of traffic, another factor that Shelby was thankful for. She waited about five minutes for a taxi to come by. She hailed it and headed back to the airport, checking to see that she had four hours until her flight left. She checked her bags in and made her way to one of the several restaurants at the end of the concourse and set down for a nice lunch before flying back to Memphis.

CHAPTER 99

An hour or so after he dropped Jackson off at the airport Will made a beeline for the office. There he rendezvoused with his partner and the Lieutenant. He recounted where they were in the interview process and admitted that they didn't have much in the way of solid leads.

"Detective Menking seems to think that you have a decent lead with the Pritchard kid from Memphis," Lieutenant Morse offered.

Will gave his partner a sideways glance, "Does he now? Well, he has a very solid alibi for the weekend the murder happened as he was in Washington, D.C. I spent time with yesterday and again this morning and have effectively ruled him out as a suspect. This may be related to him in some way, but I don't think he was involved."

"Well, who else stands out?"

"No one, really. Although my gut tells me that Jonas has gotten himself involved in one way or another. I'm going to head over there in a bit to flesh out just how deeply."

Art Menking spoke up, "I had a good conversation with Michael Carey the other day. He seems very anxious for the killer to be caught."

"And the money recovered," Will finished. "That's the only thing that barracuda is concerned about. That and the reputation of his firm. Actual concern for his client falls somewhere around sixth or seventh on the list."

"But is on the list," the lieutenant interjected.

"Yes, I suppose it is."

"He did say something the other day that didn't quite ring true now that you mention it. How about I run over there and we can meet up for a lunch after you rough Jonas up a bit?"

"Better yet, why don't you come to Jonas' with me and then we can go see the good counselor after we eat. I haven't gotten to spend nearly as much time with him as I would like."

Menking nodded. Jackson turned to the lieutenant. "I've got a couple of other people to talk to today as well. We'll catch up later this evening and get you up to speed. I checked with the tip line people, they've got nothing. Just a bunch of wackos trying to get paid. How have our net guys come along with the traces?"

Art looked at his notes. "Nowhere that I can tell. They have followed a number of different leads but they all seem to dead-end. Whoever the bad guy is knows their way around a computer."

"Did you get a sense that Pritchard was tech savvy?" the Lieutenant asked.

"I really don't think it's him, but I won't rule him out just yet. That Nashville murderer keeps popping up in my head. The way that victim and Sharon Milligan were killed seems to be too closely related to be a coincidence."

"That's an important detail. Glad you both are on the case. Now how about we get it wrapped up?"

"Thanks, boss. I do what I can."

"So what do you need from me?"

"I may need to go down to Memphis, sniff around a bit. This afternoon and tomorrow I am going to call several leads and check out the pictures we had taken of the crowd at the funeral and the graveside service. See if anything comes out of that."

"Okay, just let me know."

Will and his partner closed up their respective notebooks and headed out to the parking lot where both of their cars were parked. "Just need to make a quick call, Will. You driving or me?"

"I will, your car still smells like feet."

"It was tamales, I already told you that."

"Whatever, I've had tamales and they didn't smell like that. That's feet smell."

"Whatever, yourself. Grab your stuff and I will be right back." He wandered away for a bit and dialed. "Hello? Michael Carey, please. Art Menking. Hi, Mr. Carey, it's Detective Menking. I can't come by now, but Swift wants to come by and talk with you this afternoon. I don't know, he said after lunch. Maybe 1:30 or 2:00. Okay, see you then." He walked back over and sat down in the passenger seat.

"Who was that?"

"No one, just returning a call from your mother."

"Bite me, partner."

"Not today. Come to think of it, not ever. So..."

"What?"

"Buckle up for safety. It's the law, you know."

Will rolled his eyes as they rolled into traffic.

CHAPTER 100

"You have sauce on your nose."

"Mmpfh mmrglm meck moo."

"On your neck, too? Well, not yet, but I can fix that." He leaned over and kissed her lightly on the neck. "You really shouldn't talk with your mouth full, I don't think Miss Manners would approve. Now, tilt your head back just a bit, mmm yes, that's it. I love that little spot right there."

She chased down the huge bite she had taken with a drink of her Coke. "Wow, this IS a good sandwich. You take me to all the best places."

Jackson chuckled, "Stick with me, honey, we'll see the world together."

"From coach?"

"Hmmm, we are in coach come to think of it. I'll see if I can get us an upgrade."

"I have all the confidence in the world in your abilities."

Shelby reached into her purse and pulled out her boarding pass, handing it to the attendant waiting by the gate. By the time she boarded her plane, she had finished the second crossword puzzle and had started on the Sudoku. She was pleased that neither puzzle had caused her much trouble and was certain she would have the Sudoku done in no time at all.

Jackson and Jessica finished their lunch and made their way out of the concourse and to the ticket counter. "Hello again, Angela," he said to the woman he had spoken with earlier.

"Hello, Mr. Pritchard, is there a problem with your tickets?"

"No, but this is going to be a special trip for us; I was wondering if you could check and see if we could upgrade our seats."

"I'll check, I don't think your flight is sold out." She clattered what seemed like a thousand keystrokes. "You've got the mileage…and yes, we've got the seats. Would you like to upgrade them?"

"Absolutely, and thank you very much Angela."

"My pleasure. If you would give me back your tickets and boarding passes, I will print your new ones." Jackson and Jessica chatted for a moment while the transaction was being processed, their eyes not leaving each other for a moment. Angela interrupted them with their new tickets and boarding passes. "Your plane will be boarding in about twenty minutes, you should get through security and get to your gate as soon as you can."

"Thank you Angela, I appreciate your help today." He took Jessica by the hand and they moved quickly down the terminal to go through airport security again. It only took a few minutes and they were through and they walked briskly down the concourse until they reached their gate. A few minutes and a couple of bottled waters out of a vending machine and they boarded. They were greeted warmly by the flight staff and settled into their seats, looking forward to their first adventure together.

CHAPTER 101

Will Swift knocked on the now familiar door to Jonas' apartment. There was no answer. He knocked again and still nothing. He stood for a minute and thought, then pulled out a cell phone and dialed his number. Two rings and the door opened enough for Jonas to peek out.

"What do you want?"

"I want you to open the door Jonas. Then I want you to talk to me like I'm three."

"Not much of a stretch detective, you been taking night classes?"

"Hysterical." The door opened and the two detectives walked in.

"You need backup now, Detective?"

"Nope, just a witness that can testify to the fact that you came at me with that knife. 'Yes, your honor, it was tragic but I had to kill him. I felt that my life and my partner's were in eminent and life-threatening danger'. Sounds credible enough. Don't you think, Detective Menking?"

"I'm buying it and he's still standing here. Which knife should it be?" He started rummaging through the kitchen. "Oooh, I like this one," he cooed, pulling it out of the sharpener.

"Ha ha, very funny. Good thing that I tape record all of my visitors."

"Better thing that we have a warrant and can search the place from top to bottom. No telling what we will find. I'm certain that half of it would violate your parole. But why do we have to be combative, Jonas? Can't we just get along?"

"Uh huh. That guy in Los Angeles had videotape backing him up and the cops still got off."

"What can I tell you, Jonas? The world just isn't a fair place. Especially for ex-convicts still operating outside the law."

"So what do you want?" Jonas' voice took on a tone of exasperation.

"I want to know who you sent the picture to."

"I told you I don't know what you are talking about."

"And I'm telling you I just ordered your phone records. Had your parole officer do it as part of a random verification that you were being a good boy. Said he would have them for me in the morning. And I'm going to check and see and if there is a call at the time we happened to cross paths. I'm going to find out who you sent the picture to. And then I am going to find out why. Then I'm going to find out just how bad this person is that you were dealing with and if they are real bad I'm going to let them know you ratted them out willingly. Then I will leave you to the fortunes of chance."

"You're a cold man, you know. Does your wife know these things about you?"

"Where do you think I learned it from?" They all laughed for a moment. "Last chance Jonas. I'm on my way to a lawyer's office now. If I find out that you are two are even remotely related, I'm taking you down. Hard."

"Dude, I haven't talked to an attorney since that no-good, public defender I got stuck with when you busted me. That guy should be prosecuted for legal malpractice for using the word 'Lawyer' on his business cards."

"Cry me a river."

"Whatever, it's the truth."

"Ok, last chance. Speak now or forever hold your peace."

"Did you take that part out of your wedding vows? I'm sure like five cousins and uncles were under orders from her papa to jump up and scream 'NO!' at the top of their lungs if you had given them the option." Jonas maintained a cocky attitude outwardly while his thoughts ran wild. Shelby had said she would make sure the phones weren't traceable, but what if she had messed up? How quickly could he pack up and move...a day? Half a day? He thought to himself that he might be finding out sooner than later. "Not that I don't REALLY enjoy our little chats, but it sounds like you have a lot of work to do and I need to get moving myself. Hope you find what you are looking for. Gotta run now. Buh-Bye." Jonas herded them back out of the door and locked it behind him, collapsing in a heap onto the floor.

The next stop on their tour was the law offices of Michael Carey. Another dead end. They spent fifteen minutes or so waiting in the lobby and another fifteen exchanging pleasantries and subtle hints/threats about impeding the process of the investigation. Finally they stopped in at the Seattle PD tech center where Jeremy Gray had been hard at work trying to dig through cyberspace trying to track down the money. He literally ran across the room to where the two detectives entered. "I'm so glad to see you. I think I found your money."

Back at the Memphis airport, Jackson and Jessica's flight taxied to the runway to takeoff. There it paused to let another plane land having flown in from Seattle. It touched down perfectly and pulled around to the gate that Jackson and Jessica's plane had just departed from. The Captain announced on the overhead intercom the time and the weather and that they were oh so glad to have been of service. Shelby breathed out a sigh of relief. She was back on the ground in Memphis and back home again in time to catch the evening news. She got her bags from the luggage claim area and walked out to her car. Everything was just as she left it but the world had a different glow about it. She knew that she could take care of whatever situation came up and that gave her a peaceful feeling. Her apartment looked just as she left it and she dropped her luggage and immediately turned on the TV. The local news came and went and there was no word about any shootings in Seattle, so Shelby got back online and checked the Seattle news station websites for any "breaking" news. Finally, the fourth item that came through referenced a shooting downtown. It didn't release the name of the victim, but Shelby was dismayed somewhat to find that the TV station was not releasing any other details. A police department mouthpiece referenced a couple of leads they were tracking down, which set Shelby's heart racing. She mentally retraced all of the steps she had taken that day, careful to ensure that no traces were left behind. She went to sleep that night confident in the fact that she had indeed gotten away with it...again.

CHAPTER 102

"Okay, you have my attention now, Jeremy, dazzle me with your brilliance," Will said with an air of disbelief.

"Well, I wasn't exactly sure I was on the right track, but then on a hunch, I doubled back to where we found the two distinct trails that mirrored each other."

"Right."

"Then I found a third trail that had been made more recently."

"Can you tell me where or who it came from?"

"Not really, the IP address that whoever it was used had been washed three or four times by the time I got to it. It did come from Seattle though. Interesting thing was that halfway through that trail, it seemed like whoever had created the first trail, doubled back through and hacked the latest one."

"Jonas."

"What Detective?"

"Nothing, go ahead."

"So anyway, I planted my own little bug in the first and last tracker, same person, follow?"

"I'm with you."

"And voila, it led me straight to the money. Numbered account overseas. Very private. Getting it unlocked is another thing altogether."

"Impressive, how did you learn how to do that?"

"It's not that hard once you get down to it. My father and I used to take apart engines and put them back together. Kind of the same thing. Eliminate all the things that are working correctly and you are left with what is broken. Kind of a twist on Sherlock Holmes."

"They would have been proud. Your father and Mr. Holmes, that is. And both would probably be thoroughly confused by the internet."

Menking's phone rang and he walked away to answer it. Will looked at him with a brief flash of curiosity and then went back to the computer screen, nodding his head with a look of satisfaction on his face.

CHAPTER 103

It was dark when their plane landed. Jessica didn't have the first idea where she was, but it was warm and tropical. The few people she saw spoke with a lilting accent that seemed almost song-like at times. They had to wait just a few minutes to pass through customs and Jackson stayed on the phone the entire time. He was laughing and enjoying the conversation so she felt good. He hung up the phone and kissed her.

"What was that for?"

"It had been a while. I wanted one and thought you might as well."

"Good reason. So I can take one when the need arises?"

"I would be upset if you didn't."

"I'll do my best not to hurt your feelings."

"Outstanding. Our taxi should be here in about fifteen minutes. The ride is about twenty minutes or so. It's kind of late now, do you want to eat or wait until we get to the resort?"

"Is there something quick we can grab here?"

"Yes, right down by the water, there's a little bar that serves food. We can grab something quick while we wait."

They were paying their tab when a dark black man wearing a sailor's hat and a Hawaiian shirt appeared. "Monsieur Pritchard? My name is Marc, your taxi is waiting for you."

Jackson smiled and grabbed their bags and followed Marc with Jessica in tow. They walked to the edge of the dock and Marc climbed in a twenty-foot boat, followed quickly by Jackson. Jessica had a confused look on her face. Jackson caught it and laughed. He held out his hand to help her into the boat and said, "Water taxi."

"Oh, I thought…"

"I know. There are only a few cars or roads where we are going. A few golf carts at the main resort, but we will be walking everywhere."

Jessica was still a bit confused but she snuggled into his arm and chest as they rode. The water was smooth and they glided along the surface quickly. Jackson pointed out a few constellations and the moon that was huge on the horizon. The night sky was as black and as full of stars as Jessica had ever seen. The stars shone brightly and were crowded like an expressway during rush hour. Jackson explained that you could see infinitely more stars when you saw the night sky unencumbered by city lights. Several minutes later they slowed and pulled alongside a dock where another dark-skinned man waited for them. Jackson nearly leapt from the boat and hurried to him, both of them erupting with a roar and a huge embrace. Jessica couldn't hear their conversation and waited for the boat to be tied off. As it was, Jackson and the other man had made their way down and helped her out.

"Bon soire mes amies, my name is Jean Pierre and I am your humble servant for the next few days. Welcome to the beautiful island of St. Christophe. If you need anything, please don't hesitate to ask." He kissed her hand gallantly and motioned for Marc to get their bags. "Please to follow him," Jean Pierre gestured behind Marc and turned back to Jackson. "Everything is arranged; I trust it will be to your liking."

"I'm certain it is. Thank you, my friend."

"The pleasure is all mine. Enjoy your stay. There will be breakfast in the main hall starting at 8:00. You have the run of the place all day and your other taxi leaves around 4:30 tomorrow afternoon."

Jessica glanced at Jackson and he patted her arm in return. "I'll explain later." He looked down at his cell phone to check the time and

291

then turned it off, sliding it into his pocket. They left Jean Pierre at the dock and followed Marc to their room, which turned out to be an enormous three-room suite with an open-air balcony that looked over the water. There was a stocked fridge and one of the largest bathrooms Jessica had ever seen. Marc placed their bags on a side table in the bedroom and walked back out, opening a few closet doors and turning on the lights in all three rooms. Jackson tipped him on his way out and whispered a few instructions to him. Marc nodded and backed out of the room, closing the ornate French doors behind him. Jessica wandered out the French doors that opened to the balcony; they were identical to the ones to the front of their suite. Jackson had pulled a chair to the edge of the balcony and had his feet propped up on the railing. He was drinking a bottled water and looking out over the ocean. The roar of the surf was deafening and soothing all at the same time. Jessica played with his hair and then winked and motioned him back into the suite and into the bedroom with a coquettish look on her face. Several minutes later, fatigue caught up with both of them and they slept tightly to each other, his arms wrapped around her body.

CHAPTER 104

Jan Eberhardt paced furiously up and down the hospital hallway. The waiting room that had seemed large when she had first arrived had shrunk considerably over the past few hours. She hadn't gotten any news from the doctors since they had gone into the second surgery. After the first one had lasted six hours, a weary doctor had explained that they wouldn't have any idea on her prognosis until after 24-48 hours. The first surgery had been to remove the bullet and repair as much damage as they could while she was strong enough to handle it. Apparently the bullet had nicked a few organs and then tumbled through her body, shredding soft tissues and fragmenting a few bones along the way. The second surgery was to stop some internal bleeding and then find the damage it came from and to repair it. Jan was cried out at this point while trying to reach Jackson. His cell phone was ringing straight to voice mail, which worried her immensely. Every time she called and got it, her stress level rose a bit more. She pulled her phone out to dial again when the doctor she had spoken to earlier emerged from a doorway and removed his surgical mask. His scrubs were splattered with blood, but not enough to cause Jan to panic any further.

"She's resting comfortably. I think we repaired everything that was damaged. The bleeding has stopped and all of her vitals are as close to normal as we could have hoped. She just needs to rest and let her body heal itself. We have her in an induced coma for the next 24 hours to facilitate that process. But, when she does wake, I will have someone call you. You should get some rest."

"So she is going to be all right?"

"It's really too early to tell. She didn't regain consciousness so we don't know if there is any paralysis or nerve damage or brain damage. She lost a lot of blood and we almost lost her on the table once. Right now she is getting everything she needs in the way of care. I'm staying here tonight to monitor her and will make sure you know everything I know as soon as it happens."

"Okay, thank you doctor. I am very grateful."

"Have you called her parents?"

"I did, they should be here tomorrow. Thank you for keeping me informed. I appreciate all of your efforts. Now if you will excuse me, I do have a phone call I need to make."

She stepped out of the waiting area and into a larger lobby. It was deserted except for an elderly gentleman sleeping in one corner. She reached into her purse and retrieved the number that Jackson had given her earlier and dialed it. It rang twice and then was answered by a tired voice.

"Swift."

"Detective Swift? My name is Jan Eberhardt and I think I need your help. I know that you have been trying to reach me about Jackson Pritchard, but a dear friend of mine has been shot and is in the hospital here in Seattle. She's just out of surgery now."

"And what can I do for you, Ms. Eberhardt?"

"Mrs. actually. I would like to help you find out who is after Jackson. I was at the funeral yesterday and talked to Jackson last night and again this morning."

"Okay, so how does that help me?"

"I don't know if it helps you or not Detective, but the woman that was shot was a recent client of Jackson's. Seems rather coincidental that she was shot too."

"You have my attention. Which hospital are you calling from?"

"I'm leaving now, but I will be back at my hotel room in about twenty minutes." She gave him directions.

"We'll see you then."

CHAPTER 105

Michael Carey answered his phone on the first ring. "Douglas. I haven't heard from you in a few days, where are you?"

"Memphis, Tennessee."

"And...what can you tell me?"

"Your boy flew back here and met a woman at the airport. They caught a plane headed for somewhere in the Caribbean. Who knows where they went from there."

"It's a starting point. Get on a plane back here and get online and see if you can track where they went. I have more information on him now, so he should be pretty easy to track."

"It's pretty late here, I'll see if I can catch a red-eye. If not, I'll be back in tomorrow."

"Just get here as soon as you can." Michael threw the phone across the room and rubbed his temples. The old adage about good help being hard to find was never so true he thought. He walked over and retrieved the phone and dialed another detective.

"Menking."

"Is now a good time to talk?"

"Not really, I will have to call you back. Give me a half-hour or so."

Michael hung up again and reached for a bottle of aspirin. He swallowed three or four and chased them with a drink of scotch. He dialed one more number. It was the number of some muscle he had used before. Not too bright, but got the job done.

"Hello."

"It's Michael Carey, I have a job to do. Pack a bag for somewhere warm for a few days and meet me in my office around ten in the morning." He hung up without waiting for a response. A plan was coming together.

CHAPTER 106

Detectives Swift and Menking rang Jan's room from the hotel lobby and she gave them her room number. A couple of minutes later they knocked on the door and were greeted by an attractive but tired-looking woman.

"Good evening ma'am, I'm Detective Swift and this is my partner Detective Menking."

"Please come in detectives. I'm having a drink, can I get either one of you anything?"

They both declined and took off their jackets as they walked in. The suite was large without being ostentatious. Will made note of this as they sat down.

"So what can I do for you ma'am?"

"Well, it's about a mutual friend we have, Jackson Pritchard. I know you talked with him the other day."

"Yes ma'am."

"Well, I am afraid for his safety and in all honesty, I'm a little afraid for mine as well."

"Why is that?"

"I told you about Sharon Milligan and I believe he did too. But my friend Meredith Gregory was the woman that was shot and she spent last weekend with him. I just came from the hospital. They said the surgeries went well, but its too early to tell how she will come out of this."

"What can you tell me about Jackson that he might have left out. Anyone mad at him? Any enemies or anything like that?"

"Not that I know of…he had upset several people in the last couple of days, but not to that extent."

"You are talking about his retirement?"

"Yes, he told you about that?"

"Yes ma'am. A good idea,I think."

"Why is that?"

"Because that lifestyle catches up with everyone eventually. Anyway, that's neither here nor there. How long had Jackson and Meredith been working together?"

"That's just it, this past weekend was their first time together. I arranged everything. Kind of a reward for her for the work she had done for me lately."

"Interesting reward."

"You don't know Jackson. He is fabulous at his job. Very attentive to the smallest details. She got every penny's worth, I have no doubt."

"And you are worried that whoever shot your friend may trace that back to you?"

"That plus the fact that it happened so quickly."

"So you think he is being watched."

"Yes, I do. And if he is being watched, then whoever it is may have seen me, too."

"I understand. How long are you going to be in town?"

"It was going to be just a couple of days. I arranged for a few meetings out here for after the funeral. Now that Meredith is in the hospital I will be staying a little longer."

"I'll have a uniform watch you while you are here. Let me know if you see anything out of the ordinary. And keep me posted on your friend. Does Jackson know about her yet?"

"I don't think so. I'm a bit worried about him. I have tried calling and the phone goes directly to voice mail. I do hope nothing has happened to him."

"I hope the same thing. Did another detective or a uniformed officer take your statement regarding the shooting?"

"It was another detective. I have his card in my wallet." She went and retrieved it and handed it to Will. He recognized the name immediately and made a note to call him. "Do you need to take it?"

"No ma'am, you can hold on to it. I know that detective well." Will gave her his card and wrote his cell number on the back. "Thank you for your time; it was most helpful." He and Art headed out the door and back to his car. They headed back to the precinct where Will dropped Art at his car. Art tapped the glass and Will rolled the passenger window down.

"Let's meet early for breakfast, say seven or so."

"Why so early?" Will asked.

"I have something to show you. It may shed a light on a few things. Then we can go roust Jonas. That seems to be rather entertaining."

CHAPTER 107

The sun rose dramatically over the ocean. Jackson had awakened early and was enjoying a mug of hot chocolate and the quiet of the morning sitting on the balcony. His eyes focused on the horizon and he watched wave after wave roll in, breaking some twenty or thirty feet from the shore. This was one of his favorite things in the world, watching and listening to the ocean. He thought about that for a moment and wondered if Jessica would ever entertain thoughts of living somewhere near the ocean. "Easy now, cowboy," he thought to himself, "let's not get too far ahead of ourselves."

In the next room Jessica was stirring from a deep and restful sleep. She was momentarily disoriented but soon remembered where she was. She rolled over to find a tray with fresh fruit and muffins and she reached for a slice of pineapple. A friend had once told her to reserve her opinion on pineapple until she had it fresh on a tropical island somewhere. One bite proved that to be a wise suggestion and Jessica enjoyed the pure sweetness it provided. She got out of bed and pulled on a tank top and boxers and made her way out to the balcony. The doors were open and she could see Jackson sitting in profile, with the sunrise framing his silhouette perfectly. She sneaked quietly behind him and draped her arms around his shoulders, kissing his neck and ear playfully.

"Good morning, beautiful." He reached over and replaced his mug on the table next to his chair. Jessica swung around and lay across his lap playfully.

"Good morning to you. I think it bad manners to leave a lady in bed all alone. Terrible thoughts could cross her mind."

"I considered that when I woke up, but I didn't want to miss the sunrise and you looked so peaceful sleeping there, I certainly didn't want to wake you. So I brought you breakfast instead."

"Okay, you are forgiven. So where are we going today?"

"Well, my friend Jean Pierre has arranged for us to stay in a little grass hut over the water on a private island about a mile offshore. You can just see it from here, look." He pointed to what seemed like a speck of land on the horizon. "We can have it tonight and tomorrow. No interruptions if you like. Then I think someone else has it for the weekend."

"That sounds fun, what is there to do there?"

"Whatever our imaginations come up with."

"And the dress code?"

"Well, seeing as how we will be the only inhabitants, we can decide when we get there."

"Sounds nice. So how about our agenda this morning?"

"Well I was thinking about that hammock over there." He nodded over her shoulder to the other side of the balcony. It was an oversized hammock perfect for two. "You are invited of course. Then there is the matter of a shower. That sounds good too. Any preferences?"

Jessica got up and kissed Jackson sweetly on the cheek. She waved and walked back through the open doors. A few seconds later, he heard the sound of the shower and Jessica's voice saying something about needing help reaching a spot on her back.

CHAPTER 108

Will and Art met at their usual breakfast spot at 7:30. Art had arrived before Will and was halfway through a plate of bacon and eggs that Will swore had been served with a side of grease.

"That stuff is going to catch up with you at some point."

"I'm on the down hill part of the course already partner, may as well enjoy the trip."

"So what did you want to talk to me about?"

Art reached under the table and grabbed an envelope and set it in front of his partner. "Michael Carey has been paying me for information. I didn't know what to do about it until yesterday but I figured we could use this and the information it has helped generate to catch the killer and maybe the dirt bag lawyer as well. It's all there; I haven't spent a nickel of it."

"You should have told me from the beginning, you know."

"Yeah, it was tempting, believe me, but in the end, it was wrong."

"Okay partner, I hear you. So what does the dirt bag lawyer know?"

"He knows about Jackson Pritchard. Thinks he took the money. I think he has someone tailing him."

"Probably Douglas Jimmerson. I've already paid him a visit. What do you think about Pritchard by the way?"

"I'm with you, he's not the bad guy here. I think he is just a guy the victim knew. Doesn't seem like the murdering or thieving type."

"Right, so why is Carey all gung ho about him?"

"I guess he can't see past the money connection. That's all this guy is worried about. He sees a half million reasons to go after him."

"Okay, well let's go rattle Jonas and then the Lieutenant. We need to get this checked in and accounted for and your story out in front of it."

"Sounds good. And thanks."

"For what?"

"For being a good partner."

"It takes two to tango, brother. Always remember that."

It was a short drive to Jonas' apartment building. Will banged on the door non-stop for almost a minute. Finally the door opened and a bleary eyed Jonas stood dressed in a ratty bathrobe, a look of incredulity plastered across his face.

"Are you kidding me? Do you have any idea what time it is?"

"Yep, time for all law abiding citizens to be up and at 'em. Time for you to take a ride downtown. I'm very disappointed in you Jonas."

"What did I supposedly do this time?"

Will flashed quickly across the space between them and pinned the unsuspecting hacker to the wall. "You lied to me, Jonas. Right to my face. I know about the money trail you found. I know you have been having conversations with the person that has the money and I think the picture you took went back to them. I also think that person has KILLED at least one person and tried to kill another one in our fair city." He released Jonas, pointing a finger directly in his face. "So not only am I turning you in for violating your parole for impeding an officer in the carrying out of his duty, when I catch the person you have been working with, I am going to saddle at least one accessory to murder charge on you. You WILL be going away forever. If this second person dies, there may even be a needle in your immediate future."

Jonas swallowed hard. He pondered his options for a moment. Will's partner chimed in. "What's the matter, you look a little whiter than usual."

"Okay, God's honest truth. The hacker that got into my system contacted me. She just wanted me to go to the funeral and see if that guy was there. I did it. She said she might be coming to town and would reward me for it. I caught a glimpse of her when I got in her system and you wouldn't believe how good-looking she is. That's all I know."

"Wait, you got hacked by a girl?"

"Dude, she's good."

"Not good enough. Your favorite civil servant technician tracked her down. What else you got on her?"

"I have this." He handed Will his phone with her name and number on the display screen.

"Shelby Powers. Now see, how hard was that? Don't you feel better already?"

"Actually, I feel like I am going to throw up."

"You should get out and get some fresh air every once in a while. Might do you a world of good."

"I may just do that Detective. Hopefully it won't be at my funeral though."

Will turned to his partner. "Looks like we are going to Memphis."

CHAPTER 109

Shelby was sitting at her computer as usual. It was her early morning ritual. Wake up, brush teeth, turn computer on and stare at it as if doing something useful for hours on end. Whether it was here or at the office, it seemed she was always looking at some sort of computer screen. "Maybe when all this is over and Jackson has taken me away from it all that will change," she thought to herself. Thinking of her future love, she realized that she hadn't seen any activity from him lately. His computer had been relatively silent. Something didn't feel right and she meant to find out what. She hacked into his system and saw that nothing had changed since the last time she had been there. She dialed his home phone and got the voice mail and his cell phone rang directly there as well. This couldn't be good. On a hunch she checked his credit card accounts online and saw that he had been rather busy. The trip to Seattle was planned, but he left again the same day that he got back. It all started to make sense. She found the second ticket purchased in the name of Jessica Young, tropical island destination. The last use of his card had been at a resort on an island. St. Christophe? Never heard of it. But back to the real issue: they were traveling together. Her mind raged and she screamed loudly in frustration. "After everything I have done for him, this is how he repays me?" she asked herself. And then calm overtook her. It was time for her to finish what she had started months ago. Jackson would be hers and she would see to that directly. She searched a bit and found the island of St. Christophe. Small, only a few places to stay. She booked a room at a small, out of the way place not far from where Jackson was staying. Then she booked a flight to the same island Jackson had flown into. The timing could be tricky, but a few minutes away from that girl and Shelby was certain she could show him what true love really meant. She smiled wickedly and pulled her suitcase out from under her bed. She would have to pack tonight and get to the airport first thing in the morning. First, she took out her cell phone and dialed the number for Carlos that she had used before.

"Hello? It's Shelby Powers. I need your services again. Just like last time, it worked perfectly. Where is the other one? Probably in a trash dump thousands of miles away from here by now."

She turned her attention to packing and came up with a quick checklist. Touristy stuff. And slinky stuff for after Jackson came to his senses. Guys loved that and she wanted for him to see her at her best. In the meantime, she needed to make a couple of arrangements on her own. First, Jessica Young needed another plane ticket. One that put her on the same flight that Shelby had taken to Seattle very recently. This would take some time. She had to hack into the airlines and the credit card companies, buy the ticket and then show that it had been used. Then, the right person in Seattle would need to find out about Jessica's trip. Jonas! He knew the detective assigned to the Milligan case. Shelby smiled at how easily she could get Jonas to do her dirty work for her. Soon she would serve little miss Jessica up on a platter to the proper authorities. "After all, I am only doing my civic duty, right?" She laughed again and went to work on her keyboard.

CHAPTER 110

Mitchell Varner was a career thug. He looked and dressed the part well. Tall, stocky, with a face that had taken a few too many blows. The number he had taken paled in comparison the number he had handed out however. He had worked for several different outfits in the Northwest but was currently working freelance. He had started doing collections and petty theft work, but had earned a reputation for being someone that could be counted on to get the job done. He wasn't too bright, but one really didn't have to be in his line of work. Now he sat waiting to see Michael Carey in an overstated waiting room. Good thing too, he needed the work. About ten minutes later, Mitchell was escorted to a large office with a very harried looking Michael working feverishly at a cluttered desk. Michael spoke to Mitchell without looking up at him.

"Thank you for coming on such short notice."

"Tanks for callin'."

Michael handed him a folder with several sheets of paper in it as well as a picture of Jackson. "I need you to go find this man and have a conversation with him about a large sum of money that he has decided to take without permission. Everything you need to know about him is in there. Where they are staying, how you get there, all that."

"St. Christophe? Never heard of it."

"Been traveling much lately Mr. Varner?"

"I guess not."

"It's in the Caribbean. There is a plane ticket for this afternoon and some spending money. What else do you need?"

"Does Mr. Pritchard need to come back from the islands?"

"I don't care, I just need to get my money back. Get an account number and a password and bring them back to me. What you do with him afterward is your business. I'm not hiring you to do more though, in case you were wondering."

Mitchell looked a bit disappointed. "Ok, we'll do this your way. What's my cut?"

"$25,000 now. Another twenty-five when I get the information I need and that information gets me where I need to go. Get back to me by tomorrow night and there will be a nice bonus in it for you."

Mitchell smiled. "You're the boss."

CHAPTER III

Will called Detective Stephen Jones at his office while he and Art headed back to the precinct.

"Jones."

"Jonesy, it's Swift. How are you sir?"

"Long time no talk Detective, how's your wife and my son?"

"That's cold, haven't talked to you in what, six months and you gotta start with me? I see how it is." Both men laughed.

"So what can I do you for Will?"

"You picked up a shooting, a Meredith Gregory, business woman from out of town, right?"

"Yep, word travels fast. Who told you?"

"Jan Eberhardt. Meredith works for her. They are in town for business and to attend a funeral."

"Yeah, the Eberhardt lady is some piece of work. Asked me more questions than I asked her I think. What's your in on it?"

"I caught the Milligan case. They may be related. After talking with Mrs. Eberhardt, I was hoping to see if you had any evidence or anything concrete to go on."

"Not much, it happened in a parking garage which means there is a ton of potential evidence. The problem is that most if not all of it is probably not related at all to the shooting. We did find a few hairs on Ms. Gregory and at the crime scene that weren't hers. Checking now to see if they match anywhere. As a matter of fact, here's my partner with an envelope. Nope, sorry, not a match with anyone in the database. Definitely not Ms. Gregory's either."

"I've got a hunch about who it might be. Not sure though. I'm headed to my office to meet with the boss and then most likely headed to Memphis tomorrow. There's a woman there that I think is involved. Can you meet me there?"

"Memphis?"

"My office, knucklehead. I'll have a photo for you to take and show Ms. Gregory."

"Deal, see you in about an hour?"

"Works for me. Hey, if this helps you clear your case, you will owe me lunch or something."

"Done. See you in a bit."

Will hung up the phone and dialed Jonas.

"This is getting to be a regular thing, people are going to start talking, Detective."

"I need you to e-mail me a picture of Shelby."

"Why, a little dry spell at home?"

"Yeah right, I need it for a picture line-up. I'm heading to my office now."

"Okay detective, do I get anything out of this?"

"Besides our new friendship?"

"Yes, definitely besides that."

"Jonas, I'm hurt. I'll check and see. It's not like you were exactly forthcoming with the information. Speaking of, how's your neck?"

"It's terrific. You know, if you catch her you are going to be all over the news, just remember me when you're famous. Maybe I can get your autograph?"

"Just send me the photo."

311

CHAPTER 112

Lunch was served in an open courtyard behind the main hotel. There was a large buffet complete with all kinds of fruits and meats. Jackson and Jessica ate lightly, spending more time talking and laughing then actually paying attention to what was on their plates. Jessica noticed this and giggled.

"What?" Jackson prodded.

"I was just thinking, you might want to eat a good meal now. You are going to need your strength later I think."

"Is that so?"

"Uh huh," she smiled and looked a bit downward, lighting chewing on her fingernail. "But first, I want to go for a walk on the beach. It looked beautiful from the room."

"Whatever you want to do. A walk sounds great. I've been here a couple of times before, but haven't had a chance to check out everything on the island."

The smile left her face quickly. "So were you here for work?"

Jackson sighed. "Once, yes. The other time was when I was very young. I came here with my favorite uncle. You would have liked him. He was kind of a scoundrel."

"How long since you were here?"

"A while. Can I ask you a question?"

"Sure."

"Do we need to sit down and really talk about my previous job? It seems like you are wanting to know a little more."

Jessica blushed. "I'm sorry, I didn't mean to pry."

"It's not prying. I've already told you what I did." Jessica smiled. "What?"

"You said 'did' instead of 'do.' I think that is pretty significant."

"I hadn't really thought about it, but I guess I did."

"I'm not trying to dig, just really trying to get my arms around this. Everything is moving a bit fast, but it's wonderful all at the same time. It would just be weird if what we did was part of what you did in your former life, that's all."

"I guess I can understand that. I can say in all honesty that this place is very special to me. It's why I brought you here. I did come here once before for work, but it's only because I was pressed for time and couldn't make arrangements anywhere else on short notice. I can also say that the little excursion we are taking tonight and tomorrow will be a new adventure for me as well as you."

"Okay, that makes me feel better."

"Good, I'm glad. Now, finish your lunch?"

"Why?"

"Because you are going to need your strength." Jackson winked at her. "We better take some water and bananas on our walk too."

"Okay, I give, why?"

"Well, I wouldn't want you to get dehydrated or cramp up later either." He smiled and winked at her again.

Jessica raised her water glass and said "Cheers," before downing the entire glass in a series of gulps. "How was that?"

"You get a '10' for enthusiasm. We'll see what happens in regards to style points later."

CHAPTER 113

Will and his partner met Detective Jones in the lobby of the precinct building and walked upstairs. The Lieutenant was waiting for them in his office. "So what's the big emergency? And who is this?"

"Lieutenant Morse, this is Detective Stephen Jones, he caught a case that I think is related to the Milligan case and I asked him to meet us here so I could give him a photo to take to his victim. Stephen, Lieutenant Morse." The two men shook hands.

"Okay, so you have a lead, good. You're supposed to get leads. So what do you need me for?"

"Well, if you will follow me to my computer I will show you." The foursome moved to Swift's desk. He logged in while talking. "One of my sources was contacted by someone I had him tracking online for me. I think this person is materially involved, possibly to the point of pulling the trigger."

"Sharon Milligan was stabbed to death," Morse said.

"Yes, but Meredith Gregory was shot. Meredith Gregory was involved with Jackson Pritchard as was Sharon Milligan at one point."

"So that makes him the common denominator. Why isn't he sitting here now?"

"Because he was on an airplane when Meredith Gregory was shot. And he was in Washington D.C. when Sharon Milligan was stabbed to death."

"So what are we looking at now?"

Jackson pulled up the e-mail from Jonas and noticed it had three pictures attached. Thumbnail sketches of each revealed that two of the pictures were of her entire body in a mostly undressed state. The third was a shot of just her face. Jackson double-clicked on it, shaking his head and laughing at the other two pictures. "You are looking at Shelby Powers. She is the one we believe hacked Sharon Milligan's computer, after stabbing her to death, and took a half million dollars. If I'm right, she also shot Meredith Gregory."

"Why Meredith? Covering her tracks from the first one?"

"Not really, I don't think the robbery was the motive. I think the motive is this guy." He pulled out a photo of Jackson Pritchard.

"One of them taking him from the other?"

"A little more complicated than that. Suffice to say that he wasn't involved with either of them any longer. I think Ms. Powers is stalking him and trying to eliminate anyone she perceives as competition."

"Okay, you sold me. So go pick her up and let's talk to her."

"Well, that's what I needed to talk to you about. She lives in Memphis, Tennessee, I am pretty certain."

"Approved, you and Menking get down there, get a warrant and bring her back here."

"Thank you Lieutenant. Hey, I didn't even ask."

"Yes, but you were going to, I figured it would just save time. Check with travel to see how quickly they can get you there."

Menking hung up Swift's desk phone. "One step ahead of you boss. We are booked on the 9:00 AM tomorrow."

"Good, call me from the road and let me know when you have her."

"Will do." Jackson printed out a copy of the photo and gave it to Detective Jones. "This should suffice. Let me know if you need anything else. When are you going to go see Ms. Gregory?"

"No time like the present."

"Good, if you get a positive ID, let me know. Hell, let me know either way. That way I can add it to the arrest warrant once I get to Memphis."

"Done, and thanks again."

"My pleasure. I'll be thinking about where you can take me to lunch."

"You're on."

CHAPTER 114

Jackson and Jessica got back to their suite about forty-five minutes before they were scheduled to catch the water taxi. Jessica wanted to get cleaned up before they left but Jackson told her to just pack an overnight bag. Nothing fancy, it would just be the two of them on the island for about 24 hours.

"Can I shower first?"

"Don't need to. There is one where we are going?"

"Oh, really? This is going to be fun isn't it?"

"Yes, I think so."

They made their way down to the dock just as Marc was firing up the boat that brought them in the previous night.

"Are you taking us to the island?" Jessica asked sweetly.

"It is my pleasure, madame. Please step in this way. Monsieur, could you untie the front?"

Jackson did and they were on their way. The sun was bright and the air was warm and heavy. It felt like it could rain at any given moment. The breeze provided by the boat cooled them slightly and Jessica pressed back against Jackson, taking his hands and wrapping his arms around her. They snuggled this way for the entire ride. A few times Marc yelled and pointed out a landmark of some significance. Jackson and Jessica both nodded politely, unable to hear what he was trying to tell them over the roar of the engine. The trip lasted a bit over ten minutes and they could just barely make out the silhouette of the hotel on the horizon. They docked and Marc carried their bags into their hut and Jackson tipped him generously. "Thank you Monsieur. I will be back tomorrow evening at about six o'clock to collect you and Madame."

"No, thank you Marc. You've been extremely attentive so far and I appreciate it."

"It's my pleasure. Tomorrow night then? Please do not be late. I have to pick up another couple that evening to bring them here actually. I would hate to have them off schedule."

"We'll be packed, ready and waiting. See you tomorrow."

Jackson and Jessica stood on the dock holding hands and watching Marc motor the little craft back across the water. The day was beginning to fade into late afternoon and the air was warm and heavy. When Marc had disappeared from view, they turned and walked back down the dock and crossed the sandy beach to the walkway that led to their quarters for the evening. The hut was comprised of four rooms and stood on stilts over the water. The stretch of water was a small bay off the ocean protected on three sides by the beach. The island rose sharply from the water; as a result, high tides weren't an issue. There was a bedroom, a small sitting room, a bathroom and a fully stocked kitchen/bar. On the bay side of their quarters, there was a deck with an overhang large enough to cover three lounge chairs and a hammock. Jackson and Jessica surveyed the quarters with a smile. She turned and faced him, wrapped her arms around his neck and kissed him deeply. She pulled her face away and smiled broadly. "You did good."

"So you like it?"

"How could you not? Have you looked around? This place is paradise! It's hard to believe that yesterday I was sitting in Memphis worried about you being in Seattle and today we are here."

"It's good to get away, especially with you."

"I'm glad you think so. Now go in there and get your swim trunks on. I am going to change and freshen up a bit too."

Jackson did as he was told and was changed in a flash. "How long are you going to be?" he asked through the door.

"Don't rush a woman when she is getting ready. Why don't you look around on the beach outside and see what you can find. I'll be there in a few."

"Okay. I'm going to grab a beer, do you want anything?"

"Not yet, I'll grab a water bottle or something in a bit."

Jackson grabbed a beer and opened it, taking a drink and savoring the flavor for a moment. He walked back outside and up the walkway to the beach. The water rolled a bit about the bay, pushed around by the fresh breeze blowing in from the ocean. Jackson considered the shoreline for a moment and mapped out a quick walk down and back. He waded into the water, enjoying its warmth as it curled around his ankles. He paused to take another sip and froze as his exes fixed on Jessica's silhouette framed against the sunset. He almost dropped his beer in surprise. He was twenty feet away from her and stood transfixed as she moved shyly down the walkway at first, gaining confidence with every step. Her hair shown with the setting sun as it fell over both shoulders and was highlighted with a small white flower she had put behind her ear. She had a sarong wrapped around her waist that cascaded down around her feet. And she was topless.

"Oh my God."

"What?" she asked somewhat self-consciously.

"You are a vision."

She smiled broadly, losing any pretense of embarrassment. "And you are a charmer."

"I would like to think so, but right now I am just in awe."

She smiled again and stepped onto the beach and reached out and took Jackson by the hand. "So show me our island."

CHAPTER 115

It was nearing five o'clock in Seattle and Will decided to send Art in to talk to Michael Carey one more time to see if they could get any information out of him. They also wanted to get him on tape to hang himself in the bribery case they were working up. Will fitted his partner with a wire and they went over what he could and couldn't say to keep the good counselor from screaming entrapment. At ten after, Art walked through the law firm's front door.

He asked the bored looking receptionist to see Michael. She asked if he had an appointment.

"No, I don't. But announce me anyway, I think he will see me."

"He doesn't see anyone without an appointment."

He showed her his badge. "Announce me."

She picked up the phone and talked quietly into it. After about fifteen seconds, she hung up and waved him in.

"Detective Menking, this is a surprise. Please, have a seat." Michael Carey did not look up from the paperwork stacked in front of him.

He sat down in one of the two chairs facing the desk.

"Can I offer you something to drink? Water? Whisky?"

"How about a combination of the two?"

Michael smiled. "I prefer my water the same way." He stood and fixed two drinks, handing one to Art before sitting back behind his desk. "So what can I do for you?"

"I just wanted to give you a little heads up. My partner and I are heading to Memphis tomorrow. Going to see what we can dig up down there."

"Really, that is interesting."

"Yeah, Jackson's hometown is looking better and better."

"Well, let me save you a little time. He isn't there."

"He's not? Where is he?"

"You aren't going to arrest him are you?"

"No, just ask him a few questions."

"Okay, I have someone on the way to do the same thing. Just letting you know."

"No problem. So where is he? We are still going to Memphis. There's some background stuff we need to get too."

"He and a friend went to a little island in the Caribbean called St. Christophe."

"I've never heard of it."

"Few people have. It hasn't been publicized much at all it seems. It's on the map, though. Look it up if you decide to go."

"I will. A little tropical island work sounds kind of nice. A welcome break. Is it expensive? Not sure I could afford a place like that on a civil servant salary."

"Hold that thought, Detective." The attorney excused himself for a moment and retired through a door behind his desk that Art hadn't really noticed before. He was gone for about a minute. Then the door opened and Michael stepped through and sat back down. "Do you have anything new for me?"

"A name, Meredith Gregory. She and Jackson had a thing going and she turns up shot a couple of days ago. He might be panicking a little bit."

"Do you think he shot her?"

"I don't know. My partner doesn't seem to think so. I think there is more to this guy that meets the eye."

"I think you are correct, Detective. Here." He slid an envelope across the table.

"What's this?"

"Just a little traveling money. Buy yourself a drink with a little umbrella in it. Enjoy your trip."

Art smiled at the smug bastard across the desk. He thought to himself, "I've got you now." Aloud, he said, "I'll catch you when I get back."

CHAPTER 116

Jackson and Jessica enjoyed the late afternoon and early evening air for a couple of hours. They waded in the water, swam and splashed each other, and generally played like a couple of school kids. Jessica did have a bikini bottom underneath her sarong, but it left little to the imagination. After swimming, they rested in the sun and dozed a while, Jessica draped across his chest. Jackson awoke first and stroked her hair tenderly. She cuddled closer and moved up, kissing him softly. They watched the sunset with a very satisfied air surrounding them. The air was cool as they returned arm in arm. Jessica stepped into the bathroom and Jackson moved quickly from room to room lighting every candle he could find. By the time Jessica returned, the hut had a faint glow in every room and on the deck. She was dressed as before, but her hair was brushed out and she moved as if filled with a renewed energy.

Jackson filled a couple of tall glasses of water and placed them on the table on the deck, and then fell into one of the lounge chairs. Jessica strode out and joined him, sitting down between his legs, facing him and propping her elbow on one of his legs. They stared at each other for a few seconds, saying everything in saying nothing. Jackson broke the silence.

"So, my last birthday I spent in New York. I had worked the weekend before and decided to stay over. I had dinner one night in an Italian restaurant that one of the hotel desk clerks had recommended. The food was excellent and I had a very engaging conversation with one of the owners. She was eighty-seven years old and had cooked for forty years in the very same spot. Her daughters had taken over for her and used all of her recipes. The place was a hole in the wall but packed."

"How big was the hole?"

"Hush, this is a good story."

"Sorry, please go ahead."

"I was finishing my third plate of pasta when the old woman came and sat down. She brought a bottle of wine with her and an extra glass. I had already had a carafe on my own and was feeling a nice little buzz. The wine I ordered was good, but the bottle she brought was fantastic. She said it came from a tiny village that she had grown up in and was bottled only every five years. It was amazing. Anyway, we talked for a while and she asked me three or four times what I was doing there by myself. My explanation of being there on business didn't seem to satisfy her. We talked for a while, and after the bottle was gone, she took my hand and read my palm. At first she frowned and mentioned that I had too much pain and not enough love in my life. I couldn't help but agree with her. Then she broke into this huge smile. I asked her what she was smiling about and she didn't say a word. She called her daughters over and they looked. One of them rolled her eyes but the other one gasped and started pointing at my hand. They were all speaking Italian and rambling on and on. Finally I got them to calm down and the mother explained what she had seen. She said, 'Within one year you will find the soul that will remain by your side for the rest of your lives together'. Then they didn't charge me for dinner. I didn't think anything of it at the time. And now." His voice trailed off.

"Yes?"

"I think she saw you."

She covered her mouth with her hand, tears welling in her eyes. "Oh, is that all?"

Jackson laughed and pulled her closely to him, kissing her passionately. They stayed in the chair for a while, kissing and talking, watching the moonlight reflecting off the water. Jessica made a quiet noise kind of like a giggle.

"What was that?"

"I said, smart lady."

"Yes, I think she is."

"So how smart are you?"

"I brought you here didn't I?"

"Smart boy."

She shifted her weight and stood up and faced him. With a deft movement, she reached behind and undid the sarong, letting it slide to the floor. She stood for a moment in the moonlight; aware of the effect she was already having on him, and then smiling seductively.

"Would you care to join me?"

Jackson scrambled to his feet animatedly. Jessica tried keeping a straight face but was unsuccessful. She giggled and Jackson joined her. He leaned in and kissed her softly and then more passionately. She wrapped her arms around his neck as he pulled her closer. They stood for a couple of minutes as the passion level rose between them. Finally, Jessica pulled away and walked toward the bedroom. Jackson followed until she held up her hand, stopping him.

"The dress code is strictly enforced in this establishment sir."

"My apologies." He untied his drawstring and let his shorts fall to floor. He was fully aroused which caused Jessica to smile again.

"That will do nicely, thank you." She reached behind and took him by the hand and led him to the bedroom. They fell into bed together, Jackson kissing her neck and shoulders slowly. She moaned softly in response to his touch. He moved downward and teased and tasted every inch of her skin until he reached the soft spot between her legs. She spread them, quivering in anticipation. He lingered for several minutes, teasing and pleasing her until her body shuddered to a breath-taking climax. He paused for a moment, allowing her to catch her breath before moving up quickly and entering her with one long, slow thrust. She gasped loudly, clutching him tightly to her and scratching his back slightly with her nails. They pushed tightly together, their bodies slick with sweat, until they moved as one. Their hands and mouths joined together, they moved slowly at first and then more and more quickly as they raised the level of passion the other felt. They moved in a constant rhythm for several minutes, gradually speeding up until they reached a frenzied pace. They exploded together with loud groans escaping each of them. They collapsed together in a heap, taking several minutes to catch their breath.

"Yes, that will do nicely," Jessica said before laughing loudly. The laughter was contagious and they took a minute or two to gain their composure. Jackson got up and retrieved their water glasses, handing her one on his return. They both drank until satisfied and Jackson fell back into bed.

"Would you like anything else to drink?"

"To drink? No, I'm good. She pulled a sheet up and over both of them, creating a world for the two of them to share and explore together. Hours later, as the night turned to morning, Jackson lay very still, watching her as she slept, cuddled tightly into a ball, holding on to the arm he had wrapped around her waist. She murmured something he couldn't quite make out, working it over in his mind a couple of times. He finally gave up, leaned over and kissed her cheek and whispered, "I love you, too."

CHAPTER 117

The alarm clock shrilled loudly in the early morning hours, waking Shelby from a deep sleep. She looked at the clock and moaned, realizing she still had to pack and get to the airport. She realized this could be the most important trip of her life and everything needing to be planned and prepared just so. She disassembled the gun she had picked up the night before and wrapped the pieces in aluminum foil, just as she had done on her previous trip. Her source had charged her more than before, citing the increased risk in doing business again so quickly after the last time. Shelby had protested slightly, but not enough to raise his ire. She was sure that a person like this could NOT be trusted. She returned to her packing, adding several pieces of clothing and knick-knacks that your stereotypical tourist would take to a tropical getaway. Shelby was determined to once again be your average girl on holiday. She played the part well, purchasing a couple of outfits that were just gaudy enough to be noticeable, but common enough not to stand out. When she had finished, she admired her handiwork in the mirror. She could be any of a thousand different women, all looking for an escape from their dreary lives by taking a long weekend away somewhere. Their roads led nowhere, unlike hers of course, which was the road to bliss. She threw her packed bags in the car and drove to the airport again, retracing her previous route and parking in exactly the same spot as before. Shelby believed in omens and took these to be good ones. "A little luck can't hurt, even someone like me," she thought to herself. She moved quickly through the airport, checking in and making it to her gate with a few minutes to spare. She had brought snacks in her carry-on bag and bought two bottles of water at one of the gift shops. With about ten minutes to spare, she placed a call to Jonas on his cell while she walked down the terminal. It rang seven times without being answered, causing Shelby to contort her face. She couldn't remember a time that she had called that Jonas hadn't literally jumped to answer the phone calls from her. She left a message explaining that she would be out of pocket for a while and to call if anything happened to come up. She stood waiting at the gate until she heard, "Last Call."

Across the country, another uniformed flight attendant said, "Last call, now boarding on Flight 117 to Detroit, with ongoing service to multiple destinations." Will and Art handed their boarding passes to her as they filed by. She smiled faintly at them and thanked them for flying today. It was too early and neither was very attentive. Neither noticed Mitchell Varner boarding, unlike Mitchell, who saw the pair as soon as he reached the gate. He congratulated himself silently, remembering Michael Carey's warning that these two bozos were tracking down the same people. He went on to say that they had come to different conclusions about who was responsible, so if they could help the detectives without jeopardizing their tasks, then by all means do so." Mitchell sank back into his seat and thought about catching a little sleep. His eyes were hidden behind a pair of outdated sunglasses pulled from his jacket pocket. A long flight to Detroit followed by a longer flight to the Caribbean was not his idea of a picnic.

"It's nice to have support," Art thought to himself while scanning the airplane for familiar faces. Seeing none, he reclined in his chair until he found a comfortable compromise position to sleep in. He had replayed the tape for Will and the Lieutenant, swearing out an affidavit before the judge that had led to the sealed indictment being handed down by the grand jury. They had agreed to seal the indictment and wait to arrest Michael Carey until after they returned from their trip, fearing that the arrest would compromise their reason for traveling in the first place. "That's it!" Art said loudly, sitting up again.

"What?"

"Well, you heard it on the tape. Their guy is going to some island in the Caribbean. That's where he said Jackson and his friend are now. Shouldn't we be going there?"

"Absolutely. And I plan to call Jackson as soon as we land to give him a heads up. We have to take care of Shelby first though. If she is who I think she is, we will need to get her to Seattle before we do anything."

Seemingly satisfied, Art reclined again and closed his eyes and was soon breathing deeply. Things were beginning to fall into place on the case. And better judgment had prevailed in his taking the money from the attorney. A very wise person told him long ago that if a decision you made caused your stomach to ache at all, then you might want to rethink your decision. He fell asleep with thoughts of his mother warming him and causing him to smile.

Will wondered what his partner was smiling about as he drifted off to sleep and hoped he wouldn't start snoring. He pulled out his notes covering the case so far. There were still holes in it, but hopefully what they found in Memphis would answer all his questions. The Lieutenant had called ahead and arranged for an early appointment with one of his counterparts in Memphis. The Lieutenant he had talked to had been helpful if not somewhat disinterested. He and Will agreed that it would take no more than twenty minutes to present the case and get a search and arrest warrant if necessary. Will reviewed it again, then closed his case and followed his partner's lead.

CHAPTER 118

The sunrise reflected off the water and into the bedroom, causing Jessica to stir from a deep and satisfying sleep. She reached over and was only slightly surprised not to find Jackson in bed. She sat up and rubbed her eyes, trying to chase away the last remnants of the night before. The bed sheets and blankets were in a pile on the floor. Jessica reached down and grabbed one and wrapped herself in it and with bare feet, padded into the other rooms. She found Jackson standing in the kitchenette wearing pajama pants and an apron, working diligently on an omelet.

"Good morning sleepyhead."

"It's still early, leave me alone."

"I wouldn't dream of leaving you alone. Call it my early New Year's Resolution."

"If you keep cooking like that, you won't have much choice."

"Well, I was hungry and I thought you might be too."

"Oh, I wasn't talking about breakfast, but ok!" She winked and smiled as Jackson handed her a plate.

"What would you like to drink?"

"What do we have?"

"I have a juice you may not have had before. I had it when I was in Africa a few years ago. It's called passion fruit juice. The passion fruit is native there and delicious. It's tough to eat though, almost completely filled with seeds. Probably three times as many as in a watermelon." He handed her a glass and she took a cautious drink. He watched as a smile spread across her face. "This IS delicious!"

He held up his own glass. "To a perfect night." He took his apron off and hung it over the back of the pantry door.

"I'll drink to that."

They took their plates to the deck and ate slowly, watching a few boats crawl slowly by in the distance. They laughed and talked about the previous couple of days and then about nothing at all.

Since we only have about twelve hours left here, I don't think we should waste any more time sitting here!" He stood up and peeled the pajama pants off as he walked over to the railing. Without a word, he hopped over it and into the warm bay water. Jessica considered that for a moment, stood up and dropped the sheet she had brought out to the deck and followed him over with a splash.

They swam and splashed around for a while, working their way back around to the beach and pulled themselves into the shallows. They stood and wrapped their arms around each other, enjoying the salty taste on each other's lips. Jessica's hands fell below the water and she was pleased to find that he was fully aroused at her touch. She took him by the hand and led him up to the beach where a couple of wooden lawn chairs rested in the shade. Jessica retrieved their towels and laid them out for them to sit on. Jackson took the closer of the two and Jessica joined him. She pressed her hand into his chest as she straddled him and enveloped him slowly. They spent the next hour moving slowly together, their bodies knowing each other more and more with each passing minute. They held each other closely and pleased each other completely and exhaustingly, finishing up with a quick dip in the bay to rinse off their sweat-covered bodies. They toweled each other off playfully and walked hand-in-hand back to the deck where they crawled into the hammock and almost immediately fell asleep in the shade.

CHAPTER 119

As he had requested, the flight attendant woke Will about fifteen minutes before they began the landing cycle. He thanked her and shook the cobwebs out of his head, excused himself and headed back to the bathroom at the back of the plane. He marveled at the size of the room and how hundreds if not thousands of travelers took care of their business every day in such a cramped space. On the way back, he noticed a familiar face reclined in a chair, apparently asleep. He made his way to where the man was sitting and woke him. Mitchell Varner was groggy and didn't recognize Will at first.

"Hello Mitch, you're a long way from home. Taking a little vacation?"

"Something like that. It's been a while since I've been to Miami, I got family there."

"You have family? I figured they found you under a rock."

"Now Detective, I sense a tone of hostility. What could I have done to deserve that?"

"Not sure. What have you done?"

"I just took a little nap. It was nice. Where are we by the way?"

"About to land in Memphis. Are you getting off here?"

"Nope, going to Miami. "Were you paying attention earlier? I'm sure I mentioned Miami."

"How long are you staying?"

"Dunno, three or four days. Until the family and I get tired of each other. That usually happens pretty quickly."

"Okay, well stay out of trouble. I'm sure I will see you back home sooner than later."

"I appreciate your confidence in me, Detective."

"No problem. Remember Mitchell, experience teaches us many things, including the fact that past performance is a good indicator of future happenings."

"Okay, whatever you say." Mitchell began to gather his things. The flight attendant from earlier touched Will on the shoulder and advised him that they would be landing soon and to take his seat. After the plane taxied to a halt at the terminal, they grabbed their carry on luggage and headed for the exit. Each had checked another bag and they picked them up at baggage claim. There was a young police officer, who appeared rather bored, waiting at the back of the baggage area with a sign with Will Swift's name on it.

"Welcome to Memphis, Detective Swift. My name is Walker Patterson and I'm at your disposal today and tomorrow."

"Well, thank you Officer Patterson. This is a welcome surprise. Remind me to thank your lieutenant when I see him."

"Will do. And please call me Walker."

"Okay, Walker it is."

"So where to?"

"Your lieutenant, naturally."

"This way gentlemen, we are only about fifteen minutes away from headquarters."

They got in the unmarked squad car and headed towards downtown Memphis.

Will's cell phone rang as soon as they left the airport. His partner listened to the one side of the conversation he could hear.

"Hey, man. Yeah, we just got to Memphis. A uniform picked us up and is taking us downtown. You did? Great, how is she doing? No kidding. That's great. Do you have a copy of her statement? Awesome, ummm, fax it to me here at…Uh, hey Walker, what's a good fax number to where we are going?" He got the number and gave it to Detective Jones. "No, thank you. We'll be bringing her back soon. Yes, you still get lunch out of the deal. Bother me when I get back. See ya."

"Good news?"

"Absolutely. Jones took Shelby Powers' photo by Ms. Gregory's hospital room and got a positive ID. We have enough to take her back now."

"That's awesome. Should be a short trip then." They sat back and relaxed a bit as Officer Patterson gave them a quick, guided tour to downtown. Will dialed another number, trying to reach Jackson. He looked at his partner and mouthed the words, "Voice mail." Art overheard part of the message, as his partner tried to warn Jackson of impending company. The route from the airport was a dreary one, packed with traffic three lanes wide. Like most big cities, the roadways struggled to handle the increased amounts of traffic. Several miles of the Interstate system inside the city were under construction; a project aimed at widening the roads and relieving some of the traffic congestion. Their car weaved in and out of barrels and highway markers deftly and navigated their way to the downtown headquarters with a minimum of delay. True to their Lieutenant's prediction, they were in and out in less than thirty minutes, with arrest and search warrants in hand. The State of Washington had already filed an extradition notice, pending the suspect's arrest. A quick search and they found her home and work addresses. Will called back to his home precinct and updated Lieutenant Morse. A few minutes later, Will, Art, and their driver piled back in the car and headed to Midtown.

CHAPTER 120

Mitchell Varner's plane landed in Miami a couple of hours after leaving Memphis. He yawned and stretched and waited for the rushed horde of business travelers pressing to get off the plane first. He pulled out his phone and pressed a few buttons on the small screen. His connecting flight was on schedule and he had a ninety-minute layover to make sure he made his Caribbean flight. He opened his briefcase and spent a few minutes going over the dossier he had been given on Jackson Pritchard. "Not a bad looking guy," he thought to himself. "Doesn't look like much trouble to me." He checked the reservations for himself and then for the last known place that Jackson and the girl were staying. Confident that he would be able to find them easily, he replaced the papers and closed the briefcase, turning the combination locks off of the correct code. He joined the procession of passengers leaving the plane and entering the terminal. He made his way to his connecting flight and waited a grand total of ten minutes before boarding again. He noticed a tall, attractive brunette with long legs and a tight-fitting skirt get on the plane before him and admired her as she walked down the gangway to the plane. A flight attendant interrupted that pleasant thought as she asked for his boarding pass. He fished it from his jacket pocket and handed it to her, looking back and being disappointed as the brunette had disappeared from his view.

"Have a nice flight, sir."

"Oh, I plan on it."

Shelby Powers looked at her ticket again and noted that she was sitting in the emergency exit row. She usually requested those seats for the extra foot room they provided. With her height, every inch of space was a luxury. She stowed her carry on bag and pulled out a bottle of water and got to work on a Sudoku. She was jostled a couple of passengers as they squeezed by in the cramped aisle. Looking towards the front of the plane, she noticed a large man that somewhat resembled a gorilla. He had hair sticking out from his shirt collar as well as from each shirtsleeve. He looked back at her lasciviously and she lowered her eyes, hoping that he wasn't sharing her seat. He walked past and Shelby exhaled sharply. An older woman sitting next to her said, "I didn't want him sitting here either, dear." Shelby smiled at her and leaned back in her chair. She closed her eyes and tried to relax, wondering what her game plan would be once she reached the island. She was a little concerned that she didn't have enough time to plan her approach, but it was important to her to be there and save Jackson from making a big mistake. She was on a mission and she certainly intended to see it all the way through.

The flight lasted a little under an hour, consisting primarily of the airplane taxiing, taking off and then landing. The passengers got their complimentary beverage and a bag of pretzels and an animated demonstration of seat belts and oxygen masks from the flight crew that deviated hysterically from the normal script. The majority of the passengers thought this was funny, but to Shelby it was just another example of people breaking the rules to satisfy their own selfish egos. She wondered momentarily where the crew would stay overnight but quickly dismissed the thought. After all, she couldn't make the world a better place all the time. A few minutes after they landed, Shelby was able to exit the aircraft in the orderly fashion the crew had mentioned earlier. She made her way to the baggage claim area where she retrieved her luggage and arranged to meet the water taxi that would take her to her island destination. She looked around and was unable to find the man that had frightened her and her seatmate earlier.

Mitchell had made his way through the baggage claim much faster than anyone else and was already on his way to the water taxi pickup. The cab ride lasted only a few minutes and he paid the driver after a virtually silent ride. The water taxi was waiting and possibly the smallest boat he had ever seen. A skinny, sun-blackened young man managed his way around the craft and puttered the boat out of the harbor and off to their destination: the island of St. Christophe.

Five minutes later, Shelby Powers stepped out of a taxi and paid the driver. She found her ride, a medium-sized passenger boat that looked as if it would hold up to five people. Her driver smiled and untied the line that held the boat still, setting off for the same island as Mitchell Varner had just a few minutes earlier.

CHAPTER 121

Will stood to the side of the apartment doorway. Four other policemen to help serve the warrant had met them at Shelby Powers' apartment. As she was a murder suspect, they had weapons drawn, just in case. The Memphis officers would enter first, followed by him and his partner as they were out of their jurisdiction. After repeated knocking, the door was forced and the contingent entered. A quick search revealed they were alone in the apartment. Will and Art walked through and checked the bedroom and bathroom. "She's gone," Will announced.

"Why do you say that, Detective?"

"All her personal items are gone. Toothbrush, toothpaste, make-up bag. It looks like clothes have been taken out of the closet too."

"So now what?"

"Jonas."

"Jonas? He's home in Seattle."

"Right, but he can get in." Will dialed the number.

"Hello, Detective."

"It's like you were waiting on my call, Jonas."

"Not waiting, I just figured you would call, I mean, it is a day that ends in the letter 'Y'."

"Cute, fire your computer up and hack in to her computer."

"Who, Shelby? I like my computer not fried thank you."

"She's not here. I'm in her apartment as we speak."

"Really? Can you bring me back something sexy of hers?"

Will laughed in spite of himself. "You're a sick man, Jonas."

"You may be right, but it's SOOOOO much fun. Have someone turn the computer on, you have to be able to spell 'Power" so you are disqualified."

"It's already on."

"Okay, give me a minute. What am I looking for?"

"She's traveling somewhere, I want to know where."

"Just one pair of panties?"

"Jonas…"

"I know…the information. Give me a second." Will could hear the clicking of Jonas' keyboard as he navigated through the security system. "Ha, she hasn't changed her challenge question or password."

"She's been too busy."

"Obviously. Okay, she caught a flight out of Memphis today, heading to Miami. From there she caught a connecting flight and a water taxi. She is in St. Christophe."

Will turned to his partner and put his hand over the phone. "Didn't you say that Carey was sending Mitchell Varner down to the Caribbean?"

"Yep, it was an island I hadn't heard of before."

"Well, guess where Shelby Powers went?"

"Really? She must be tracking Jackson somehow."

"I'll bet that somehow is right over there." Will nodded in the direction of her computer and then held up the dossier they had put together. "It says here that she works in a computer repair shop. I'd bet a month's salary that she is our hacker and knows where that money is."

"You make more than me."

"Then you would be getting odds. How nice is that?"

"No bet. So where does that leave us?"

"We take and inventory the evidence here and ship it back home. Did you happen to pack a bathing suit?"

"No, why?"

"Because we are off to this island that no one has ever heard of."

"Nice."

CHAPTER 122

Dinner was to be served in a small courtyard off the rear of the resort. Jackson checked the clock and saw their reservation time was rapidly approaching. Jessica was getting ready in the bathroom. He glanced at the clock again, "You know we are supposed to eat in like five minutes, right?"

"Hey, perfection takes time. And since perfection isn't an option, you get me."

"Same thing as far as I am concerned."

She opened the door and leaned against the frame suggestively. "You're sweet, a little impatient, but in a cute way." A snug, form-fitting white sundress accentuated her newly tanned shape beautifully. Jackson stared momentarily and then dropped the glass of water he was holding. Jessica snickered, covering her mouth with one hand. "So...you like?"

"You are stunning. Oh my God. You're the most beautiful woman I have ever seen."

"Talk like that will change my mind about dinner."

"You aren't hungry?"

"I'm starving. But room service is sounding more and more appealing."

"That does sound good, but my fragile male ego is much more in favor of showing you off to the other guests, staff and everyone else on the island. You have to give me that."

"Ok, I will give you that, and a few other things. Now what are you going to give me?"

"Wouldn't you rather know how many?"

Jessica smiled. "I do love a man with confidence."

"It's all about the fit."

"And I love how well we fit together. A bit more snug than I have experienced before if you must know."

"Flattery will get you everywhere."

"But will it keep me here?"

"It will…after dinner though." She smiled anyway.

Dinner was a luau complete with a bonfire and torches. They mingled with the other guests and talked with several of the staff, including the owner, an older man with an English accent that Jessica found adorable. He smiled a lot and invited them to his table, where they enjoyed dinner and drinks for a couple of hours. Jackson was getting antsy and made an excuse to pull Jessica away. They walked hand-in-hand down a manicured walkway that ended at the beach. They left their shoes behind and enjoyed the contrast of the feel of the sun-warmed sand and the cool water as it lapped against the shore. They talked about the trip so far and the possibility of going sailing or scuba diving before they left. They came upon a couple of chairs and sat, enjoying the breeze off the ocean.

"So what do we do when we get back to Memphis?"

"What do we do about what?"

"Well, it would seem that things have changed a little bit for both of us." She squeezed his hand gently.

"Yes, I would agree."

"After this trip, the Blue Monkey seems like a dead end."

"I don't know, you liked the job didn't you?"

"Yes, but getting drooled over by drunken fraternity boys and overage adolescents seems a little pointless. It's just a job"

"Did you ever perfect your drink?"

"You mean 'Liquid Courage'? Would you believe I haven't yet?"

"Well there's a reason to go back right there, wouldn't you say?"

"Maybe, or we could just stay here?"

"I could get used to that. We would definitely save money on clothes."

"You're bad."

"I really wasn't talking about that. Just about beach weather in general."

"Well, that's a shame. The other is infinitely more appealing. To my way of thinking any way."

"Mine too. But just lying around on the beach for a living would get rather boring. And to be honest, I can't see you being happy doing nothing. I haven't seen many soup kitchens or anything around here."

"You're probably right, did you have something else in mind?"

"Maybe, how married are you to Memphis?"

"I'm not. You said 'married'."

"I did. I kind of like the idea of your dartboard. Anywhere you would like for me to aim for?"

"Well, I do like the water. The beach is good too. Suggestions?"

"California?" She wrinkled her nose and shook her head.

"Okay, do you have a preference of which coast?"

"I guess not. But this isn't just my decision."

"True, I would like to be somewhere close to lots of outdoor things to do."

"That doesn't really narrow it down much. Might rule out Siberia."

"Are we thinking globally?"

"Well, I guess not. That could be interesting though."

"I guess the dart will just have to decide. It seemed to work pretty well for you." He leaned over and kissed her.

"I think so too."

"I think we should make our way back to the room."

"I like how you think."

The walk back was picturesque, waves crashing on a moonlit shore. They found their shoes and rinsed their feet off at the edge of the beach and made their way to the resort. Jackson checked at the front desk for the availability of scuba lessons and arranged for them both for the next day. He put in a wake up call for 9:00 just to make sure they would get breakfast before their lesson. They reached the door and Jackson pressed her against it, kissing her neck and shoulders while standing behind her. She opened the door and reached around it, finding the "Do Not Disturb" sign and hanging it on the knob. She pulled Jackson into the room and closed and locked the door.

CHAPTER 123

Mitchell Varner woke early. He had found and followed Jackson and his girlfriend the previous night before retreating to his hotel room. He had made a note of their room number as well as what she looked like to make the following days work that much easier. Flying always made him tired, so he slept soundly. His game plan was simple, watch their room today, wait for the guy to leave and grab the girl. Then go back and talk to the guy to get him to cooperate. He'd get the info and get back to Seattle and get paid. He stopped at the front desk and asked about breakfast. The clerk directed him to a little out-of-the-way restaurant that served fruit and muffins. Nothing greasy. "What kind of restaurant doesn't serve grease for breakfast?" he asked himself. The coffee was good by any measure and he drank two cups. He paid the tab and made sure to hit the bathroom on his way out. He bought a newspaper and walked around the island a bit before it was too busy, noting pathways and the shortest route back to his hotel room as well as to the water taxi. That reminded him of his last arrangement to take care of. His walked down to the water taxi stand and asked if they could be on stand by as he might be ready to travel on short notice. The men that worked their were largely unimpressed until Mitchell handed

345

them each a one hundred dollar bill. "At your service, sir," one of them exclaimed. Mitchell took one of their cards and told them that after he called, he would want to leave within ten minutes.

"Any bags?" he was asked?

"Just a small one, I travel light."

"Could you bring it here now?" We could be already for you once you were ready to go."

"Deal. Let me finish packing and I will bring it right over." Mitchell made his way to the room and packed in a flash. On the way back to the docks, he noticed Jackson leaving the resort dressed to go running. "I should have known," Mitchell said to no one, disgusted with the self-interest everyone seemed to be taking lately. "He probably has a lifetime supply of bottled water at home." Noting that he was by himself, Mitchell hurried down to the water taxi and dropped his bag off. He made his way back to the resort without being seen and came in through a side entrance, taking great care not to run into anyone. Mitchell took the back stairs and moved quickly to the front door of Jackson and Jessica's suite.

He knocked on the door lightly and called out, "Room Service."

A few seconds later, Jessica came to the door and answered through it. "I didn't order any room service."

"No ma'am you didn't, but Mr. Pritchard did. Said it was a surprise. I wasn't supposed to tell you."

"You're secret is safe with me," she answered, opening the door. As soon as the chain was off, he bulled through the door, catching her in the jaw and stunning her. She was dressed and he escorted her down the back stairway and to the pathway that took them back to his hotel room. He had a surprise for her all right. A roll of duct tape along with some handcuffs waited for her there. Since it was early, they didn't cross paths with anyone and made it back to the room safely. Jessica had recovered somewhat and tried to pull away from his firm grip. She had a fearful look in her eye, which Mitchell attempted to reassure.

"Don't worry, sweetheart. If your boyfriend plays ball then we won't have any trouble at all. I'm not after you or him, just after some money that he knows something about."

"He doesn't know about any money."

"Sure he doesn't; he got you down here on his good looks alone."

"Well, kind of…not everyone has to have money or whatever to get the girl. Sometimes being who they are is enough."

"Whatever, sister. I am going to go pay him a little visit and he and I will hash out all the details." With that, Mitchell put duct tape across her mouth and cuffed her hands around the leg to the sink in the bathroom. Jessica sat on the floor and once her abductor left, broke into tears, unwilling to let him have the satisfaction of seeing her cry.

Shelby Powers made her way across the island and to the resort when she saw the scary hairy man from the airplane walk quickly by. She stopped and watched as he was walking with a woman that didn't seem to have any idea where she was going or what she was doing. Ducking down behind a row of hedges, her eyes grew larger when she realized it was Jessica, the woman from the bar. Her mind raced with possibilities ranging from Jessica leaving Jackson to Jessica being taken somewhere by this man. She covered her mouth at that possibility and had to fight her instinct to cry out when Jessica crumpled to the ground in a heap. She watched as Mr. Scary picked her up with ease and carried her into the hotel at the end of the path he was walking on. He peeked out the door to make sure no one had seen him and then retreated again into the interior of the hotel room. Shelby left her hiding place and raced to the resort where Jackson and the woman were staying. She reached a house phone and picked up, asking for Jackson's room and was dismayed to find that he wasn't in. She hung up without leaving a message and headed to the front desk where a front desk clerk and maintenance man were in the middle of a heated conversation. The lilt of their island accents was usually quite musical to Shelby's senses, but now she was in a hurry.

"Excuse me, but I need to find Jackson Pritchard and he isn't answering his room. Have either of you seen him?"

"We aren't supposed to discuss the whereabouts of our guests, Madame. If you are friends, you could wait maybe?"

"I would, but this is possibly an emergency?"

"Possibly? Either it is or it is not, ya?"

"Okay, I am about 90% sure it is. Can you tell me?"

The pair looked at each other before the woman answered. "Monsieur Pritchard left almost forty-five minutes ago. He was dressed in jogging attire."

"Do you know which way he went?"

"No, I am sorry I don't."

"It's okay, thank you for your help."

"It is my pleasure, Madame."

Shelby rushed outside and scanned the horizon to see if she could see him. He was out of sight for now. Having a thought, she made a series of educated guesses about his whereabouts that led to a set of footprints made by running shoes that led down the beach. She followed them at a brisk walking pace, gradually speeding up to a jog. She made it a mile or so down the beach where it came to a point and turned off in the other direction. As she rounded the bend she heard voices coming from off the shoreline. She moved stealthily closer to find that Mr. Scary and Hairy was holding a gun on Jackson and badgering him about an unnamed account sitting in a holding area in an anonymous bank based in Switzerland. Not knowing about the account, Jackson couldn't answer to his satisfaction. Frustrated and rapidly losing patience, the man cracked Jackson across the cheek with the butt of a pistol he had hidden under his belt. Jackson fell to the sand like a rag doll. He sat, pulled himself up and onto his feet and gathered his thoughts. "No Jessica means no deal. So where is she?"

"She's safe, doing well actually. Sends her regards."

"You bastard, if there is so much as one little hair out of place I will stalk you until one of us is dead."

"That sounds like a challenge I would be up for."

"Or I could just beat the crap out of you right now." Jackson stood to his feet again, feeling a little wobbly from the blow to the head he had taken. Mitchell took the pistol out of his belt and pointed it at Jackson.

"I had hoped not to have to shoot you, but you leave me with no alternative. Now, I am going to count to three and if you haven't given me what I need, I will put a bullet through your brain and watch you die. Then I will go back and get much better educated with your girlfriend and show her how a real man treats a whore. Until she gives it to me."

"She doesn't know anything. I don't know anything."

"Of course you don't. That's why you are down here at some out of the way island that no one has ever heard of. That's why I found you in a swank hotel with a huge suite overlooking the ocean."

"And the thought never crossed your little pea brain that I could have made my own money and paid for this on my own?"

Mitchell paused for a moment, narrowing his eyes to small slits. He chuckled and said, "Whatever." He raised the gun back up and stepped towards Jackson, pressing the gun between his eyes. "Okay, back to the point. I'm going to count to three and then I'm going to shoot you if you don't tell me what I want to know."

"I'm telling you I don't know what you are talking about."

"One."

Jackson voice rose along with his heart rate. He had to figure out a way to give him something to get out of the situation. He looked up and down the beach, seeing no one. "If I knew, I would tell you, I swear."

"Two. I almost believe you." He cocked the hammer of his gun. "Almost. Now would be a good time to say a quick prayer, if you are a praying man. He shifted his weight, preparing himself for the shot.

"Look, I have money. I can replace whatever it was that was stolen."

Mitchell shook his head. "They always beg and then try to make deals. Last chance to tell me." Jackson shook his head. "Suit yourself. Thr..."

BOOM! The noise was deafening and a shockwave blew over his skin. "Wait," Jackson thought as he opened his eyes. He moved his hands over his body checking for something, whatever. There, lying on the ground in front of him was the man with the gun. A pool of blood was forming in the sand, flowing from the hole in his head. He looked to the right and saw Shelby Powers standing with a gun in her hand and her arm extended at a 90-degree angle from her body. A thin stream of smoke drifted out from the barrel.

"What? How did...where did...what the hell are you doing here?"

"Saving you from him. And from yourself."

"From myself? What are you talking about?"

"There's no time for that. Someone will have heard the shot, I have to go."

"What? Wait. I have to find Jessica. Do you know where she is?" Shelby was walking away and stopped at the mention of her name. "You do know. Where is she? WHERE IS SHE?"

She sighed deeply. "He is staying at the hotel just down the beach from you. The one with the big awning out front. I am sure she is there."

Jackson stepped over to the body and rolled it over. His face was covered with sand. The man smelled of sweat and alcohol and his eyes and mouth were both open with surprise. Jackson checked his pockets and found a key with a room number stenciled on it. He looked up and Shelby was gone. He thought about running after her, but Jessica was more important. The hotel was a short run down the beach and he burst through the doorway, ran up a flight of stairs, finally reaching the room. He opened the door and looked around to the pigsty the man had turned his room into. What he did not see was Jessica. Jackson turned to leave but stopped when he heard a whimpering coming from the bathroom. He burst in to find Jessica handcuffed to the sink and crying.

"Jessica! Oh my God I was so scared." He gently pulled the tape from her mouth and kissed her. She sobbed and breathed heavily.

"I knew you would come. I think he threw the key back on one of the tables in the other room." Jackson went back in the main room and found the key and unlocked the handcuffs. "Where is he?"

"He's dead."

"Oh my God, did you?"

"No I didn't, but someone I know did."

"Who?"

"A woman I know from Memphis. She works for the computer company where I have my laptop serviced."

"What is she doing here?"

"I don't know exactly. She said she was helping save me from myself?"

"What does that mean?"

"I don't know exactly. It's a good thing she was here though, you and I could both be dead by now."

"Was she a client? Or did you two date?"

"No and no. We didn't date, but we did hook-up one weekend a very long time ago. She kept trying to make something more of it."

"So she's been stalking you?"

Jackson paused as the realization hit him, "Yeah, I guess she has been."

They left the room and descended the stairway, leaving the hotel and stepping back into the sunshine. They looked up the beach and saw that a small crowd had gathered around the body. A uniformed officer was moving everyone back and outlining the area with tape. Jackson took Jessica by the hand and they headed in the other direction. The walk back to their hotel was short and they hurried through the lobby and up the stairs. They opened the door to their suite and came face to face with Will Swift.

CHAPTER 124

"Hello Jackson. How's your vacation going?"

"Not so good Detective if truth be known."

"You don't like the islands?"

"I love them. Everything was going great until that guy showed up."

"What guy?"

"You don't know? I figured that's why you were here."

Jackson and Jessica led the two detectives back down the beach to the body. It was covered with a tarp. The crowd of bystanders had grown larger and they pushed their way through. Will and his partner showed their badges to the police officer and introduced themselves. No one noticed that Shelby Powers was watching the scene from half a mile away through a pair of binoculars.

"So what do we have here?"

"One dead white man. He's been shot in the head. We haven't had a murder on this island in years."

Jackson spoke up, "It wasn't a murder. He was going to kill me and someone shot him."

Will looked back at him. "Who shot him?"

"A woman from Memphis that I know."

"That wouldn't be Shelby Powers would it?"

Jackson's head whipped around in surprise, "How did you know?"

"We've already been to Memphis to arrest her. I'm pretty sure she killed Sharon Milligan and she tried to kill Meredith Gregory."

"Meredith? When?"

"Just after the funeral. She's going to be fine, though."

Art walked over the body and uncovered it. "I know this guy. It's Mitchell Varner, didn't you say he was on our flight to Memphis?"

"Yes," Will answered, shaking his head.

"Guess he won't be on the return flight. Well not sitting in the passenger section anyway."

"That's cold, partner."

"Sorry, long trip. You know how traveling makes me cranky."

Will looked back at Jackson, "Why don't we go back inside and we can try and figure this whole thing out." Jackson shook his head and they walked back down the beach. A few minutes later, they were sitting in the balcony off of their suite. Will started.

"So you saw Shelby shoot Mitchell?"

"I didn't watch her pull the trigger. But he was getting ready to shoot me and I closed my eyes. There was a loud explosion and the next thing I know, he is on the ground with a hole in his head and Shelby was standing behind him with a gun in her hand. It was surreal."

"Why was he going to kill you?"

"That's what I didn't get. He kept demanding to know the password to some bank account somewhere. He insisted I knew and was going to get it out of me one way or another."

"But you don't know it?"

"I don't have the first idea what he was talking about."

"I didn't think you did. When was the last time you answered your cell phone?"

"It's been a few days."

"I tried to reach you to warn you. Some other people were calling too. I know Jan Eberhardt tried for a few days."

"Is she ok?"

"She's fine. She is watching over Meredith in Seattle."

"God, it's my fault."

"No, it's Shelby Powers' fault. We have her computer and some other evidence we gathered in Memphis. It has been shipped back to Seattle. I was hoping to bring her back with us, but obviously she wasn't in Memphis. So we found out she was here. Apparently she is gone again. How long ago did she leave you?"

"It's been a couple of hours now I guess.

"There's no telling where she is then. We'll put the arrest warrants on the wire and see if we can get her picked up somewhere. In the meantime, it's probably a good idea to get you packed up and checked out and on your way somewhere else."

The uniformed policeman sat quietly and had taken notes the entire time the conversation had been running. His Caribbean accent was not quite as pronounced as Jean Pierre or Marc's, but at the same time carried the same lilt and relaxed cadence. "I am convinced. We can close the book on this case. I will call a few friends around the islands to see if we can locate this Shelby Powers. The body will be held until tomorrow to make sure the autopsy is properly done. Will you be making the arrangements to ship it back to the United States?"

Will answered. "Yes, it will take a few minutes to get that arranged. It will be done, though."

"Splendid, then unless you need anything else, I will leave you to your arrangements. I do hope you will enjoy what's left of your stay."

"Thank you," Jackson replied. "You have been most helpful in this matter." He checked his cell phone and found that he had 17 unheard messages. He scanned through them, shaking his head at the unfortunate timing. There were five from Detective Swift and six from Jan Eberhardt. He hung up and picked up the room phone and pressed the "zero" key. Jean Pierre answered.

"Hello Jean Pierre. Listen, I hate to do this, but our plans have changed a little bit. We need to leave tonight if that is possible." There was a long pause. "It is? Great. What time do we need to be ready to go?" He looked at his watch and nodded. We'll be downstairs then. "Okay, we have an hour and a half to pack and be downstairs. Jean Pierre will have a water taxi waiting for us to take us back to the main island. We can try and catch a plane from there.

"Already done." Will hung up his phone. "The four of us will fly into Memphis tonight. Pack, make sure we have everything we need and then fly to Seattle the next morning."

"Seattle, why would we go there?"

"Well, it's where I live first of all and I miss my wife. Second of all, I am hoping we can catch up with Shelby Powers and take her back there with us as well. Finally, there is another case I am going to ask you two to testify in."

"What case is that?" Jessica demanded.

"The man that hired the guy that kidnapped you," he pointed at her and turned his attention back to Jackson, "And tried to get bank account information out of you with a gun. We have already indicted him, now we are going back to arrest him. I need you two to testify to what happened here."

"And if we don't want to go?"

"I would hope that you would want to come just as a good citizen. But if you refuse, I can detain you under protective custody since there was an attempt on your lives. Then a court could order you to testify. I'm not sure why you wouldn't though, this is no big deal."

"NO BIG DEAL? I get hit in the head, handcuffed and gagged in a bathroom and he gets accosted at gunpoint and you say it's no big deal?"

"Did you say accosted?" Jackson asked with a bewildered look on his face.

"You hush, and yes I did."

"Just checking."

"I know you have been through a very traumatic experience. I'm saying the court proceeding in Seattle is no big deal. I'm on your side and have been since we met. But Jackson, you are the common denominator and I don't want to have to detain you. If that happens and the evidence comes out about your old job, that is simply going to raise questions that you might want asked and definitely don't want to answer. I'm sure you just want this to be over and done with."

"We do," Jessica sighed. "I have plans for him far away from Memphis."

"You do?" Jackson raised an eyebrow.

"Yes, we talked about this already!"

"Oh yeah," he turned to Will. "Do you have a dartboard on you?"

"I'm sorry?"

"Inside joke. We can find one soon enough."

Jessica smiled from ear to ear. "Are you serious?"

"Absolutely. The sooner the better."

"Wow, okay then. Let's get going, we're burning daylight?"

Jackson shook his head. "Are we in an old western? Who says burning daylight?"

"You two are a bit crazy, you do know that, right?"

"Maybe, Detective, but in the best way possible."

"Been there; happy for you. Ok, lets get to work."

CHAPTER 125

Shelby was already on an airplane back to the States by the time the alerts hit the network. She had altered her appearance somewhat as an added precaution. It was amazing how much an added scarf here or an extra bit of padding around the midsection could change one's appearance at first glance. She checked her watch and noted that she had an hour or so left on her flight. The events surrounding the last couple of days had sufficiently worn her out. The seat laid back sufficiently enough for her to get comfortable and fall quickly asleep. The image of the scary hairy guy's head exploding after she pulled the trigger seemed to be stuck in her head. Over and over the image appeared and began to move in slow motion. It was like watching a movie with someone else controlling the remote control. Shelby hoped that the scene switched soon. Then Jackson's face appears. The look on it was too terrible to stomach. It was a combination of horror and revulsion without the gratitude one would expect from someone that saved your life. It was a look of a person seeing a monster. The scene shifted again. Now the scary hairy guy was standing and holding the gun, although now he wasn't aiming it at Jackson. He was aiming it at HER. Shelby twitched in her seat. The scary hairy guy was laughing. Jackson stood

357

next to him shaking his head and laughing as well. The scary hairy guy asked Jackson if it was ok and Jackson motioned in her direction as if giving him the go ahead. The gun loomed closer and closer to her head until she couldn't see the barrel any longer. The feel of cold steel pressed against her temple let her know where it was. She begged him for her life. He just laughed. She watched as his finger pressed against the trigger and began to squeeze. "It's time," he mouthed. She saw but didn't understand what he was trying to tell her. "It's time, wake up!" She felt a hand on her arm and tried to shake it off. She sat up in her chair and screamed "No!" and looked around the cabin of the airplane.

"I'm so sorry ma'am," the flight attendant sounded sincere. "But we have landed and it's time to get off the plane."

"No, it's ok. I was just having a bad dream. Thank you for waking me up."

"You're welcome. Had a busy vacation?"

"Something like that." Shelby looked around at the empty airplane and shook the cobwebs out of her head. She gathered her carry on bag and walked to the doorway. It was early evening and the nap had refreshed her immensely. The cell phone in her pocket rang and she looked and saw it was Jonas.

"Hey, stranger. How is the wet Northwest?"

"It's wet. Where are you?"

"Memphis, why?"

"Because I've been trying to reach you. They are after you."

"Who is after me?"

"The cops. They were here busting my chops and asking me questions about you."

"What kind of questions?"

"They think you shot someone. And stabbed someone else. You didn't did you?"

"No, don't be silly."

"Good, I didn't think so and told them that. They wanted me to give up where you were."

"And what did you tell them?"

"The truth, I didn't know. But I think they are there now, looking for you. I think they have a warrant and everything."

Her heart sank. "I need you to do something for me."

"I'm not going to get in trouble am I? My favorite detective keeps waving my parole in front of me. And if you did anything he said, that means my going away for a while."

"Did he mention that you working for him and tracking me down without a warrant constitutes an illegal search? And that any evidence that comes out of that is inadmissible?"

"No, but he's not investigating me. He's investigating you. So if I do anything outside of that, it doesn't apply."

"But he isn't going to fuck you nearly as well as I am going to."

"Ok, you said the magic word, what do you need?"

"I need to know where that detective is and where he is going."

"Well, he's in Memphis. And then I would guess he is coming back here."

"Ok, interesting. So if I can make it up there, do you have a place for me to crash?"

"Absolutely, does my face work for you?"

"It will for a good long while. We'll need to sleep at some point though." She rolled her eyes, thinking how easy it was to manipulate a boy.

"No problem."

"Okay, I need to get some money and take care of a few loose ends. I may head your way and I may not. I'll call you and let you know."

"So what do I do until then?"

"Find out where your friend is exactly and then let me know."

"Done."

Shelby hung the phone up, her mind racing. There were so many things she needed to take care of and she wasn't exactly sure where to start. She walked over to a pay phone and dropped some change in it; dialing the phone number her computer was attached to. It rang and rang without anything picking up. She knew that meant her computer was no longer hooked up. They were onto her. It was time to disappear with her true love. Once she explained everything including being his savior, both literally and figuratively, she was certain he would be more than ready to go with her. First, she needed money. She looked up the location of the nearest Western Union and drove there. She was sure that her credit cards would be watched along with her license plate. But she needed to get somewhere quickly and couldn't chance renting a car. She would have to be careful. It was a short five-minute drive and she made it there without incident. She called the secure phone number to the bank where she had set up the numbered account and reached a manager. The entire transaction took less than five minutes and she left with almost $10,000 in her pockets. She would have gotten more, but she was limited in how much they would advance her at such short notice. She got back on the interstate, heading west. Twenty minutes later she was in Arkansas. She stopped at an information center and found a U.S. Atlas. A few minutes later, she had mapped out a road trip to Seattle and headed west with a Honda Civic full of gas, some snacks and a 12-pack of energy drinks. It was time for her to claim what was rightfully hers.

CHAPTER 126

A bleary-eyed Jessica opened the door to her house, comforted by the familiarity of its sights and smells. The last couple of weeks had been a whirlwind and her head seemed to spin uncontrollably. Three different times on their trip back from the islands, she had almost broken down in tears. If not for the man following her through the door, she would have certainly lost it. She stopped short in the doorway, causing him to run into her.

"You did that on purpose."

"I certainly did. Now drop those bags and wrap those arms around me. I need a hug."

"You could have more than that if we didn't have chaperones tonight."

"I kind of feel better that they are going to be here though, don't you?"

"I guess so. Are you hungry? It's kind of late, but I could go pick something up for everyone"

"Now Jackson Pritchard, I believe it is well outside of your upbringing to suggest that you would be in charge of hospitality in my house." She smiled to show she appreciated his gesture. "If you think these gentlemen are going to come in my house and eat take-out, you have another thing coming. Now, are you hungry? It won't take me long to throw something together."

He sat down and she went to work in the kitchen. Will and Art joined Jackson and Jessica smiled at the feeling of feeding an army again. Her house had been the house that all the kids had wanted to hang out at because she always fed them. That had contributed to the popularity of her son. He had taken it from there and done well. Her ever-present smile broadened at the reminiscence, as if she had experienced the most pleasant of daydreams. It all seemed a lifetime ago however, and the reality of her current situation loomed large and weighed heavily on her. She focused her attention on her kitchen for now though, and an hour later, the foursome sat around her kitchen table, with heaping bowls of pasta, salads and bread crowding them.

"Thanks for dinner Jessica, we could have ordered out though."

"What fun would that be? Besides, you guys get to wash the dishes."

"Deal."

Jackson smiled at her and then turned his attention to Will. "So what have you found out?"

"Well, she was on the flight back to Memphis, we traced that on her credit card. From there, she seems to have disappeared. Memphis has two units watching her apartment and we will grab her when she comes home. She will have to come home sooner or later. There is a decent amount of money in her accounts and she will have to get at it at some point."

"What if she doesn't?"

"Well, then she would have to disappear from the grid. It happens. If someone really doesn't want to be found, then they won't be. The good news is if she is hiding, she is less likely to go after anyone that knows her. The survival instinct is a very powerful thing."

"So you are saying that we don't have anything to worry about?"

"No, I'm not saying that. I'm saying it's less likely that you have something to worry about. But there are no guarantees, especially when you are dealing with someone that is a little bit off?"

Art laughed. "I'd say she's more than just a little 'off,' wouldn't you partner?"

"Maybe, but she's not acting irrationally. She's thinking ahead and trying to cover her tracks. SO that makes her rational, which usually means that the fight-or-flight instinct is working. In situations where rational people find themselves unprepared for the situation they are in, their typical response will lean the way of flight."

"I hope you are right," Jessica said. "Although I enjoy your company gentlemen, I would as soon be alone with Jackson right now."

"I understand very well. We'll fly out late morning and be in Seattle tomorrow afternoon. Our lieutenant is checking to see if we can get in to see the judge tomorrow afternoon or the next morning. You'll do your bit before the grand jury and then you should be done."

"Should be?"

"Just keeping the possibility open. As far as I am concerned, your work for the Seattle Police Department will be finished. Memphis may want to talk to you about anything she might have done here."

"But I don't have any clue what she might have done. I only saw her at her office except for the one weekend we were out."

"I understand. And the Detective I spoke to here is aware of that. They still might want to talk to you."

"Okay. So when do we leave?"

"Our flight leaves at 11:00. That should give you two plenty of time to sleep in."

They finished dinner and true to their word, the two Detectives pitched in to help clean the kitchen. Jessica dug out some blankets and extra pillows for them and they made impromptu beds on her two sofas. Art agreed to take the first watch to make sure no one tried to ruin an otherwise lovely evening.

Will wandered off and called his wife and son and spent several minutes getting caught up on the happenings in their household. Everyone seemed relieved that his trip would soon be over. He said his good nights and told his wife how much he loved and missed her and then hung up. He then dialed a much-dialed number as of late and waited for two rings before he heard the familiar voice.

"Good God detective, yes I will sleep with you if it will make you go away."

"I think you have mentioned something like that before Jonas and it concerns me. Not getting enough lately?"

"When have I ever gotten enough?"

"Good point. I was just checking in to see if you had heard from our friend."

"I wouldn't imagine she would call you her friend would you Detective?"

"I guess not, but that's not what I asked you, now is it?"

"No, it's not. And no, I haven't heard from her. I figured you swooped in and snatched away any chance I would ever have of sleeping with her."

"I'm sorry to put such a crimp in your style Jonas, but I am trying to catch a killer."

"Yeah, whatever, outside of me, you have barely caught a cold."

"She shot someone else Jonas. Down on the island. This time, there is a witness."

"Really?"

"Yep, the funny thing about this one is that she could claim self-defense this time. Defense of another anyway."

"So she saved someone?"

"You know I can't comment, Jonas. If you talk to her, tell her to come in and see me. I will do what I can for her. Anyone that defends someone else isn't a bad person. I think she is just a little misguided."

"If she calls me I will tell her Detective. Maybe you aren't such a bad guy after all."

"Don't tell anyone Jonas, I do have a reputation to protect."

"Your secret is safe with me."

CHAPTER 127

Jessica awoke early and slipped out from under Jackson's arm. She paused for a moment and drank in the comfortable silence of her own house. She made her way to the front door to retrieve the newspaper. An hour later, she had perused the paper and had her morning coffee. She thought for a moment and began to cook for her guests again. Jackson came in and greeted her with a kiss. The detectives followed half an hour later or so and grumbled their good mornings. Jessica teased them like she had done with her son for many years. The banter over the breakfast table came fast and furiously. Everyone ate and helped clean up afterwards. They had eaten, in Jessica's words, "a good southern breakfast." With a few hours before they were scheduled to leave, Jessica and Jackson excused themselves and went to see Mike and Max. Mike was extremely unhappy with the bump on her head and the story of the abduction and kidnapping. He repeated his warning to Jackson to take care of his girl "or else."

"You aren't nearly as upset as I was at the time, trust me. To that point, we now have a traveling police escort."

"Really?"

"Well, yes, kind of. They are actually taking us back to Seattle to give a statement in a couple of different cases."

"I see." He turned to Jessica who was busy getting a tongue bath from Max. "How long will you be gone this time?"

"A couple of days, I'm not exactly sure, is that ok? I can call Melanie if you need a break."

"Nah, Max and I are good buddies again. Take your time."

"How is the Monkey?"

"It's good. Your regulars have been asking about you. I am guessing you have about fifty bucks waiting there. They leave you tips even when you aren't working."

"That is interesting. Let me guess." She named the four absentee tippers and Mike just shook his head. "What can I say, they love me."

"It's true," Mike said to Jackson more than Jessica. "So, bring her back and keep her regulars and me happy." The pair exchanged furtive glances. "What? You are bringing her back to us, right?"

Jessica spoke first. "Well, we are coming back. But how long we will stay afterwards? I can't say for sure."

"You're leaving? Where are you going?"

"We aren't sure yet," she looked at Jackson, "right?"

"Yep, it all depends on the flight of a randomly thrown dart."

"You're kidding," Michael said flatly.

"Would I kid you?"

"And to think I bought you a sandwich."

"I said thank you, and tipped the staff well."

"Too well, apparently; you're taking one of them with you."

"It wasn't just his idea, Mike. I have been here for a while now and it's time to see what else is out there for me."

"I guess so. So I guess I need to hire someone then?"

"Probably. It will take you about two seconds to replace me."

"Nice try. My girls aren't easily replaced. I told you that when I hired you."

"You did, and thank you for everything. We just need to go somewhere and start 'us' in a new place."

"I think I understand."

"I knew you would; you're a sweetheart." Jessica stood and kissed his forehead.

"Thank you, now go away."

They made their way back to Jessica's house and picked up the detectives. The drive to the airport was quiet and the flight uneventful. The travel weary foursome left Seattle airport together in Art Menking's department issue sedan. The day itself hadn't worn them out, rather it was the accumulation of stress and travel over the past several days.

Will called the office from the car and found that they couldn't get in front of the judge until the morning. They made arrangements for Jackson and Jessica to be put up in a hotel and dropped them there. Uniformed officers were assigned for the night through the next day to ensure their safety. Will hung up the phone and addressed the pair wearily. "They will be here in the next hour or so."

"That's fine," Jessica said. "I'm ready to crash and do nothing."

"I was actually thinking about going to the hospital if that's okay. I called yesterday and Meredith is doing well. I'd like to see her and Jan."

"It's okay with me," Will said.

"Me too," Jessica answered.

"I was kind of hoping you would go with me," Jackson shuffled his feet nervously.

"Really? Why?"

"I don't know. It just seemed right for me to want you with me."

"That's sweet. But both women were clients, right?"

"Yes."

"I'm not sure I am ready for that."

"Ok, whatever works for you."

"I'm not saying 'no,' I'm just not sure."

"Not to butt in kids, but we are going to get out of your way. I'll call you in the morning to make sure you are ready. Why don't we pick you up at 8:30?"

"Ok, we'll see you downstairs."

Jackson and Jessica watched the pair leave the hotel before grabbing their bags and heading up to their room. The elevator was quick and the

367

door opened with the first swipe of their room key card. They dropped their luggage and plopped down on the king-sized bed.

"On second thought, the bed is kind of nice."

"It is, isn't it?"

"Yes, and I plan on wasting the majority of the available space in it tonight."

"How do you plan on doing that?"

"Well, where are you going to be sleeping in it?" Jessica pointed to the side of the bed away from the window. "So right about there?" He moved her over to the spot and pressed her down slightly until she was laying flat. "Then I will be right about here." He moved as closely to her as he possibly could without being on top of her.

Jessica laughed loudly. "Okay, I get it. It takes me a while sometimes."

"Apparently." He laughed and ducked the play slap that was already on its way. He tackled her and rolled her over straddling her with his knees on either side of her chest. They both laughed and collapsed in a heap. Jackson kissed her sweetly on the tip of her nose and then with a bit more passion an inch or so lower. They stayed that way for a few minutes until Jackson broke away. "I really should go. It's the right thing to do."

"Yes it is. Am I dressed okay?"

"You're coming?"

"There's a phrase that we should both get comfortable with: 'Where you go, I go'."

"It has a nice ring to it."

"Ya think?"

He kissed her again. "Yes ma'am, I do."

"There you go with the 'I do's' again. Be careful, someone might overhear you saying that and get the wrong idea."

"I'll remember that in case I get asked that in a pressure filled situation. How was the delivery, believable?"

"It will do in a pinch. Your tone could stand a bit of work."

"Thanks."

"No problem."

"Okay, let's see about a cab then."

CHAPTER 128

Michael Carey paced back and forth in his office. He pressed the intercom on his desk. "Are you sure I don't have any messages?"

"No sir. I checked the first couple of times you asked and nothing has come in since."

"Okay, let me know as soon as anyone does call."

"Yes sir." She hung up the phone and rolled her eyes. "What part of your instructions do you think I didn't get the first five times you told them to me?"

Michael sat back down in his chair and checked his computer again. No e-mails. No messages. No nothing. He should have heard something by now. He wouldn't dial the number on the off chance that Mitchell Varner had gotten arrested or worse. Michael's mind raced with possibilities. He got arrested. He found the money and ran. He never left Seattle. Shaking his head, he reassured himself that Mitchell was a worker. He would complete the task and get back as soon as he could. Case closed. Nothing to worry about.

Across town, Jackson and Jessica stepped out of the cab and into the hospital lobby.

"Did I mention I hate hospitals?

Jessica laughed. "It's a bit late for that, don't you think?"

"I suppose."

"We should stop and buy flowers."

"Why?"

"Because it's what you do. You had such good manners only a week ago. Are you going to be one of those guys who goes to pot as soon as he gets what he wants?"

"I'm sorry," he said shaking his head and not seeing how hard she was trying not to laugh. "I'm just not thinking clearly."

"I should say not since I am over here trying not to laugh myself silly."

"You're not nice."

"Yes I am, I'm very nice."

"You are that. And you're right, flowers are very appropriate." They stopped in the gift shop and bought an elegant arrangement with a vase and made their way to Meredith's room. Arriving there, they found another armed guard, this one watching her door and the comings and goings. Jackson showed his identification and they let the pair in.

"Jackson!" Meredith exclaimed. "Oh God, don't look at me, I have been in a hospital bed for a month it seems."

"You look great," he leaned down and kissed her forehead. He paused for a moment, not knowing exactly what to say or do next.

Jessica rescued him. "Jackson brought something to brighten the room up." She took them from him and cleared a place on her bedside table. "There, that does the trick I think."

Meredith smiled broadly. "They are beautiful. Thank you Jackson!"

"We brought them actually." Jackson looked in Jessica's direction and frowned slightly.

Jessica held up her hand. "I just picked out colors…that is a woman's prerogative."

"I'm sorry. Meredith…" Jan popped her head out of the restroom. "And Jan, this is my friend Jessica Young. Jessica, this is Jan Eberhardt and Meredith Gregory."

Jessica shook both their hands and very politely said, "I have heard a lot about both of you. It's a pleasure finally meeting you."

"The pleasure is ours. What say we get better acquainted?" She took Jessica by the hand with the intention of leading her out of the room.

Jackson looked a bit perplexed over his shoulder. He looked at Jan coolly. "It's okay that she stays. I don't have any secrets from her."

"Really?" Both women looked flabbergasted.

"Really, she knows pretty much everything. Plus I reserve the right to retain editorial power over what stories she tries to tell you."

"Pretty much?"

"Well she hasn't asked for references from former clients or anything. The rest I can pretty much fill in on my own." He turned his attention back to Meredith. "How are you feeling?"

"Much better. I am back on my feet for an hour a day and just getting stronger as quickly as I can. I have work to do."

"I am sure that work will wait. I am certain that Jan could have someone pick up the slack for you since you got SHOT." He raised his voice intentionally to make his point.

It didn't work. "No need to shout, I haven't aged that much since I last saw you."

"Hopeless," he muttered, rubbing his temples, "Completely hopeless."

"Hopeful," she corrected, "but I expect you remember that."

Jackson turned to Jessica and explained. "In Jan's world, there are two kinds of people. First are the people that see a situation and let it be governed by whatever the natural limitations of the people involved. Second are the people that see their limitations and attempt to break through and do something new or unexpected. Some people call them dreamers. Jan calls them…"

"Hired." Jan interrupted with a laugh. She turned to Jessica. "I try to hire people with an outlook that leads to questioning, gathering information and then making the best possible decision. I think that's important in all kinds of decisions. Business, personal, or some kind of combination therein."

"So you want people that don't allow themselves to be limited by what they see? Sort of think-outside-the-box people?" Jessica asked.

"Something exactly like that," he nodded.

"I can see why you and Jackson got along so well." Jessica said.

"And I am starting to see why he likes you so much." Jan turned to Jackson, "She's sharp."

"Yes she is."

"Except for being taken in by you, that might show a character flaw." She winked to both, letting them know that she was teasing.

"We can't all be perfect."

"That's true, but you all can keep trying." Jan had a smug look on her face. They all shared a laugh.

"Did everyone forget about me over here?" Meredith asked loudly. All FOUR laughed that time. "So where are you two going from here?"

Jackson thought for a moment before answering. "Well, we have to talk to the judge tomorrow and hopefully get an idea about what they need to catch Sharon's killer."

"So they have a suspect?" Jan asked.

"I don't know if I can give details, but yes, I think they know who it was."

Meredith was shaking her head. "I meant what is next for you two when all this is over."

"Oh that," Jackson chuckled, "I'm not sure. I think we are going to leave Memphis and start over...again. I'd like to close that chapter of my life and start fresh somewhere new. Some place new and maybe some place old at the same time. New for us but maybe a fixer-upper house or a business or both that can occupy our time for a while." Jackson subconsciously reached out and took Jessica's hand.

"That sounds nice. If you need help, let me know. The pay is good with what I do, but there seems to be a bit of risk involved."

"Tough job," Jackson said dryly.

"Tough boss," Meredith countered.

"Tough clients," Jan answered both. "They need tough people to take care of them in return."

"I hear you. I think she qualifies though, don't you? I mean, how many of your people have been shot?"

"Six."

"What? Are you kidding me?"

"I get that a lot. Yes, I'm kidding."

"I was going to say, must be hell on your insurance rates."

"Yes, but is saves me a ton in retirement pay outs."

"You're awful. Funny though." Jackson turned his attention back to Meredith. "So when are you leaving?"

"Doctor said probably the day after tomorrow. There's a symposium I need to be at early next week, so that will give me plenty of time to travel and rest beforehand."

"Good, is there anything you need?"

"No, but you're sweet for asking." She turned to Jessica. "You're a pretty lucky woman, you know?"

"I think so. The jury is still out on him though." They laughed, both looking at Jackson.

"Wait, how and when did I become the topic of conversation here?"

"Just now and just because," Jessica wrinkled her nose in his direction. "You should feel lucky that everyone here is a fan of yours."

"I know...and I do."

The nurse poked her head in. "Okay, time to rest. You three... out!"

Jackson and Jessica said their good-byes and caught a cab back to the hotel. It was dark in the cab and Jessica cuddled close to Jackson. "Soooo, They were nice."

"Yes, they seemed to like you too."

"Can I ask you a question?"

"If I said no, would it stop you?"

"No."

"I didn't think so. Shoot."

She paused for a moment, choosing her words carefully. "Well... why me?"

"What do you mean?"

"Why me? Those women are beautiful and powerful and have money and they are smart and..."

"Is there a pause button anywhere?" Jackson scanned back and forth over the cab.

Jessica feigned taking offense. "I'm serious, they have so much to offer."

He snapped his fingers. "You're right, driver can you turn around and take me back to the hospital?" The driver slowed as if to turn around. "Sorry, never mind. The hotel please." Jessica punched him in the shoulder. "You started it. You are right; they have an incredible amount to offer. But they don't have anything to offer to me. What they have to give, I have seen before and it's not anything I want. Their world is about money and prestige and power and who is climbing what ladder and how fast and who is wearing what and blah, blah, blah."

"And I offer you…"

"You offer me you. In a very short time you have shown me more of yourself than anyone I can remember. And it's a beautiful self."

"Thank you."

"No, thank you."

The cab pulled up to the hotel and they went upstairs. The uniformed officers had set up shop outside their room. They talked for a minute until Jackson and Jessica understood the ground rules.

"We aren't planning on going anywhere. Might be a quiet night. We're about to order dinner, do you want anything?"

The officers declined, thinking twice about their decision when the food was delivered. Jackson and Jessica ate, watched part of a movie and then cuddled together, him spooning in behind her, falling fast asleep before the final credits rolled.

CHAPTER 129

The second article that Jackson had gotten published was a tongue-in-cheek piece that measured the decibel level of hotel telephones during their automated wake up calls. He had gotten several e-mails thanking him for his assessment. The hotel they were staying in apparently didn't adjust their volume as he had suggested in his article. Jackson shot up out of bed on the second ring, "Hello? Hello!" He heard a computer generated beeping in his ear and placed the phone back on its cradle. He fell face first back into his pillow, struggling against the pull of the comforter. "I hate wake up calls."

"Me too. Unplug the phone."

"Can't, we have a breakfast date."

"With?"

"Detective Swift."

"Who gets the shower first?"

"Why should we take turns? It would be a more environmentally friendly use of water if we shared."

"That's the best idea I have heard all day." Jackson threw the covers back up over his head and Jessica laughed. "C'mon, I'll make it up to you in the shower."

An hour later, they met Will in the restaurant and ordered breakfast.

"My you two look rested and refreshed. Sleep well?"

"Something like that. And I love the oversized showers here," Jessica added.

"Well good, I'm sure they have a comment card or something you can fill out."

"I'll make sure and do that."

Their food was delivered and Jessica noticed the small banquet placed in front of Will. "Don't they feed you at home, Detective?" Jackson asked with a raised eyebrow.

"She tries. I love my wife more than I could ever explain. But, she just can't cook very well. She's getting better at dinner, but breakfast is still awful."

"You poor thing!" Jessica frowned at him.

"What?"

"There's another cure for that you know."

"What?"

"You could, I dunno, COOK!"

"I tried! It hurt her feelings. I tried to cook her breakfast and she told me it wasn't any good. So she won't let me."

"How do you get around it then?"

"I go to work early and tell her I will grab something."

"Smart move," Jackson said with a mouthful of food.

"What?" Jessica looked surprised.

"For him, I love eating bad breakfast."

"So would you cook?"

"I think I have already demonstrated by willingness and ability to work hard in the kitchen."

"You cooked well too. I appreciate that in a man."

"Why thank you!"

"You're very welcome!"

"I'm not sure which makes me more sick, you two making goo goo eyes at each other or my wife's cooking. And this conversation is our little secret."

"What secret?" Art asked walking to the table.

"Nothing, just enjoying our breakfast."

Art leaned in conspiratorially, "You know, his wife is an awful cook. He sneaks breakfast in his car."

Jackson and Jessica smiled.

"You know?" Will looked shocked.

"How could you not? You have had me eat breakfast at your house more times than I care to remember."

"It's awful."

"I know. I forgive you. Now we have to go and see the judge."

"One more piece of bacon?"

"Take it with you."

Jonas was awakened by his cell phone. It took him five rings before he could find it. He tried to answer the TV remote before finding and answering the phone.

"Vampire Hotel. No one should call this early."

"Cute, Hello Jonas."

"Shelby? Where have you been?"

"Here and there, have you been looking for me?"

"I thought you were coming to see me?"

"Maybe I did?"

"You're in town?"

"Maybe. I need a favor."

"You seem to need a favor all the time from me."

"You should be flattered. I never ask favors of anyone."

"So what is it?"

"I need to know if the guy you took pictures of is in town?"

"Why?"

"Something is going on and I need to know about it."

"Can't do it. "

"What?"

"You heard me, can't do it."

"Why not?"

"Because you haven't told me anything about what's going on. And because that detective is going to arrest me and throw the key away."

"But I need…"

"I need something in return. You have given me exactly no reason to do anything."

"I know. But I am in town. And I would like to see you, just not today. I have to take care of a couple of things."

"Ok, how am I going to find your boy?"

"I have a feeling he is going to be with your boy." Shelby described Will from memory from what she saw at the islands. "See where he is going to be and call me back?"

"I'll see what I can find out."

The courthouse was typical in design. Neoclassical in style, adorned with columns and a big flight of concrete steps. Will and Art escorted Jackson and Jessica in through a side door and directly to the judge's chambers. Will checked his watch and found they had twenty minutes before the deposition. He excused himself and stepped into the alley and punched a number into his cell phone.

"Detective, I was just thinking about you."

"That can't be a good thing. Have you found anything out?"

"Nope, nada."

"So why were you thinking about me?"

"I was hoping I would see you so you could watch me dial the girl's phone number and therefore believe me when I left yet another message."

"I would have liked to have been there, I am sure it would have been a completely different message."

"Maybe. Especially if you had brought me a thong of hers like I asked you."

"You're still a sick man, Jonas."

"Thanks, I work hard at it."

"You're welcome. I have to go back to work."

"Say hello to that cute Sergeant at the desk for me."

"I'm not at the precinct, I'm downtown, not entirely too far from you. As a matter of fact, you and I spent several lovely afternoons together here once upon a time."

"The courthouse. Maybe I will come down and buy you lunch."

"I won't be here that long, but thanks for the offer."

"I won't do it again."

"I believe it. Find out what I need and let me know soon."

"You got it boss."

Jonas hung up and immediately called Shelby. "I have something for you, what do you have for me?"

"Depends what you have."

"He's at the courthouse."

"Thanks, I will call you tonight and we can plan for tomorrow."

"Ok, I will…" Click. "Fuck." Jonas didn't expect to hear from her, but why would that be different from any other girl on any other night.

Shelby parked a block away from the courthouse. She was nervous but knew that this was her last shot. She had to have a few minutes along with Jackson and could only think of this way to make it happen. Surely he would be able to see the logic behind her actions and would forgive her. She had forgiven him for his dalliances with the other women. It was his job after all. And she had saved his life, twice if you thought about it. Once for real on that island and then again by getting them the money they would need to live on so he could quit doing that nasty job. Of course he would forgive her. She just needed a few minutes alone.

The judge finished his questioning and Jackson and Jessica were excused from the room. They sat outside on a bench and waited for the detectives. Jackson got them both Cokes to drink. Fifteen minutes later, Will and Art emerged all smiles.

"Good news?"

"Absolutely. We got warrants for the man who had you followed and we indicted Shelby Powers in absentia for the murder of Sharon Milligan and the attempted murder of Meredith Gregory. She may be tied to an unsolved murder in Nashville, too; we are having her computer records shipped there as well."

"Sounds like a good day. Your mother would be very proud. What about what happened on the island?"

"My mother would be proud. I talked to the detective there before we left. The official report classified the shooting as justifiable self-defense. Or defense of another in this case. The files will be on hand in case there are further questions. Shall we go celebrate somewhere?"

"Somewhere with a map please."

"What?"

Jackson pulled Jessica closely to him and explained her comment. Will and Art both nodded and smiled. They made their way to the exit. The sun was bright and blinded them as they stepped outside. Art went to get the car. Will led the down to the steps and pulled out his cell phone. "I need to make a quick phone call."

Shelby's heart fluttered in her chest. She spotted Jackson and "SHIT!" she screamed loudly, banging her hand on the steering wheel. "SHIT! SHIT! DAMN! FUCK!" He was with that woman AGAIN. She grabbed two fistfuls of hair and screamed again. Tears streamed down her face, contorted with anger.

Jessica asked Jackson "Did you hear something?"

"Nothing stands out. What did it sound like?"

"Like someone in pain."

Shelby threw the car into drive and stomped on the accelerator.

Art pulled up to the curb across the street from the courthouse. Jackson and Jessica motioned to Will and he waved to them in recognition. They stepped into the street and towards the car. A woman screamed. Time stood still. Jackson saw the oncoming car out of the corner of his eye, grabbed Jessica and threw her towards the hood of Art's sedan. He braced himself for the impact but was hit first from behind. A searing pain shot through his left leg and he heard the squeal of a skidding car and two gunshots. Then everything went black.

CHAPTER 130

Jackson woke up with a terrible dry taste in his mouth and a splitting headache. His leg felt as if someone had torn it from his body and then reattached it with duct tape. He rubbed his eyes and gathered his wits about him. He was in a hospital bed and his leg was in a cast. Jessica was sitting across from his bed in a chair and sleeping soundly. Jackson looked to his left and found Will in the neighboring bed. Art was pacing back and forth across the room and a pretty black woman sat in a chair next to the bed, bouncing a young boy on her lap. Meredith sat in a wheelchair watching his TV and Jan stood in the hallway, visible through the propped open door, talking animatedly on her cell phone.

Art noticed Jackson stirring. "Well, well, look who is up."

Jessica shot up with a start and nearly jumped into Jackson's bed, hugging his neck. "Don't ever do that again. You scared me to death!"

"Did you not make it to the car?"

She popped him playfully in the chest in response. Then she kissed him. "How are you feeling?"

"Ok, my head hurts and my mouth feels like I drank a pitcher of sand. So what happened?"

Will spoke up. "You tried to be the hero. I couldn't have that, so I pulled the same trick you did. Apparently you weigh more than she does. So we both got hit." Jackson noticed that he had a matching foot cast along with one for his arm.

"Thanks man."

"No, thank you. Both of you. We couldn't have done what we did without your help."

"What happened to Shelby?"

"Well, my sharp-shooting partner here nailed two of her tires and caused her to run headfirst into a telephone pole. Not much give with those. She got a nasty bump on the head and split her lip open and a cell for one in our lovely jailhouse. No bail. She's not going anywhere soon. I hear her attorney has already started making noises about an insanity plea. This thing won't see the inside of a courtroom is my guess."

It was Jessica's turn to talk. "So you are finished with us?"

"As far as I know. I think we know everything you did at this point." He turned back to Jackson. "You didn't know about the money did you?"

"Nope, why?"

"She opened up a joint account with the money she took from Sharon Milligan. Apparently it was going to be some kind of wedding gift. A dowry I suppose."

"Nice. Maybe I should have given her another chance." He winked at Will who stifled a laugh.

Jessica scoffed playfully. "She never kissed you like I have and she never will. No one will."

"Hear hear."

"Well, the doctor says that you are both well enough to leave today. I asked him for a second opinion on the definition of 'well'. He had a confused look on his face, makes you wonder about what they are teaching in medical schools. Anyway, I have a little something for our new friends to remember us by."

"Art you big softie, what am I going to do with you?"

"Nothing, hopefully. My partner got put in a hospital bed and your girlfriend got hit in the head because of your stalker."

"And I would like to keep my husband in one piece." Jackson's head turned as the woman next to Will spoke for the first time.

"I'm sorry, Jackson this is my wife, Christiana. Baby, this is my new friend, Jackson Pritchard."

"My pleasure," Jackson bowed deferentially.

Art cleared his throat. "We did get you two something as a going away present." He brought a box out from under Christiana's chair and placed it in Jackson's lap.

"For us? You shouldn't have."

"Go ahead, open it."

Jackson peeled the paper back to reveal a U.S. map and a dartboard and dart set like you would find at any good English pub. He held them both up and smiled. Jessica covered her mouth with her hands as tears welled up in her eyes. Everyone else applauded.

Will broke the silence. "So where to?"

"Dunno. Let's see."

Art took the map and unfolded it and pinned it to the wall next to Jackson's bed. Jackson turned his back to the map and threw the dart over his shoulder.

"So where are we going?" he asked.

CHAPTER 131

The sun set on another gorgeous North Carolina summer day. Jackson lounged in a chair on the back deck and watched Jessica jogging on the beach with Max in tow. The tide rolled in and chased their feet, Max chasing it back into the ocean and returning to Jessica's side, tail wagging in triumph. She reached down and scratched behind his ears, praising him and laughing at the same time. Jackson stomped his foot on the wooden floor, testing it as the cast had been removed earlier that day. The lighthouse provided the perfect backdrop to the view and he smiled at their surroundings. Jessica ran right up to the deck and stopped about six inches from his face. She reached down and kissed his lips softly.

"Hey you."

"Hey yourself. You stopped too soon."

"What? Why do you say that?"

"Because I love watching you. You are quite stunning. Even if it's just your silhouette."

"You're hopeless, you know that?"

"I do. I'm hopelessly head over heels in love with you."

She smiled broadly and reached down and kissed him again. "I love you too, baby. I need to go check on dinner. Melanie will get upset if I make her do too much of the work."

"Did she sleep with the UPS guy that came by yesterday?"

"I don't have any idea what you are talking about," she said with a smile while shaking her head "yes."

Jackson sighed deeply. "I feel like your old boss, taking calls from the trail of broken-hearted men she leaves behind."

"It's tough being you."

"We have a bed and breakfast to run, not a house of ill-repute!"

"That reminds me, we are having the Dalton reception here this weekend. Did you get the stuff while you were in town?"

"Yes, right before I had my cast taken off. It IS tough being me isn't it?"

"I'll make it up to you later."

"I love it when you say that."

"I love that you make me want to say it every day."

She kissed him again and left him with his thoughts. His head turned and his eyes fell upon the map that Will and Art had given him. The dart held up one corner. Will figured that the dart might just stay put there for a while. It was a good thought and it filled him with a comfort that he hadn't experienced before. He loved her and was loved in return. What could be better than that?

CHAPTER 132

"And in conclusion, it is the finding of this board that Ms. Powers be released from mandatory in-patient care. The past five years have been quite a journey for you Shelby. You have made amazing progress and it is the hope of the board, as well as me personally, that you continue the steps you have taken here and do something positive with your life. Dr. Johnson would like to make a statement for the record before we adjourn today. Dr. Johnson?"

The frazzled-looking doctor leaned forward in his chair and took a deep breath. "Normally, we as a board do not make comments specific to these cases once a majority decision has been reached. I do want to go on the record in this case however. It was and remains my recommendation that Ms. Powers not be released from our care. As her primary therapist, I have spent hundreds and hundreds of hours with Shelby and while agree she has made progress, I do not agree with the board in that she is ready for the outside world. I fear that she will either fall back into a similar pattern and begin acting out again as she did before, or that she will be entirely too naïve and trusting and be taken advantage of in a world she won't recognize." He turned and spoke directly to Shelby. "I'm sorry, but I believe that what I am saying is for your own good."

Several seconds of silence passed. "Thank you Dr. Johnson. The board has heard your arguments already and…"

"I'd like to speak if I may," Shelby broke in. "I want to thank Dr. Johnson for all his time and effort and understanding. I can honestly say I wouldn't be sitting here if it wasn't for him. It me be an irregular request, but I would like to continue my treatment with him…with you Dr. Johnson, on an outpatient basis if that's possible."

The doctor stood and called the board into a huddle behind their table. They talked for just a few moments and returned to their seats. "While yours is an unusual request, the board approves and sees this as further validation for our original decision. If there are no more statements or any further business here, we are adjourned."

EPILOGUE

Jonas parked the car outside the hospital for the last time. Today marked the end of five years of coming and visiting and being frustrated by the progress and relapses of a beautiful but traumatized woman. No family had ever turned up and claimed her. Once a week, he made the drive and sat and waited for her to walk through the door. Some days she wanted to talk. Others she just sat for an hour and cried. Or looked into space not noticing Jonas at all. Last week, she had smiled timidly at him when he walked in and revealed her secret after a few minutes of him prying it out of her. She was being released! He had gone home afterwards and cleaned his apartment from top to bottom. He had no idea what an apartment for a woman was supposed to look like, but he hoped to be shown in short order.

The door opened and she walked out. She was dressed in black in the same clothes they had arrested her in. They hung off of her loosely as she had lost several pounds while in the hospital. Jonas scrambled out of the car and opened the door for her as she slid into the passenger seat.

"Thank you, kind sir."

"My pleasure."

He walked around to the driver's side and sat down. He had left the keys in the ignition and fired the car up.

"Actually I owe you a lot of thanks. Thank you for coming and picking me up. I think they sold my car after it had been in the impound lot for so long. It was kind of dinged up though, so I'm sure they didn't get much for it. And thank you for visiting me for five years. You're a special guy, Jonas. And I am going to make sure everyone knows it."

"Where else would I go? I love you, you know that." Jonas headed back in the direction of his apartment. It was a short drive if you caught the traffic the right way.

"I know, but I haven't told you that before and I wanted to. So thank you, again, for everything."

"It was nothing really."

"Well, your pleasure comes when we get to your place. Do you have any idea how long I have been waiting to get you in bed?"

"At least a day or two I hope."

"You're on the right track. A little longer though."

"So then what?"

"I don't know. The bathroom maybe? You said the apartment wasn't that big, so our choices would be somewhat limited."

Jonas laughed. "I love how you think. I was actually referring to what you and I do. Are you going to work or just relax for a while? Would you want to travel? I don't have a lot of money you know. My freelance work has been a bit slow and I think the good detective is still a bit upset with me that I couldn't find you before you went after the guy and his girlfriend."

"You'll live...and so will he. And don't worry about money, we are all set."

"How do you figure? The police and the courts took back all that money that you had taken. Did you have a lot of savings before or something?"

"No to the last question, and as far as the first one goes, they took back everything they knew about. That attorney wasn't going after a half million dollars. He was going after the five million that he didn't tell anyone about. His ego or his greed or whatever just wouldn't let him do it. So we have been earning interesting on that for five years now. That's kind of exciting wouldn't you say?"

"I would say. So then what?"

"I'm not sure. Live a life. Get a job. Do something worthwhile. I think I would enjoy that. Maybe teach some poor kids how to use computers. I'm sure there is some program somewhere like that."

A few minutes later, they pulled up in front of Jonas' apartment building. The term shabby chic still applied, despite the continued conversations that Jonas had with the landlord. Soon, it wouldn't matter. They climbed the stairs, each carrying one of her suitcases. They got to the apartment and talked for a while before Shelby brazenly walked up to Jonas and wrapped her arms around his neck and kissed him passionately. It lasted for nearly a minute as they became intimately familiar with each other, more and more so with each passing kiss. Jonas felt nervous and clumsy and demonstrated both traits while attempting to undress Shelby for the first time. She giggled a bit at his touch and moved his hands away, preferring to concentrate on him instead. She undid his shirt and jeans and slid both to the floor. Anticipation got the best of him and their first time together proved to be a very quick encounter.

Jonas excused himself and went to fix them a glass of water. She lay in bed for a few minutes until the enormity of her surroundings began to overwhelm her. She slid out from under the comforter and wrapped it around her, wandering into the kitchen. Jonas stood naked as the day he was born, drinking from a tall glass. He handed it to her and she took large drink before handing it back to him. She stood silently, an awkward silence filling the apartment.

"Sorry if that wasn't long enough," Jonas offered. "It's been a while since my last…confession." He laughed weakly, trying to hide his embarrassment.

"It was great, don't worry about it."

"Okay, thanks. You know what? I think this calls for a celebration. I have a bottle of wine I have been saving for a little while. It's not the best, but I think it will do. Would you like some?"

"Sure, what kind?"

"I'm not exactly sure…I'm not what you would call a connoisseur. It doesn't have a screw top so I am guessing it must be good." He reached up to a cabinet over the refrigerator and pulled out a dust-covered wine bottle. He filled two mismatched glasses three-quarters full with a dark red wine. He handed her one and cleared his throat. "If I learned anything from my old man, it was to make a toast and then finish my glass. About the only thing that bastard taught me." He raised his glass. "So here's to you and me. Through the lips and over the gums, watch out stomach, here it comes." He turned his glass upwards, draining it completely. She followed suit, grimacing at the bitter taste in her glass.

"It has been a while since I have had a drink. Feels like it went straight to my head."

"Are you ok?"

"I'm not sure. I feel…kinda…dizzy." She stumbled and place her hand on the counter to keep from falling. "Whoa. What…what's going on?" Panic began to creep into her voice.

Jonas reached into another cabinet. He retrieved a small brown bottle and handed it to Shelby. She held it close to her face, but was unable to make out the lettering. "It's sodium cyanide. A potent and pretty fast-acting poison." He walked across the room, locking the dead-bolt on the front door. "I was onto you a long time ago. It was obvious you were using me from the get go. And I found the money you were hiding. It's quite safe now, thank you for hiding it so well. The Seattle PD would never have found it. The genius that attorney hired wasn't going to even come close. But I did. I found a lot of other interesting things in your computer before they shut it down too. No family to speak of. No one that will miss you once you go missing after getting out of prison. Just another ex-con that has fallen off the grid, gone underground. Are you feeling okay? You look kind of pale. Don't worry, you will be in a coma soon and won't feel a thing. Here, why don't you sit down." He pulled out a chair and helped her sit. She slumped over onto the table in front of her, knocking over the glass of water Jonas had just placed there. "Where was I? Oh yeah. You had a parole officer assigned to you this morning. I got to their office before they had checked in and deleted you from their records. Bottom line? No one is going to miss you. I've talked to a buddy of mine with a boat and scheduled a late night fishing trip tonight. He goes out all the time. Heads out the night before, throws out the anchor and sleeps on the boat. Gets up at the crack of dawn. Says the fishing is best then. Do you like fishing? Guess it doesn't really matter. Oh, you're foaming at the mouth. Here, let me get a towel and get that for you. I don't know if you can hear me still, but this will all be over soon. I appreciate all the research you did on those women. They look like some pretty easy targets. As rich as they are, I am sure they won't miss a little money here or there. Seems like I will be sitting pretty for a while." Shelby slumped further down in the chair until falling out of it and onto the floor. He regarded her momentarily then returned to his computer, checking a couple of entries and e-mails before logging off. He had a lot of work ahead of him and a foolproof plan to carry out. Get rid of any evidence of the crime while leaving traces that she had been here. After dark, take the body to his friend, along with a sizable payment, and return home with food for two people. Be surprised when she is not there and then log on the computer to see if she can be traced online. IF anyone comes looking for her, "Yes, she was here. And talked like she was going to be here for a very long time. I went out to get us something to eat and when I got back she was gone. And she took a couple hundred bucks I had stashed in the kitchen. I don't know what I did, but if you find her, tell her she is welcome to come back." Jonas the victim. He liked the sound of that. He had played that role before and he played it well. He turned his attention back to the screen and accessed a file on the computer with the information he had downloaded from Shelby. A large group of women with a very large net worth. The list was complete with all the information he would need to get started in separating them from very modest amounts of money. For now. "Yes, a lot of work to do indeed."

The End

Manufactured By: RR Donnelley
Momence, IL USA
July, 2010